CRAVING OF THE SANDS

A RUNEBREAKERS NOVEL

CEARNACH GRIMM

Cover illustration by Steve Worthington

Cover design by Jessica Bell

Edited by Gina Kammer, Rebecca Zornow, Lionel Barter.

Chapters 59 to 74 are in part based on the earlier short story *Craving of the Sands*, written by Cearnach Grimm and W. Lawrence.

ISBN: 979-8-89196-013-8 (ebook)

ISBN: 979-8-89196-014-5 (paperback)

ISBN: 979-8-89196-015-2 (hardback)

Printed in China.

Nervous Rocket is an imprint of Sagaflare LLC, Sheridan, WY 82801.

ABOUT THE AUTHOR

Cearnach Grimm is an author of fantasy and science fiction. He worked as an international journalist for more than ten years, writing more than 1,500 articles on things like rabbit breeding and Egyptian tombs, before transitioning to screenplays, comic books, short stories and novels. Above all, he believes in the health benefits of chocolate cake. After extensive traveling, he currently lives in Europe. *Craving of the Sands* is his debut novel.

ABOUT THE RUNEBREAKERS

Noblemen of Renown and Taste, Prepare to be Astounded!

Announcing the Legendary... Runebreakers!

In the grand and glittering annals of adventuring history, there arises a group so daring, so audacious, so overwhelmingly prone to collateral damage that even the gods themselves occasionally look away and whistle.

Behold, the Runebreakers!

When subtlety fails and diplomacy falls flat on its over-polite face, the Runebreakers stride in. Their philosophy? Simple. Their motto? Even simpler: *Storm in, Fight, Loot, and Drink!*

Why, you might ask, should you, a noble of exquisite judgment and refined sensibilities, employ such a rambunctious band of sword-swinging, spell-slinging ruffians? Allow us to illuminate the unique advantages of hiring the Runebreakers for your next quest or endeavor:

1. Guaranteed Action

When you send in the Runebreakers, things will happen. Structures may collapse, and landscapes may be irrevocably altered, but *things will happen*. Guaranteed.

2. Efficient Problem Solving

Every quest is a path to ale! While other adventurers might prolong quests unnecessarily so they are able to bill you more, the Runebreakers are always eager to get back to drinking. This means: They get to the heart of the matter with unmatched speed. They will use advanced wit to find a shortcut you surely have missed!

3. Treasure Redistribution

The Runebreakers believe in the free movement of wealth. Specifically, wealth moving from old, dusty hoards into their pockets (and, by extension, possibly yours, if you're quick about it).

4. Party Expertise

Their post-victory celebrations are legendary. Should your quest conclude successfully (or at least noisily), expect a feast for the ages. Caution: hangover remedies recommended.

5. Risk Management

Nothing quite refines one's appreciation for life and property like the thrill of knowing it could all go up in flames at any moment. Hire the Runebreakers and discover new heights of existential awareness!

~

Client Testimonials

"Well, they did resolve the bandit issue... sort of." – Lord Tremblay of Yondervale

"I have never seen such enthusiastic looting. My treasury will never be the same." – Duchess Ophelia the Befuddled

"They drank all my best wine, but the stories they left me with are priceless." – Count Reinald of the Rift

~

So, esteemed noblemen, if you crave excitement, thrill, and a dash of unpredictability in your otherwise meticulous life, look no further. The Runebreakers are ready to charge forth, swords raised and mugs ready.

Hire the Runebreakers Today! *(Insurance highly recommended. Not responsible for incidental kingdom restructuring.)*

Runebreakers: When you need chaos with a side of competence.

To E., for enduring so much with me and offering the best variety of experiences, from mild to wild, and always being the highlight of my life at every occasion. Incidentally, very similar to cheese.

CHAPTER 1
ANOTHER ONE BITES THE DUST

Wilhilm's soul would twitch if he still had one. As it happens, there is only a sorry mess of it, too little to twitch anyway after being ripped apart by an excess of magic.

He is supposed to repair his soul with gnome magic tonight, but instead of catching a gnome, he watches his gnome-catching golem rampage through the forest clearing. The golem is a marvel of magical engineering but Wilhilm can only gape at the terrifying embodiment of unbridled fury in horror.

Blast the eldritch darkness!

Once in fifty years, the green moon is in conjunction with Antares and everything is perfect for the gnomish ritual of Tak'Andoo, the refueling of magic. Catching a gnome now would mean the gnome would be filled with fresh magic. The perfect moment to squeeze it out and use it to fix his soul.

But now this! *This should not happen!*

A golem is supposed to obey. Obeying is what it is made for.

Determined, Wilhilm clutches his wand. He needs a gnome, and he needs it now!

And yet, the golem rages in defiance of its orders. Standing nearly ten feet tall, its body is a jigsaw of jagged rocks and gleaming metal plates, fused together in ritual executed by the skilled hands of Ronny's Wizardry ("If you find a lower rate, we'll match it"). Every movement sends a shudder through the ground, and the sound of grinding stone accompanies its thunderous steps. It's punctuated by a unique, high-pitched whine, almost like the keen of a trapped animal echoing within its core.

Something has gone wrong. But what? Wilhilm followed the manual's copious instructions religiously. The golem is supposed to catch a gnome. Everything worked fine until a few minutes ago, when the golem suddenly whizzed out of control. Now it's uncontrollably wreaking havoc through the forest to the next hamlet, and depending on how long it would run, the next hamlet after that, and the hamlet after that.

Its eyes, two burning embers set deep within its craggy face, flashed with an otherworldly light, fixed and unyielding. The mouth, a mere slit in the rock, seems almost an afterthought, yet it gives the golem a semblance of a snarl as it lunges forward. There is no mercy, no understanding, only the relentless pursuit of its quarry.

"It's not responding to the control rune!" Wilhilm shouts, his voice barely carrying over the deafening noise.

"I'll axe it!" Mormak the Dwarf yells back, one of his two axes at the ready. He's a wall of muscle and determination, but even he seems daunted by the golem's relentless advance. Sweat already glistens at his brow. Mormak has long stopped trying to cover up the bald patch on his head. Neither is he concerned about the constant breath of ale surrounding him. Worrisome in a human, prodigious ale breath was actually an indication of good health of a dwarf in the prime of his life. Sort of.

"No," Wilhilm shouts back in even more horror. "It's a rental!"

Wilhilm's mind races, his magical senses probing the golem's arcane mechanisms, careful to use only the faintest bit of magic, making sure not to upset the roaring well of hidden turmoil inside of him. He feels the pain immediately, albeit only a tiny tug, digging deeper from where his soul used to be into the sad rest of it. But there is no way around it. Casting magic requires him to pluck small pieces of his soul, like petals from a daisy, and sacrifice them.

Only, a couple of years back, he didn't just pluck, did he? No, he tore, giant chunks, greedily, too greedily. Ultimately, he has ripped his soul apart, and it never really recovered.

On the contrary, it is getting worse. Week by week. As if the raging magic that occupies the hole where his whole soul used to be is eating tiny bits of what's left, trying to devour it all. Even whispering to him at times.

That's the problem with Wilhilm and magic. He never liked it. For his taste, it has too much a mind of its own.

There was reason he ripped his soul apart though. *Lysandra.* The moment freezes him, the magic still roiling inside of him. *Lysandra. The love of his life...*

As much as he tries to forget her, the memory of her still haunts him. She stood at his side when he fought the Witch King. She died protecting him. Wilhilm pushes the memory of her back into the darkest chamber of his mind. He has more immediate concerns now!

Fixing the golem is essential, or he would need to pay off a whole lot of damage suits, very probably requiring more money than he could ever work off (unless, perhaps, he found a legendary artifact like the Rubber Chicken of Longevity.)

The creature is no ordinary construct; its purpose is specific, and the magic binding it is convoluted and strange. Of course, nothing is too complicated for Wilhilm. With enough time in the relaxing atmosphere of his study, a stack of books before him, he could figure it out. But the pressure to ease his soul and Mormak's constant bellows are stressing him out in the field.

An intricate network of runes and glyphs, barely visible to the naked eye, dances across the golem's surface. They pulse and shimmer, a symphony of mystical energy that binds the golem's form and fuels its relentless drive.

This wasn't the first time that Wilhilm shopped at Ronny's. And it wasn't the first time that, within the first hour, he came to regret it. He has to contain the golem somehow. The lowest rate will mean nothing if he can't catch a gnome.

The arms of the golem swing like battering rams, each blow capable of leveling trees or smashing boulders. The fingers, articulated and surprisingly dexterous, end in razor-sharp talons that glisten with a metallic sheen. They clamp close, designed to seize and hold with relentless strength. Its legs, thick pillars of stone and iron, move with an unnatural grace, propelling the golem forward in a relentless march. The feet, broad and heavy, leave deep impressions in the earth.

The acrid smell of churning earth and the metallic tang of scraped iron mingle, underscored by a faint whiff of ancient magic, like ozone mingling with the musty scent of old parchment.

"Did you try turning it off and on again?" Mormak says.

"I've heard that helps when there's a problem with machinery."

"I'm trying to, but there's nothing in the manual!" Wilhilm declares. He hates to use his magic. The good thing about the second-hand golem is, he doesn't have to use his own. He just needs to focus a little and he can tap into the operating artifact of the golem. It's a small drop of magic but enough to allow him to see through the ethereal layers of the golem, seeking the core that holds its commands. The sensation is like diving into a labyrinth, twisted and dark.

The golem lunges again and Mormak's strength is put to the test as he holds it at bay with his axe. Every second counts, and Wilhilm's focus narrows to a pinpoint.

Suddenly, his magic wells up inside of him like a storm. *Not again.* As if his magic is somehow able to smell it might be needed. Even for this little bit of magic that under normal circumstances wouldn't require any focus at all, Wilhilm must fight through the pain, tame the resistant cyclone inside of him. A dark fog evaporates from the Wizard's skin, almost too fast to be noticed. Wilhilm pulls the sleeves of his robes half way over his hand, grasping at the cloth as if to hold the fog in, and focuses on the arcane layers of the golem's inner workings, while at the same time trying to suppress his own magic from doing anything stupid.

"There!" he cries, finding an ethereal simulacrum of a switch within the golem's magical core. With a word of power and a gesture of finality, he flips it.

CHAPTER 2

TINY DANCER

The effect is immediate. The golem's eyes dim, its body freezes in place. The grinding of gears gone, the forest falls into a sudden, eerie silence.

Wilhilm stands panting, the realization slowly sinking in.

Oh no. We wrecked it, he thinks.

Fantastic, absolutely fantastic. Once in fifty years came the opportunity for the gnomish ritual of Tak'Andoo, and he blew it.

That means no gnome for him. No fresh gnome magic to repair his soul. And, to make matters worse, a wrecked golem would take at least a hundred years to pay off. He might even have to sell his library of rare books with gems like *Soul-Rifting: How Not To Do It, How To Win Familiars and Influence Demons, The Seven Habits of Highly Successful Wizards* and *How To Tame Your Magic.*

As Wilhilm surveys the downed construct, his ears catch a faint, peculiar noise. He dismisses it as the creaking of an ash or the rustling of crunchy autumn leaves, but then it comes again—clearer this time—a muffled thumping. It's too rhythmic, too insistent to be a mere trick of the wind. Then, an accompanying high-pitched whine, muted, but clearly a voice.

It's coming from the golem itself. Wilhilm's pulse quickens as he follows the noise to a hidden compartment on the golem's back.

Opening the compartment with a twist of the knob, he discovers a small cage, and within it, a furious gnome, jumping up and down, his voice a stream of curses and demands. The gnome's tiny feet thump against the cage floor. Wilhilm's heart leaps. A gnome! He has a gnome!

How wonderful! He *can* heal his soul!

And, he won't have to spend a hundred years paying Ronny back after all.

"What took you so long?" the gnome snaps, his eyes gleaming with anger and impatience. "Get me out of here, you gibface! Hornswoggler! Such a meater, using that big brute to catch me! It's not fair!"

The cage is an intricate piece of engineering, at odds with the slapdash composition of the golem's body. It's designed to hold without harming. Carefully, Wilhilm ejects the cage from the compartment. The mechanism releases with a soft click. The thumping stops as the gnome stares up at Wilhilm, then spits into his face.

A LITTLE LATER, the gnome stands at a mere three feet tall, but what he lacks in height, he more than makes up for in character. His round face is dominated by a prominent, bulbous nose that, even in repose, looks red and slightly inflamed. His eyes, a twinkling shade of hazel, are almost overshadowed by bushy white eyebrows that seem to have a life of their own. They twitch and waggle with every emotion, from curiosity to irritation.

"So, just to summarize," the gnome says, "you want me to use my magic to heal your soul, thereby endangering, no, sacrificing my life? With nothing in return? Sounds like a very intriguing offer, but I'm afraid, my finance guy would not approve."

"But..." Wilhilm says.

"You have a finance guy?" Mormak interrupts. "I thought gnomes are their own finance guys."

"Gold doesn't procreate just like that. The good old times when a rainbow would do the trick are gone. Gold needs to be set to work nowadays," the gnome says. Deep creases line his cheeks. His skin wrinkles as he frowns, like leather exposed to the sun for too many years.

"Let's circle back to you doing magic for me," Wilhilm says. He tries to give the gnome his best severe stare, but finds his eyes distracted by the gnome's mop of unruly silver hair that seems to defy any attempts at grooming. It spills over his pointed ears, which stick out prominently on either side, the tips slightly curled.

Wilhilm lowers his eyes purposefully. Dressed in a patchwork of mismatched clothes, the gnome wears pants that are a tad too short, exposing hairy feet that have never seen shoes. His tunic is dotted with stains and sport a few holes.

"I don't think you're getting anywhere," the gnome says. "I have no magic to give to you."

"That's not possible. You're a gnome. Every gnome has magic, at least some. And today is Tak'Andoo, where all gnome magic rejuvenates and your magic is strongest."

"In theory, yes," the gnome says.

"In theory?" Wilhilm eyes him suspiciously. Gnomes

are known for their trickery but they would not trick him. No, no, no. Wilhilm was far too clever to be tricked by a gnome.

"I, errr, I have issues. *Medical* issues."

Wilhilm bows down, so he's face to face with the gnome. He knows gnomes need forceful handling. Wilhilm musters up his best intimidating wizard stare.

With darting eyes that widen to twice their usual size, the gnome stands frozen, like a tiny statue caught in an unfortunate pose.

"You will learn to fear my magic! If you resist me," Wilhilm starts, "your feet will squeak like a rubber duck with every step."

The gnome's rosy cheeks drain to a pale shade. His hands start to tremble uncontrollably, making a gentle, rustling sound against the fabric of his clothes.

"You'll wake up with daisies growing out of your ears every morning," Wilhilm continues.

A series of rapid, shallow breaths escape from the gnome's mouth. He looks like a mouse who has just spotted a looming cat, unsure if it should dart or play dead.

"Your fingers will..."

"Stop it, stop it, I have... I can't!" the gnome eventually relents.

"Why can't you, what's wrong with your magic?"

"Don't make me say it!"

"Tell me, or I'll curse your tunic to..."

"Fine! I have... I have premature evocaculation. Happy now?"

"Premature... what's that?" Wilhilm asks. He has never heard the word before.

"Premature evocaculation. It means, I release my magic accidentally, prematurely, if I'm under stress."

“But you’re not under stress!”

“Let a golem a thousand times your size catch you, and then we’ll talk again about stress!”

Wilhilm stands up. He stares at the gnome. *Oh that’s why the golem acted up.* A sudden release of gnome magic. And while a gnome-catching golem should be magically insulated from that, Ronny probably took some shortcuts.

“But I have another idea to repair your soul,” the gnome says. “One that works, money back if it doesn’t!”

“What kind of idea?” Wilhilm asks, intrigued.

CHAPTER 3

HEARD IT THROUGH THE GRAPEVINE

The gnome, with a complete lack of self-consciousness, inserts a stubby, dirt-caked finger deep into one nostril. He digs with a concentration that's almost admirable, his face scrunching up in determination. Every so often, he pulls his finger out, inspecting the treasure he's unearthed before flicking it away and resuming his quest.

"You're quite the digger," Mormak murmurs admirably.

"Your idea is...?" Wilhilm says.

"Do you know what Echo Stones are?" the gnome asks.

"Of course," Wilhilm says. "A way to communicate over long distances. They come in pairs. We had a pair, but one ended up inside of a whale, and then in another dimension, and so the one we still have is pretty useless without its counterpart."

"Uh," the gnome says.

"What do you mean 'uh'?"

"I gather you're not quite on top of the recent developments in Echo Stones?"

"Recent developments?" Wilhilm says. "Echo Stones are

magical artifacts that date back a hundred years! We got ours from a dragon's hoard."

"You are aware, aren't you, that a dragon's hoard is not a sigil of quality? I mean, those places are basically just huge dumps. As long as it sparkles, it's there. And everything comes with pre-owners. But still, people are like, '*Oh, I got this from a dragon's hoard,*' like it's something special. Like '*Want to take a bite from my apple? I just got it from the trash.*'"

"They're Echo Stones! They're basically all the same."

Wilhilm feels a gentle tug at his robes, then another one, and another one. The repeated pulls have a rhythm akin to the distant tapping of a hammer on an anvil, calling for the wizard's attention.

Looking down, Wilhilm finds himself meeting the deep-set eyes of the dwarf, surrounded by a thicket of bushy brows and an unkempt beard. Right, Mormak was still there. He has almost forgotten about the dwarf. Mormak, eyes earnest and filled with intent, convey a wordless message, underscoring the importance of the moment. A message Wilhilm unfortunately doesn't get.

"What?"

"Don't talk to him as much," Mormak whispers a bit louder. "Gnomes are master merchants. Before you know it, you'll spend money."

"I got this," Wilhilm says, then eyes the gnome. "Why are you asking about Echo Stones?"

"As it happens, I'm in the Echo Stone biz!"

"There's a business for Echo Stones?"

"I work for Cheese," the gnome says, and Wilhilm senses the distinct pride behind his words.

"I only work for ale," Mormak says. "And occasionally for gold that I can convert into ale."

“No, I mean I work for the company named Cheese. Never heard of it?”

“Cheese? Who would name his company after something to eat?” Wilhilm shakes his head, and the gnome rolls his eyes.

“You need to get in more,” the gnome says, rattling the bars of the cage.

“In?”

“You’re, like, out in the woods all the time. You need to dive into city life, learn how the world is changing!”

“What do Echo Stones have to do with getting my soul back together?” Wilhilm asks.

“Not any Echo Stone, but Echo Stones made by Cheese! Cheese re-invented the Echo Stone. Imagine it as your gateway to a connected universe of conversations!”

“I prefer silence, just like in the perfect library,” Wilhilm says. “A universe of blah blah blahing sounds like torture. So, erm, back to the matter at hand. What’s with the healing my soul thing?”

“We call them...” The gnome pauses for effect. “EyeStone.”

“EyeStone? What do eyes have to do with it?” Wilhilm asks.

“Figuratively,” the gnome assures. “Because they’re like a far-seeing eye.”

“It’s not bad, actually,” Mormak murmurs.

“Back to healing my soul. What about that?” Wilhilm presses.

His mind works furiously. He has a gnome. Does the gnome have magic, or not? Does the gnome lie or does he tell the truth? It is always so hard to tell with gnomes. But he needs gnome magic to heal his soul, and he needs it now. *Wants* it now. Wilhilm has to make some kind of deal.

"The connected universe is the best," the gnome continues. "Think about it this way—there's a constant conversation going on—if you're there or not. You can tap in and tap out whenever you feel like it. Aren't you tired of missing out on the latest news, stories, and updates from your friends and allies? And what about the hassle with messenger birds, magic scrolls, untrustworthy postriders, and delayed communications?"

"Postriders are a nuisance, but nothing compared to messenger birds. Much too nosey for my tastes," Wilhilm says.

"See, we're getting somewhere! Now, let me out of this cage and we can proceed with the EyeStone transaction."

"I still don't understand how it can help me fix my soul. I get the distinct feeling you're trying to distract me."

"This is the perfect solution for you," the gnome insists.

Was it possible the gnomes found a way to pass on their magic using an Echo Stone? Why would they? Of course, they would, Wilhilm corrects his own thoughts. If there was money in it, of course the gnomes would do it.

The gnome smiles at him. "Thanks to the gnome magic running through the Cheese Echo Stones, your soul will rejoice! Set me free and you will be healed."

"As soon as I remove the cage, you can move freely and just escape," Wilhilm says.

"I would never!"

"But if you promise you won't leave without my permission, you're bound to that promise!"

"Am I?"

"I've read about it!"

"Guess it must be true then! So, what happens to me if I break this promise?" The gnome grins. "Just hypothetically, of course."

"Not sure, probably you'll turn to goo or something."

"Not a fun way to part with this world."

"But you would try to escape, of course?"

"Absolutely not. I hereby promise not to leave without your express permission before you have your EyeStone!"

"I accept," Wilhilm says solemnly and opens the cage.

CHAPTER 4

SOMEBODY'S WATCHING ME

Wilhilm and Mormak stand in the small clearing, their forms etched in sharp relief by the pale moonlight. Wilhilm examines the Echo Stone the gnome gave him. It's roughly oval, but with edges that are imperfect, as if nature herself crafted it with purpose. The surface is a deep obsidian black, but when he moves it around, swirling patterns of deep blues and violets emerge, reminiscent of a night sky sprinkled with distant galaxies. It looks a bit like a goblin's attempt at making a pocket mirror. For the aesthetically challenged.

Upon closer inspection, Wilhilm notices tiny, silver-flecked veins running through it, pulsing faintly, like the gentle rhythm of a heartbeat. The texture is surprisingly smooth to the touch, yet it holds a peculiar warmth, defying the usual coldness of ordinary stone. It's weighty, grounding, and when held one could swear they feel the faintest vibrations emanating from within, a whisper of the magic locked inside.

The Echo Stone he owned previously, was made from a different material, a little lighter, and not so smooth. It seemed like someone invested a lot of time in getting the new exterior right and not just the magic.

To the untrained eye, the EyeStone might seem like a mere decorative artifact, but for those attuned to magic, they'd recognize the depths it holds. A single indentation, small and circular, sits on one side of the stone, acting as a conduit, a focus point for the arcane energies stored within.

On the back, there's a small engraving: a wheel of cheese that someone took a bite off.

Of course, the gnome charged a heap of gold and, of course, after the transaction concluded, he disappeared. Wilhilm should have listened to the "before you have your Echo Stone" part of the gnome's promise not to escape. But anyway, now he had this piece of gnome magic, ready to use.

The stillness is broken by a frantic rustling. Emerging from the dense undergrowth, two figures burst into the clearing. Their breaths come in ragged gasps. Sweat glistens on their brows, and their usually composed demeanors are replaced with looks of exhaustion and mild panic.

Wilhilm knows them better than he would have wanted to. Gadisa Tar'Anomin, a Rogue, and Dakaria Galzur, a Druid, their two companions, finally arrive. Wilhilm raises his hand in greeting.

Even in a realm known for its abundance of unique characters, Gadisa stands out. A strong, big, and bald fellow at first glance, it's the lack of eyes that throws people off. A bronze blindfold is held in place by screws on either side of his head. A lose leather strip is fastened to it and bound behind his head, seemingly added as some kind of decoration. He wears striped culottes, the rest of his body exposed. Tubes run from his back to his torso, and small plates are embedded into his chest.

Gadisa, clutching a side stitch, leans on a thick ash for support, his chest heaving. “By the spirits...” he pants, “I hope you have something to eat for us.”

Dakaria, wipes her brow, her usual grace momentarily absent. “You said... meet in the forest,” she gasps, casting a playful glare at Wilhilm. “You failed to mention...which part.”

As a druid, Dakaria wears a hunter green dress that compliments the green gloss that occasionally shows on her dark skin when the sun hits at just the right angle. Her long, pointy ears—as long as those from elves in the feywild—mark her as an elf, or “kind of an elf” as she herself puts it.

“You should have been here an hour ago!” Mormak says, a touch of anger in his voice. “Where have you been? The whole thing is done by now!”

“We ran into supply issues,” Dakaria says. Her voice is melodious and serene, reminiscent of a gentle breeze rustling through ancient trees. There’s a natural, soothing quality , evoking the calm of the moonlit glade they stand within.

“Supply issues? What issues?”

“We passed a tavern, and they had deer for half the price,” Dakaria explains.

“I didn’t even get to eat,” Gadisa growls, his voice an accusatory tone, as if he had been denied the visit to his mother’s deathbed.

“You ate so much, the innkeeper turned pale!”

“Ph, I had a tiny appetizer,” Gadisa puffs.

“So, you have the gnome? What’s next?” Dakaria asks. “Can he stop those shadows evaporating from your skin?”

“He explained to me they’re a side effect,” Mormak whispers to her. “Something to do with a hole in his soul.”

Use it. Use the EyeStone, a sudden voice in Wilhilm's head urges. He would be surprised, if it were the first time he heard a voice in his head. As it happens, he constantly hears whispers and voices, a fact he attributes to the magic within him. Since his soul had mostly evaporated, he feels it has worsened, like the magic inside nestled and expanded where once his soul rested.

"I say, let's eat something. I'm sure there's deer around somewhere, perhaps even a small boar or two," Gadisa says.

"Or let's get back to that tavern," Mormak murmurs.

"We don't have the gnome, not anymore, but he gave us this," Wilhilm says and extends his arm so Gadisa and Dakaria can see the Echo Stone.

"What are you going to do with a single Echo Stone? Without its counterpart, you can't connect to anything," Dakaria says.

"It's gnome magic. They call it *EyeStone*. He said I can activate it and connect to some network of Echo Stones, and whatever happens will help me heal my soul."

"Sounds like a sales pitch," Mormak grumbles.

Wilhilm stares at the EyeStone, holding it with both hands. He is filled with profound anticipation. His fingers tremble slightly, not from fear, but from expectation. The air around the EyeStone seems to hum with latent energy, as if the very fabric of reality awaits his command. His heart beats a rhythmic drum in his chest. There's a moment of pure, exhilarating potential.

"I have to try this now," he says. "I can't wait any longer. This might just be the answer to my problems."

"We're waiting," Gadisa says. "I mean if it's not too long. Otherwise, just find us in the next tavern. Or we're doing a barbecue right here. I'm sure I can find something to impale and roast."

Wilhilm takes a moment to steady his nerves, focusing his gaze on the subtle indentation of the Echo Stone. With a determined exhale, he presses his finger against the groove.

Almost immediately, he feels a sharp, unexpected sting, as if the stone sprouted a tiny needle. Pulling back, he notices a bead of blood welling up on his fingertip. The stone seems to drink in the crimson droplet, its previously dormant veins igniting with a fervent silver glow.

Strange. The Echo Stone he worked with previously did not need blood. *Why does this one?* Wilhilm wonders.

"What is your name?" a voice ask him. There's no image.

"Hello? Who's there?" he asks.

"What is the name you want other members of the EyeStone network to see?"

"Like a pseudonym?"

"What is the name you want to use?"

Wilhilm pauses for a moment. "I'm Wilhilm Grindto... no, make it Wilhilm the Wizard... no, sorry, I want something crisp. Make it... MagicWilly."

"MagicWilly. Confirmed."

As the warmth of the stone intensifies, a vast expanse of murmurs envelop him, like the distant sounds of a crowd heard from underwater. Moving images spring up on the surface of the stone. It's a young witch stirring a potion in a cauldron.

"FastPotion challenge! My three fastest potions! One, Potion of Healing. Even though it's incredibly useful, this basic healing potion is also probably the most commonly brewed. Ingredients include simple herbs. I always include wolf berries."

"Erm, ok, I guess," Wilhilm says. "My name is Wilhilm. I'm a wizard."

"Two, Potion of Climbing. My favorite recipe includes boiled gecko legs and a bit of salt and pepper. Tasty and effective!"

"Interesting, not a big climber myself," Wilhilm tries again. "So, who am I talking to? And where are you?"

"Three, Potion of Animal Friendship! My go-to version uses pheromones of cats. Now you! FastPotion Challenge!"

"Me? Um," Wilhilm says. "Fast potions are not really..."

The moving image shifts, and this time he is connected to a gnome.

"If you have gold, don't spend it," the gnome says. "I know, it's counterintuitive, but that's how it works! Every adventurer goes through their loot in a weekend when instead what they should do is invest wisely."

Interesting. It's not a real connection. Unlike a regular Echo Stone where one person speaks directly to another, Wilhilm isn't really connected to the witch or to the gnome. It's more like he sees images that happened in the past. He can't influence it; he can't interact with it. When he moves his hand, the connection is immediately replaced by another, allowing him to skip ramblings he doesn't care about.

There are all kinds of people in the network. Witches and wizards, bards (a lot of bards!), artificers...

Reality around him appears to blur and recede, replaced by the sensation of standing at the threshold of an immense auditorium bustling with voices. The more he watches, the more his spirit seems to drift *into* the network.

Each syllable, each intonation feels amplified and connected by myriad threads of consciousness. Wilhilm hears laughter, solemn oaths, arguments, and sweet nothings, all existing simultaneously in this mesmerizing soundscape.

Zeroing in on one particular strand, he discerns a conversation between two scholars fervently discussing alchemical properties. It is as if he had leaned into their very minds, privy to their most immediate thoughts.

Amidst the enthralling mosaic of voices, an undertone tugs at Wilhilm. Dissonant whispers seemed to beckon him from the shadows of the network, their source, elusive. They seem to come from everywhere at once, weave through everything. Wilhilm can't exactly make out what they're saying or what language they're in. But they seem hostile. Then, suddenly, one sentence becomes clear.

Meet Your Destiny, Wilhilm.

Alarmed, Wilhilm severs his connection to the network. The stone's pulsing light diminishes until it returns to its dormant state. Breathing heavily, Wilhilm examines his finger, the tiny puncture already starting to heal.

CHAPTER 5
NEED YOU TONIGHT

Wilhilm feels a lot better after using the Echo Stone. It's as if the very air around him has turned into a cascade of light bathing him despite the fact that it was still early morning, and the sun was only just starting its climb. He inhales deeply, absorbing the feeling. Did it already start to heal his soul? Probably it's the residual high of gnome magic. But then Wilhilm realizes it's more than that. The Echo Stone hums gently in his hand, almost as if purring in delight. And the sound, bizarrely enough, resonates within him.

He feels as if a tiny knot inside his damaged soul, a knot he wasn't even fully aware of until now, has loosened. The feeling is subtle but profound, like the first rays of sunrise seeping into a long, dark night.

Wilhilm smiles, realizing that the gnome might have been right. This kind of magic does wonders for his soul. It transmits a piece of gnomeish joy, an arcane optimism that knits the soul.

He reaches into the folds of his robe and retrieves a small leather pouch, worn with age and etched with enchantments. With a flick of his wrist, he sends it tumbling to the ground before him.

As the pouch lands with a soft thud, Wilhilm's heart quickens with anticipation. He watches—even though there's nothing new about it—with wide, awe-filled eyes as the pouch begins to tremble, the leather rippling as if stirred by an invisible wind.

In mere moments, the transformation begins. The leather pouch unfurls and expands, growing and stretching as though it were a living thing. The seams part, revealing vibrant, embroidered fabric of deep azure and shimmering gold. From the pouch's mouth, tall wooden poles shoot forth, anchoring themselves firmly in the earth. The once small pouch now stands as a magnificent travel tent, its peaks crowned with ornate finials.

This never gets old.

The magic tent is his favorite artifact. Wilhilm looks over to where his companions lie in their own meagre tents, then with a graceful sweep of his hand, the flaps part, revealing a luxurious interior filled with plush furnishings, soft cushions, and a warm, inviting glow.

"Did I promise too much?" a voice asks. "Do you feel already how your soul is coming back together?"

Wilhilm jumps up, startled. It's the gnome again. "You... how do you... how did you come in here?"

"I just want to make sure that I have satisfied customers!" the gnome says.

"It does help a little, I think," Wilhilm admits. Then he bites his lip. Never let a gnome know you're satisfied with a purchase. It always leads to upselling! "It's too early to say," he hurriedly adds.

"Not yet convinced? Then you should do a cast of your own. That's the word for those short bursts of moving images that are hurled through the network. Casts. By the way, I like the name you chose as your alias in the network. MagicWilly is an impressively bold choice."

"You want me to send a message to the network? To everyone? Saying what?"

"Think of something original. You're a wizard. Do magic. Tear deep into your soul, being connected to the network might accelerate healing."

"Might?"

"Will. Probably will," the gnome says. "Try it!"

Wilhilm doesn't like the idea. He doesn't want to be seen by so many people at once, nor does he want to do magic. He wants to stay away from magic as far as possible. He prefers using artifacts that have their own magic and don't require his own magic, like his magical tent.

The EyeStone sits atop the small, ornate table before him that is, in wondrous fashion, always there when he activates the tent's magic. It glows dim for the moment, waiting for activation.

"If you want your soul to heal, you should give it a spin," the gnome says again.

Wilhilm sighs. He hates it. Not only since his soul ripped apart, but long before that. Even as a little kid, he always felt like magic was about to overpower him, to make him do things, things he didn't like. But it got worse, so much worse. His magic now tried to make him *do* things.

But well, if it took magic to get things fixed, he probably should try.

"It's not as if I'm battling marauding orcs today. Might use a bit of harmless magic," Wilhilm muses. "Perhaps share a bit of wisdom with those people out there, take the edge off these tough times."

He considers what spell to demonstrate. A fireball? No,

too risky and honestly too cliché. Maybe he could summon an ethereal creature? No, that could scare the younger viewers. Then it dawns on him—a classic illusion trick, something playful and innocuous, yet still enchanting. A rabbit out of a hat! It's a mundane magic, but therein lies its charm.

Wilhilm positions his wizard's hat on the table next to the EyeStone. His fingers brush over the worn felt of the hat, reminiscing momentarily about the countless battles and adventures it has seen.

Taking a deep breath, he activates the EyeStone. The aura brightens, signaling the start of the cast. It was the network's turn to watch.

CHAPTER 6

OOPS I DID IT AGAIN

Wilhilm sees his own reflection looking back at him, and next to his face, there is a rapidly climbing number, the number of people watching him. When it reaches a hundred, Wilhilm hesitates for a moment. What is he supposed to say?

"Good evening, fellow seekers of mystery and magic," he starts. After the first words are out, he feels more confident. "This is my first cast and I will show you some basics, the kind of magic that made us all fall in love with spells in the first place."

His heart pounds in anticipation, not from danger, but stage fright. Will they love it? Will they hate it? No matter, he decides. All that counts is that this will result in a repair boost for his soul. Hopefully.

"Let's make some magic," he whispers to himself.

Wilhilm's fingers hover over the brim of his hat as he utters the incantation. It's a simple spell, one he's done countless times before for small crowds or friends. A touch of Elvish here, a smattering of Draconic there—a language he's always found well suited to spells of illusion and whimsy.

The problem Wilhilm has with magic is the next part. Soulrifting. Tearing fragments from his own soul to open an inter-dimensional rift just big enough to pull some magic through to this dimension. It's a painful, often dangerous process, but it's also incredibly potent—if he can endure it.

His fingers twitch in the air as he continues the incantation, a low murmur that only he understands. He feels the initial tugging sensation at the center of his chest, like an invisible hand clutching at his heart. He steels himself, already anticipating the piercing pain that is to come. But when the tearing finally begins, it's more agonizing than he ever before.

His soul is injured, still mending from its past fractures. As the rift forms, it's like pulling apart a wound that has only just begun to heal. The interior of the tent blurs in his vision, spots of darkness close in from the edges. A strangled gasp escapes his lips.

A piece of his soul rips away to fuel the spell. A burst of magical energy floods from his hands, lighting up his tent with an ethereal glow. The spell is powerful, more potent than he expected and the cost is high.

Wilhilm staggers, almost falling to his knees. The wound in his soul feels like it's been burned, cauterized by the very magic it birthed. He feels the weave of magic pull taut. It was painful, but he did it. At least the virtual audience will be delighted.

But something feels off. The magic coursing through him feels too... substantial. *Wait, is that the pull of Conjuration?*

He realizes, with a rising sense of dread, that the Draconic word he used might have been all wrong.

In the Draconic language the word for “rabbit” is Zhafrindorix, which means “swift-footed one” as opposed to Zhafindorux, which translates to “sovereign of the skies”.

He didn't say rabbit as he’d thought, but rather dragon.

The energies constrict and snap. The hat on the table shudders, wisps of silvery mist rise from it. Wilhilm’s eyes widen, and he tries to break the spell, to force the magic back into the manageable box of illusion, but it’s too late.

With a thunderous roar and a whoosh of tempestuous air, the hat explodes into shreds of fabric. The tent tears and the furniture crashes under the weight of the summoned being. Looming over Wilhilm’s now broken prized belongings is a full-sized red dragon. The wings extended in a span that dwarfs the remnants of his tent, its eyes wise and yet bewildered.

Somehow, the dragon’s neck has looped and twisted upon itself in ways that would baffle even the most seasoned contortionist. Now, with a knot that seems to defy all laws of anatomy and possibly physics, the dragon is well and truly stuck.

He puffs, he huffs, and he lets out a low, frustrated growl that sends small gusts of wind. Each attempt to wriggle free only tightens the knot further, turning what was meant to be a regal movement into something that resembled a particularly confused pretzel.

“You...errr,” Wilhilm starts, but doesn’t know how to continue.

“You just wait a moment,” the dragon roars. “I need to sort this out... Bloody materialization spells, something goes wrong every time.”

The dragon’s eyes have a distinctly cross-eyed look as they try to focus on the knot that somehow involves both his left wing and the tip of his tail. His claws, usually weapons of great destruction, are now employed in a series of increasingly desperate but entirely futile attempts to untangle the mess.

The dragon pauses for a moment, then clears his throat, and looks down at Wilhilm, then around at the torn tapestries and shattered remnants of the ornate table. "Why have I been summoned?" it rumbles, its voice a cascade of mountains crashing into the sea.

The EyeStone, miraculously still intact but knocked off to the side, captures this all. Comments of his live cast come in, an absolute chaos of shock, awe, and hundreds of small hieroglyphic depictions of dragons.

Wilhilm gulps, mustering as much dignity as one can when standing next to a house-sized creature of myth and legend. "A simple mistake in translation," he says, his voice tinged with awe and humility. "Even wizards are allowed those, I believe?"

The dragon momentarily catches sight of his reflection in the shards of the tent's mirror. If dragons could blush, this one surely would have, for the image staring back at him is not the fearsome beast that he probably thinks he is, but rather something that might have appeared in a book titled "The Adventures of Knotty the Dragon."

The dragon let out a sigh—an enormous, world-weary exhalation that sends ripples of air Wilhilm's way. He gives one last, half-hearted tug at his neck, which only serves to shift the knot slightly to the left, before resigning himself to his fate.

"Who are you talking to anyway on that EchoStone?" the dragon inquires. "Who is at the other end of this Echo Stone?"

"These are your fans! Thousands and thousands of people watching you right now!" Wilhilm moves the Echo

Stone to show the head of the dragon. “Say hello to the audience,” he pleads with the dragon.

“Hello,” the dragon says, then reconsiders and growls ferociously as the dragon begins to dissolve back into the ether from whence it came.

Wilhilm looks back at the Echo Stone. The viewers have skyrocketed, and among the frantic exclamations are comments like “BEST MAGIC EVER!”, “Someone sign this guy up for a magic show!”, and “MagicWilly is the best”.

As he’s left standing in the aftermath, amid the ruins of his tent, adrenaline still pumping through his veins, Wilhilm can’t help but feel a certain exuberant satisfaction, despite the potential mortal danger he just put himself in.

The Dwarf and the Rogue crawl out from their much smaller tents.

“What kind of noise was that?” Mormak complains. “We’re trying to sleep!”

“The number of your fans is sky-rocketing,” the gnome says. “Keep it going. The more fans you have, the better your soul will heal. You’ll see.”

“I’m not doing that a second time,” Wilhilm says. “That dragon might have killed us all.”

The gnome looks back, incredulous at Wilhilm’s refusal. “But you have to cast again, you just went viral.”

CHAPTER 7

LISTEN TO YOUR HEART

"Going viral? What does that mean?"

"It means everyone is crazy about you. Go back and watch the reactions," the gnome responds.

In his tent, canopy ripped open, Wilhilm taps the surface of the EyeStone. Instantly, a cascade of voices, images, and emotions sweeps over him, pulling him into the vast network of which he had recently become an unexpected star. Everywhere he turns, it's all about him: the audacious wizard who dared to summon a dragon on a live cast.

"Did you see that?" one voice exclaims. A replay starts, the majestic silver dragon bowing down, its scales reflecting light like a shimmering sea.

"Wilhilm's the real deal!" another voice chimes in, the admiration palpable.

A flood of pride and exhilaration swells within Wilhilm, sending a tingling sensation from the top of his head to the soles of his feet. This...this is oddly satisfying. Not just the admiration, but the validation that he's not just another wizard in the vast world of magic; he is special.

He swipes through countless comments, each one feeding his newfound ego. "Wilhilm for Archmage!" one comment reads. Another gushes, "Never seen magic like that before."

A grin stretches across his face, his heart racing in his chest. Lost in the sea of praise and adulation, Wilhilm momentarily forgets his past struggles and doubts. Here, in the luminous glow of the EyeStone network, he feels invincible, cherished, and most importantly, seen.

Among the sea of voices and the bustling chatter, a singular melody emerges. It is soft at first, like the whisper of the wind through a dense forest. As Wilhilm tunes into it, the voice becomes clearer, its notes cascading like a gentle waterfall. It's enchanting, ethereal.

Wilhilm stops scrolling, captivated. Every fiber of his being seems to lean towards this voice, trying to grasp its essence. The song feels like it surrounds him, as if he's submerged in a vast ocean of sound. It doesn't come from any one direction in the network; it's everywhere and nowhere all at once. The beauty of it tugs at his heartstrings, and a pang of nostalgia hits him.

He closes his eyes for a moment, letting the voice wash over him. His heartbeat syncs with the rhythm of the song, and for a moment, all the chatter, the admiration, the viral acclaim, it all fades away. There's only the song and the deep, inexplicable connection he feels to it.

A sense of yearning fills Wilhilm, a desire to find the source of this voice, to know the person behind this bewitching melody. Who could sing with such raw emotion, such depth? While he listens to it, the fresh tears in his soul feel to heal already. As the last note lingers, fading slowly, Wilhilm is left with a sense of purpose. He has to find this singer.

Wilhilm's fingers skim across the network's interface, driven by a compelling urgency. Amid the myriad casts, he spots one that seems to glow more brightly than the others. Tapping on it, the voice he'd been searching for fills the space around him, but now it's paired with an image.

A beautiful woman is singing, her eyes closed, lost in the music. Wilhilm's heart stammers in his chest as he takes in her features. Those familiar eyes, that curve of the lips, the cascade of her hair—it's like seeing a ghost.

Lysandra.

The wound in his heart, never fully healed, throbs with fresh pain. But as he watches, the minute differences start to become apparent. It isn't Lysandra, but the resemblance is uncanny.

He continues to watch, captivated. Every note she sings, every graceful movement she makes, draws him in deeper. Her user name reads: Seraphina. There is something more below it—*Meet Me In Upper Bunningsworth At My Community Event!*

Emotion surges within him, a maelstrom of sorrow, longing, and newfound fascination. Lysandra's memory still clings to his soul like a haunting refrain, and seeing Seraphina—so like her yet distinct—adds a complex layer to his grief.

As Seraphina's song concludes, Wilhilm is left in a daze, the weight of his past colliding with the present. The soul connected him with...something. With everything. With everyone. It felt for a moment like the healing of his soul accelerated.

For a moment, a memory resurfaces. Lysandra, her eyes

alight with determination, stands before a Witch King. Her sword gleams in the dim light. She moves with a dancer's grace, each step a calculated strike against her foe. Her laughter, a sound he once cherished, rings out amidst the clash of steel. She's fearless, a tempest, a warrior born from the heart of battle.

But then, the scene shifts, darkens. A demon, its form a whirlwind of shadows, emerges from the chaos. Lysandra turns, her sword raised, but the demon is too swift, too powerful. Wilhilm's heart clenches as he remembers the demon's hand reach for her, its fingers tendrils of pure darkness.

In that harrowing moment, Wilhilm's world shattered. The sound of her battle cry, cut abruptly short, echoes in his mind, a ghostly reminder of loss and failure. He closes his eyes, willing the memory away, but it lingers, a scar upon his soul. He closes his eyes tighter, as if the physical act could somehow shut out the past. Deep breaths in and out become his immediate focus, a lifeline to the present, then the memories are gone again.

He needs to know more about this Seraphina, not just for her likeness to Lysandra, but for the unique magic in her voice that's ensnared his heart—*no, don't think of her like that*—the unique magic in her voice that has the power to heal him.

The final note of Seraphina's song lingers in the air, its beauty echoing in the silence that follows. Then, as if someone has snuffed out a candle, the world around Wilhilm comes rushing back, cold and uninviting. The gentle hum of the EyeStone network, the ambient sounds of his surroundings, and the faint buzz of magic in his ears seem almost jarring compared to the ethereal realm he'd just been a part of.

His heart, which swelled with emotions during the song, now feels heavy, weighed down by longing. The image of Seraphina's face—so similar to Lysandra's, yet distinctly her own—stays imprinted in his mind. With every beat of his heart, he's reminded of the confusing amalgamation of past and present, the intertwining of sorrow and newfound intrigue.

He takes a deep breath, trying to ground himself. But the air he inhales seems lackluster without the magic of Seraphina's voice. A sense of urgency grips him. He needs to hear her again, to be lost in that paradise once more, even if it means facing the shadows of his past.

Upper Bunningsworth it is! Thankfully, it would only take half an hour to get there by horse.

The pull is undeniable, and Wilhilm knows it might either heal old wounds or deepen them further.

"What? Are you serious?" Mormak asks incredulously.

Wilhilm and his friends stand in the clearing. His tent artifact has transformed back into a pouch. A couple of bluebirds sit on a nearby tree, singing, but in Wilhilm's mind, every singing pales to the memory of Seraphina's voice.

"What is it... Where does he want to go?" Dakaria asks while packing her bag.

"Upper Bunningsworth," Wilhilm says.

"You really want to go to a dreadfully rotten hamlet like Upper Bunningsworth for a *concert*?" Mormak summarizes. "We never go to concerts!"

"We did once," Dakaria says.

"That was different," Mormak quips. "We just went

there because we were on a quest and we had to stop an assassin."

"And you ended up befriending him," Dakaria reminds him.

"He happened to own a brewery!"

"We're going to a concert?" Gadisa cuts in. He just returns from what Wilhilm likes to call *his morning routine*, if only to have a word that would prevent him from thinking about details.

"It was the most beautiful song I've ever heard," Wilhilm says. "Like a fast track to soul healing."

"If it helps him...," Dakaria says. "Don't be so hard on him guys."

"I don't understand, you never did magic. You didn't even talk about magic for the last year. I remember that you magically lit a candle once. So what's the fuss about magic and souls suddenly? Can't we just leave things as they are?"

"Believe me, I would love to," Wilhilm says. "But the wounds in my soul, that's an old wound. It never healed, instead it got worse and worse. If I don't find something to heal my soul, it might just destroy me."

Wilhilm doesn't feel comfortable going into more details. So he doesn't say anything about the voices in his head, urging him to do things. He doesn't mention the shadows his skin keeps giving off for a couple of weeks now. They had seen them anyway.

And he doesn't tell them how, at night, he tastes and smells the sands of the Zal'qaran desert, like he did all of those years ago. He doesn't tell them how the sands started to call out to him again. How he feels its deep and evil craving to get back at him.

"We don't have anything to eat," Gadisa points out. "Is there anything to eat in Upper Bunningsworth?"

"I've heard they have the best meals at concerts," Wilhilm lies hurriedly.

"Then it's settled, we're going," Gadisa decrees.

"Nobody ever asks for ale. If not for me, we'd never have any ale," Mormak grumbles.

CHAPTER 8

SPIRITS IN THE MATERIAL WORLD

The grand hall that will house Seraphina's performance blazes with opulent chandeliers and glimmering lights, painting the room in golden hues. Velvet drapes, gilded mirrors, and mosaics adorn the walls. Wilhilm would have thought a community event would be less posh and more, well, *communal.* Here, everyone looks distinguished. Their voices blend into a symphony of excited chatter. Musicians play soft tunes in a corner, but the true excitement is building around the stage where Seraphina is set to perform.

Wilhilm, draped in his usual blue robes, walks through the entrance with his entourage: Mormak, Gadisa and Dakaria. They glance around, absorbing the extravagance of the event.

"I smell food," murmurs Gadisa, his eyes twinkling.

Mormak grunts, adjusting his armor. "Too many frills for my liking. Give me a good tavern and a sturdy drink any day."

Wilhilm smirks. "Well, we're here now. I'm sure you will enjoy it." His eyes scan the crowd, searching for a familiar face or two. But amidst the sea of elite nobles and influential merchants, his gaze settles on a figure standing by the stage. Seraphina herself.

Even from a distance, her beauty is unmistakable. Dressed in a flowing gown that shimmers with each movement, she looks like a star descended from the heavens. Raven-black hair cascades down her back in soft waves, and her eyes, a deep shade of sapphire, sparkle with a mischievous glint. She is surrounded by admirers, each vying for her attention.

Mormak nudges Wilhilm. “That's her, isn't it? That singer? She’s quite something.”

Wilhilm nods slowly, an unfamiliar sensation grips his heart.

Movement from a shadowy corner near the edge of the stage catches his attention. Turning his eyes away from Seraphina almost physically hurts, but these figures in the shadows alarm him on some level. Three slender figures, draped in flowing gray robes, stand huddled together. Even in the dim light, their skin seems to glow with a soft, arcane luminescence, a deep purple mingling with twilight blue.

Stitchsuckers.

The fabric of their robes, Wilhilm notes, is almost insubstantial, like a woven fog. It flutters even without a breeze. In place of hair, the Stitchsuckers’ thread-like tendrils float around their heads, swaying and dancing as if they are in constant communion with unseen magical currents. The tendrils shimmer as they absorb ambient magic.

Their eyes, though partially obscured by the shadow of their hooded robes, are captivating. Each pair among the three are different—one’s crackle like lightning, another’s shimmers like a mirage, and the third burns with the slow intensity of ember. They scan the vicinity, clearly attuned to the rich fabric of magic that will soon permeate the air during the performance.

Wilhilm is used to them—Stitchsuckers live off magic, needed magic to survive. They make up one of the oldest families of Tiringar, holding a high position in the Academy. Still, he feels a twinge of unease. The proximity of the Stitchsuckers to the stage means they're in prime position to siphon off the magical energies that will be unleashed during Seraphina's performance.

As the Stichsuckers move closer to the stage, Seraphina's voice rises above the din. "Ladies and gentlemen, thank you for joining me this evening. I promise you a performance like no other."

The crowd hushes, the anticipation palpable. The soft strains of a harp begin to play, and when Seraphina's voice echoes through the hall, Wilhilm feels that odd pull again, a connection he can't explain. Everything else fades into the background.

The audience collectively takes out their EyeStones. It's an odd movement to make, given that they all can just look at the stage and hear Seraphina.

The glow of the stones cast a mesmerizing pattern of lights across the hall. Wilhilm realizes that some of them look different, and their owners encrusted them with diamonds and runes. Each pulses with a power that connects them to the vast EyeStone network.

Wilhilm, too, retrieves his Echo Stone, feeling the subtle hum of magic beneath his fingertips. As he activates it, the stone's screen reflects Seraphina's image. She stands poised on the stage. Comments and hieroglyphic icons flow rapidly across the bottom of the screen, live reactions from those who watch here or elsewhere. Words of admiration, hearts, and musical notes flutter by. The sheer volume of engagement is overwhelming.

This is powerful magic, Wilhilm muses. It alters reality. Through the EyeStone, Seraphina's performance doesn't just take place here. It takes place at numerous places at once, everywhere where people hold onto their EyeStones. It almost seems to collapse space itself.

"What do we do now?" Gadisa asks. Are we supposed to look at rocks too?"

Mormak grumbles. "In my day, we'd just watch with our eyes and clap with our hands."

Wilhilm tries to settle into his seat and focus his mind on the upcoming performance. The constant babbling of Mormak and Gadisa starts getting on his nerves. "Can't you just shut up for a moment?" he hisses.

"We need find something to eat and drink," Mormak says, puffing. With a jolt, he jumps up. Gadisa follows him looking for a buffet.

Wilhilm is glad Mormak and Gadisa are finished distracting him from the performance because with every note Seraphina sings, the virtual applause grows louder, echoing the real-life claps and cheers of the audience present.

The combined experience is surreal. Attendees aren't just passive spectators they are participants in a shared experience, uniting both the physical and magical realms. Through the EyeStone network, the boundaries of space and time seem to blur, allowing fans from all corners of the realm to unite in their admiration for Seraphina's artistry. It comes to Wilhilm in a rush: this is the new age of performances, a blend of magic, technology, and art that none will ever forget.

But there is something else too. Tiny whispers rippling

through the network. The same whispers he heard once before when the evil voice said something about his destiny. At first, the thinks it's only in his head, but they seem to come from every side at once. Faint and weak, but present.

His fingers dance over his EyeStone with now practiced precision, attempting to hone in on the elusive whispers. Every time he feels he's close, they slide away like quicksilver.

Determined, Wilhilm closes his eyes, begrudgingly shutting out the live performance. He imagines himself as a beacon, sending out waves of magical energy, trying to latch onto the faintest echo of the whisper.

Suddenly, a thought strikes him. Instead of chasing the whispers directly, why not trace their impact on the network? Just as one might follow ripples in a pond to locate a stone's impact, he will find where the whispers culminate by detecting the disruptions in the magical currents.

His fingers move with renewed purpose. The stone glows brighter, and a web of interconnected lines sprawl across its surface, showing the flow of magical energies. *There.* One focal point pulsates from a concentration of power. It is building, amassing an energy that is dangerously close to critical.

Wilhilm's eyes snap open, immediately locking onto Seraphina. Her posture, her grace, everything about her seems like the epicenter of this power buildup. Wilhilm jumps off his seat. Rushing forward, he prepares a spell to divert the overwhelming energy, to prevent the impending magical detonation.

Again magic! He hasn't done so much magic in... well, not since that fateful moment when he lost Lysandra.

Don't try to pretend you don't like it. You love it when I pulse through your veins, another voice resounds in his head. It's not the whispers in the network, but a voice he knows only too well. The contorted magic inside of him.

As Wilhilm focuses on the spell, ready to tear into his soul once again, his senses pick up on something amiss. The energy isn't emanating from Seraphina but from something behind her. His eyes widen in realization. A backup singer bathed in the shadows of the star performer is the true focal point. The energy around her swirls in a vortex, threatening to consume her.

Wilhilm lunges, his hands glow with dispelling magic. He feels something deep inside of him howl and groan. Too much, too early? It doesn't matter now. He has mere moments to act if he is to prevent a catastrophe.

The backup singer's aura shimmers with an outward manifestation of the unchecked magical energy swirling within her. Initially, it's a soft, almost ethereal glow, like the first rays of dawn. But as seconds pass, it rapidly intensifies, changing from a soft blue to a violent shade of crimson.

From where he stands, Wilhilm can hear the faintest of hums, separated from the worldly noise. The sound of magic. A tightly wound string on the brink of snapping. The ground beneath the singer starts to crack. Tendrils of smoke waft up from the fractures as if the very ground is unable to withstand the energy she's emanating.

The spotlight surges, a blinding wave of incandescence that turns the stage into a sudden tableau of terror and disbelief. Though the vortex swirls around the backup singer, she clings to her lyrics like a musical lifeline. Her voice breaks, the sound akin to a delicate glass figurine shattering upon a stone floor. It's a sudden, jarring interruption, a discordant note in the symphony of chaos that now reigns.

In the front rows, the audience recoils as one. A woman in a vibrant red dress throws her arms up, her opulent jewelry sparkling in the harsh light, as she turns her face away, her expression contorted in fear. A young couple clutch at each other, stumbling backwards, their eyes wide with shock.

Wilhilm looks at Seraphina. She seems to stand frozen, almost like her spirit has left her body.

Gasps and screams rise in a crescendo, echoing off the walls of the hall. A man near the center aisle stands abruptly, knocking over his chair, his mouth open in a silent shout of terror.

The backup singer's skin takes on a luminous quality, becoming almost translucent. Beneath it, a network of blue veins pulsate with unnatural brightness, like a web of glowing rivers. Her eyes, wide with terror, flash with the same fiery intensity as the power that consumes her.

The temperature in the immediate vicinity spikes dramatically, causing the red velvet curtain to smolder and the wooden floor chars. The very air begins to warp and waver. It's as if reality itself is bending, distorted by the sheer force of magic.

With a heart-wrenching scream, the backup singer's form starts to disintegrate. It's not a sudden explosion but a gradual unraveling. Wisps of energy lift from her being, spiraling upwards in shimmering strands. Her form becomes less and less solid, her outline blurring as if she's made of sand carried away by a fierce wind.

Nice. That's the kind of action I like, the voice in Wilhilm's head whispers.

And then, with one final, ear-piercing shriek, the singer

combusts completely. The intense light fades, replaced by a thick, heavy silence. Where she once stood, there's now only a smoky, charred outline on the stage, a haunting reminder of the catastrophic melding of magic and human frailty.

Seraphina tumbles and Wilhilm moves in to catch her.

CHAPTER 9

BLAME IT ON THE BOOGIE

The self-combustion of the backup singer throws the hall into a frenzy. People stumble over one another in their rush to escape the fiery spectacle. Smoke billows and obscures the panicking mass from Wilhilm.

All he sees is Seraphina's face. Its gone ashen, the color draining away. The strength leaves her knees, and with a soft gasp, she starts to crumple forward, the weight of shock and sorrow pushing her down.

Wilhilm, moving with a swiftness that belies his usually calm demeanor, lunges forward, covering the distance between them in mere moments. A tiny mouse scuttles away causing Wilhilm to nearly stumble over it, but just in time, his left arm slides around Seraphina's waist and the other cradles the back of her head.

As he steadies her, their eyes lock and, for a heartbeat, the world narrows to just the two of them. Seraphina's eyes, vibrant before, now glisten with unshed tears. Yet, even in her distress, there's a depth to them, an endless expanse of emotion that draws Wilhilm in.

They are the eyes of someone who's seen the world's wonders and its tragedies. Eyes that speak of tales untold and dreams yet to be realized. For Wilhilm, looking into them is like being caught in a tidal wave, an overwhelming rush of memory and emotion.

There is something else in those eyes, something that more than just reminds him of her. He feels like he sees some part of *Lysandra* in there. Of laughter shared under moonlit skies, of soft touches and whispered confessions, of a love that burned brighter than the sun—they all come flooding back.

Memories of a love lost seven years ago he thought he'd buried deep within the recesses of his mind. Memories of the moment of her death... It's as if he can almost hear the sands whispering to him, calling out to him.

We miss you, Wilhilm. Don't you miss us? We want you back, you only narrowly eloped our grasp. Next time you won't be so lucky.

The pain of that loss led him to construct walls around his heart but now, as he holds Seraphina, those walls crumble. The intensity of the moment, the raw vulnerability in her gaze, and the undeniable connection they share evokes feelings in him that he believed were long dead.

Forget it, don't think about it. What's past is past, he tells himself.

There's a haunting beauty in the way Seraphina looks at him, a mixture of gratitude and an unspoken understanding. Even amidst the chaos, there's a sense of serendipity in their meeting, a twist of fate that neither can ignore.

"Thank you," she whispers. Her voice feels like a gentle caress–soft, melodic, and ensnaring.

"I... erm... I happened to be close, trying to save this pour soul," he stammers. A rush of blood runs to his face.

"What happened?" Seraphina asks, looking in horror at the stage and then at the panic across the room as if she just comes out of a dream and hasn't realized anything that happened on the stage.

But Wilhilm can only focus on her eyes.

He shakes his head. *Don't get sidetracked,* Wilhilm tells himself. *You need to understand what happened.*

"Why did she combust?" he ventures, realizing it is a stupid question the moment it comes out of his mouth.

The aftermath of the combustion still leaves a hazy cloud of smoke. The three Stitchsuckers stand out like statues in the midst of the rapidly emptying concert hall. One by one, they turn to face Wilhilm, their robes whispering softly against the ground. But it's not their movements that send chills down Wilhilm's spine—it's the synchronized, melodic tone of their voices as they speak. A way entirely unique to Stitchsuckers.

"*You-wove-that-thread,*" the first one intones, every word a different pitch, like notes in a scale.

"*Magic-misdirected,*" hums the second, their voice oscillating like a pendulum.

"*Guilt-be-your-shadow,*" the third hisses, each word stretched thin.

The combined effect is eerie, like an unsettling song, and the accusatory notes of their voices pierce the air. Wilhilm feels a weight on his chest, as if the atmosphere around him has thickened. Those that are still left in the grand hall pin him in place with their gaze at the trio's allegations. Panic flutters in his chest, mixing with indignation.

I did not, Wilhilm thinks vehemently, searching for a voice amidst the tightness in his throat. The tendrils of the Stitchsuckers' hair seem to twitch and shiver in response to his emotions. The gravity of their insinuation is clear: not only has magic gone awry, but they might pin it on him, though he has nothing to do with it!

They're all staring at him. Then—movement.

Amidst the disarray, two Lepusian rogues move with purpose. They're easily distinguishable by their lapine features—long ears, sharp eyes, and agile forms. Their fur, a sleek shade of midnight black, hints at their affinity for the shadows, while the leather armor they wear is form-fitting, allowing for maximum flexibility.

And they're coming right for Wilhilm.

CHAPTER 10

I FOUGHT THE LAW

One of the Lepusian's whiskers twitches as he darts forward to swiftly place himself between Wilhilm and Seraphina. He shifts Seraphina behind him, using his body as a protective barrier. His companion moves to Seraphina's other side, completing the defensive formation. Their eyes, sharp and wary, scan the surroundings for any imminent threats. If not for the rest of a carrot sticking out of his mouth, he would appear rather intimidating.

Wilhilm, still reeling from the intense moment he has shared with Seraphina, attempts to follow, protesting, "Wait! Let me check—"

But the second Lepusian, without even looking at Wilhilm, interrupts, "Our job is to protect her, mage. Stay back."

Their nimble feet dance over the grand hall's floor, moving Seraphina away from the scene with a speed that seems almost unnatural.

The swiftness and precision with which they operate

make it clear that these Lepusian rogues are no ordinary guards. They are elite.

Strange. Who would send elite guards to Upper Bunningsworth?

The soft thud of boots approaches Wilhilm from behind. An unyielding grip squeezes both his shoulders. Wilhilm tries to twist away, but two more pairs of hands clutch his arms, their grip surprisingly strong for their furry fingers. More Lepusian guards.

Their long ears, usually upright and animated, droop slightly in concentration. The silver and blue tunics shimmer in the shifting light, signifying their status as protectors of Tiringar. The capital's influence and protection stretches as far as hamlets like Upper Bunningsworth. But why would the Patriarch be interested in guarding a concert here?

"You're under arrest for the unauthorized use of destructive magic and causing the death of a woman," announces one of them. His voice is gruff, and the whiskers on his snout twitch in apparent disdain.

"But I didn't—" Wilhilm starts, his voice strains, desperate to be heard.

"Save it for the Patriarch," the guard cuts him off.

Wilhilm's heart races as the Lepusian guards bind his hands in front of him with iron shackles coated with a silvery thread—spellguard shackles designed to dampen magical abilities.

"Is this a new fashion, self-combusting? Did we miss another trend?" Gadisa asks, climbing onto the stage and approaching Wilhilm, sweat glistening on his green skin.

"I don't understand young people anymore. Back in my time, we set fire to our enemies, not to ourselves," Mormak chimes in.

"You set fire to yourself, last week," Gadisa replies.

"Nonsense, you stupid hornswoggler! You set fire to me, because you wanted to use me as a torch, while you were healing my wounds with that artifact."

"See? You burned, same thing," Gadisa says.

"You realize I have just been arrested?" Wilhilm chimes in.

"For?" Gadisa asks. "For... cheese, perhaps?"

"How would someone be arrested for cheese?"

"All this talk about cheese confuses me," Gadisa says.

Dakaria arrives at the stage, out of breath. "Wilhilm! What's going on?" she asks. "You suddenly jumped up and ran on stage. Why?"

Wilhilm looks at her surprised. "Didn't you hear the whispers?"

"What whispers?"

"Those... unintelligible whispers, something magic, just before she started to burn up... O right, you don't have an EyeStone, but I swear, there were whispers. It was getting worse and worse."

"No one else seemed to hear anything," Dakaria says.

"I really enjoy chatting with you, but does any of you care that I have been arrested for causing the combustion?"

"Stop whining," Mormak says. "They arrest us constantly. Never deterred us before. Can they put you behind bars somewhere with good ale? They only have fancy colored alcohol in tiny glasses here. You know, those glasses that shatter on touch."

"On a dwarf's touch," Dakaria murmurs.

"They tasted alright." Gadisa shrugs.

"You ate the glasses?" Mormak asks.

"Stop it," Wilhilm says. It's too much to endure the constant bickering of his companions. "I need to think."

One of the guards coughs. “Sorry to interrupt your discussion, but we have official business here.” He coughs again, and continues in a more formal tone. “We’re taking you to Tiringar, where you will stand before the Patriarch.”

As the guards march Wilhilm away from the scene, the whispers and stares of the crowd burn into his back, and the accusatory chants of the Stitchsuckers echo hauntingly in his ears.

“Tiringar sounds fine,” Gadisa says, keeping pace alongside Wilhilm and the guards. “And he’s kind of our friend, the Patriarch, I mean.”

“We need to go to Tiringar anyway,” Dakaria says. “That’s where they make those Echo Stones.”

CHAPTER II

TAKE ME HOME, COUNTRY ROADS

Wilhilm has visited the city of Tiringar many times, but never like this—shackled and shadowed by Lepusian guards.

As they pass the formidable walls of Tiringar, he can't help but feel a bitter twist in his gut. Memories of past adventures within these walls clash with his current state of disgrace. Not all of them were a triumph, but at least he was free. Like that time, when the Rogue accidentally had burned down the city and most of it needed to be rebuilt.

Or when Patriarch bestowed the title 'Heroes of the City' upon them for saving Tiringar. (Thankfully, he had never learned how Wilhilm, Gadisa, Mormak, and Dakaria had kind of almost caused the downfall of the city.)

Happy memories of a different time!

The clinking of his chains seems to mock Wilhilm, a constant, grating reminder of the glaring injustice that was done to him.

However, no one watches him being marched into the

city. In fact, the city itself is different than he remembers. The streets of Tiringar, once bustling with life and activity, now bear a ghostly quiet. People are there, but they are mere shells of themselves, their eyes fixed on the EyeStones in their hands, oblivious to the world around them. The vibrant chatter and laughter that once filled the air are replaced by an eerie silence, punctuated only by the occasional murmur or chuckle directed at a stone's screen.

This is not the Tiringar Wilhilm knows well, the dazzling amalgamation of magic and machinery!

Towering clockwork structures stretch towards the sky, their ornate architecture intertwined with brass pipes and cogwheel embellishments, but the gears rotate more slowly. The pistons hiss, their symphony off. Arcane-powered streetlamps cast a warm glow, illuminating the vibrant marketplaces where peddlers hawk their steam-powered gadgets and clockwork contraptions to shoppers that only stare at their Echo Stones. The scent of coal and oil punctures the winding alleyways less that it usually.

There is a reason that Tiringar could do what other cities couldn't: It houses the Nexus, the remains of a colossal Elder brain, which once led a Brainreaper colony. The brain's neural pathways now serve as corridors, with synaptic clusters acting as reading rooms. The accumulated knowledge of the brains consumed by Brainreapers throughout the ages were accessed by Tiringar's elite, most prominently the Neural Navigators.

Wilhilm's eyes are drawn by a splash of vivid color amidst the drab cityscape. It's a Netherling absorbed in his EyeStone. The Netherling, with her rich indigo skin and horns that curl back like the gnarled branches of an ancient tree, stands out starkly against the muted tones of Tiringar's streets. Her tail is tipped with a tuft of hair the color of a midnight sky. It sways gently, betraying the only sign of life in her otherwise motionless form.

The Netherling taps rhythmically on the stone's surface. Her long nails flash like polished obsidian. Her eyes, a deep crimson, are fixated on the glowing screen with an intensity that borders on reverence.

Mormak walks alongside Wilhilm with a light step. His heavy boots thud solidly against the cobblestone streets of Tiringar, a rhythmic counterpoint to the clinking of Wilhilm's shackles.

"Ask her what's wrong here, what's everyone doing," Wilhilm whispers to the Dwarf, and gestures his head at his guards. "They probably won't let me."

Mormak nods and walks up to the Netherling. "Madame, can I ask you something?"

"Uh," the Netherling replies, her eyes still glued to the Echo Stone.

Wilhilm's thoughts wander off. *Seraphina*. He can't seem to forget her. When he closes his eyes, he still sees her face right in front of him, so close he can almost touch it. But this is not the right time for distractions.

"Could I just ask a question?" Mormak again says.

"In a moment," the Netherling says, then laughs aloud at her EyeStone.

After a while, it becomes clear that this "moment" will not come any time soon.

"You hornswoggler," Mormak says, putting his hands on the Netherling's right horn and yanking it up. "I'm talking to you!"

Wilhilm feels the attack a moment before it happens. The Netherling, with a cunning glint in her eyes and a wicked smile playing upon her lips, darts forward in a sudden burst of speed.

"Dodge," Wilhilm shouts in alarm.

In one fluid motion, the Netherling unsheathes a gleaming obsidian blade. Its serrated edge catches the light with a menacing shimmer. She lunges towards the Dwarf, her blade aimed at his throat.

CHAPTER 12

WE WILL ROCK YOU

In mid-attack, the Netherling's eyes fall on Wilhilm, and she stops.

"MagicWilly?" she asks. "Are you MagicWilly? Why are those guards around you? Are those your bodyguards?"

Wilhilm feels a blush rising. He doesn't like that at all. He prefers an aura of calm and depth. Blushing isn't part of that!

A Feathermaul looks up from his EyeStone when he hears the name mentioned. "It's MagicWilly, alright," he says.

"MagicWilly?" another voice repeats

The assembling crowd should know him for his vast years of service to the city, of course, but it turns out a few moments on the EyeStone community had far bigger impact.

"I want to do a cast with you," the Netherling says, holding her Echo Stone up.

As rumors of MagicWilly's arrival spread like wildfire, intrigued onlookers converge. With each passing moment, more people are pulled towards what they see as an enigmatic celebrity, their eyes filled with fascination.

If only Seraphina could see how his fans admire him. Or even better, if Seraphina would look at him like that. Or even better, if she would look at him like he looked at her.

The streets become congested as throngs of people surge towards the epicenter of the gathering, their eagerness and determination creating a palpable energy that electrifies the atmosphere.

Every corner and alleyway seems to overflow with spectators yearning for a glimpse of the renowned spellcaster who summoned a dragon. Families, merchants, and scholars find themselves swept up in the tide of anticipation, all driven by an irresistible desire to be near Wilhilm.

The more people push in, the more uncomfortable Wilhilm feels. It was nice to be recognized, but this is madness. All that for just one cast!

As the crowd swells, the thoroughfare strains under the weight of the convergence. Narrow streets become packed to the brim, making movement difficult as the masses press ever closer to the Wizard's location.

Wilhilm dodges outstretched hands and desperate pleas for attention, his heart pounds with the need to escape the overwhelming crush. His own guards propel him forwards, straining to push through.

The alleys are cramped, the ancient buildings leaning inwards as if to close off the path ahead. His breath comes in quick, sharp gasps as he pushes forward, each step a desperate bid for freedom. The brush of fingers against his cloak, the grasping hands, they all add to the urgency thrumming through his veins.

The guards are struggling to keep hold of Wilhilm and they push back at the crowd with their free hands.

Wilhilm's eyes dart around, seeking the quickest route, a slightest gap in the crowd to exploit. Every shout, every sudden movement from the crowd sends a jolt of adrenaline surging through him. The need to escape, to break free from the confines of these walls and the sea of bodies, is overwhelming, driving him onwards with a relentless, desperate energy.

"They're going to crush us!" Dakaria cries out.

"I'll cut us a path with my axe," Mormak volunteers. Wilhilm shakes his head.

"Don't hurt them," Wilhilm says. "They just love me! It sounds strange, but this is love—just too much love."

Dakaria nods. "Come on, try this direction, it looks less crowded."

Wilhilm looks for his guards. They are shoving people back, getting entangled in the mass of fans. Fear and determination drive Wilhilm forward, still bound by chains. He searches for an escape route, his eyes scanning for any opening that will grant him respite from the suffocating crowd. Finally, he spots a grate leading to the sewers, a narrow gateway to safety. He catches Dakaria's gaze, as she seems to have the exact same idea.

"We need to go under. There's no chance making it out alive here."

Wilhilm again looks for his guards. He can't see them anywhere. They are somewhere, swept up by the sea of people.

"Wait, we should wait for my guards!" Wilhilm looks back. "We can't just leave them behind, right?"

"Come on," Mormak says. "We'll meet them in the palace. Where else would they go? They certainly won't mind if we arrive first. But let me hack those shackles away."

With a swift movement of one of his axes, Wilhilm's spellguard shackles come off. He didn't even hear the axe grinding the iron.

Wilhilm makes a dash towards their escape route. Elbows brush against bodies, and the press of people threatens to overwhelm him. Yet, his determination pushes him and his companions onward, their will to survive propelling them through the suffocating mass.

Finally, Wilhilm reaches the grate, wrenches it open, and slips into the darkness below. The sound of rushing water echoes through the tunnels. The air shifts from the clamor of the city to a damp, stinky smell.

"It stinks," Mormak states the obvious.

Breathing heavily, Wilhilm takes a moment to gather himself. In the dim light, he and his companions exchange glances. He knows they must continue onward, venturing deeper into the depths of the sewers, away from the clamor and pursuit above.

"There's food," Gadisa says after a moment. "A lot of food swimming here."

"We don't eat that," Dakaria says. When Gadisa still tries fishing something out of the murky water, she rephrases her statement. "Don't eat that. Let's move on."

CHAPTER 13
CASTLE WALLS

Wilhilm and his companions step into the entrance hall of the Patriarch's palace and their footsteps echo upon the polished marble floor. The hall stretches out before him, vast and majestic, adorned with gleaming chandeliers and ornate columns that reach towards the lofty ceiling.

Sunlight pours through the stained-glass windows, casting a kaleidoscope of colors across the marble surfaces, illuminating the hall with a resplendent glow. The air is infused with an aura of regality, each breath mingling with a hint of intrigue. And something else, especially around the companions: the fine parfum of the city's sewage.

"Good thing we still have this 'Heroes of the City' thing still going on," Dakaria says. "Otherwise, they might have preferred to throw us into the alligator pit rather than let us in."

"If they only knew," Mormak sighs.

The walls are adorned with artwork and tapestries that depict heroic tales and historical events, from the Attack of the Giant Alligator to the Incident of the Hollow Teddybear (a giant stuffed bear, seemingly left as a gift at Tiringar's gates). Busts and statues of revered ancestors stand on pedestals, their stern gazes seemingly overseeing the proceedings within the hall.

"They stare at my belly," Gadisa says.

"I don't think it's your belly," Wilhilm muses. "Probably it's more the fact that you haven't washed your culottes in, like, forever."

"Has anyone ever found anything conclusive on the longterm effects of washing?" Gadisa says. "Until there is no evidence, I will not believe in it."

"Stop," a guard's harsh voice calls down the hall. "That's the fugitive we were tasked to bring before the Patriarch."

Wilhilm turns. His guards! Finally, they arrived. The guards are hurrying toward them, panting, their uniform in tatters, sweat on their fur.

"A fugitive?" Wilhilm says. "How can I be a fugitive, when I'm right where you want me to be?"

"But you walked here on your own," the guard states.

"I don't think this is against the law," the second guard says after a moment's thought. "I think if he was walking backwards, that would be against the law."

"I'm not walking backwards," Wilhilm says, wondering what walking backwards has to do with anything. "And now, hurry up. You have to lead me to the Patriarch to face my punishment. How does it look when I arrive without guards? What is the Patriarch supposed to think when you slack off?"

The guards cough in embarrassment. Again, they put spellguard shackles on him, then lead the way.

The hall's dimensions seem to expand as they move deeper. The ceiling soars high above, painted with scenes of celestial wonders and mythological beings, giving the illusion of an infinite sky. The soft glow of crystal chandeliers cast a warm and inviting light. Layers of luxurious rugs provide a cushioned path amidst the grandeur, muffling the group's footsteps.

"I hope he remembers how helpful we have been," Gadisa murmurs. "He can be moody at times. The Patriarch, I mean."

"I have a good feeling about this," Mormak says.

Again, Wilhilm's thoughts wander off to Seraphina. He wonders how she copes with the attention of crowds. Perhaps he should try and find out where she is. Just to make sure, of course, that she is fine.

Each step brings him closer to the imposing double-winged doors at the end of the hall end. He pauses, his gaze tracing the carvings on the doors, mostly depicting dwarves drinking and dancing. Their tops nearly brush the arched ceiling, itself adorned with vivid frescoes: scenes of a radiant sun god, nymphs and satyrs in a verdant garden, a tempestuous sea goddess, and the grand depiction of the kingdom's creation unfold above him, the colors so vivid that they seem to pulse with life.

As hands of two guards press against the cool, heavy doors, they swing inward with a low, resonant creak. Wilhilm steps forward, his eyes widening as the chamber reveals itself. He's greeted by a room so vast, its farthest corners lurk in a soft, golden haze. At its heart lies a colossal mahogany table, its surface a mirror to the world above, reflecting the flickering lights of the crystal chandeliers. Each step Wilhilm takes sends tiny reflections scurrying across its polished expanse, revealing years of history etched in its wood—battles won, treaties signed, secrets whispered. Wilhilm can't help but feel a little veneration of the decision that were taken here.

Seated at the head of the table is the Patriarch clad in regal attire. He exudes an aura of authority. Surrounding the table, a select few council members, each distinguished in their own right, sit in quiet conversation, their attention momentarily diverted by the arrival of the adventurers.

CHAPTER 14
UNDER PRESSURE

As Wilhilm and his three friends approach the table, there's hardly any commotion. The council members casually glance up, then down again to their EyeStones. Only a Stichsucker sitting at the Patriarch's side keeps on staring at Wilhilm. The Patriarch's gaze darts from one to the next, hungrily soaking in every aspect of the scene before him.

"May honor go with you," the Patriarch greets them in the traditional fashion.

"Better honor than a sharp stick in the eye," the Rogue replies.

Wilhilm cringes. Before the Rogue can continue lowering Wilhilm's chances of fair treatment, Dakaria talks over him, replying with the standard response. "When the Ruler calls, all beings answer."

The Patriarch lets the Rogue's reply slide, and instead focuses on Wilhilm. "Wilhilm Grindtosser! What a joy seeing you! Or shall I say, MagicWilly? Quite the following you've built!"

"Too kind, Sir," Wilhilm replies, feeling slightly honored. "Let me guess, you are PatriarchOfTiringar01?"

The Patriarch laughs out, a sharp and concise laugh, cutting through the murmur of conversation like a well-honed blade. "Indeed, I am! There's a slight issue with someone already using PatriarchOfTiringar, but I ordered the Assassin's Guild to take care of it."

"*Death-brought-he*," the Stitchsucker cuts in.

The Patriarch gives him an unhappy look and sighs. "This is the esteemed Kel'zorath Vrallax, Keeper of the Lore," he introduces the Stitchsucker.

Wilhilm isn't quite sure what the title *Keeper of the Lore* entails, but it sounds important. For a moment he ponders what to say, but decides that there might be some kind of formal greeting required of him that goes with that title, so instead he just smiles and nods.

"Kel'zorath seems to accuse you of using magic to kill a singer at some concert," the Patriarch says.

"*See-it-happen-my-brethren, truth-it-is-not-conjecture*," Kel'zorath says.

"Thoughts indeed travel fast in the Stitchsucker community. But it was nothing of that sort," Wilhilm defends himself. "I heard whispers and then I rushed to the stage to..."

"*Set-on-fire-he-did*," Kel'zorath says and coughs.

The Patriarch sighs a deep long sigh, while he buries his face in his hands. "Wilhilm, so your defense is that voices in your head told you to do it?"

"No. I mean yes, there were whispers, but I went on stage to save Seraphina," Wilhilm says. Kel'zorath seems to have something stuck in his throat, he is still coughing.

"Bring him something to drink," the Patriarch orders,

and a moment later, a Feathermaul lackey in orange robes enters, the typical brutish bulk of his kind.

The lackey moves with an unsettling fluidity, its massive paws barely making a sound on the marble floor. He brings a bubbly blue drink. And not the benign blue of a summer sky or the gentle blue of a robin's egg, but a deep, vibrant blue that seems to shimmer with a life of its own.

For a moment, Wilhilm thinks he sees a tiny, iridescent creatures swimming within its depths, but this surely must be a trick of the eye. *Right?*

Bubbles rise to the surface with an eager enthusiasm, popping with little puffs of what could have been smoke or the spirits of the recently departed. It has a scent that was equally perplexing—a heady mix of violets, burnt sugar, and something faintly metallic.

"Kel'zorath, I hear you love Azure Ambrosia," the Patriarch says. "And don't forget our culinary motto. Drink at your own risk!"

Azure Ambrosia. Wilhilm has heard of it, though never seen it. The inventor, reputed to have been both a genius in alchemical circles and a terrible cook, had left the recipe behind as a parting gift—or perhaps a curse.

"My problem is," the Patriarch continues, "when the security of the Nexus is concerned, I can't really go against one of the Stitchsucker families. Not if I want my brain to stay intact, that is. If they say it happened, it's as good as a fact."

"But it isn't fact!"

"As I said, there is nothing I can do..."

Desperation, as far as feelings go, is a rather sly and persistent emotion. It creeps up on you like an unwelcome relative, the sort that borrows money and never leaves. And in that moment, standing before the Patriarch, it wraps itself around Wilhilm like a damp, uncomfortable blanket.

"But... but... but...," Wilhilm says. "You have to listen to my side of the story."

"In the finer workings of Tiringar justice, this is not a legal requirement," the Patriarch replies. "The way I see it is that Kel'zorath will insist on offering your brain to the Brainreapers of the Nexus."

Wilhilm feels it in the tightening of his chest, the way his breath comes in short, panicked gasps, each one a little more frantic than the last. His mind races, conjuring images of every possible outcome, none of them good, all of them ending in a variety of unpleasantness that would make even the most hardened adventurer squirm.

The Patriarch shrugs. "This is just how things are."

Kel'zorath takes a sip from the blue drink. His face twists in contemplation, then amusement, as the drink's peculiar flavor spreads across his palate. But the amusement is short-lived. Suddenly, Kel'zorath coughs again, a violent, hacking sound that echoes through the room. His eyes bulge in surprise and alarm as he shoots up from his chair, the goblet clattering to the floor, its remaining contents splashing harmlessly.

His hand flows to his chest, while he twitches and jerks. His face turns a worrying shade of purple, veins standing out starkly against his skin.

CHAPTER 15
KNOCKIN ON HEAVEN'S DOOR

Wilhilm watches on in horror, while the room remains undisturbed and the eyes of the council continue to be glued to their EyeStones, as if Wilhilm is the only one who can see that Kel'zorath is indeed in trouble.

Just when Wilhilm wants to shout out for someone to help, Kel'zorath's knees buckle. He sways for a heartbeat, then collapses to the floor with a final, shuddering breath. And still, nobody seems to take notice.

"I can't do anything...except of course, if the accuser would suddenly pass away. O did he just do that? So sad. This causes some hassle with the Stitchsucker community, no doubt," the Patriarch says conversationally. "But laws are laws. Well, seeing that the accuser has passed away, I can regrettably only declare that there is no legal grounding to go ahead with the prosecution."

He waves for the Feathermaul lackey. "Bertram, would you clean up and remove the body? And make sure there are no traces of that... drink."

The lackey's feathers bristle and talons click ominously

on the polished marble floor. Clutched in its powerful beak is Kelzorath's left arm. The Feathermaul, seemingly unfazed, drags Kel'zorath away. His muscles ripple under a coat of mottled fur and feathers. Wilhilm watches on, but finds it hard to form a coherent thought. With one final heave, the Feathermaul disappears through a side door.

The Patriarch turns to the guards. "What's this nonsense? Remove the shackles."

Wilhilm has trouble keeping up. Did the Patriarch just poison a Stitchsucker? But why? To save him? That seems unlikely. The Patriarch would never do anything without getting something out of it.

"Allow me," Dakaria chimes in, "there's an urgent issue we need to discuss with you."

"What coincidence, there's an urgent issue I need to discuss with you," the Patriarch replies.

"Does your issue also have to do with Cheese EyeStones?" Dakaria inquires.

The Patriarch and the Council laugh. "Everything has to do with the Cheese EyeStone. We're over the moon. Best product to ever come out of Tiringar. Everyone uses it!"

"Do you know who made it?"

"Of course, the gnomes make it. This little one..."

"They're all little ones," Gadisa says.

"Bereton," the Patriarch calls to someone in the Council, "what's that gnome's name?"

"Dipple Nimble Retchbucket, Sir," the man—Bereton—replies.

"That's the one," the Patriarch says triumphantly. "Well, Wilhilm, did you think about how your new influence can help the splendid city of Tiringar?"

"My influence?" Wilhilm says.

"Who is this Dimble...Dipple Nibble... Dimple Nimble..." Dakaria says, trying to get back to the issue at hand.

The Patriarch ignores her, and instead focuses on Wilhilm again. "Thanks to your immense following, you can promote the reputation of Tiringar...and... Bereton, finish the sentence!"

Bereton looks up from his Echo Stone, confusion on his face, as if awakened from a deep dream. "Sorry, Sir, I wasn't listening, FunnyOrc23 just cast something wild. Crazy. Look!"

"Tapton!"

"Sorry, Sir, I can't listen right now, there's a new cast of TheColorfulBard," the man replies.

"Lady Aston," the Patriarch calls.

"Sir?"

"Have you been listening?"

"With half an ear, yes, Sir, with the other I was focusing on the new casts," Lady Aston replies.

"Then finish the sentence!"

"The Honorable Lord Patriarch was about to say you can promote the reputation of Tiringar and the near perfect rule of its beloved Patriarch, but, of course, his modesty prevents him from praising himself," Lady Aston says.

"Me? Promote the city? How?" Wilhilm asks.

The Patriarch and what members of the council are looking up from their EyeStones nod gravely.

"You could collab with FunnyOrc23—might double your audience," Bereton says.

"So, what is it you exactly want me to do?" Wilhilm asks. "Say something like... Travel to Tiringar. In Tiringar, the possibilities are endless. Brace yourself for an experience that will test your limits, immerse you in a world where the boundaries of imagination blur, but where you always can sell a limb when you're short of gold?"

The Patriarch shakes his head. "All perfectly fine sides of our beautiful city, but nothing as... obvious. I was thinking about you performing your casts here in the city—some of our famous landmarks in the background, visiting some of our restaurants—so people will feel compelled to search out these locations on their own."

"I... well, I'm not sure... I mean, this would be immense pressure," Wilhilm says.

"I see, we agree on this, perfect. You will promote our fine city, and I see to it that these ridiculous and unfounded charges against you will not resurface."

"I didn't... I mean..."

The Patriarch rises from the table with the grace of a well-practiced statesman. His movements are swift yet deliberate. As he stands, the finely woven fabric of his robe fall into place, cascading down with the precision of a master tailor's handiwork. With a flick of his wrists, he claps his clothes, smoothing out any imperceptible wrinkles.

"Wilhilm, walk with me, so we can talk about the details."

The Patriarch strides out into the adjacent chamber, and from there out into the garden, his presence as commanding as ever, his robes trailing like whispers of authority. Behind him, Wilhilm trails, each step a study in barely contained agitation.

There is something the Patriarch doesn't tell him. At least, not in front of the whole room. Wilhilm's grip on his wand tightens and loosens in an erratic rhythm, the knuckles blanching with each squeeze. Occasionally, his lips press into a thin, displeased line, only to be followed by a quick exhalation, a silent but eloquent display of his inner turmoil.

"Are we supposed to come along?" Gadisa whispers.

"Why wouldn't we? We're pleasant to be around. Everyone wants to be with us," Mormak says.

"We're happy to follow," Dakaria calls after the Patriarch.

"We need to speak privately," the Patriarch whispers to Wilhilm, while they pass red tulips. "I need your help."

CHAPTER 16
SECRET GARDEN

The Patriarch's garden is breath-taking. Wilhilm has heard so much about it, but despite his previous visits at the palace never entered it before. The air is thick with the scent of blooming flowers, each more vibrant and unique than the last. Wilhilm's fingers itch to reach out and touch, to feel the hum of life that courses through every leaf and petal.

Above him, the branches of towering trees intertwine like the vaulted ceiling of a great cathedral, their leaves rustling in a symphony of whispers. Gadisa, Mormak and Dakaria are hurrying closer. *Don't let them do anything stupid, dear Gods.*

"What is bothering your Eminence?" Wilhilm detracts himself by addressing the Patriarch.

The Patriarch directs Wilhilm toward a vine-covered archway. "What did you see when you entered Tiringar? Is this still your city?"

"The very same merry old city, Your Eminence, full of steam-powered wonders, organ-stealing creatures, and the strongest undercurrent of magic in all of the lands," Wilhilm replies.

When they reach the archway, the garden seems to come alive. Not in the mundane, chlorophyll-filled sense, but in the manner of a creature just woken from a long, luxurious nap and suddenly very interested in its guests. The vines, previously content to be mere decoration, now seem to stretch and yawn, their tendrils curling with a sentience that suggested they had been biding their time for just such an occasion.

The Patriarch stands at the center, the vines curling around him in a manner that is almost reverent. The vines form a small chamber. "Come closer," the Patriarch says, "this part of the garden is a sanctum. It will shield us from curious eyes and ears."

To Wilhilm's right, the bulky shape of Gadisa starts a fight with one the vines. A particularly enthusiastic vine repeatedly jabs him in the posterior with what could only be described as botanical zeal. Gadisa yelps and shuffles forward with surprising speed for a man of his girth. He moves into the sanctum.

Meanwhile, Dakaria's eyes are wide with admiration. She extends a hand, allowing a tendril to wrap gently around her wrist. Another vine, apparently taking its job very seriously, drags Mormak by the ankle toward the closing sanctum. Mormak's protests are muffled by the sheer indignity of it all, his beard bristling with affront.

As the final tendrils interwove and the sanctum completes itself, Wilhilm can't help but feel admiration. The vines form a living wall, their leaves rustling with a sense of purpose, creating an intimate space. The Patriarch smiles at them.

“As I was saying, the city, unfortunately, has become almost unrulable. Everyone is glued to their EyeStone. They don’t care for anything anymore. People come in late for work, leave early, some even demand salaries when they have perfectly fine arrangements like a bed and a healthy breakfast from their employer,” the Patriarch complains. “Some don’t show up at all. But it’s especially dire for restaurants.”

“For restaurants, Sir?” Gadisa asks. “This reminds me... I’m hungry.”

“You wouldn’t believe,” the Patriarch continues. “They show up, wave their EyeStone, and expect free food in return.”

“I’m not sure I understand. What has free food to do with the EyeStone?” Dakaria chimes in, absent-mindedly stroking a vine that cuddles up to her.

“Something about it bringing in more customers if they talk about it on the EyeStone network,” the Patriarch explains. “They perpetuate that they bring in customers, so they demand free food in exchange.”

“Huh. But the owners can refuse, right?” Wilhilm asks. What a wild thought. Food for free, just because you use an EyeStone.

“It’s not so easy. If they refuse, they talk about the restaurant anyway, but in a manner less favorable. Let’s just say it involves mice.”

“But I’m sure the EyeStone reels in taxes?” Mormak says. “It does fill up your treasure chamber good. Right?”

“This used to be the case. Lots of taxes. Unfortunately, they brought in a tax gnome, and you know how much of a nuisance they can be. They established some scheme, and now officially, all EyeStone transactions take place in the Zal’qaran desert.”

Wilhilm shudders at the mere mention of the

Zal'qaran desert. It brings back memories from the time he lost Lysandra. He finds it advisable to not comment on the Patriarch's comments on tax gnomes, though. As far as he understands, the Patriarch employs tax gnomes himself.

"But why can't you just send your guards in? Or the Imperial Revenue Service?" Wilhilm asks.

"Ew, pesky bastards," Mormak grumbles when he hears the Imperial Revenue Service mentioned.

"I'm in a bit of a difficult position. As the Patriarch of Tiringar, I embrace successful entrepreneurs. And people just love the EyeStone. So, if I act against Cheese, people will hold it against me. There even might be a rebellion. People are *very* attached to their EyeStones."

Suddenly, the picture completes for Wilhilm. The Patriarch wants to get rid of the EyeStone business for tax evasion, but he fears the backlash of the population.

"This seems to be more of a fiscal matter," Wilhilm carefully says. "I don't quite understand how I can be of assistance."

The vines crack the tiniest bit. Wilhilm looks around but sees nothing. Probably a bird that crashed against the sanctum outside.

"Well, you and your friends... you *break* things. And by things, I mean buildings, towers, libraries, even cities," the Patriarch continues.

"That's a very lose interpretation," Wilhilm says. "Most of those things were very unfortunate random mishaps."

"All I want for you to do is to break Cheese," the Patriarch whispers while he puts his index finger to his mouth.

"Huh. The problem, Sir, might be that we can't really *deliberately* break things. They more like break when they are not supposed to break," Wilhilm tries to explain.

"I don't care how you do it. But it's very important to me."

"Important... how?" Mormak chimes in. "Gold-important or ale-important?" These are the two main categories for Mormak to prioritize and it is always clear what his number one category is.

"I've heard that there's a problem with your soul?" the Patriarch addresses Wilhilm.

"Nothing much really," Wilhilm hurries to say. "A bit of scratches here, a bit of fissures there, a bit of rags and tatters in between."

"You know, there's some ancient knowledge in the Nexus. And my people tell me there's something that might help you in the vastness of the Nexus."

"Something that might help me? What did you find?"

"I could show you, but unfortunately this whole EyeStone business keeps me busy. So, I will really only come around taking you until after this is all has been dealt with."

"So, you want us to..."

"Shshsh," the Patriarch admonished. "I'm just stating facts or merely listing facts."

Wilhilm nods slowly. He still thinks the Patriarch is not telling him everything he knows. But it's clear to him now why the Patriarch protected him from the Stitchsucker. And now the ruler wants something in return—and would, as kind of an additional pay, help him fix his soul. For the Patriarch, everything is a business. That's good enough for Wilhilm now.

"Fine," Wilhilm nods.

"There is the matter of payment for the rest of us," Mormak says. "I mean, fixing the wizard's soul, that's all nice, but what's in it for us?"

"I'm sure we'll find something," the Patriarch smiles.

"I would prefer to know upfront," Mormak sets in, but Dakaria flicks his ear. "The Ruler commands, we obey," she says.

"What are you doing? I don't want to..." Mormak protests.

"Doesn't matter," Dakaria whispers.

"Fine," Mormak sighs.

"There will be food, right?" Gadisa asks but his question is largely ignored.

"Let's go straight to the source and pay this gnome a visit," Mormak says. "I hear they have a good tavern right next door."

The Patriarch nods, and the vines around them pull apart, allowing them to leave.

CHAPTER 17

MATERIAL GIRL

"That must be it," Wilhilm says, pointing at the building before them.

A half-eaten wheel of cheese adorns the façade of the building. Below it, the symbols for "Cheese Re-Invents the Echo Stone, Meet the EyeStone" are spelt out in over a dozen languages.

Wilhilm slides his Echo Stone back into his pouch which he had taken out while they walked, just to check if Seraphina had been visible on the EyeStone network. He was disappointed to see she hadn't published a new cast since that horrific incident at the concert. It's worrisome. *He really should look for her.* Just for her own safety, of course.

But for the moment, the entrance of the building beckons Wilhilm with its towering double doors. Carvings depict griffins and dragons using Echo Stones, even a mouse with an Echo Stone in the right corner. As the sunlight dances across the doorway, the handles and hinges catch the light, revealing an understated luster of gold. This subtle glint, more burnished than bright, mirrors the city's hidden wealth and long-standing prosperity. It suggests a realm within where luxury and legend intertwine.

Wilhilm can't help but feel a sense of anticipation. The building's magnificence serves as a harbinger of... well, *something*—exactly what is for a topic of discussion, but that something would probably involve EyeStones and, perhaps, cheese.

Inside is as silent as the inner sanctum of a temple. Arched windows adorned with delicate stained glass filter colorful beams of light into the interior, casting a soft glow upon the marble floors and walls. Over a dozen gnomes in blue robes bustle around, serving customers in whispers.

"Are we supposed to talk?" Gadisa whispers.

The high-pitched voice of a gnome greets them. "How can I help you?"

"We want to talk to Nimble...Timble...Fimble," Dakaria starts.

"Dipple Nimble Retchbucket," Wilhilm says.

The gnome laughs. "Sure, everyone wants to talk to him. But while the universe inflates to the size of your self, why don't you talk to me?"

"They think there might be something wrong with the EyeStones, or with the network," Wilhilm says, pointing at his companions as if he had nothing to do with it.

The gnome looks at him, then smiles. "Isn't that you, MagicWilly?"

Wilhilm nods, and then lowers his voice. "Let's not make a big fuss, we don't want chaos in your store, right?"

The gnome nods and gets back to the issue at hand. "Something wrong with our EyeStones, how?"

"Well," Dakaria says, "they seem to impact people... and

not in a good way! They get all moody, and we saw someone combust."

"Self-combust in the middle of a concert," Mormak adds.

The gnome smiles again and looks at Dakaria. "Moody? Self combustion? Isn't that a little... old-fashioned... for a young lady like you?"

"How's not wanting people to be possessed by something evil old-fashioned?" Dakaria asks.

"I mean, you're assuming people don't want to change, don't want to become the best version of themselves while others cheer them on," the gnome says.

Wilhilm wonders if they came to the right place. Gnome ethics can be particular—as long as gold is involved, they're happy to accommodate for pretty much anything. Still, intentional evil spells? That seems so far removed from the little engineers bustling about in their blue coats, it's just not plausible.

"I don't mean... I mean, I'm talking about physical changes," Dakaria insists.

"Show me your EyeStone, and I will personally look it over."

Something else might be going on, perhaps not even related to the gnomes, Wilhilm thinks.

"I don't have one," Dakaria says. "But I know this from... general observation!"

Wilhilm looks around. Those gnomes seem to know their stuff. They're busily attending to their customers.

The gnome nods gravely at Dakaria. "No EyeStone? Impossible." He looks at Mormak and Gadisa. "Don't any of you have one?"

CHAPTER 18

SHOP AROUND

"I have an EyeStone," Wilhilm says and shows the gnome his Echo Stone. "Everything's okay with mine. I didn't burn yet."

The gnome smiles. "Of course, but none of your companions own one? Let me suggest this: MagicWilly, I will offer ten percent off to your friends. If you aren't satisfied in any way, I pledge a full return of your gold. This way, you can confirm for yourself that everything is in order, and if not, we can investigate the matter right away."

"Why can't you investigate now?" Dakaria asks but Wilhilm glances at his Echo Stone in time to see that Seraphina has put a new cast on the network. Behind her are the city walls of Tiringar. Wilhilm's heart quickens.

He steps away from the others as Dakaria goes back and forth with the gnome. "Meet me in Tiringar," Seraphina says in her cast to her fans. If Seraphina's in Tiringar as well, Wilhilm actually stands a chance of bumping into her.

He pulls out of his revery to hear the gnome say, "I can only look into individual EyeStones, and since Wilhilm says everything is okay with his and I can't confiscate an Echo

Stone from someone you may have met on the street, you need one to show me what's wrong."

"I don't like that. It sounds too much like selling to me," Mormak mutters.

"And like spending gold," Gadisa adds.

Dakaria has a shrewd look on her face. "How much is one of these?"

"Think of it more as an experience rather than a price tag," the gnome says.

"But how much gold is it?"

"Just let me remind you that I'm offering a world of new experiences, of new connections, of quality time spent. These are things money cannot typically buy!"

"But how much...?"

Oh no. Once a gnome is in selling mode, it is really hard to stop him. Or to hold steadfast and not give in to the marketing. Wilhilm hurries to shove his fingers into his ears.

"How much is your life worth, really?" The gnome's voice comes muffled. "Or that of your companions? Or your last adventure? See, it's so hard to put a price tag to experiences."

"HOW MUCH?" Gadisa asks in a voice so loud it resonates from the marble and makes the room shake. Wilhilm's fingers do nothing to shut out the rumble.

"600 gold," the gnome says hurriedly, gesturing to the Rogue to calm down.

"But that's... that's... like 50,000 gold for all of us," Gadisa says.

"1,800," Mormak corrects him, "but still a lot. Too much." He lowers his voice and speaks to the gnome. "And you only negotiate with me. Never with the Rogue, you understand? Never with the Rogue!"

The gnome nods, yet turns back to the Rogue. “Do you see how everyone eyes your culottes?” he asks Gadisa.

“What’s wrong with my culottes?” Gadisa says.

“Nothing, nothing at all. Still, one might think, I mean not me, of course, but—” he gestures toward the room, “—they might think you haven’t washed them for a very long time.”

Gadisa sighs. “There are no long-term studies on the effects of washing,” he says with the tone of a well-worn subject. “All this water and soap and rubbing them on a washboard might just ruin the fabric. It takes all the... minerals out. The good stuff.”

“But they don’t know that, do they?” the gnome asks.

The fingers in his ears don’t do a very good job. Wilhilm can still hear everything, and he feels like his hands are twitching and itching to get to his purse and buy something from the gnome.

Calm. He has to remain calm. That is most important of all.

Wilhilm again glances at his Echo Stone. Seeing Seraphina, he cautiously takes one finger out of his ear. “Watch this space. I’ll reveal soon where to meet me,” Seraphina’s cast promises.

Gadisa meanwhile, continuing to argue with the gnome, shakes his head. “Someone tells them to wash their stuff, they go ahead, wash it. Where I’m from, people never wash anything.”

“Because they live underwater,” Mormak murmurs.

“What if they knew washing is not good?” the gnome says. “What if, no matter where you showed up on your travels, people knew about that, and supported it?”

“But how? Not unless I talked to them about it... and I can’t talk to all of them!”

Oh no. That was it. The Rogue walked right into the trap. Wilhilm knows now he is lost. He is the gnome's victim, ready to be manipulated into a sale. Deep inside, Wilhilm's empathetic. *Poor soul. This is what happens when you talk to a gnome.*

And the gnome goes in for the kill.

CHAPTER 19

HUNGRY LIKE THE WOLF

"You *can* talk to all of them at the same time, can't you?" the gnome says, waving an EyeStone in Gadisa's face. "With this little device, you can tell people the truth about washing. And while not all of them will immediately believe you, some will."

"Someone always will. People believe the stupidest things, especially if it's not far off from how they perceive the world," Dakaria says. "That's hardly a good thing. It's much harder to make them understand the true nature of things. Because truth is messy and complicated and interdependent on so many facts—so much knowledge, so much insight."

"Like what for example?" the gnome asks innocently.

Oh no. Not her too! Wilhilm waves at Dakaria from behind the gnome and makes faces. This whole conversation is littered with dangerous sales traps like a dungeon is littered with skeleton warriors.

"Trees, for instance," Dakaria says regardless of Wilhilm's gesturing. "People don't understand how trees are alive. How they talk to each other, though much slower than our communication is. That they use the network of their roots, the fungi close to them, and their fragrances, to speak."

"Enlighten me."

"Take caterpillars. If they chew the leaves of a tree, they respond by releasing a special blend of aromatic compounds to the air. The compounds attract some species of wasps that inject their eggs into the bodies of those caterpillars. When the wasp egg hatches, the larva feeds on the worm's internal organs. They die, the trees are saved. Problem solved."

That is interesting, Wilhilm thinks. He should listen to Dakaria more often. Then he catches a gleam in the eye of the gnome and realizes she is lost too.

"Wow," the gnome says. "I did not know that. Did you know that?" he asks the Dwarf.

Mormak shakes his head. "Trees? Never talked to one of 'em. My axe knew lots of them, though, by, errr, direct contact."

"See, he didn't know! But isn't that fascinating?" the gnome says.

Dakaria blushes a little, and nods. "It is fascinating."

Wilhilm realizes he still has his fingers in his ears. He retracts them—they're not doing much good anyway—and lets a sigh slip out at Dakaria's downfall.

"Wouldn't you want to tell more people about trees, to educate them?" the gnome asks.

Wilhilm can see the salesman's breathing quickening as the closure of his deal nears.

"It would be beneficial," Dakaria says.

"It would! Most definitely!"

"But I don't have the time," she says, "not while I'm out doing quests, trying to make a living."

"But with a Cheese EyeStone, you can educate everyone, even while you're out questing. Where's the harm? Try it. Best case, you teach some people. Or, you do find out something's wrong with our product. In that case, you come back to me and together we will fix those issues, make the world safer. At any rate, you make life better. Isn't that something?"

Dakaria takes the Echo Stone and looks at it. "I suppose, I could try," she murmurs.

"Huh," Mormak says. "I'm the Chief Gold Officer of this bunch, and if I say no, you can sweet talk them all you want, I'm not releasing the funds."

Right! The Dwarf! He might turn the tide. Wilhilm has never seen him coaxed into anything. Not even gnome magic can sway his stubbornness. There is hope, after all.

"But surely you see the advantages?" the gnome asks. "A strong, experienced, and handsome dwarf like you? All the realm would love to watch your axe moves, I suppose."

"I bet they would. But I'm not spending 1,800 on that! And you know why?"

"No, why?"

"Because then my funds for ale would be gone! And a dwarf can't run on anything less than ale." Mormak pauses for a moment. "Well, beer will do the job too. And lager, and porter, and stout. And even wheat, if it's a real emergency."

"Oh, but did you know you can get a life's supply of ale with one of these?"

Mormak looks suspiciously at the gnome. "How so?"

"Every modern brewery understands that they need to take advantage of this exciting new opportunity in marketing," the gnome explains. "With a knowledgeable spokesman like you, every brewery in Tiringar would be happy to supply you with ale for the rest of your life, as long as you keep talking about them on the network."

"Free ale? Just like that?"

"In trade for EyeStone casts advertising their drink."

"I talk about ale most of the day anyway, right?"

"You do," Gadisa says. "Even if I want to talk about our next meal, you keep on talking about your next ale!"

Mormak thinks for a moment. "Okay, 1,800 minus the ten percent you promised, that makes 1,620. Let's just round it and make it an even 1,500 because who wouldn't want his price to be a nice round number?"

The gnome nods. "1,500 it is. And you'll be getting the latest EyeStone generation. You'll have so much fun!"

Wilhilm sighs. He looks at his own Echo Stone, and a question forms in his mind.

"There's one thing I always wondered," he says slowly.

"What do you want to know?" the gnome asks.

"Could I send a cast, not to everyone, but to a specific person?"

The gnome shakes his head. "Currently, that's not possible. As you might know, all Echo Stones connect to the same counterpart. We're working with this counterpart to mirror the casts back to everyone else. It's a complicated installation, involving a lot of mirrors. The system doesn't allow you to choose to which EyeStones your cast goes."

Wilhilm sighs again, thinking of Seraphina.

CHAPTER 20

UNDER COVER OF THE NIGHT

At the doors of Cheese, Wilhilm leaves his companions behind in favor of wandering the bustling streets of Tiringar on his own. He wants to be ready for when Seraphina's cast announcing her location goes live. He might even—randomly, of course—run into her once he sees the background of her next cast.

As the sun begins its slow descent, the sky transforms into a canvas of ethereal beauty. Streaks of orange, pink, and deep purple paint the horizon, casting a warm, otherworldly glow over the cobblestone streets.

Dark, wispy shadows begin to seep out from Wilhilm's skin, an eerie visual manifestation of the turmoil within. The shadows are not thick or overwhelming. The shadows, like tendrils of smoke, emerge in sparse, sinuous trails, curling away from his arms in a ghostly dance.

Wilhilm focuses on his Echo Stone, trying to calm down the magic inside of him. The gnome magic really does wonders for his soul. Whenever he feels the magic act up in him, the Echo Stone seems to calm it down.

While looking down at his Echo Stone, he bumps into

something hard. He can just make out a splash of vibrant color as he juggles his Echo Stone to keep it from falling. Looking up, he finds a large, glossy poster plastered against the weathered brick wall of a local apothecary. The paper has a slight sheen, distinguishing it from the array of other advertisements and notices.

The poster is dominated by an alluring image of Seraphina. Raven-black hair frames her face and sapphire eyes sparkle with a mix of mischief and allure. Wilhilm takes in the gentle curve of her cheek and the softness of her lips, slightly parted as if she's about to share a secret. It's a face that has haunted Wilhilm since the night of the performance.

Beneath the image, flowing, elegant script reads, "Seraphina: The Voice of Ages. Witness the Enchantment at the Horse Inn." The dates of her performances are detailed below, confirming she's performing in the city for the better part of the month.

For a brief moment, Wilhilm feels an odd sensation—a mix of elation and anxiety. It's like the universe calls out to him. This can't all be happenstance. First, he sees Seraphina doing her cast and now, he sees her poster on the wall. This is destiny. It is like the universe wants him to see her again, to speak to her.

But with that comes memories of their last encounter: the intimate moment interrupted, the backup singer's tragic fate, and the protective Lepusian rogues.

Wilhilm reaches out, his fingers grazing the smooth surface of the poster. The texture, combined with the image before him, makes the memories of that night feel even more tangible. He takes a deep breath, making a silent vow that he will find a way to see her again and ensure her safety (of course).

The first concert date listed is the day after tomorrow. An eternity.

Don't exaggerate, he tells himself. *And compose yourself!*

Wilhilm reluctantly leaves the poster behind and meanders through the labyrinthine streets of Tiringar. The city's blend of traditional structures and machinery paints a vivid picture of its storied past and its forward-looking aspirations. He treads on worn cobblestones, lined by houses adorned with flowering window boxes and intricate wrought ironwork. In contrast, statuesque stone edifices, engraved with tales of old, cast long shadows over the lanes, standing as silent guardians of countless secrets. The city is alive with a cacophony of sounds: vendors shouting about their wares, children playing and laughing, even the distant strum of a lute from a nearby tavern. Yet, amidst the urban symphony, Wilhilm's mind is a whirlwind of its own.

With every step, Wilhilm contemplates Seraphina's potential link to the shocking incident at the performance. Could she have been the target? Or did she possibly know more about what had transpired? But each hypothesis is invariably interrupted by the recollection of Seraphina's mesmerizing eyes. Their depths, reminiscent of moonlit oceans, seem to have etched an indelible mark on his psyche, refusing to fade.

The possibility of their paths crossing again not only intrigues him but evokes an emotion he hadn't anticipated.

He keeps bringing out his Echo Stone, staring at it, until eventually, Seraphina indeed casts. She's drinking a colorful liquid in front of a market stall. "Enjoy the Tiringar market with Luminescent Liqueur," she whispers.

Wilhilm replays the cast multiple times. Seraphina is out on the streets, just like him. With any luck, he might run into her. Using the background to guide his steps, he tries to find the spot where she took the cast.

Damp cobblestones gleam beneath the muted glow of awakening streetlamps. The dim lights etch ghostly outlines on the timeworn stalls. Wilhilm continues through the market, stopping every so often to reference Seraphina's cast.

A peculiar luminescence catches his eye. It's from a small stand tucked away near the mouth of an alley. Wilhilm approaches and pauses in front of the stand, eyes locked onto a gleaming, effervescent drink.

The vendor, a wiry man with an ageless face and nimble fingers speaks, "The Luminescent Liqueur of Tiringar. Drink, and witness truths you dare not utter."

"Oh, hello," Wilhilm replies, not wanting to be rude, but not interested in the tinctures.

That's it. There is where she should be. Or was, probably just moments ago. Wilhilm eyes the four narrow alleys, each of them crowded with people. It seems impossible to find her.

Wilhilm consults his Echo Stone. No new cast.

"Is it about a woman?" the man behind the stall asks. "If so, I have the right drink for you."

Around them, the streets quiet for the night. Taking a deep breath, as if bracing himself for an enchantment, Wilhilm purchases a glass—trying the brew Seraphina recommended might make her feel a little closer.

He takes a sip. The liquid dances on his palate, its magic intertwining with memories. He blinks, and then, amidst the shifting shadows, he sees her.

Seraphina.

CHAPTER 21

EVERY BREATH YOU TAKE

"MagicWilly?" Seraphina's voice echoes across the vast expanse of their shared past. It's even softer than he remembered. "Is the universe playing tricks, or is this fate?"

"Wilhilm, for my friends."

She smiles "I hope no one's about to go up in flames this time."

"We didn't have time to finish our conversation," Wilhilm says. "How do you feel? After all that happened?"

"We all have to do what we have to do. And all I can do is sing. I could as well stop living if I stop singing."

"Was this the first time you've seen that combustion happen?"

"Is this the kind of small talk you use on women? Talking to them about people on fire?"

They share a glance and a profound connection surges between them. "I've missed our magical duels, the promises whispered under the ancient oak," Wilhilm says. "Careful, there's a mouse by your foot." Wilhilm can sense that he's not quite making sense, but his thoughts are suddenly blurry.

Seraphina looks down. "Cute. I'm not afraid of mice." She walks up to the stall, reads the label on the bottle the same color as Wilhilm's drink. Then she says to the merchant, "The tear of an ice giant, mead, and two drops of truth serum? That's what you're selling to him?"

"One of my best drinks," the man exclaims. "Fancy a shot? Always on the house for you, my dear Seraphina."

Seraphina gracefully waves her hand and turns back to Wilhilm. "Magical duels? Oaks? Willy, I'm not her, whoever you are thinking about," Seraphina says. "Though, the depths of your feelings are...remarkable."

Wilhilm takes a step closer, eager to continue their conversation about feelings, of which he is suddenly having a remarkable amount of, but they're interrupted by a hooded figure brushing past, muttering about a lost door.

Seraphina muses, "Ah, a Neural Navigator. They're cryptic, but where would Tiringar be without them?"

The two continue their walk.

"Do you recall," Wilhilm whispers, "the time we uncovered the Circle of Shadow's intent to unbind the city's core magic?"

Seraphina chuckles, "Your question isn't for me, but I've heard of the tale. I would have loved to be her. To see how half the council ended up speaking in rhymes for a week."

Her shared laughter is a melody. Wilhilm continues on, fueled by the strange drink. They walk past the Fountain of the Evening Battle, depicting three Netherlings with crossbows, and sit next to it for what feels hours. Later, they walk again, and the longer they do, the more taverns on their way close their windows and lock their doors for the night.

Yet, as dawn approaches, reality intrudes. The weight of unspoken words and missed chances presses between them.

Seraphina finally breaks a silence that has grown. "Wilhilm, it was nice feeling like you knew me. Unfortunately, all things come to an end. When your drink wears off, you realize I'm just me. I'm just Seraphina."

Wilhilm takes a deep breath. "Your eyes are different."

Seraphina smiles, tears glistening. "The drink is losing its effect. I'm not her."

"Then let's have another."

Suddenly, Seraphina whispers again, her voice like the soft rustling of leaves. "You can't drink your magic away. Magic is what's bothering you, right?"

Wilhilm stiffens, eyes widening in surprise and apprehension. "What makes you say that?" he responds. His voice is forcedly casual as he tries to mask the anxiety that bubbles beneath.

Seraphina smiles enigmatically, her eyes searching his face. "There's a story in every heartbeat, Wilhilm. Yours beats... differently around magic."

What does she know? Wilhilm tries to maintain his composure. Every fiber of his being screams at him to deny it, to maintain the walls he has painstakingly built over the years. He changes the subject hastily. "Look at that wall there. Exquisite craftsmanship, isn't it? Just the right amount of wally, wouldn't you say?"

But Seraphina is not to be deterred. She takes his hand and pulls him closer, into a corner near a gurgling fountain adorned with mermaid statues. "There are many things about you, Wilhilm, that people shouldn't know. And yet..." She trails off, letting go of his hand to trace a finger down the side of his face.

The intimacy of the gesture stuns him. The air between them grows thick, their eyes lock in a silent understanding, and for a brief moment, the marketplace seems to fade away.

“Wilhilm, there’s no shame in fear. But there are shadows around you, more troubling than a simple fear of magic.”

Though he tries to meet her gaze, his eyes betray him. They dart away, filled with a mix of fear and astonishment. How could she know?

Seraphina tilts her head, studying him, her voice lowering to a soft murmur. “The past is a sly creature, Wilhilm. It weaves its tales even in places you’d least expect, but you should know, Wilhilm, I sense a shift in the winds. A disturbance. Something is on the horizon, something foreboding. I fear it will alter the very fabric of our lives.”

He stares at her, taking in her words, his heart pounding louder in his ears. Before he can respond, Seraphina takes a step closer and places a delicate hand on his arm. Her touch is cool, but it sends shivers down his spine.

CHAPTER 22
ANOTHER BRICK IN THE WALL

"I don't know the nature of this coming storm, nor its intent," Seraphina says to Wilhilm, her voice laced with concern, "but I feel it. A tremor in the ether. A darkening of the skies even on the brightest of days. You might be able to stop it. But only if you find Soulshade."

Wilhilm, reeling from the weight of her revelations and the intensity of the moment, manages to nod. "Soulshade... wait, what's Souldshade?" he begins, trying to find the right words, "What are you talking about? How do I prepare for something when I don't even know what it is?"

"You know what Soulshade does, right?" Seraphina asks.

"I have no idea what you're talking about," Wilhilm says.

She looks at him, almost reproachful. Perhaps with a tint of disappointment.

"I really have no idea," Wilhilm repeats.

"You know, there's something inside of you, right?"

"You mean, my magic?"

"Something that whispers to you?"

"Oh yeah, my magic."

"Come on, you know, deep inside, that magic doesn't whisper, Wilhilm."

She bends her head, bringing her lips to his ear. She starts to softly sing. Her voice dances gracefully between notes, each one pulling Wilhilm deeper into the melody. It isn't a song he recognizes, but it feels ancient, as if it has been passed down through countless generations. The lyrics, though foreign to his ears, convey a tale of love, loss, and cheese.

Each verse seems to be woven just for him, capturing the depths of emotions he feels he could never express. Her voice is haunting. It echoes with raw emotion and pain, but also with hope and resilience. The crescendos falls like waves crashing against cliffs.

His fingers find his Echo Stone without dropping Seraphina's gaze. He feels the tiny jab on his finger to activate the stone and lifts the EyeStone to catch the song. It pulses with a soft, radiant light. It is as if the stone itself comes alive, resonating with Seraphina's melodies.

Wilhilm feels an almost magnetic pull from the stone, an invisible tether drawing him in. The atmosphere grows thick, the very air vibrates with anticipation.

As the song's energy meets the stone, a cascade of shimmering light surges forth, branching out like roots seeking nourishment. This radiant network extends in all directions, connecting to other Echo Stones scattered across the realm. A luminous web is formed, binding stone to stone, land to land.

Wilhilm can feel it—a subtle shift in his consciousness. It is as if a door in his mind, previously locked and hidden, is suddenly flung open. He is no longer an individual entity but part of something vast, expansive, and interconnected.

It's a hive of minds, a sensation that is overwhelming, yet not intrusive. It is a collective consciousness, a tapestry of individual threads coming together to create a rich and intricate pattern. Wilhilm can sense the thoughts and feelings of others, and he knows his own is here, but he can't find it, it feels like—something breaks away from him. He ceases to exist as an individual within the hive mind. New perspectives offer glimpses into lives and experiences far removed from his own.

The song is the catalyst, the bridge between individuality and collective understanding. As Seraphina's voice echoes through the EyeStone network, it becomes an anthem, a call to unity, binding all those connected to the network in shared emotion and purpose.

Wilhilm is... spread out. Like butter over too much toast. He is here, there, and everywhere, part of an endless conversation where everyone talks and no one listens.

"Ok," a voice says in the distance. Wilhilm smells faint traces of cheese in the air.

Amid the chorus of harmonious voices flowing through the EyeStone network, a singular, dark whisper emerges. It is faint, a shadow against the luminous backdrop of the collective consciousness. Wilhilm tries to resist the call of this enigmatic whisper but its siren-like allure is impossible to ignore.

CHAPTER 23
DON'T FEAR THE REAPER

Wilhilm finds himself standing on the precipice of a vast abyss within his own psyche. He struggles to close out the other voices and narrow in on the whisper. He begins tracing this mysterious thread through the network, pushing past memories aside and thoughts not his own. The deeper he delves, the louder and more insistent the whisper becomes. The whisper is now a cacophonous scream, echoing from the depths. The hive mind hums in the background. Wilhilm is as good as alone here.

He finds himself in an eerily familiar setting: Ishmaara, seven years back, a maelstrom to the demon dimension. There, amidst the swirling energies and the chaos of battle, he sees himself—a younger version, brimming with determination and a naivety that now seems almost alien to him. He's wearing a blue cloak, wand out.

The younger Wilhilm moves with a fluidity not yet eroded by years of eating and avoiding too sudden movements. His much younger hands weave complex patterns in the air and his spells cut through the din. An immense rift, a snarling wound in the fabric of reality, pulsates before him. Even now, from this distance in time, the rift is an abyssal maw seeking to devour all it touches. He can't help but stare into the rift, the inescapable black, threatening to spill out.

The scene is gone in an instant. It is quiet. Dimly lit. He is in his childhood bedroom, shadows playing tricks on the walls. He remembers this room, remembers the nights he'd lay there, paralyzed by terror. Terror that his magic could act up, as if flames could burst out of him any moment, devouring everything he holds dear.

He feels the sands whispering, he feels the desert calling out to him. *Come back here, Wilhilm. You belong here. You belong to us.* He can almost feel grains of sand on his tongue, the mineral smell of the desert sand in his nose.

And then he sees it. Sees what Seraphina wants him to see. In the room's center stands a hulking figure with eyes like burning coal and a grin that stretches impossibly wide. The demon is an abomination of nature, a grotesque blend of humanoid and beastly features. Its skin is a ghastly shade of blackened red, pulsating as if molten lava courses just below its surface.

Huge, leathery wings unfurl from its back, jagged and torn with the scars of battles from eons past. They flap lazily, casting the monstrous shadows, making the demon appear even larger than it is.

A cold sweat forms on his brow, his throat is dry with terror. Every instinct screams at him to flee, but he is rooted to the spot, entrapped by the sheer malevolence radiating from the creature. The realization that he is in the presence of a being from the very bowels of the abyss, a creature of unspeakable evil and power, is overwhelming.

"Did you truly believe you could escape me by looking away?" it taunts.

All of his life, Wilhilm has feared his magic. His subconscious must have spun that terror into the shape of a demon.

And while those thoughts rush through Wilhilm's mind, he knows none of them are true. He never saw that demon as a child, it just fiddles with his memories. Seven years ago, this is what he brought back. Before he closed the rift. The thing is real. He feels it.

Devastation washes over Wilhilm. The euphoria of the collective connection is shattered, replaced by a deep-rooted dread. Here, amidst the grand tapestry of minds, he has discovered his deepest, darkest secret.

His demon is real.

"No, no, no. This can't be happening!" Wilhilm panics.

Seraphina's voice cuts through the noise. "You have to see."

"No," Wilhilm cries out. "No, stop it!"

Suddenly, he's back in the street in Tiringar, people eyeing him as if he were a drunk wandering the street.

"Seraphina?"

He is met with silence. The weight on his arm is gone. He blinks, refocusing his vision and looks around frantically. Seraphina is nowhere to be seen.

His eyes dart from stall to stall, searching the almost empty streets. But it is as if she has melted into the shadows, vanished like a mirage. The lingering touch on his arm, however, was real enough to remind him that their conversation isn't just a figment of his imagination.

He runs a hand over his face. A demon? Inside of him?

He has to be sure. And thankfully, he knows just who to look for.

CHAPTER 24

ALL TOGETHER NOW

When Dakaria sees a heart finally float across the smooth scrying screen, she feels her own make a little jump. Then chastises herself.

How stupid! There is no objective meaning in how many people like her casts. Or, in her case, how few. And yet, she feels small jabs every time she checks how her casts are doing and realizes, they're not doing well enough.

What a shame. Personally, she found her last cast the best she did so far. In it, she described how two trees outside of the city have agreed to help a third tree that, unfortunately, stands on bad ground with little nourishments. But, connected by their roots, they pumped preprocessed sugar through the root network to help the third.

It was a touching, quality story. And yet, it didn't reel in nearly as many viewers as the casts of her companions have so far. Gadisa especially was doing quite well, but more and more, his casts took a stranger turn (they have, in fact, been strange from the start, but nothing compared to their current state).

With every cast, he claimed something even more

outrageous than the one before. Baseless fantasies about washing being a social construct. How it's a tool used by the rich to cement their power. But people did not only believe it, they savored it. They promoted it. For some even, it becomes their life, a philosophy they've adopted to model their lives after.

At least Mormak didn't lie. So far, all Dakaria had seen him do is drink. He makes a bit of a show around it, but basically every cast is just him downing one ale after the other. And though it is funny at times, Dakaria doesn't count those kinds of casts to come close to her level. She puts a lot of thought into each of her casts. New information she is sure people didn't have before.

However, people seem to support the simple and entertaining casts a lot more than those that require more effort to think and focus. How strange. Dakaria can't fathom not wanting to learn something new about nature. And yet, so few in the network seem to really want to know things.

On the other hand, she does have her community. A small, but loyal audience of other casters and watchers who react to every cast she does. And those folks are actually meeting up in person. Small gatherings of other creators to talk about their casts.

"A few of us are meeting this evening at the Growling Boar in Tiringar," one of those new friends—WitchLydia—announces in her latest cast.

Dakaria hesitates a moment.

"As it happens, I'm in Tiringar," she responds in a public reaction.

Half a dozen reactions come up immediately.

"Would you want to meet up? To talk about what we do, perhaps evaluate possible collaborations and help each other grow."

Dakaria hesitates for another moment. It is a strange thought—meeting people she only knows from the casts. Then again, why not? She is curious to get to know those people. And perhaps learn more about what is going on in the EyeStone network.

"Sounds fun," Dakaria says back. "Count me in!"

Fortunately, the Growling Boar is in the old city center, only a few moments' walk away from the Inn the companions chose to stay in.

The sky is darkening outside when Dakaria heads out.

Two kids hop through an alley, singing a children's song about the Nexus. "*In the heart of old Tiringar town, / Where knowledge sinks deep and floats around, / There's a path made of thoughts, so vast and wide...*"

As the kids hop on, their voices slowly drown out. "*Where dreams of the ancient ones reside. / Oh, walk the brain's path, step light, step true, / For memories old will feel so new...*"

Dakaria's steps slow as she nears the Growling Boar. The heavy wooden sign, featuring a crudely painted boar, creaks gently in the evening breeze. Her heart beats a nervous rhythm, a fluttering bird trapped within her chest. Was it a good idea to meet those people in person?

As a druid accustomed to the solitude of nature and the quiet companionship of her fellow adventurers, the idea of meeting other casters, fans even who only know her through the magical network of the Echo Stones, is both exhilarating and daunting. Her fingers twitch at her side, instinctively seeking the comforting texture of leaves or the rough bark of a tree.

Will they be kind? Will they see her as she truly is? Or as the persona she's projected herself in her casts? Will they be jealous?

Taking a deep breath, she smells the familiar scents of

spiced ale and wood smoke that waft from the tavern. She steels herself, drawing on the strength and calm of the forests that have always been her sanctuary. Pushing the door open, she steps into the warm, bustling interior.

The noise of conversation and laughter washes over her, grounding her. Her eyes scan the room, taking in the faces that turn towards her, some with recognition, others with curiosity. This is it, she thinks, the moment of truth. She immediately recognizes most of the other casters. The crowd includes Sheeren the Netherling, Tongo the Feathermaul, the twins Zuri and Guri the Wyrmkins, and Athea the Human. There was also an elf she doesn' know. Dakaria files a mental note to avoid her.

As she draws closer, an unsettling detail becomes apparent, sending a chill down her spine. Each of them, engrossed in their conversations and laughter, is emanating shadows that seem to evaporate off their skin, like steam rising from a hot spring.

CHAPTER 25

WHISPERING SECRETS

Dakaria pauses, her heart thumping in her chest. The shadows coming off the casters' skin swirl and twist, forming ephemeral shapes before dissolving into the air. She's seen this before, they were exactly the same type of shadows that Wilhilm has.

Her mind races, thoughts tumbling over each other. Are they in danger? Fear mingles with a sense of duty within her. These are other casters, people who have listened to her, who have formed a connection with her through the Stones. She feels a responsibility towards them, a need to understand and possibly help.

Tongo the Feathermaul is the first one to turn. Golden feathers cascade down Tongo's face, blending seamlessly into the thick, coarse fur of its bear-like body. Tongo's beak is softened by a gentle, almost amused expression. He raises a feathered arm, waving with an amiable awkwardness that brings a smile to his lips. One by one, the whole group turns and waves.

Swallowing her apprehension, Dakaria steps forward, her druidic instincts kicking in. She must approach this mystery with both caution and an open mind. The shadows might hold answers, or they might be a warning of things to come. Either way, she knows she cannot turn away.

"Greetings, Dakaria! What are you looking at? Have you seen a demon?" Tongo asks. Dakaria notices a peculiar pattern of blue feathers on Tongo the Feathermaul's chest. They form a distinct, almost rune-like shape, a leaf caught in a gentle breeze.

"The shadows, you all have those shadows," Dakaria stammers. Looking at the faces around her, she sees their confusion. That must have seemed the weirdest greeting ever. They probably think she's crazy. Dakaria points at one of those shadows.

"These? Pah, these are the new normal. If you cast a little longer, you'll have them too," Zuri and Guri both say simultaneously in a deep baritone voice.

Intrigued, Dakaria sits between the Wyrmkin twins. "What are they? What do they do?"

"Nothing,“ Sheeren the Netherling says. "They're just there." A gentle, almost imperceptible glow emanates from her fingertips. This soft luminescence, flickering like the light of distant stars, seems to pulse in rhythm with Sheeren's heartbeat. She must have a deep, intrinsic connection to some form of magic.

Sheeren opens up her hand, presenting her fingers, and when Dakaria looks up, Sheeren smiles at her. She has realized Dakaria was staring at her. How embarrassing.

"Isn't that a bit... unusual?" Dakaria tries to resume the conversation about the shadows.

"It's just something that's connected to the magic that keeps those things going," Athea says. A faint, almost ethereal, herbal scent clings to her clothing and skin. This aroma, a blend of lavender and rosemary with a hint of sage, is not overpowering but rather soothing.

"What kind of magic? How do the EyeStones work?" Dakaria asks.

Everyone looks at her for a moment, then bursts into laughter. "We wish we knew," Tongo says. "Cheese hasn't revealed their secret."

"Come on, get something to drink first," Sheeren says. "It ′s self-service."

"Self-service, how does that work here?"

"Where have you been the last couple of weeks?" Athea asks.

"Well, I'm out there adventuring, you know, quest after quest. I only recently returned to Tiringar."

"Oh, that explains it." Sheeren laughs.

"It's not terribly complicated," Tongo says. "Basically, with everyone busy either doing their own casts, or watching casts, there's less and less people to do those tedious jobs."

"No tavern wrenches anymore." Zuri and Guri nod both simultaneously.

"Better this way, you'll see," Athea says. "Basically, you're tapping your beer yourself, and you'll be doing the payment all on your own."

"It's fun," Sheeren promises.

While they go behind the bar for their beer, Dakaria eyes her new friends' shadows suspiciously. There is no obvious pattern in how they move. It seems more like erratic bursts of fog.

"What do you like best about the network?" Sheeren asks Dakaria. "For me, it's definitely the music. It's as if you're pulled out of your body, as if you can see the world from different perspectives. The moment when we all feel like a part of something bigger. Nature perhaps."

"Music?"

"You know Seraphina, right? She is well known for the experience of merging minds through song. It's transformative. We all become one, as we are intended to be," Sheeren says. "I'm sure you've heard about her."

Heard? Dakaria remembers only too well, and she knows a wizard who can't stop talking about that certain singer... but Dakaria is more interested in the shadows. "Do you feel any different, I mean, with these... shadows?" Dakaria asks Sheeren.

"You're a little obsessed with those, huh? As I said, they're perfectly normal. You'll see. Some say, they are connected to the self-combustions but I don't believe that. I mean, it's pure conjecture to say those self-combustions have anything to do with the EyeStone network at all."

"Self-combustions?" Dakaria asks. *Plural.* So Seraphina's backup singing wasn't the only one. "How many have there been there?

Tongo chimes in, before Sheeren can answer. "My uncle had self-combustion long before the EyeStone. And my great-grandfather died of self-combustion."

"Weren't they vampires who died from sunlight exposure?" Sheeren says, flicking her tail.

"So what? One kind of self-combustion is better than another?" he shoots back.

Dakaria sighs. "How many self-combustions are there?" she asks again.

"Nobody knows," Sheeren says. She pauses for a moment and nervously touches her horns. "The first one was at StoneCon."

"What's StoneCon?"

"You really aren't up-to-date, darling. Cheese does this big event whenever they release a new EyeStone generation. It's called StoneCon. They invite some of us casters, depending on how well we're doing."

"And this is where the first self-combustion happened?"

"They don't want you to know, but I was there," Sheeren says, lowering her voice to a whisper.

"BigTower, one of the first and most influential casters in the network, literally burned up. He was doing a cast live from StoneCon," Tongo says.

"You mean like someone cast a fireball?" Dakaria tries to clarify.

"Self-combustion, they said. But there was nothing willing about it, trust me. I was right there beside him when it happened just when MagicWilly's first cast went on."

CHAPTER 26

LIGHT MY FIRE

Self-combustion, Dakaria thinks, it's not a one time thing. Despite what the other casters insist, it keeps happening.

"Do you want the pale ale, too?" Athea asks. It takes Dakaria a moment to realize it's her turn. She nods and Athea pours her a pale ale.

She takes her first sip. It's good. She's just raising the glass to her mouth again when a shrill shriek pierces the jovial atmosphere of the tavern like a discordant note.

The piercing cry cuts through conversations and halts the movements of patrons mid-gesture. It lingers, reverberating through the air, leaving an eerie echo that seems to freeze time itself.

"Oh no. No, no. Not them," Sheeren whispers.

Dakaria follows her gaze and realizes that the shriek came from both of the twins.

"We have to get them out, now," Sheeren says.

"What? Why?"

"It's what they told us at StoneCon, to get them outside," Sheeren says. She turns to Dakaria.

Dakaria moves toward the twins, but it's already too late. The flames burst forth from their very being, consuming their form with an unnerving and rapid intensity. The air fills with the acrid scent of burning flesh and the crackling sound of flickering flames. Onlookers stand frozen in shock.

As the flames dance and lick at the twins, their anguished cries echo through the air. Half the crowd stands, shocked, as they witness the gruesome scene. The man closest to the twins drops his Echo Stone and turns to run, bumping into a woman in a cloak, knocking her to the ground. That sets the entire crowd off and within a split second, there's a rush to the door.

Athea's voice trembles with urgency as she spots the keg of water nearby. "Quick, get this water to them," she cries out.

Sheeren's voice, clashes with Athea's frantic energy. "There's nothing we can do," she says, her words slicing through the chaos like a cold blade. Her gaze is locked onto the inferno. "You can't extinguish it. You can't stop it." Her hands hang limply by her sides.

Dakaria steps forward, her eyes ablaze with determination. *Not extinguish it?* There surely was a way to end this with magic. With a deep inhalation, she closes her eyes and lets her senses attune to the weave of magic that surrounds her. Her nostrils flare as she draws in the air, searching for the faint whispers of power that dance upon the winds. With a swift incantation and a wave of her hand, she calls forth the power of her spell to quench fire.

As the scent of magic fills her lungs, it intertwines with her own essence. The fragrant notes of arcane energies become a symphony in her mind, each strand of magic carrying its own unique scent, its own distinct signature.

With her heightened senses, Dakaria can discern the elemental essence of fire, the crackling warmth, and the smoky tendrils that curl through the air. Amidst this fiery symphony, she seeks the discordant notes, the distorted scent that signifies the unnatural blaze engulfing the twins.

But as the words of the spell leave her lips, a sense of unease creeps within her, a flicker of doubt that taints the air she breathes. The scent of the spell twists, morphing into a dark and unsettling presence. Dakaria's eyes widen, realizing that her magic has encountered an opposing force, an enigmatic power that resists her command.

A cloud of dark shadows materializes from the heart of the blaze, twisting and writhing with an eerie hiss. The Druid's eyes widen with a mixture of shock and disbelief as she realizes the depths of the power she has unwittingly awakened. The shadows surge toward her with a chilling velocity, their dark tendrils reaching out like claws hungry for destruction.

Dakaria is violently thrown back, propelled through the tavern wall with an explosive force. The whole building shatters beneath the impact, showering debris onto the street outside. She lands roughly, the breath knocked out of her, her left arm bruised.

Dakaria struggles to regain her senses, pain coursing through her body. Her mind races, grappling with the intensity of the encounter and the profound darkness she now faces. Dakaria stands, staring into the flames, clutching her left arm while around her people moan and cough, and new spectators are attracted, using their EyeStones to live cast the fire. A distant bell alerts the city to the fire.

CHAPTER 27
WE CAN WORK IT OUT

Sheeren grabs Dakaria's arm and drags her away from the burning building. Clusters of spectators form in the dark street, awash with the amber shadows of the fire. "You can't do more," Sheeren says. "Believe me, I've been around when it happens. You can only hurt yourself."

"This is connected to the EyeStones!" Dakaria cries out. "Why? Why don't you all just stop using them?"

Sheeren's face is dark with grief, but now it becomes defensive. "Why would the EyeStones have anything to do with it? There were monsters and magic long before Cheese created the EyeStone. It's something else entirely." She pauses. "Something demonic."

Dakaria looks back at the sound of commotion. It's the city guard, clad in their distinctive crimson and gold uniforms. There are at least a dozen of them, forming a tight circle around the Growling Boar, ensuring no one re-enters. Black smoke billows out of the window next to the door, gradually shifting to a ghostly gray before slowly dissipating. Dakaria watches intently, analyzing the transformation of the smoke. It feels like it holds significance. But what can it mean?

Dakaria's still pondering what she should do next, how involved she should get, when three hooded figures arrive at the scene. They pass the guards, barely acknowledging them, and enter the Growling Boar. Neural Navigators. Sorcerers working for the Nexus—the colossal brain under Tiringar and keeping the secrets of ancient generations, the source of Tiringar's wealth.

What does the Nexus have to do with the Echo Stones? Did the guard call in the Neural Navigators because of their ancient knowledge? Or is there more to it?

Dakaria approaches the entrance to the Growling Boar, but a guard steps in her way. It was a particularly nervous Lepusian. His foot thumps rapidly against the ground.

"Difperfe," the guard says, the word coming out mangled because he's chewing on his lower lip with his protruding teeth.

"I'm a Druid, I'm sure I can help," Dakaria offers.

"Difperfe. We are required to take anyone into cuftody who refifts our orderf," the anxious guard says.

Dakaria nods apologetically. Something is going on, something the city doesn't want anyone prying into. Or at least, someone high up in the city's administration. How else is it possible the guards swoop in so quickly as if the Neural Navigators were on standby?

She will find out—Zuri and Guri deserve that—but she needs her companions for that. Dakaria turns away from the guard. "I do hope, I can get Mormak and Gadisa to do something useful for once," she murmurs to herself.

~

BACK AT THEIR INN, Dakaria knocks at Mormak's door.

His voice comes through the wood panels. "I'm working."

"I need you," Dakaria shouts back.

"Come back later."

Typical of the Dwarf! He is probably just sitting there and drinking beer!

Dakaria knocks at Gadisa's door.

"Not now, I'm changing the world," Gadisa says. "Go away."

Dakaria groans, then something Sheeren has said comes back to her.

The music that makes all minds merge. You should definitely give it a try.

That phenomena might be the way to warn everybody about the shadows and the combustions.

Or, even better, to find a way to the minds of her companions, get them on her side, and then warn everybody.

In Dakaria's room, she flips through casts until she finds a piece of Seraphina's music. As the melody wafts from the Echo Stone, Dakaria closes her eyes, letting the notes wash over her. She imagines the harmonies are the whispering winds through the leaves, the rhythms distant thunder. And then, something shifts. The music isn't just something she hears; it's something she feels, deep within the very marrow of her being.

Her thoughts, always vivid, now entwine with emotions and fragments she doesn't recognize. The borders of her consciousness blur as other minds meld with hers. Dakaria's usually steady heart races, her breathing grows shallow, and the overwhelming sensation of being connected to others—truly connected—envelops her.

Images flash before her eyes: a sunset she's never seen, a childhood memory of a place she's never been, the sharp pang of a heartbreak she's never felt. The emotions accompanying these visions are raw and unfiltered, a cacophony of joy, sorrow, hope, and despair.

Amid the swirling thoughts, there's a gentle undercurrent, a grounding force that feels like an old friend. It reassures her, its presence a soft reminder that, despite the chaos, she's not alone in this vast mental expanse.

She wonders if they too are experiencing her memories, her dreams, her fears. The notion is both exhilarating and terrifying. As the song reaches its climax, the noise inside her head grows louder, more insistent.

Dakaria tries to steer her own thoughts, to reach out and search for his companions. She clings to the memory of a meadow she once rested in, the soft buzz of bees, the fragrance of blooming wildflowers. She uses that moment of clarity to hold on to herself, retain a shred of consciousness. It allows her to scan the sea of minds for one she recognizes.

There. Gadisa's mind.

She drifts toward it, focusing, trying to become one.

CHAPTER 28
SMELLS LIKE TEEN SPIRIT

With a jolt, Dakaria realizes she has reached Gadisa. Now, can she talk to him? There must be a way to contact him.

"And that's why you should never wash your clothes," Gadisa summarizes to finish his cast.

As Gadisa disconnects from the EyeStone network, Dakaria feels an abrupt sense of disorientation akin to the sudden drop of a leaf in the autumn wind. She senses the weakening of their mind-merge. It's like watching a bridge made of mist fade away, the path between their minds growing fainter, more tenuous.

But then, amidst the fading connection, Dakaria notices something—a single thread that remains active, a lingering filament of Gadisa's mind. It glows with a residual energy.

Interesting. So, even if you're not using the EyeStones, the network literally stays on your mind, Dakaria muses. Seizing this opportunity, Dakaria focuses her attention on this solitary thread, using it as a lifeline. Determined, she hikes up this thread, metaphorically ascending the fading path back into Gadisa's mind. It's a delicate, almost ethereal experience, like walking on a strand of spider silk, fragile yet surprisingly resilient. She feels a rush of sensations—Gadisa's residual thoughts and feelings, his recent mental activity.

And then, just like that, she's Gadisa.

Her sense of self melts away. She thinks his thoughts, feels his emotions. She remembers she wanted to tell him something. Something important, but she just can't remember what it was. It's as if her brain has shattered in fragments and she has to piece it back together.

Gadisa reaches down with one meaty hand, his fingers disappearing into the waistband of his underpants, his enchanted undergarments, and begins the rummage. There is a certain art to it, honed over years of practice. As his hand delves deeper into the infinite folds of fabric, he encounters the usual assortment of bric-a-brac: a couple of gold coins, an old map that might lead to treasure or a particularly well-hidden pub, a half-eaten sandwich (he briefly considers finishing it off), and what felt suspiciously like the handle of an axe.

Finally, after what feels like an expedition worthy of its own ballad, his fingers close around the hilt of the Dragonteeth Dagger. He pulls it out with a satisfied grunt. The dagger is a vicious-looking thing, all jagged edges and dark magic. It's his most treasured artifact. A weapon that allows him to attack the shadows of his opponents, a fitting weapon for a rogue.

Satisfied that the dagger is still very much in order—sharp, deadly, and with a faint hum of menace that suggested it is just itching for a bit of action—he nods to himself. Then, with the casual air of someone storing away a particularly comfortable pair of socks, he slides the dagger back into his magical underpants, and returns to his EyeStone,

A few symbols pop up on the screen. Mainly it's hearts and smiling faces. He would have to wait a while for the comments to build up.

Gadisa watches some of the other casts as he waits. Increasingly, food is featured. A Wyrmkin smiles into the camera. He seems to be sitting in a tavern. "And this, dear followers, is Drakescale-Stuffed Quail. A masterpiece of culinary creativity, the meat is expertly stuffed with a delicate blend of drakescale, fragrant herbs, and spices. The combination results in a succulent fusion of flavors, where the slight gaminess of the quail is complemented by the subtle hint of the exotic drakescale."

Gadisa is intrigued and hungry at the same time.

"It's another spectacular dish offered by the Wyrm Inn in Tiringar."

Tiringar? Right where he is!

Gadisa leaves his room and knocks on the door next to his. "Mormak? I'm hungry."

The answer comes through the door. "I'm casting, no time."

Strange enough, Mormak has never before turned down a request to go to the tavern.

Well, Gadisa is hungry now, and their own inn-keeper points him in the direction of the Wyrm Inn. It's in Flamecrest, the Tiringarian quarter most heavily inhabited by Wyrmkins.

Nestled within Flamecrest district, the tavern is more modest than the more opulent establishments nearby. The weathered stone and sturdy timber gives the façade an earthy tone. A wooden sign swings gently above the entrance, bearing the tavern's name WYRM INN in boldly carved letters. Soft lamplight spills through the small windows, casting a warm glow onto the cobblestone street below. Vibrant hanging baskets of Dragon's Breath flowers adorn the exterior.

When Gadisa enters, nobody turns to watch him. Most of the guests sit in front of their dishes, Echo Stones pointed at their meals. In the bustling narrowness of the tavern, a small Wyrmkin waiter weaves skillfully through the throng of patrons.

Clad in a crisp, neatly pressed uniform that matches the establishment's aesthetic, the waiter's scales shimmer in hues of vibrant red or iridescent blue, reflecting their unique ancestry. One waiter carries a heavy tray laden with a steaming plate on which a tentacle seems to move. His scaled tail sways gently to maintain balance.

"A table for one," Gadisa says.

"Certainly," the waiter replies, pointing at a free table in the corner. "My colleague will be right with you."

Gadisa sits and scans the inn to find his waiter. One of them seems to be approaching him. The waiter, towering over the other patrons, moves with grace. His emerald scales shimmer subtly in the tavern's dim light, while his gold-piercing eyes scan the room with attentive care. A friendly, toothy smile, reveals sharp fangs and softens his fearsome appearance.

"Sir, happy to see you here," the waiter greets Gadisa. "First timer? If you make a positive cast about one of our dishes and it's likely to attract new customers, we will take ten percent off your order."

"I will eat less?"

"No, not all," the waiter hurries to explain. "I mean, you will pay ten percent less. But you will eat the same amount."

"What about, I eat ten percent more?"

CHAPTER 29

DON'T STOP ME NOW

"Eating ten percent more? This can also be arranged, of course," the waiter says with a smile.

"Arrange it. What can I have?" Gadisa asks. As he looks forward to a reply, he realizes how hungry he is. So hungry. Ever since he left his river at home and an artificer installed this tubes to make him able to breathe air, he feels hungry. All the time.

"Today, I recommend the Wyrmfire Grilled Salmon and the Basilisk-Eye Salad followed by a fine Dragonfruit Sorbet."

"Salad?" Gadisa asks with disdain in his voice.

"What sets it apart is the inclusion of basilisk eyes. The basilisk eyes add a unique burst of flavor, infusing the salad with a subtle tang and a hint of mesmerizing enchantment," the waiter explains.

"Fine, I'll try it, but put the ten percent more on the salmon," Gadisa says. He watches the waiter scuttle away and spots three patrons hunched in a corner over their Echo Stones. All three of them give off faint hints of the same shadows he saw on the wizard a couple of times in the past.

Gadisa files away this information. They might be the same kind of wizards, the kind that never properly do spells. Before he can think more about it, his meal arrives. The main waiter smiles at him and bows while a different Wyrmkin waiter brings large plates and sets one on the table.

"As you can see, a shimmering silver salmon fillet takes center stage, kissed by the flames of a wyrmfire grill. The fish's flesh is perfectly cooked to a buttery texture, infused with a mesmerizing smoky flavor and a touch of heat from the mythical flames."

Then the second plate is set in front of Gadisa. With the Basilisk eye in the middle, it's hard to miss which one this is.

"And for dessert, a Dragonfruit Sorbet. A refreshing finale to the feast, the vibrant pink sorbet made from the luscious flesh of the exotic dragonfruit, offers a tantalizing blend of sweet and tangy flavors, punctuated by subtle floral undertones," the lead waiter announces.

The table groans under the weight of such lavish feast. The aroma of the seasoned salmon fills the air, drawing the attention of everyone in the vicinity. Gadisa's stomach growls and he can't wait any longer. He nods at the waitstaff and starts on the salmon first.

The first bite of the Wyrmfire Grilled Salmon sets Gadisa's taste buds ablaze with enchanting flavors. The perfectly cooked fish, its flesh tender and flaky, yields effortlessly to the gentle pressure of the fork. The rich, buttery texture of the salmon melts on Gadisa's tongue. There's a slight tang of citrus.

Gadisa savors the flavor that explodes on his tongue.

And in this moment, Gadisa's dining experience becomes a performance. The onlookers, captivated by the sight, are astounded by the finesse with which Gadisa savors each bite. Patrons begin pointing their EyeStones at Gadisa.

Gadisa notices and states, "Follow me, I'm NoWashRogue."

Gadisa savors the last of the salmon, transforming the simple act of eating into a mesmerizing display of grace and appreciation. However, when Gadisa moves on to the first forkful of the Basilisk-Eye Salad, nothing has prepared him for the vibrant explosion of flavors. The crisp freshness of the greens provides the perfect backdrop for this enchanting creation. As the taste buds tingle with anticipation, the unique centerpiece ingredient, basilisk eyes, adds a delightful burst of flavor.

Gadisa's excited *oohs* and *aahs* are caught by dozens of Echo Stones at the same time. He glances at his own and sees some of those casts live.

"NoWashRogue enjoying his lunch at the Wyrm Inn," one states matter-of-factly.

"NoWashRogue gobbling down his salmon as if it's the first time he eats," another describes more vividly.

As the sorbet gently melts on Gadisa's tongue, it releases a burst of vibrant tropical flavors. The luscious flesh of the dragonfruit infuses the sorbet with a refreshing blend of sweet and tangy notes. Each spoonful offers a juicy, succulent sensation that transports Gadisa's senses to a sun-kissed paradise.

When he's finished, the waiter hurries to thank him. "This was a true spectacle. My guess is we will be booked for months in advance," the waiter says. "And of course, this meal is free of charge. You're always welcome here."

"And the ten percent?"

"You will always get ten percent more off your dish, sorry, you always will get ten percent more of your dish."

"Thank you, I guess?"

"You're welcome. And of course, I just followed you, NoWashRogue. Very interesting cast about washing. If I'm honest, I was suspicious whether this human behavior to over-wash and under-wear should be adopted across all species. Very enlightening, Sir, very enlightening!"

As Gadisa leaves the Wyrm Inn, he looks at his EyeStone. The screen lights up with a constant stream of people who send hearts or smiling faces or thumbs up for his video.

Eventually, they will all know the truth about washing. Stomach full, he plans to do another cast just right before bed.

CHAPTER 30
FAME

When Dakaria awakens the next morning, she feels still sleepy and groggy. She tries to sit up, but her body feels frozen in place. She tries to move her arms. Not possible. Then she realizes something else... she doesn't *have* a body.

Oh no. She's still *in* Gadisa's head. She needs to get out. How does she do that? Before the panic can set it, Gadisa seems to awake as well and Dakaria's sense of self is completely washed away again.

Gadisa starts his morning with more casts. He replies to his many followers, elaborating on certain aspects of not washing your clothes, and blocks a number of noisy people. They're trying to convince others that washing will do no harm, and might even be beneficial for their health.

When he goes out for lunch, the city has changed. Especially the Street of Laundresses. Someone has painted slogans across the shops. Gadisa reads a few of them: *Washing is swindle. Soap is a lie. They only want your money.*

Sudsilla Scrub-a-Dub, known for her relentless dedication to removing even the most stubborn stains, nails her windows shut.

WrinkleWitch Wanda, known for her knack in banishing wrinkles from clothing with a flick of her wand, listlessly directs nails and a hammer to shut her shop down.

Iron Maiden Irma, known for her unmatched strength and precision when it comes to ironing, discusses her plight with a small group. Her powerful arms that used to effortlessly glide over fabrics, gesticulate in the air with frustration.

"That's simply not true. Everyone knows a scrub is good from time to time," she says to a crowd.

"What for?" someone shouts at her. "It's not good for the common man, I can tell you that. To wash clothes, you either have to spend money on the likes of you, or you have to buy a washboard and soap. And who profits?"

There are approving shouts of "Hear, hear!" from the crowd.

"Follow the money," another one adds. "It's all just a business. An unnecessary business. The common man does not profit. You only take his money away with soap and washboards and laundry services."

"Your mother runs a soap shop, John," Irma shouts back. "Your own mother!"

"Not anymore, she doesn't," is the reply. "She's seen the error of her ways, how she's been used!"

"Used by who?"

"You know by who!"

"I don't," Irma says. "And who's supposedly behind this whole soap conspiracy? Who would do something like that?"

"The powerful," someone else says. "They make more and more money by creating this illusion. They make us think washing is good, so we return to them the hard-earned money they gave us for our work. We're practically working for free! Listen to NoWashRogue, he spills the whole truth!"

Gadisa can't help but smile at being mentioned by a complete stranger in the street.

"But I'm not rich," Irma says.

"The people behind you are! You're being used! They brainwashed you, same as us!"

"There's no-one behind me, there's only the wall," Irma retorts.

Someone appears at Gadisa's elbow. "Aren't you NoWashRogue?" a small Netherling asks.

"Me?" Gadisa says.

At the sound of his voice, eyes turn. Big, green, tubes protruding from his body. He's not hard to recognize.

"NoWashRogue, NoWashRogue." Whispers run through the crowd, getting louder and louder, and suddenly a whole throng of people pushes their way to him. Even Gadisa, more than a head taller than humans and a lot heavier, can't counteract the weight of dozens of people pushing into him at the same time.

As the crowd converges, Gadisa becomes engulfed in a sea of bodies. Hands reach out from all directions, brushing against Gadisa's tubes and clinging onto his shoulders. The air becomes thick with sweat and heavy with the collective breath of the mob.

Gadisa's heart pounds with a mix of exhilaration and nerves. Each step becomes a struggle, as the crowd pushes and pulls in a chaotic dance. He is caught in the midst of a whirlwind, swept along by the adulation and frenzy of his admirers.

Amidst the chaos, a strong arm grabs Gadisa. "Come, now!"

With an unexpected surge of strength and determination, Gadisa fights his way through the throng, breaking free from the suffocating embrace. He's led once more into the darkness of the sewers.

In the dim light, he realizes who the strong arms belong to.

"Iron Maiden Irma?" Gadisa says.

"So, you're the one who started all of that?" she asks. Her voice is deep and raspy, each word tinged with a rough-hewn quality, like the sound of gravel being stirred.

"I'm just voicing my opinion."

"But you had to do it on those stone things, hmm? People will believe anything if it allows them to be lazy," Irma says.

"But washing is..."

Irma holds up her hand. "I'm not here to discuss washing with you. It's probably useless anyway. I just can't have people die in a mass panic in my street, you know. No matter how crazy people turn, we're still people." She gives Gadisa one last frown. "Try to find your way out, and don't get eaten by an alligator," she says, then climbs back up.

"Fortunately, we had to use the sewers more than once to escape some angry... clients," Gadisa calls after her, but there is no reply. He sighs and traces his way towards the inn.

In the dim light of the sewer, he thinks he catches a wisp of shadow emanating from his skin.

He stares at his arm. Everything looks normal. Then another shadow drifts off.

"What's that?" Gadisa murmurs. "I should see a healer."

The thought of those evaporating shadows stays with Gadisa all the way to the inn.

Eventually, Gadisa lies in bed, surrounded by the comfort of darkness. Yet, he stays restless. A tormenting symphony of indistinct whispers seem to echo from the depths of the night.

Like fleeting shadows, they dance at the periphery of his consciousness, teasing and taunting. They are maddeningly incomprehensible, an enigmatic chorus that defies understanding. Gadisa strains to decipher the words, to make sense of the voices that invade his thoughts.

As he tosses and turns, the whispers escalate from faint murmurs to an unsettling noise. His frustration mounts when, even as the whispers get louder, they remain just beyond the threshold of understanding. They become an insidious presence, a constant reminder of their elusive nature.

Sleep slips through Gadisa's grasp like a wisp of smoke. His eyelids grow heavy with weariness, but the persistent whispers, well, persist.

As dawn approaches, the whispers gradually recede, retreating to the ethereal realms from whence they came. The Rogue's mind, weary yet determined, finally finds a moment of respite. Gadisa drifts into a fitful slumber, his dreams intermingling with the fading echoes of the night's indistinct murmurs.

In the realm of dreams, Gadisa suddenly understands the whispers.

"You're not good enough, you're not popular enough. Others can do more—are more. You are useless," the voice says. "Get up. Make more casts. Become more popular."

Gadisa opens his eyes, sits up straight and lunges for his EyeStone.

Something, in his mind stirs.

In *her* mind.

She's not Gadisa. She's someone else. She is Dakaria.

She has to get out.

CHAPTER 31

BAD MEDICINE

The door to the Chime Chamber creaks softly as Wilhilm pushes it open. He's met by a gentle rush of air, as if the room itself is exhaling a welcome. The sweet tinkling of bells and chimes fills his ears. Sunlight dapples through the windows, casting flickering patterns of light and shadow on the rustic wooden floor. Each step he takes makes various wind chimes hanging around the chamber sway lightly.

The Chime Chamber and its owner Klink have often helped Wilhilm in situations where the problems were just a little beyond the scope of Wilhilm's Alma Mater, Tiringar's Magic Academy.

Klink's figure stands out among the cascades of hanging chimes. The Tanaku healer turns, and Wilhilm notices the soft feathers on his head ruffle slightly. A pair of shiny, curious eyes meet Wilhilm's, their depths reflecting wisdom and a hint of mischief.

"Wilhilm," Klink greets him a voice not his own, a hint of warmth in the otherwise neutral tone. Tanaku, due to their unique nature, replicate voices they've heard before, and Wilhilm wonders for a fleeting moment whose voice that once was. A previous patient no doubt.

"Klink," Wilhilm responds, a waver betraying his unease. "I... I need your help."

Klink tilts his head, much like a bird analyzing a curious object. He repeats in another voice, a woman's gentle tone this time, "Help?"

Wilhilm nods, swallowing hard. "There's... something inside of me. I'm not sure, but it feels dark, menacing. Like a shadow, or maybe... a demon."

Klink steps closer, the chimes singing with his movement. He gestures to a cushioned bench in the middle of the room, hinting for Wilhilm to sit.

"I will have a look at it. Unfortunately, there is so much damage done to your soul. There was a reason magic once was banned. So many magic users forever lost because they ripped too many shards off their soul to tap into magic," Klink sighs.

Wilhilm takes a seat, steeling himself for whatever examination is to come. Despite his wariness, he trusts his friend.

Klink looks at him, a determined gleam in his eye. From a drawer in a nearby table, Klink pulls out a circular artifact, a ring of multicolored gems that sparkles even in the dim light of the Chime Chamber. Each gem is a different hue, and they all seem to be pulsing, alive in their own right.

Klink starts humming a melodic tune, a tune that Wilhilm recognizes from his childhood, one that had soothed him during stormy nights. The room's chimes pick up on the melody, amplifying it in a gentle chorus. As the Tanaku healer moves the bejeweled ring closer to Wilhilm, the gems glow, their illumination intensified by the song.

"Do you know of something called a Soulshade?" Wilhilm asks. "Is it a serum that might help? A plant?"

Klink stops for a moment. Then shakes his head. "Soulshade is a dark path," Klink says. "It's a forbidden spell, lost to time. Only the Nexus might still harbor some remnants of it."

Wilhilm watches, his breathing uneven, as Klink rotates the ring between two primary feathered hands, letting each gem hover over him one at a time. A cascade of colors dances across Wilhilm's vision—deep blues, radiant reds, ethereal greens, and more. With every transition, Wilhilm feels a different sensation—warmth, cold, a light tingling. It's as if the gems are peeling back layers, searching, probing into the very core of his being.

Wilhilm can't help but close his eyes, bracing himself for what the ring might reveal. Every rumor he had ever heard about soul-seeing, every hushed whisper about the horrors that could be uncovered, floods his mind. The possibility of a demon residing within him fills him with a fear so potent, he feels almost paralyzed.

The gems' glow bathes him, and he imagines them creating a radiant web, mapping out the intricacies of his soul. He wonders what Klink sees, what secrets are being laid bare. Is there a dark stain marring his spirit? A lurking shadow?

A heavy silence envelops the Chime Chamber, broken only by the musical hum of the chimes and Klink's soft, rhythmic breathing.

The gems' intensity starts to wane, their luminescence dimming as Klink finishes the examination. But Wilhilm doesn't dare open his eyes yet, too afraid of the truth that awaits him.

Klink steps back, the ring of gems now dim and seemingly lifeless in his hands. For a long moment, there's only silence. Then, in his unique manner of mimicry—a patchwork of voices and tones he's heard over the years—Klink speaks, "There's a shadow, Wilhilm." The voice shifts. "A dark one."

Wilhilm's eyes snap open, searching Klink's own for any sign that he might be joking. But the Tanaku's eyes are somber, and a chill of dread washes over Wilhilm. "A... demon?" he manages to whisper.

Klink nods, and in a low, almost mournful voice borrowed from Wilhilm's own past, he confirms, "Yes, it's deeply entwined with your soul."

Suddenly, the whispers that had been distant murmurs in Wilhilm's mind become deafening. Shadows dance on the walls of the Chime Chamber, seemingly emerging from within Wilhilm himself. They converge. Dark tendrils wrap around his vision, choking out the light. Panic sets in. He tries to shout, to call for help, but the shadows inside him tighten their grip, stifling his voice.

As the room grows darker, Wilhilm becomes aware of a force moving his hands. They act of their own accord, reaching out and wrapping around Klink's feathered throat. The Tanaku's eyes widen in shock, but instead of fighting back, there's a look of deep sadness in them. The room's chimes ring out in a frantic, chaotic melody, their sounds blending with Klink's strained gasps.

The strength of the shadows is overwhelming. Wilhilm tries to fight, tries to regain control, but it's like battling a tempest. The harder he fights, the stronger the demon becomes, its whispers turning into roars of triumph. The world tilts, the walls of the Chime Chamber seeming to close in, and just as Wilhilm feels himself being pulled into the suffocating darkness of his own mind, his consciousness slips away, leaving only the chilling sound of the chimes and the muffled struggles of the Tanaku healer.

CHAPTER 32

HAVE A DRINK ON ME

Dakaria has managed to launch herself from Gadisa's mind and drifts aimlessly through the vast expanse of minds within the network, trying to find her way back to her body. Each of the other minds is a distant shimmering star in an endless night sky. It's a sprawling sea of consciousness, thoughts brushing against her like fleeting whispers in a crowded room. A pang of loneliness courses through her, a realization that she is but a speck in this vast, overwhelming universe.

Just as despair threatens to pull her under, a familiar hum resonates through the network. It's soft and almost imperceptible at first, like the distant strum of a lute, but she recognizes it immediately—the comforting cadence of a soul she knows. Relief washes over her as she moves towards that resonance. She's eager to leave the cacophony behind and dives right into the mind she knows.

It's Mormak, in his own room at the inn, his door only a dozen paces away from Dakaria's. Mormak's room is full with dozens of kegs. So full that even he has problems turning around. He looks at the keg before him, then back at the pink gnome.

"Could you stop smiling?" Mormak asks. "Your smile unsettles me."

"I'm not smiling. I just have a friendly face," the gnome says.

"You want me to sell this piss to people?"

"You're not selling, you're promoting."

"It tastes like piss. It's not ale at all."

"It's a new taste. Our market research indicates that people crave something new."

"Nothing wrong with the taste of ale," Mormak says.

"It's Elderglow Ale, a remarkable concoction of flavors crafted exclusively for adventurers seeking a taste of the extraordinary. This exquisite ale combines the essence of rare herbs and fruits, harnessing the magic of nature to create a drink unlike any other," the gnome says.

Mormak stares at him.

"Brewed with enchanting Elderglow berries plucked from ancient vines that thrive in the heart of mystical forests," the gnome continues, "this ale radiates a captivating purple hue. Each sip carries the sweet and tangy notes of the berries, offering a burst of refreshing and invigorating flavors reminiscent of untamed wilderness."

Mormak still stares.

"Any questions so far?" the gnome asks.

"What kind of herbs are in there?"

"With a secret blend of herbs known only to the master brewers, this ale unveils subtle hints of aromatic spices and delicate floral undertones. These carefully selected herbs enhance the complexity of the brew, awakening the senses with every sip."

"And you want me to work with that?"

"Do one of your wonderful casts with that. People love you. Everyone who wants to drink ale or beer or anything, they all listen to you, waiting for you to suggest their next fix. And this is where our new Elderglow Ale comes in. It gives your audience something new to look forward to. It will fortify your reputation."

"People only see the keg, right?"

"Sure."

"So, when I spill all of this into the next, let's say pig trough, and I refill it with real ale, nobody will know, right?"

"I suppose... but don't you want to taste this fantastic new brew?"

"I just want to make sure that if I do this, I'm paid ten kegs of real ale. Not this stuff. You have real ale, right?"

The gnome nods. "Sure, we have standard pale ale."

"Good enough."

When he opens the door to bid his farewells to the gnome, Mormak sees the wizard coming up the stairs.

"Wilhilm," he calls out, but the wizard doesn't show any reaction. The wizard seems deeply trapped in his own thoughts, murmuring to himself.

Mormak hurries to the top of the flight of stairs to wait for Wilhilm. Dark shadows billow around the wizard, and for a moment, Mormak imagines they could grab him. Instinctively, he takes a step back.

"Wilhilm, I have a little—let's say—medical question," Mormak says.

The Wizard continues his way, still showing no response.

"Hey, Wizard, I'm talking to you," Mormak says, crossing both arms across his chest.

Even from under the hood of his coat, dark clouds evaporate off Wilhilm's skin. Mormak can't see Wilhilm's face, but for a moment, it seems like two small red dots deep beyond the dark clouds are the only features of his face that are left.

Mormak arches his eyebrows in concern, then Wilhilm's face is brightened by a small, leaded glass window, and Mormak shrug off his earlier impression. "So, about my health problem," he continues.

"Don't touch it all the time. Just let it hang. Try the bark of a guaiacwood tree, make a tincture from it, and gently rub it on it," Wilhilm finally replies. His voice sounds darker than usual and far away.

CHAPTER 33
WITH OR WITHOUT YOU

Mormak feels his face reddening. "No, not that," he says hurriedly. He rolls up his left sleeve and points at the dark shadows evaporating from his own skin. "That! I have the same shadows...clouds...fog whatever that you have."

Wilhilm stares a moment at Mormak's arm. It seems like the shadows descend from him and muster around Mormak as if the shadows were a living thing. "Disturbing," Wilhilm says at last.

"Disturbing? That's it? How do I get rid of it?"

"Rid of it?" Wilhilm laughs a dry laugh. Then his voice changes into a raspy whisper. "I try to fight it. I don't know how for long I can. It gets stronger and stronger."

"Can I like wash it off?"

"Wash it off?" Wilhilm echoes.

"Yeah, I mean, if it helps. I didn't want to try, you hear all sorts of bad things about what washing does to your body these days, but if it helps...Have you tried washing yours off?"

“You can’t have the same thing I have,” Wilhilm says. “I got it... elsewhere. And now, move aside, the pressure is getting greater and greater. I need the answer.”

“The answer to... what? Look, I’m sorry if I mocked you before about those EyeStones,” Mormak says. “They’re perfect for getting ale.”

“I should have known. Everything in this city always revolves around the Nexus. We should have gone there first. Everything is connected.”

Mormak tries to make sense of the wizard’s ramblings for a moment. How do they connect to anything he said? Then he decides, there is no connection. The wizard’s mind is somewhere else.

Mormak steps aside, and Wilhilm hurries into his room, heavy wooden door left open behind him. Wilhilm shakes the cloth off his Echo Stone, and starts doing a cast. While he speaks, the shadows, like little tornadoes, wander into the Echo Stone.

When Wilhilm sets down the Echo Stone, he pulls back his hood. He’s just his normal self again.

“So, that’s how you get rid of it. The shadows, I mean,” Mormak murmurs to himself.

He hurries back to his room, takes up his Echo Stone and positions the keg of Elderglow Ale in front of him.

“Greetings, everyone,” Mormak says. “I just received a keg of a new and exciting ale. I will a do a new tasting soon, but wanted to share the news right away.”

While he talks, he monitors the shadows. The ethereal black fog begins to emanate from his weathered skin in greater quantity. The tendrils of darkness curl and twist, undulating with an otherworldly energy, as if imbued with a life force of their own. Instead of dissipating into the waiting embrace of the Echo Stone clasped in the Dwarf's hand, it grows denser, its ebony essence coalescing and expanding.

As if drawing sustenance from some unseen source, the fog billows outward, like ink spreading across a canvas. It swells and deepens, its once-translucent veil transforming into an impenetrable shroud of darkness. Then, in an eerie reversal, the ominous clouds begin to sink back into the very skin from which they emerged. The fog melds seamlessly with his flesh, merging with every pore, every crevice, as if reclaiming its rightful place.

In panic, Mormak stops the cast. “It’s getting stronger,” he cries out to nobody but himself.

He recalls what happened to Wilhilm just a moment ago. “The stupid hornswoggler, he’s the one creating the shadows, pouring them into the network,” Mormak says. “He’s responsible. It’s his doing!”

He jumps up to confront Wilhilm, then sits down again. What if it is true? What if it is the Wizard’s doing? It could only mean that his friend has fallen to dark magic. Better to not confront him on his own. Better to get the Druid and the Rogue onboard first! And if the wizard would send fireballs their way, it would be better if a taller person stood in front of Mormak.

The Dwarf rolls the cloth around his Echo Stone and stores it under the hay mattress. He knocks at Gadisa’s door.

“No time,” Gadisa says.

“Urgent matter. I invoke right of party assembly.”

“What..? You can’t! I’m busy!”

“Right of party assembly!”

“Fine! Granted. Where and when?”

"One hour, The Thirsty Atlas."

"They have no snacks!"

"Then bring some! One hour, Thirsty Atlas."

Next, Mormak knocks at Dakaria's door. There's no reply.

CHAPTER 34
SWEET DREAMS ARE MADE OF THIS

Mormak pushes open the creaky door to Dakaria's room. The warm, dim light from the single window casts an amber hue over the scene, revealing Dakaria sprawled out on the wooden floor, her hair fanned out like a halo.

A sharp pang of alarm shoots through him. "Dakaria!" he cries out. He kneels beside her, his rough hands gently cradling her face. Her skin is alarmingly cold to the touch, and her usual vibrant energy seems sapped, replaced by a vulnerable stillness. He scans the room for any signs of struggle, any hint of what might have happened, but everything appears undisturbed.

There is a flicker of recognition in him.

This is not her.

This is him.

Her.

This is me.

With a jolt, Dakaria tries to get back to her own self.

Dakaria's eyes flutter open, the blurred edges of her vision gradually taking form. And what she sees almost makes her wish she'd stayed unconscious. Mormak's bearded face looms large, his wide eyes shimmer with unshed tears, and his nose—a prominent feature at the best of times—appears even more exaggerated from her position. The Dwarf's brows knit together in a look of exaggerated concern. He resembles a particularly worried potato.

She blinks, attempting to process the sight. Why was Mormak so...close? She could count each individual hair in his bushy eyebrows and smell the remnants of his lunch—a not so pleasant combination of pickled herring and...was that onion?

"What... who... what happened?" she says.

Mormak blinks back his tears when he sees she's all fine. Then he remembers, he needs to save the world. Or at least the wizard. "I invoke right of party assembly," Mormak says.

"Huh. That important?" Dakaria says, still sprawled across the floor.

"More than you can imagine! One hour, The Thirsty Atlas."

"I will be there."

~

Mormak sits comfortably at a worn wooden table. Before him rests a Zoroan Pale Ale, its frothy head beckoning like a siren's call. He lifts the mug, feeling the familiar heft and coolness of the handle against his calloused hand.

As he brings it to his lips, the rich, earthy aroma of the ale floods his senses. He takes a hearty sip, letting the liquid gold cascade over his tongue. The ale is robust and full-bodied, a perfect blend of bitterness and subtle sweetness.

Mormak takes a moment from his own merriment to cast a curious glance toward the forlorn figure huddled in the corner of the bustling tavern. His gaze fixates on a depressed Tanaku, recognizing the telltale signs of melancholy in its slumped posture and somber demeanor.

There's something familiar about the Tanaku, and it dawns on Mormak that he has seen him before. Right. DrinkingBird33! What happened to him? He was one of the big casters.

Leaning against the sturdy wooden table, the Dwarf's eyes soften with a mixture of empathy and intrigue. He observes the Tanaku's feathers, usually vibrant and lively, now dull and ruffled, mirroring the bird-like creature's downtrodden spirit.

What weight burdens the avian being? What silent sorrows have veiled its normally vibrant mimicry with a haunting silence?

Carefully, Mormak rises from his seat His footsteps carry him toward the Tanaku. With a gentle yet determined expression, he takes a place opposite the creature, allowing a moment of silence to bridge the gap between their worlds.

"Not the drinker yourself, hm?" Mormak says.

"Can't find the joy for it," DrinkingBird replies. "Can't find the joy for anything these days."

"What happened to you?"

"I'm just not good enough. Not good enough for anything. As hard as I try, nothing works out."

"Naw, you're one of the big ones," Mormak says.

"I'm still so small. So insignificant," he sighs. "I will end it."

"End it? What? How?"

"I will rapidly flap my wings to create a whirlwind of

feathers, and then I will just stand there, mouth open, and my feathers fill up my mouth until I suffocate. Isn't that a beautiful way to die?"

"Death by feathers? Not sure how well that would work... I'm more of an axe guy myself."

"You want to take your own life with an axe?"

"What? My own life? No, I wouldn't be able to drink ale if I did that, right? No, I mean, I'd rather use an axe than feathers, and instead of killing me, I prefer killing monsters."

"That your way of showing empathy?"

"You want an ale?"

"Which one are you having?"

"It's the Zoroan Pale Ale," Mormak says.

"Not bad. You should ask for the Zulupian Pale Ale, though. Even better," DrinkingBird says. They order one and then another, until Dakaria shows up. DrinkingBird moves to the bar.

"Where is the Rouge?" Mormak asks.

The door opens, and Gadisa comes in.

With a confident swagger in his step, he enters the tavern. Behind him, through the open door, he drags a sizable grilled boar, its hooves scraping over the dirt of the street, then the polished floor of the establishment.

The patrons, caught off guard by this unconventional sight, pause mid-conversation, their eyes following the peculiar duo.

Undeterred by the quizzical glances and laughter that erupts around them, Gadisa skillfully maneuvers the boar towards a corner of the tavern. His movements, though somewhat awkward, reveal a certain grace born from experience.

Amidst the mingling scents of ale, and the earthy musk of the boar, the Rogue finally comes to a stop.

"What?" he says under Mormak's enquiring stare. "You said to bring my own snacks!"

Mormak sighs. "I guess that's on me," he says.

"Where's Wilhilm?" Dakaria says.

"This is about Wilhilm," Mormak says, and quickly recounts how Wilhilm's Echo Stone swallowed his shadows and distributed them over the network.

"You're sure that's what happened?" Gadisa asks, while he takes bites off the boar.

"You're not serious. It can't be Wilhilm who pushes all of those shadows into the network. Everyone has them. You two have them as well. Where would Wilhilm procure so many shadows," Dakaria points out. Then she stops, as an idea comes to her.

"Reflective amplification," she murmurs.

"Reflection? Like a mirror?" Mormak asks.

"Like a scrying mirror, an artifact similar to the Echo Stones," Dakaria says. "There are Magical Theorists who say that under the right circumstances, routing magic through inter-connected scrying mirrors enhances the power of that magic."

"So, Wilhilm does poison the network," Mormak insists.

"If he does, there has to be immense power somewhere. It can't be just his magic. We all know he barely has any," Dakaria says.

"But then, where—mmmmph—does this power come from?" Gadisa asks while chewing on his boar.

"I don't know. Perhaps there's some amount of natural amplification? Like how a black cloak intensifies the heat on a summer day as opposed to a white cloak, something that's on him that amplifies what he puts in," Dakaria says. "But I have no idea about theoretical magic. I'm sure, though, that the Nexus is involved somehow. Tiringar has the strongest magic undercurrent of any city, and that's because of the Nexus. Has to be the Nexus."

"Well, anyway, no matter what the cause is," Mormak says, "there's only one solution."

"We need to stop Wilhilm from using his Echo Stone," Dakaria says.

"If we must, we will use force," Mormak says, stroking his two axes.

"Or we just feed him," Gadisa says. "He's so skinny, some snack here, some snack there, that might do him some good. Pump up his physique. Make him forget shadows."

CHAPTER 35
LEAN ON ME

I will call him Derek, Wilhilm thinks.

Avoid using its real name. This is important.

So it is true. He's harboring a demon. All of these years since he fought against demons, trying to save Lysandra. The demon must have managed to give him false memories to hide his presence.

So, give him a nice pet name in return. Something unthreatening. When Wilhilm thinks of the demon next time, fear shouldn't have a chance of overwhelming him and erasing the memory of what's really going on with him again.

Derek? But my name is Malphasar.

The images of Klink resurface. Did he kill him? Did the demon kill him? Someone did. Klink is dead. And he feels guilty for it. He looks at his hands, covered by swirling shadows, and imagines its blood circling the air around his hands, marking them, sending a sign to the world—*this is me, Wilhilm the Murderer.*

Wilhilm stares at the Echo Stone in front of him. Casts

filled with misinformation. Comment sections overtaken by slanted views. And the more he watches, the more he forgets the little of Klink that still lingers on his memory.

There is a strong community making argument that the health advantages of washing have never been proven and further that washing is a conspiracy to keep people poor. Another theory claims the lizards were never defeated, still rule the world, and control the weather. And a third theory maintains that they all just live in a simulation created by the Guild of Illusionists.

He stares at the EyeStone for a moment. What does this thing actually do? It sucks up magic, seems like it absorbs the demon's magic as well. And it creates... *something*. A network of minds that fights over pretty much everything even though most of them are convinced that they are being lied to.

"There's no type of storage gem," Wilhilm murmurs. "Strange. If it were an artifact, there should be something holding magic."

Perhaps it was an arcane singularity effect. The EyeStone might have been created with gnome magic, and the accumulated magical energy perhaps creates a miniature distortion in the ether. This distortion then could act like a vacuum, drawing in nearby magical energy.

Might be. Could be. Perhaps. It is nothing more than a guess. And it doesn't explain everything. Deep inside in the network... he felt magic. When the demon acted out... it's hard to remember, he feels immense pain and knows he's done something to Klink, it seems the pain prevents him from calling back what exactly happened...

At any rate, when the demon acted out, it took magic from somewhere... from deep within the network.

He has to have a closer look into the EyeStone itself. But first of all, he has to find out what it is made of. That might give him some clue about why it sucks up magic...and then what it's doing with that magic.

Amidst the maelstrom of thoughts plaguing him, he recalls a name: Vexatia Cogsworth, an alchemist. Good old Vexatia. She would be able to help.

Wilhilm leaves the inn and directs his steps to Vexatia's lab. He eventually arrives at a door which is only half his height. There's a small sign with scrawled writing that reads, "Knock thrice if you're tall, twice if you're small." Wilhilm knocks three times.

No sooner had his knuckles left the door for the third time, did it burst open to reveal the diminutive form of Vexatia, a kobold. Her large goggles are pushed up to her forehead, and her bright yellow eyes, magnified by the lenses, inspect him with fevered curiosity.

"Oh! Wilhilm, always the thrice-knocker!" she declares, her scaled tail twitching behind her. As she says this, her pet firefly, Fizzlewick, buzzes around Wilhilm's head as if inspecting him on behalf of the kobold.

Taken aback, Wilhilm sets on to chase away Fizzlewick, while Vexatia gesticulates wildly, hands waving about dramatically, "You look terrible! What happened to you? You've the look of someone in need of some alchemical assistance! Or perhaps a trap for unwelcome guests? Maybe a potion to calm your nerves?"

Wilhilm blinks, struggling to find his words. However, before he can speak, Vexatia, not waiting for an answer, suddenly yawns theatrically." Oh, but first, would you mind if we moved this chat inside? I feel one of my genius naps coming on."

And just like that, Wilhilm finds himself ushered into the cluttered world of Vexatia Cogsworth, Tiringar's most unpredictable alchemist. The space is dimly lit by a series of colorful glass lanterns hanging haphazardly from the ceiling. The soft glow from each lantern seems to originate from fireflies similar to Fizzlewick. Shelves run the lengths of the walls, every square inch covered with vials of liquids in every shade imaginable, oddly shaped gears, countless springs, and various unidentified trinkets. The scents are overwhelming—acrid, sweet, smoky, floral—all intertwined. In one corner, a still is distilling a neon green liquid that bubbles and pops, emitting small puffs of purple smoke. On a nearby countertop, glass tubing connects a myriad of beakers and flasks that simmer and froth with mysterious concoctions.

The room's floor is barely visible beneath a scatter of blueprints, scribbled notes, and the occasional stray tool. A couple of half-assembled gadgets, momentarily abandoned, fill the room, their purpose unclear but their design undeniably ingenious.

A massive wooden table stands in the middle of it all, laden with countless alchemical spills, mortars and pestles, tubes, scales, and a tiny forge. Above the table, hanging hooks hold dried herbs, crystals, and what look to be desiccated bat wings.

Fizzlewick zips around Wilhilm in enthusiastic, erratic patterns. The darting firefly leaves a trail of soft glow in its wake, creating fleeting sketches of light in the air.

In one corner, a cozy-looking hammock stretches between two sturdy bookshelves, its presence confirming Vexatia's claims about her midday naps. Above the hammock, a small sign reads, “Genius at rest.”

However, what captures Wilhilm's attention most is the contraption in the center of the room. It's a large, elaborate device with multiple levers, rotating gears, and a series of bells and whistles, quite literally. At its base, a plate reads, "The Dreamer's Concoction Machine."

CHAPTER 36
WEIRD SCIENCE

Wilhilm finds Fizzlewick's enthusiastic buzzing to be more than a little obnoxious. The firefly seems to have taken a particular liking to Wilhilm's ears.

"Shoo! Away with you!" Wilhilm exclaims, swatting at the tiny creature with his hand, but Fizzlewick, as if considering it a game, only darts out of reach at the last moment, circles around, and dives back in for another pass.

Wilhilm's attempts to ward off the persistent firefly turn into a dance. He twists, turns, and jumps, trying to dodge Fizzlewick's playful advances. "Why does it have to be so... so spirited?" Wilhilm mutters to himself.

Vexatia can't help but chuckle. Her goggles reflect the glimmering dance of Fizzlewick's light. "Oh, don't mind Fizzlewick," she says with a smirk. "He's just trying to get acquainted. In his own... persistent way. So, how can I help you?"

"Could I use your lab? I need to examine something, my EyeStone actually."

"Will you set the lab on fire like the last time?"

"I didn't... I mean, it wasn't intentional!"

"Let's rephrase that... Will you randomly set my lab on fire this time?"

"Definitely not," Wilhilm assures.

"Fine," Vexatia says with a sigh. "You know the way."

Wilhilm nods and descends the stairs to the curiously cluttered basement, while he continues to stare at the Echo Stone.

Wilhilm thinks back to his teachings, the principles of magic, and how the flow of energy should be harmonious, especially with artifacts as refined as Echo Stones. Yet, why was there an underlying dissonance that makes the hairs on the back of his neck stand up?

Rubbing his temples, he thinks about the right approach to examine the EyeStone. Meddling with Echo Stones wasn't child's play. But if not him, then who? He has the skills, the knowledge, and most importantly, the drive. If someone can break it, it's surely him.

What would Lysandra say if she were here? The image of her flits through his mind. He remembers her warm smile, the depth in her eyes, and the lessons she imparted about the balance of magic. Would she warn him of diving too deep, or would she encourage him to uncover the truth? Remembering her death immediately brings back the memories of the demon, the constant reminder of how much was sacrificed, and a new thought creeps in.

It isn't memories, because it hasn't ended yet, he thinks. *As long as I have the demon, its influence still endures, working toward something catastrophic.*

It is clear to him now; he has to investigate the source of this corruption. He has to find the connection to the demon. He has to cut the bond, finally putting an end to something that has started almost seven years ago.

Somehow, the EyeStone is involved, sucking in the demon's energy. For whatever nefarious purpose.

Wilhilm carefully places the EyeStone on the table, its glossy surface catching the ambient light. Drawing a small, sharp tool from a mount on the wall, he positions it on the stone's edge, applying gentle pressure to scrape off a minuscule fragment. The motion is delicate, akin to an artist carving a miniature sculpture.

With the fragment successfully separated, Wilhilm holds it up to the light, scrutinizing its structure. The reflects a myriad of colors as it catches the light from different angles. He carefully transfers the fragment into a glass vial, which contains a few drops of a translucent amber liquid known as Thirium Ether, a rare solvent used by magical researchers to analyze magical properties.

Next, he reaches for a second vial containing a silvery fluid named Lunar Essence, which reacts with magical elements. He slowly drips three drops into the first vial. Wilhilm then pauses, drawing a deep breath as he mentally reviews the alchemical combination.

Sealing the vial, he gently shakes it, allowing the contents to mix thoroughly. He watches intently, looking for any change in color, consistency, or any other unusual signs that would give away the stone's properties or composition. The vial's content starts to swirl in shades of violet and cerulean. The liquid mixture sparkles as the tiny fragment dissolves.

"Demon magic," he mutters to himself, noting the unusual shimmer of Ulthril in the vial. "Because, of course, it is. Nothing in my life is just...easy."

A sudden, chilling gust of wind sweeps through the room, snuffing out the candles. Wilhilm's heart races as the temperature drops and the shadows grow darker, more menacing.

CHAPTER 37
LIKE A VIRGIN

As abruptly as it begins, the gust ceases. Wilhilm's eyes adjust to the dimness, only to widen in astonishment. There, not three paces from him, stands Seraphina, just as if some magic has whisked her here.

Her raven-black hair flows freely, and her silvery eyes hold a stormy, intense gaze. Her imposing presence makes the room feel the size of a teacup. "You've found the Ulthril, then?"

Wilhilm's first instinct is to leap up, to question how she entered so silently through the closed door. Yet, awe paralyzes him, rooting him to his chair at the lab table. The stillness in the room is charged with a tension that makes his skin prickle.

"Seraphina—" The name leaves his lips as a breathless whisper, a mixture of a question and an exclamation. He tries again to get his voice working. "How... Where do you come from?"

Seraphina stares at him, her gaze unwavering, as if she is trying to communicate something beyond words. It is an intense moment, one where Wilhilm feels the world around him blur, leaving just the two of them in this pocket of reality. "I will always find you, Wilhilm," she says.

Is it a promise? Or a threat?

Before he can muster the courage to voice any of the thousand questions running through his mind, Seraphina moves, her steps almost soundless on the wooden floor, her form ethereal like a wraith. As she approaches, Wilhilm feels the temperature in the room gradually return to normal, yet the atmosphere remains thick with unsaid words and unexplained occurrences.

Wilhilm coughs. He tries to break the ghostly feel of Seraphina's dramatic entrance by starting a conversation. "Did you know the EyeStone has ties to demon magic?"

"Does that surprise you?" Seraphina asks.

"What do you know about it? Who are you? You're more than a singer..." Wilhilm breaks off, distracted by what he thinks is a small mouse running into a dark corner of the lab.

Seraphina picks up on his thoughts regardless. "Ulthril, the Demon Stone, isn't that what they call it?"

"Its frequency is naturally tuned in to their dimension," Wilhilm says. "That's why it's used by those calling on demons..."

"Don't we all call on demons, some more, some less?"

"Are you trying to distract me? I'm talking about dark magic here!"

"Says the wizard harboring a demon."

Wilhilm sits up straight but she continues.

"Everyone is ready to sacrifice their soul. To give a little bit of themselves. Some know it's to demons. Some give it away for power from a different dimension, not knowing who or what lurks over there. Isn't it funny how everybody just takes, no matter where it comes from?"

"Magic is... difficult," Wilhilm says.

"Did you know, when the Dragons ruled, Ulthril was at the heart of their most powerful artifacts? But even before... When the Eldaris ruled..."

"The Eldaris might be real, but there's no proof that they had any civilization before the ancient dragons," Wilhilm says.

Before he can protest further, she goes on, voice dripping with mischief. "It's of no consequence if you believe facts, or not. They don't stop being facts. Anyway, beyond the dubious joy of watching ogre opera or gnome game nights, these Echo Stones can elevate us."

Wilhilm's face contorts. "Elevate... us?"

"When you're in the network, don't you feel connected? Connected to so many people who share your interests. Who like you for you. So many minds thinking alike. Don't tell me you didn't feel it. It happens to me when I sing. Suddenly, I can not only see into their minds. I become... one with them."

"It's demon magic!"

"Think about what makes demons so powerful. Isn't it the fact that a dozen of them can act like one? That they connect to a hive mind? Look at us. Even if we're facing an army of demons, we still manage to quarrel and scheme against each other. One demon is dangerous enough, but even a dozen, they're almost invincible."

Seraphina pauses for a moment and approaches Wilhilm's EyeStone. "Now imagine that kind of power for humans. Hundreds of thousands of us connected by the same strong unifying will. Humanity could act as one in one harmonious, synchronized action. We could achieve everything. There is so much power in harvesting demon magic."

"For the cost of our individuality."

"Spoken like a true wizard, focused only on himself. I bet your Druid thinks differently. She'd value the connection of all things over self-interest. But you make it sound so dirty." Seraphina shrugs with a sly grin. "Think of the power... of how we would be able to shape a new humanity. To stand up against dangers looming in the shadows."

"But we always stand up against looming dangers from the shadows, it's basically why the Adventurer's Guild was founded," Wilhilm protests.

Ignoring him, Seraphina continues, "One mind, think about that."

Despite himself, Wilhilm has to think about it. All life connected by one mind.

"I told you before. There's something going on, but it's something other than demons. It feels bigger. World-changing. Demon magic, I think... it's only part of it. We will need all the help we can get to withstand what's coming."

"What's coming? What are you talking about?"

Seraphina smiles. "You are looking for the evil element inside the network, and I think it's time you learn where it's coming from."

Suddenly, the wicks light again. The dim candlelight creates flickering shadows on the walls, adding a sense of serenity to the chamber. The soft glow illuminates the subtle contours of Seraphina's face. Her glossy tresses catch the occasional glint of light, and Wilhilm is reminded again of how very much she looks like the woman he once loved.

CHAPTER 38
WHO WILL SAVE YOUR SOUL

Seraphina meets Wilhilm's gaze for a fleeting moment, her eyes expressing a vulnerability he has never seen before. "You have to see, Wilhilm. Don't fear your magic," Seraphina says.

Wilhilm's relationship with his magic has always been a tenuous one marked by trepidation. The power at his fingertips has always been an overwhelming one.

But Seraphina's statement ignites a spark of realization in him. It challenges the narrative he has constructed about his own abilities, the narrative that his magic is something to be wary of, a force that could spiral out of control at the slightest provocation.

In that moment, as her words sink in, Wilhilm feels a shift within himself. It's as if a door has been unlocked, revealing a path he's been hesitant to tread. The possibility that he can view his magic not as a threat, but as a gift—an integral part of who he is.

Wilhilm's heart races. The atmosphere in Vexatia's cluttered room becomes heavy with tension. His lips almost mutter an incantation to allow him see the magic tapestry of the world. He stops himself just right before he can do magic. Instead, he rummages through his pouch. It's bigger from the inside than from the outside, and he sinks in head first, with both arms sorting through various items, until he finds what he is looking for. A small ring with just one activation of the Arcane Eye left, the spell that will allow him to see the magic setup of things around him.

Wilhilm's eyes become silvered mirrors, reflecting nothing and everything at once. The Arcane Eye forms in his mind's eye: a shimmering, ethereal orb that is his to command. It drifts upward, passing through walls and barriers as if they were mere mist. He sinks into it, leaving his body behind. Somewhere back in the room, there's Seraphina, taking care that nothing happens to his body, no doubt.

Wilhilm thinks of where he wants the eye to travel, visualizes the corridors of the EyeStone network, and searches for any hint of what he seeks. From this remote vantage point, he watches, a silent observer, all while still anchored in the cramped, potion-filled room. He watches Seraphina. She moves his chair with him in it to the middle of the room. Probably to make sure he won't hit anything when his body slides out of the chair and onto the floor.

A part of him is cautious, wary of the drain that soul-rifting places on his essence. Another part, the curious, hungry part, revels in the power and potential of it all. He's a ship's captain navigating uncharted waters, and the thrill is intoxicating.

The abstract weave of the EyeStone network sprawls out beneath him. From his vantage, he sees his shadows—tendrils of inky darkness—spiraling toward the heart of the network, attracted like iron to a magnet.

There's a moment of hesitancy, before his shadows

touch the EyeStone. And then, with a silent fervor, they are drawn in.

Wilhilm watches, spellbound and horrified, as the black tendrils, the very essence of his demon's powers, continues in the network, seeps toward the threads of magic that bind the other users to the network. The shadows weave their way into the individual threads of magic connecting every user in the network. Each connection they touch turns a shade darker, imbued with the same demon magic that courses through Wilhilm's veins.

The weight of realization lands heavily on his shoulders. *I did this,* he thinks. The shadows, the interconnected web of demon magic, they were born from him. He is the epicenter of a storm he did not intend to create.

A rush of emotions washes over him. There's a burst of pride in the sheer power he has unleashed (W*here does this feeling come from?* he wonders), but beneath that lies dread, the knowledge of the unpredictable nature of the demon magic. There's vast network of people, all unknowingly bound together by the magic he brought into being, that stand as a testament to both his potential and the danger he wields.

What have I done? The question echoes in his mind, a haunting refrain. The enormity of his actions weighs on him, the unknown consequences looming large. Every person connected to the network, has become a part of a vast, shadowy tapestry. And at its center stands Wilhilm.

The pull of the Arcane Eye diminishes, tethering Wilhilm's perception back to his own surroundings. The walls of Vexatia's room sharpen into focus along with the myriad scents of alchemical concoctions. For a moment, the vastness of the network and the weight of his own actions threaten to drown him. He blinks hard, desperately trying to anchor himself to the here and now.

Above him a churning mass of demon shadows loom like storm clouds ready to burst. They ebb and flow with Wilhilm's emotions, twisting and darkening in response to his inner turmoil.

A small rustle from the corner of the room catches his attention. There, beneath an overturned beaker, is the same tiny mouse. Its whiskers twitch, and its beady eyes lock onto Wilhilm. The little creature stands still, perhaps sensing the formidable magic emanating from the wizard.

Then, something miraculous happens. The oppressive cloud of shadows, which moments before seemed unyielding and omnipotent, begin to recoil. Like waves meeting a cliff, they draw back, seemingly respecting the small space the mouse occupies. Wilhilm watches in astonishment, a small smile creeping onto his lips despite the situation.

Do demons fear mice?

Then, rest of the shadows disappear into the EyeStone, and the mouse scuttles away.

The once again familiar room stands stark, and the very air feels dense, like a thick fog pressing down upon him. He has been a part of something vast and infinite, only to be snatched back into the limited confines of his own mind.

He slides off the chair and sinks to the floor, grappling with the realization of his solitary existence. The connection he has felt, the unity with the world around him, is now just a fleeting memory. Still, the connection to the collective of minds is strong. Whether he wants it or not, it feels so... *right*.

"That was enlightening, wasn't it?" Seraphina says.

"It's me. It's been me all along. The moment I joined

the network, I started to poison it. All of those shadows—the EyeStone *devours* them..."

Seraphina puts a hand on his shoulder. "Don't fear the truth, Wilhilm. This means you can do something about it. Who if not you? And you know how... Did you find the spell I told you about? Soulshade?"

Wilhilm slowly shakes his head. "Not yet... It's a forbidden spell. How will that kind of magic do anything to help it..."

Seraphina smiles. "You will figure it out. Don't fear."

And then, she's gone. Just like a figment of his imagination.

Surprised, Wilhilm jumps up, hitting something on the table. A vial drops to the floor, and there's a series of cracks, adding to a loud *boom*. And before he knows it, there's a fire in the basement.

Vexatia rumbles down the stairs.

"Wilhilm Grindtosser, what did I tell you about not setting my basement on fire?" she coughs while the fire quickly spreads. Fizzlewick zigzags hastily through the room.

"It kind of just happened," Wilhilm defends himself.

Vexatia rummages through the top shelf, and lets out a triumphant cry when she finds a glass of what looks like silver sand. Wilhilm catches a quick glance at the label. It says, "In case Wilhilm visits." She throws it into the flames and with a poof, they suddenly subside.

"Wait... Did you call that thing...?" Wilhilm starts.

"Out, out, out," Vexatia counters. "Leave, leave now! And learn how not to set things on fire before you return!"

CHAPTER 39
UNDERGROUND

The Nexus. Tiringar's unending library, an unending pool of knowledge. That's where Wilhilm is headed to find information on *Soulshade*. It's the only place an ancient forbidden spell would be sealed away. The Nexus is magically hidden in the ground under Tiringar, but Wilhilm has been there before and knows the way.

His footsteps echo against the wet stone of Tiringar's labyrinthine sewer system. The dim glow from a magical pendant only barely lights the way. The noxious odor is nearly overpowering; a blend of mildew, waste, and something metallic, an acrid hint of iron. The entrance to The Hollow Echo—a sort of antechamber to the Nexus—is located in the deepest recesses of the city's sewers, but Wilhilm has almost forgotten how convoluted and vast these underground channels could be since his last visit.

As he continues his descent, the smooth bricks of the city's constructed sewers give way to natural stone tunnels, carved out over millennia by rushing water. The air becomes cooler, denser, and the sounds more muted.

He thinks of the demon and shivers. The demon—it still is hard to admit it to himself—almost overpowered him several times. Especially after he returned from Klink.

Klink. The very thought sends pain down his spine, and for a moment, the fog in his mind lifts, and he can see his hands around Klink's throat, before the images disappear again.

The pressure within his soul yields since he uses the EyeStone, but now Wilhilm knows the price. He saw how he spreads the darkness through the network, how he is at the center at everything. It weighs on him like a ship anchor, sunk deep in a sea of guilt, pulling him down with its weight. He can only hope that this spell Soulshade will put an end to it.

Hours in the sewer labyrinth seem to drag. Wilhilm's initial methodical tracking of every turn and twist becomes challenging as the paths start to look eerily similar. Occasionally, he stumbles upon skeletal remains, silent remnant of adventurers who have met their doom within these depths. Wilhilm shivers.

After what feels like an eternity, the narrow passage he is following opens abruptly, the tunnel's roof soaring upwards, and the walls stretching out on either side. Wilhilm has found it: The Hollow Echo. The cavern is immense, a yawning expanse of darkness where every sound is magnified tenfold. Even his own breathing reverberates eerily back to him.

The vastness of space is almost dizzying. The pendant's light barely pierces the blackness. Here and there, patches of luminescent fungi paint an otherworldly glow on the walls, guiding Wilhilm's path towards the cavern's centerpiece: the Concealed Crater.

Drawn to it, Wilhilm cautiously approaches the edge,

peering down into the swirling vortex of colors below. He feels a tide of magic inside that vortex. Wilhilm takes a deep breath, trying to calm his racing heart.

This is it.

The heart of the Nexus awaits him below.

Wilhilm stands on the precipice, the vastness of the Hollow Echo surrounding him. He looks around until he finds the rock that will open the veil to the Nexus. It's a smooth gray rock that goes so well with its surroundings that it took him two hours to find it the last time. There's one feature only that rock has, and that's a coin slot on one one side.

Wilhilm picks a silver coin from his pouch and inserts it into the coin slot. Of course, the Patriarch established a Nexus tax. Because, why not make money here? Wilhilm feels a pang of anger, and it increases when nothing happens.

"What's wrong?" he murmurs.

"What's wrong?" a voice says. "You're giving me a silver coin and you're asking me what's wrong?"

Where is the voice coming from? It can't be the rock. Can it?

"Who's there?" Wilhilm asks.

"Come on, you're staring right at me!" the rock says.

"But... you're a rock! You didn't talk last time!"

"Just because I won't talk doesn't mean I can't talk. And why wouldn't I be able to talk? Is there a law against it? Did I miss something?"

"Talk all you want," Wilhilm counters, still a bit surprised. "But why don't you open the veil?"

"Inflation," the rock says.

"Inflation?" Wilhilm echoes.

"Prices go up everywhere, especially now with everyone

engulfed in the EyeStone and nobody willing to take up a decent job anymore."

"But I gave you a silver coin! It was a silver coin last time!" Wilhilm curses, then takes another silver coin from his pouch.

"Let met stop you right there. That won't do it."

"What do you mean? Two silver coins is double the price!"

"It's one gold coin now."

Wilhilm takes in a sharp breath. "One gold coin! That's not inflation! That's robbery!"

"You don't *have* to go to the Nexus, you know. Nobody's forcing you to. You can go to that silver mine you're obviously coming from anytime."

"Do you have any idea how long a decent person has to work for a gold coin?"

"Do you have any idea how long a decent rock has to work for a gold coin?"

Wilhilm sighs. He won't get far with this rock. He takes a gold coin from his pouch and puts it into the coin slot. "There, but now give me back my silver coin!"

"I'm sorry, no takesies-backsies," the rock says.

Three runes light up in the air. The runes blaze brightly. Their combined energy creates a web of interwoven light that begins to spiral towards the center of the cavern. The ground trembles.

Then, with a thunderous sound, the magic of the runes begins to unravel, its layers peeling back one by one. The Concealed Crater, masked by powerful magics, now lies exposed.

Wilhilm leans over the edge to gaze down into the heart of the crater. The way forward is now clear.

Hesitantly, Wilhilm climbs down into the Nexus, the

cavern's entrance giving way to an awe-inspiring chamber. The very air seems to shimmer with energy, pulses of light dance across the vast space. Towering spires of crystal jut out from the floor, each one aglow with a soft luminescence.

He gazes around, a sense of reverence filling him. Every corner of the Nexus seems imbued with magic, with history. This is the very heart of Tiringar's magic, the epicenter of its power. The remains of a colossal Elder brain.

Wilhilm's fingers brush lightly against one of the crystal spires. It hums under his touch, resonating with his own energy. His footsteps echo lightly as he delves deeper into the Nexus. The soft glow of the crystalline spires around him casts eerie shadows, playing tricks on his eyes. It's within this shifting play of light and dark that a familiar silhouette emerges

Standing gracefully among the luminous crystals is Zyphoria, the guardian of the Nexus. Her skin, an otherworldly shade of mauve, contrasts starkly with her flowing silver robes. The pallid skin glistens slightly, like the belly of a deep-sea creature. Her head is elongated and bulbous, tapering to a point at the top. It's devoid of any hair or familiar human-like features. Most striking are the tentacles that wriggle and writhe around her mouth, each one thick and sinuous, like grotesque worms seeking prey. They undulate with a life of their own, moving with an unsettling, hypnotic rhythm. The tentacles frame a mouth that seems to be a gaping maw of darkness, a pit leading to an unknown abyss.

Wilhilm hasn't seen Zyphoria in years but the guardian is impossible to forget.

CHAPTER 40
LET'S GET IT ON

Where eyes should be, Zyphoria only has deep, empty sockets, shadowed and inscrutable. The lack of eyes renders her expression unreadable, a blank canvas that somehow conveys a sense of ancient intelligence and malevolence. It makes her face all the more unsettling—as if she perceives the world in a manner beyond human understanding.

When those empty sockets fixate on him, and Wilhilm feels an almost imperceptible tug at the edges of his consciousness. It's a gentle probe, a mere brush against his mind, but enough to remind him of what she is.

The Brainreaper's reputation for devouring brains is well-known. Even with the history they share, even if Zyphoria has left her brain-reaping evils long behind her, the primal part of Wilhilm can't help but be wary.

Wilhilm scans the surroundings past the imposing figure of Zyphoria, drawn inexplicably to the shadows beyond. There's another itch at the back of his mind, a niggling sense of something amiss. And then he spots them

—figures cloaked in gray, their forms insubstantial as if made of unraveling threads.

Stitchsuckers.

There are three of them, standing as silent sentinels behind Zyphoria. Each exudes an aura of hungry anticipation, ethereal tendrils subtly waving as though seeking out streams of magic to devour.

He swallows hard, his throat dry. Their presence shouldn't be a surprise to him. The Stitchsuckers occupied the top ranks among the Neural Navigators and they greedily flocked to magic like moths to light.

Wilhilm watches as the foremost Stitchsucker glides forward. Its tendrils undulate around its ambiguous form. The very air seems to hum, charged with the raw energy of the Nexus, but now tainted with an underlying menace.

"*You-weaver-of-spells,*" the Stitchsucker intones, its voice echoing in a haunting chorus as if spoken by many. "*Magic-strings twisted, you did. Darkened they have.*"

A second Stitchsucker moves to its companion's side, joining the chorus. "*Ripples and whirls in the stream, caused by you. The net-song is off-tune. Shadows where light once danced.*"

The third remains slightly behind, its tendrils waving more frenetically. "*Dark strings, dark casts, echoes of a demon's whisper. Why, spellbinder, why?*"

Wilhilm's heart races, his palms growing damp.

Kill them, kill them all. They don't deserve to live. Derek's voice booms in his head.

The dark thought shocks Wilhilm. He's not the killing type.

But you did kill your friend Klink.

"I didn't kill him," Wilhilm murmurs.

Oh yes, you did.

Trying to ignore the Stitchsuckers, Wilhilm turns his focus back on Zyphoria.

She lifts a slender hand in greeting, her fingers long and delicate, adorned with rings that pulse with a magic of their own. “Wilhilm,” she murmurs, her voice a soft, sibilant whisper that seems to resonate inside his head more than his ears.

“Zyphoria,” he finally greets her. Zyphoria just stares at him, showing no sign if she heard the mind conversations with either the Stitchsuckers or the whispers of Derek. Wilhilm tried to keep the unease from his voice. “It’s been... a while.”

The subtlest of smiles plays on the edges of her tentacles, a gesture that over time he’s come to recognize as her version of warmth. “Indeed. But it’s a pleasure our paths cross again.”

Wilhilm nods at her in acknowledgment. As much as Wilhilm feels uncomfortable in her presence, he knows that the long-lost knowledge buried in the Nexus is worthless without her.

“No need for a long catch-up, I gather?” Wilhilm says. His tongue is dry. What does she know? What does she see in his mind?

“I guess, it’s better you tell me,” Zyphoria replies. “As it is, I’m not allowed to reap brains in this position. Something about insurance.” She comes closer. “There’s a part of you that evades my probing, something dark, but I know better than to insist.”

“The EyeStone network,” Wilhilm says hurriedly. “I want to find out how to clean it from my.... from evil influences.”

“The Nexus holds immense knowledge, but the EyeStones are recent. The Neural Navigators are on high alert. The Patriarch ordered them on stand-by. The investigate the Self-Combustions, but have yet to find the matching snippet of knowledge." She pauses. "But I sense you're looking for something more specific."

Wilhilm clears his throat, trying to regain some semblance of composure. "I've been told there's a... thing called *Soulshade*."

Zyphoria tilts her head slightly. "There are many forbidden things in this world, Wilhilm."

"Forbidden?"

"You're looking into legacy spells, so to speak."

This is taking too long! We need the spell. We need it now. NOW!

For a moment, Wilhilm stops. Derek wants the spell? But won't the spell expel him? Stop his influence? Just when he tries to hold on to this thought, something in his mind shifts, and fogs the thought out of existence.

Hurry up, Derek urges.

Wilhilm tries to ignore the voice—Who knew demons were so impatient with long conversations?

"Can you grant me access?" Wilhilm asks.

"What would you need with a spell like that? It almost damned our world once before."

Wilhilm hesitates. This doesn't sound like the spell he's looking for. "Are you sure there aren't two spells by the same name? Mine should be harmless. Just let us look over it together."

"There's nothing I can do for you, Wilhilm. The spell is sealed. Knowledge, they say, is neither good, nor bad, but there is a surprising high number of people who use knowledge for their own gain. As guardian, I have responsibilities."

Slay her, and her kind, and everyone that is here. This is unacceptable. We don't allow insubordination. When we command, every being obeys. We want the spell. We need it. We need it now.

The whispers are incessant, a relentless assault that wears at him. Beneath them, he feels the trap of corruption and madness. And then, again, he feels the desert calling out to him. *Come back. We want you back.* Images of him under heaps of sand fill his mind, sand pouring into his mouth, his nose, his ears, until he can't breathe anymore...

Wilhilm's head throbs with the strain. His head feels too small, invisible walls closing in as the demon's voice echoes in his skull. It's a battle fought in the silent depths of his being, unseen, though the air around him seems charged with the tension of his struggle.

CHAPTER 41

DANCING IN THE DARK

"I need to see what the spell does... just look at it...," Wilhilm pleads.

Zyphoria doesn't realizes how important this is to him. Seraphina told him this would make things better and he trusts her. He has to make Zyphoria understand. Make her see that he's right. "Zyphoria, most of my soul has been torn away. This spell can help me. I need... I need to see it."

"Did you ever consider looking into yourself to solve your problem?" Zyphoria asks. She extends her fingers, and instinctively Wilhilm shrieks back.

"Don't probe me... I don't want to... lose control."

"I have lived so many lives, have memories to last me generation, and they tell me that often, the real solution lies in ourselves, not around us." Zyphoria's tentacles twitch again and a low shiver runs through them. "And I feel there's something inside of you that is part of this."

Ignore her lies. Take the spell. Take it now. No matter what it takes.

Suddenly, Wilhilm feels rage rise up deep inside of him, rage striving to take control, rage pushing with urgency.

"What's inside of me... My own problems, they have nothing to do with it. Nothing at all!"

Zyphoria's eyes light up for a second. "Open your eyes, Wilhilm. Don't close them to the truth. Open your eyes, and you will see that you are part of the problem, and thus, you are part of the solution."

You indeed are part of the solution. Take the spell. Take it now. You need it. We need it. The world needs it.

"Be quiet," Wilhilm shouts out loud, grabbing his head with both hands as if it was something he could just pull off and throw away.

Zyphora ignores him. "There is something, let me see... I can almost taste it...,"

Wilhilm relaxes his hands and looks up. The Stich-suckers are still standing there, as if frozen in time. An undercurrent of trepidation courses through him; his senses, honed by countless encounters, scream at him to react, to protect himself. Yet, there's a strange allure in her unhuman face, a pull he finds hard to resist.

As if reading his uncertainty, Zyphoria glides gracefully towards him, the movement so fluid it's as though she's part of the shadows themselves. The Brainreaper's tentacles gently reach out, caressing the contours of his face with an unexpected tenderness. Instead of cold and clammy as he'd expected, the touch feels oddly warm. Almost comforting.

Wilhilm's eyes widen in surprise, but his body refuses to react. A soft paralysis begins at the point of contact where the tentacles secrete a numbing substance and radiates outwards. His arms drop limply to his sides, his legs buckle, but he doesn't fall. Zyphoria's tentacles cradle him, supporting him in a gentle embrace. The sensation is intimate, like a lover's touch, but terrifying in its implications.

One absurd thought floats to the surface of his consciousness: *This is the strangest hug I've ever received.*

As the paralyzing substance spreads through Wilhilm's body, the lurking demon inside him senses the impending danger. It refuses to be subdued by an external force, especially a creature that would dare to rob it of its host.

Wilhilm feels a sudden, white-hot surge of fury, but it isn't entirely his own. It's the demon's rage fueled with the instinct of survival. With a ferocity that catches even the poised Zyphoria off-guard, shadows explode outward from Wilhilm. They coalesce into grotesque grimaces and razor-sharp talons.

This part of the Nexus, already dim, plunges into an almost impenetrable darkness as the shadow tendrils lash out. Zyphoria's tentacles, previously gentle in their caress, now snap defensively, seeking to ward off the shadow onslaught. The two entities—one of darkness and one of an ancient, insatiable hunger—clash in a fierce dance with Wilhilm's consciousness caught in the crossfire.

Wilhilm feels the demon's visceral delight in the battle, its primal need to dominate. The Brainreaper's psychic pulses reverberate through the room, each burst fighting to fend off the shadows and reach Wilhilm's mind.

"*I will not be devoured!*" The thought—whether Wilhilm's own or the demon's—echoes loudly in his mind.

Tendrils of shadow plunge towards Zyphoria, piercing her defenses, wrapping around her tentacles, constricting and pulling. The Brainreaper lets out a shriek, a sound so otherworldly that it chills the very marrow in Wilhilm's bones but the shadows are relentless.

With one slash, the shadow talons tear into Zyphoria,

ending the Brainreaper's reign in a final, gruesome moment.

As quickly as came, the shadow recedes, leaving Wilhilm slumped on the floor, panting heavily. The weight of what has transpired, the sheer force of the demon's rage, leaves him drained.

As the fog of demonic influence slowly recedes from Wilhilm's mind, a chilling clarity begins to settle over him. His eyes open to the grim reality of his actions. There, before him, lies the lifeless body of Zyphoria. Wilhilm's heart plummets into an abyss of shock and despair. His hands tremble at his sides. He stares at Zyphoria's still form, the once intimidating figure now rendered hauntingly inert, the tentacles that had always writhed with an alien life now limp and motionless.

Before Wilhilm can recover, the Stitchsuckers stir. They speak in an overlapping chorus, each voice starting just a beat after the previous one, creating a ripple effect of sound.

"He did it... it was him..."

"...The energy, the darkness..."

Like ripples in a pond after a stone's thrown, the increasing volume of their chatter draws the attention of the few other beings in the Nexus. Mutterings and gasps rise as the news seems to spread. Heads turn, fingers point, and whispers multiply, each eye focusing on Wilhilm.

Panic bubbles inside Wilhilm. He's cornered, exposed, a spectacle for all to see. The demon within him senses this vulnerability too, feeding off the anxiety and fear. It roils and churns, eager to lash out, to silence the chattering Stitchsuckers before they cause any more damage. The shadows quiver, almost like tentacles.

He feels a growing compulsion to command the demon, to unleash its wrath on the Stitchsuckers.

I need to leave... I need to get out of here, Wilhilm thinks frantically, his gaze darting around, searching for an escape. But the chorus of the Stitchsuckers grows ever louder, drowning his thoughts, and he feels the pull of the demon, eager to once again take control.

"*It was him... the darkness, it consumes his soul. It consumes us. The corruption spreads. He is the catalyst of ruin. This act of BLOOD IS THE BEGINNING. THE WORLD TREMBLES ON THE PRECIPICE OF HIS MADNESS. HE WILL BRING IT ALL CRASHING DOWN. INTO THE VOID. INTO THE VOID. HE IS MAD. INTO THE VOID. We must act, or all shall be lost to his descent.*"

Wilhilm feels the entity surge forward, claiming dominion over his body. Shadows emanate from him in monstrous faces, elongated talons, and coiling tendrils. Wilhilm needs to save himself. Is it so bad to let the demon help with that?

CHAPTER 42

KILLING ME SOFTLY WITH HIS SONG

The barrage of demonic shadows catch the Stitchsuckers off guard. They attempt to meld with the magic threads around them, trying to draw power. But the demon shadows are too quick, too fierce. One by one, the Stitchsuckers are ensnared by the writhing darkness. Their unique voices, moments ago so full of conviction, are silenced abruptly, leaving only the echoes of their last words.

But the demon's appetite isn't sated.

Half a dozen Neural Navigators storm in, and Wilhilm's demon lashes out. The first Neural Navigator barely has time to utter a spell of protection before the shadows engulf him, snuffing out the incantation on his lips and leaving him lifeless. Two others break down beside him.

In the aftermath of the shadow's ruthless onslaught, the Nexus lies in eerie silence. Among the scattered possessions of the Neural Navigators, the EyeStones of the unfortunate souls lay scattered on the ground. As Wilhilm's demon shadow sweeps across the scene, it touches each EyeStone in turn. The stones, which had been lifeless, suddenly flicker to life, but not with their usual warm glow. Instead, they ignite with an ominous light, a deep, pulsating crimson that seems to pulse in time with some unseen, dark heartbeat.

Heart beating wildly in his chest, Wilhilm unwraps his own EyeStone, driven on by Derek. Even before he gets the cloth off, it glows with a fierce intensity. The EyeStones pulse in synchrony, drawing from deep within the network. It's a kind of magic Wilhilm has never felt before—this energy isn't the same as those from another dimension. No shreds of his soul torn to pieces. No tear in the ether. No smell, no taste of another world.

Where does this energy come from?

It seems to be siphoned directly from the very heart of the EyeStone network. The stones feed him, their energy channeling through him in waves, making him feel both incredibly powerful and disoriented.

Part of Wilhilm revels in this newfound might, a dark exultation shared with the demon. But another part, the still-human side, watches in abject horror, unable to intervene or halt the onslaught. *What have I become?* he thinks, the weight of guilt pressing down, even as the rush of power threatens to sweep him away.

Then, Wilhilm feels an overwhelming exhaustion setting in. The stones dim as the energy dissipates. He sinks to the ground, surrounded by a battlefield of dead bodies. The once-lustrous corridors of thought and synaptic chambers now bear the scars of the demon's fury. Silence rings deafeningly.

The Nexus, with its vast repository of knowledge, lies open before Wilhilm. He stares at it, too exhausted to move, when something echoes through his mind. Then, he understands. The demon that now shares his psyche, the one that killed the Brainreaper, it holds parts of the remnants of Zyphoria's consciousness. The key.

Guided by this alien, yet intimate presence, Wilhilm navigates the intricate neural pathways of the Nexus. It feels as though he's delving into a dense, multifaceted web, with threads of thought and memory intertwined in an impossibly complex tapestry. Each synapse he touches radiates knowledge, sensations, and experiences —entire lifetimes worth of wisdom. The demon's greed drives him relentlessly towards the prize: the Soulshade spell.

A distant, yet familiar memory surfaces—Zyphoria's memory. With it comes the sensation of cold tentacles, the taste of alien emotions, and the intricate weavings of a particular spell. Following this spectral trail, Wilhilm delves deeper, feeling like he's both the hunter and the hunted as he chases a fragment of a memory through a labyrinth of thought.

There's so much knowledge here, so much of it stored here, but lost elsewhere. So much to learn and understand. He dimly remembers the Patriarch telling him about a spell that would help him... he must have been talking about Soulshade.

Finally, within a secluded synaptic chamber, he finds it —a glowing node of magic and knowledge. The spell that might hold the key to Wilhilm's salvation lays before him. It pulsates with power, the arcane symbols shimmering invitingly.

Wilhilm examines its structure. It is a Conjuration spell, tied to dimensional travel.

How would this spell help him? He had expected spell of Abjuration of Evocation. A spell of Conjuration seems... too easy for his problem. Banning the demon to another plane, perhaps. Was that what it was about? But why was this spell banned and so closely guarded then?

We have what we need. Leave. Leave now.

Everything in Wilhilm rings in alarm, but he can't find the why in his thoughts, there's so much fog obfuscating his memories. It doesn't matter now. He has to go. Flee. So many lives lost... such carnage.

The spell is worth it. Leave now.

Wilhilm touches the synapsis holding the spell, and the light turns into a scroll dropping to the floor. He picks it up, then turns and traces his steps back. A crystal in the corridor reflects his image back. He moves closer and sees a new Wilhilm. Dark shadows shroud his head like a hood. There's gray turmoil in his eyes, the pupils red.

Wilhilm's heart hammers wildly against his chest, each beat an urgent plea to flee. The very air around him feels stifling, thick with unseen threats and encroaching shadows. Panic, like an insidious vine, wraps itself around his thoughts, squeezing tighter with every passing second.

His feet move before he"s consciously made the decision, stumbling over the uneven floor of the Nexus. All he can focus on is the overwhelming need to escape. To be anywhere but here.

His robes flutter around him, catching on ancient terminals and artifacts as he dashes through the neural pathways. The very walls seem to pulse, the remains of the colossal elder brain watching him with unseen eyes. Every slight movement in his peripheral vision, every soft sound, feels like a predator lunging at him.

He barely registers where he's going, careening down pathways. And with each frenetic step, one thought, one desperate plea, dominates the rest:

Get out. Get out now.

CHAPTER 43

BAND ON THE RUN

Wilhilm makes it back to the alleys of Tiringar. The sweat that gathered on his back during the battle and escape now feels cold in the open air.

Derek feels like a tempest, writhing and churning inside, seeking an escape. Wilhilm fights hard to keep control of his body. Sharp pangs akin to a thousand tiny needles pierce through him. They radiate from the core of his being, snaking outwards through every fiber, every cell. The sheer intensity of the pain is overwhelming, causing his vision to blur and his knees to buckle. It is as though his very essence is being torn asunder, every fragment of his soul being scrutinized and stretched.

Gasping for breath, Wilhilm stops in a dark alley and tries to center himself, to anchor his thoughts, but the magic's turmoil is relentless. Memories, both cherished and painful, flash before his eyes in rapid succession—the warm touch of Lysandra's hand, the weight of the Echo Stone in his palm, the menacing glare of the Witch King.

As the convulsions continue, a singular thought pierces through the chaos: *Control. I must regain control.* Drawing upon every ounce of his strength and training, Wilhilm uses the EyeStone and starts chanting an old mantra, one taught to him during his earliest days of magic training.

Every spell I make, every soul I break

Every step I take, magic's my heart's stake

Every single day, with every price I pay

Every word I say, magic finds its way

Slowly, the torment begins to subside. The sharp pangs dull, the visions fade, and the street around him settles. The shadows leak back into the EyeStone. He did it again. He fed the demon's energy into the network. Panting heavily, Wilhilm slumps to the ground, drained but alive.

This has gone on long enough. He has the spell now. He can end this. He must end this.

Yes, cast the spell.

No, not now.

He's arrived at an immense building. The Horse Inn, standing tall and venerable, is a juxtaposition of age-old architecture and cutting-edge magical innovations. The warm light from its windows casts a gentle glow onto the cobbled streets, revealing the inn's stone exterior with vibrant stained-glass windows.

Wilhilm is surprised that his feet took him here, then he remembers that this is the inn Seraphina chose to stay.

Seraphina.

Wilhilm pushes the heavy oak doors open, revealing the bustling common room filled with chatter, laughter, and the strumming of a lute in the background. The comforting aroma of roasted meats and spiced mead fills the air, momentarily distracting him.

However, his gaze is soon drawn to the reception desk. In stark contrast to the typical innkeeper one might expect stands a golem. Its imposing structure carved from a pale, marbled stone stands out against the cozy backdrop of the inn's interior. Magic runes glint along its arms and torso, signifying the enchantments that grant it life and cognition. Wilhilm shivers at the memory of his last interaction with a golem.

"Good evening, sir," the golem intones in a voice deep and resonating, though oddly gentle. "How may I assist assist-assist you?"

"I'm here to see Seraphina," Wilhilm replies, trying to maintain a neutral tone.

The golem blinks slowly. Its voice crackles. "Cereal cleaner? We do not serve breakfast at this hour. Would you prefer a dinner menu?"

Wilhilm, eyebrows raised in surprise, tries to clarify. "No, I meant Seraphina. I need to speak with her."

The golem tilts its head. "Speak with a hyena? We don't house animals here. Are you sure you're in the right inn?"

Exasperated, Wilhilm enunciates, trying to make himself clear. "Sera-phina! The person! I need to speak to her."

The golem nods, though its voice still falters with static. "Serrated cleaner? We have cleaning utensils available for purchase if you require."

Wilhilm takes a deep breath. This is a particularly dumb golem, and Wilhilm feels his frustration turning to rage. Shadows waft around him, dangerously condensing. His eyes catch a tiny plaque.

Ronny's Wizardry, Second Hand Golems. If you find a lower rate we'll match it.

Of course. One of Ronny's golems, a second hand one at that. No wonder it doesn't work properly.

"Is there a human, or any other sentient being, I can speak to about guests?"

The golem looks at him blankly for a moment before chirping, "Best quests? We have a board with recommended activities for tourists."

Wilhilm groans exasperatedly. "Could I leave a message for a guest, please?"

The golem brightens. "Yes, message for guest. Please proceed." It seems that, at least, was a command it could comprehend.

"Meet me tomorrow. I need your help. Found a way to stop this."

"Got it, sir."

"Are you sure?"

"I'm not sore, but thank you for caring."

Wilhilm turns around and leaves the Horse Inn before he turns the whole place into a burning inferno.

CHAPTER 44
IN THE AIR TONIGHT

Wilhilm sits cross-legged on the cold stone floor of his room in his own tavern, the arcane scroll of the *Soulshade* spell unfurled before him. His fingers tremble. The scroll seems to pulse with an inner life. This is the temporary form the Nexus has given the spell. If done nothing, it would fade away. The only way for Wilhilm to salvage it, is to transform the spell back into ethereal energy and commit it to memory.

The words are in an ancient Wyrmkin dialect.

Wilhilm puts both of his hands onto the scroll. There is a long, drawn-out sigh—an exhalation of pure, distilled melancholy—as the scroll awakens fully. The words quiver slightly, as if even maintaining their form is an unbearable burden.

"Oh, it's a wizard, what a surprise," the spell mutters, the text almost slumping under the weight of its own sadness. "Of course, it is. Who else would it be? Do you know how long nobody was interested in me? Have a guess!"

Wilhilm looks around, half-hoping someone else might

suddenly appear and take over this clearly doomed conversation, but there's no such luck. He presses down a little harder, as if that might somehow inject a bit of energy into the lethargic script. It doesn't.

"Hey, don't lean on me like that. If you don't want to answer my question, what does that say about you, have you thought about that? It is a simple question about time." The scroll ripples with a despondent flutter, like a particularly morose flag in a nonexistent wind. "But what is time anyway?"

"You know that you will fade away if I just go away?" Wilhilm asks. "You'll die if you don't cooperate."

"O wow. That's your approach? Blackmailing the poor innocent spell? What do they teach you at your academies these days? Not empathy, not courtesy, that's for sure."

Force it into obedience, do it now, Derek booms.

"Hey, no need to send a demon after me," the spell counters. "Okay, what do you want," it asks, with the air of someone who knows they won't like the answer but feels compelled to ask out of a sense of grim duty.

Wilhilm sighs. He hates spells. Most of them are extremely obnoxious when it comes to learning them. "I need to learn you. And I need to learn you fast. Someone has built a network of Echo Stones that basically uses my demon's energy, and whatever the purpose, I need to make it stop."

The spell sighs. "It's so sad, you know. Here I am, a spell that is almost as old as this world; long before the planes were the way they are today, I held the world together. I made the structures you know today. And then, they put me away, like a third-rate spell for a hundred and fifty-four years. And when finally someone comes along, it's a third-rate wizard who doesn't even know me! Who has no idea what I can do!"

This will be a long evening, Wilhilm thinks.

Unacceptable! This has gone on long enough, Derek booms. *Yield now! You are a spell! You are supposed to be used!*

"Wizard, you know, if you want to stop the demon, doesn't it strike you as odd that the demon wants me to be used? Just saying," the spell says. "I mean it would strike me as odd. But, of course, I'm a very brilliant spell. Too brillant for this world in which nobody really understands me."

"It is odd," Wilhilm says. He tries to gather his thoughts. This feels like a trap. He feels like his mind fogs, but this time, he can fight it back a little while longer. "Derek, you killed in the Nexus to get this spell. You wouldn't do this for a spell that expels you, except—are you suicidal? Do you want to talk about it?"

His mind is fogging again, and now he can see it. Derek tries to make him stop thinking about how odd this is.

"You will just have to answer me this time," Wilhilm says. And then, there it is. The image of Lysandra, engulfed in shadowy tendrils. *Lysandra.* Wilhilm's thoughts disperse, and a moment alter, his memories fog. He feels like he was thinking about something important, just a moment ago. Now it's gone.

Learn the spell, Derek says.

The spell sighs a long desperate sigh. "Fine," it eventually says. "I have never worked with a completely useless wizard before, but I guess that's just what the world has come to."

The room is filled with a brief, luminous glow, and then, it fades. The scroll turns to ash, disintegrating into the still air of the room, while the spell flows into him through his nose, his ears, his mouth.

Wilhilm exhales, feeling a newfound connection. It's as if a part of him had been dormant, and now, it has awoken. The sense of power is intoxicating.

He rises, his legs slightly unsteady. The Soulshade spell feels like a bridge to a deeper, older magic. For a moment, he thinks of Zyphoria, and the pain of her death pulsates in him. The thought of her stings him greatly. He wants to cry out, but then something fogs his memories of her.

"So, you've memorized it," Seraphina says.

Wilhilm is startled at Seraphina's abrupt appearance.

"I figured you wanted to see me," she said in place of a greeting.

"Figured? I think I was quite clear from the message."

"Do you mean the part about eating two yarrows? Or about you riding cereals like hyenas?"

"I hate that golem," Wilhilm groaned. "You know, Ronny used to be a decent wizard."

The glimmering surface of Wilhilm's EyeStone, situated right at the center of the room, casts ghostly reflections on the walls. The pulsating light adds a surreal feel to the ambiance.

Wilhilm hesitates. He pushes back his usually neat hair now more disheveled than a haystack in a storm. Seraphina stands beside him, her inquisitive eyes darting between the Stone and him. A lock of her own wild, curly hair playfully obscures one eye, but she makes no move to brush it away.

"Do you think...?" Wilhilm begins, but trails off.

Seraphina leans in, her voice low and teasing. "Think? Oh, you must know by now thinking is overrated, especially around these parts."

He gives her a mock stern look. "It's a Conjuration type of spell," Wilhilm says. "Its structures are similar to portal magic."

"It hasn't been cast in a hundred and fifty years," Seraphina responds. "Guess, we will find out together what it does."

"A hundred and fifty-four years," Wilhilm automatically corrects. "It feels like portal magic, the application seems simple. But I need you. The spell will open a rift and send all of that demon energy where it came from. That is if Derek—if the demon—doesn't stop me."

Seraphina nods, determination on her face. "I see. You want me to sing, so everyone becomes one, and you can pull out the demonic energy as one thread."

Wilhilm nods. "If I'm right—and that's a big if—your music will establish a connection, something like a mega cast that will draw everyone in, will glue the threads of demonic energy together as one. I can hitch a ride on that connection and blast the demonic elements through the rift."

"It sounds like a plan."

Yes. Start it now. Cast the spell.

Seraphina takes his face in her hands, forcing him to meet her gaze. "You're a clever, clever wizard. I trust you."

He swallows hard, placing a hand over hers. "And I trust you. More than I've trusted anyone since... her."

She sighs, resting her forehead against his. "Let's do this."

Wilhilm hesitates for a moment. Something doesn't seem right. Suddenly, there was this plan in his mind, like someone put it there. Seraphina just accepted it. And the demon urges him to go on. A huge alert shrills in his mind. He's being set up. But then his mind fogs again and he loses the thought.

There's a faint trace of cheese in the air.

"Yes, I will cast the spell," he hears himself say.

CHAPTER 45

LOVE IS A BATTLEFIELD

Wilhilm and Seraphina stand before the EyeStone, both determined in the way that only people who have just realized they've run out of options can be. The plan, if one could call it that, is simple: with Seraphina's knack for weaving minds together, she will collect the demonic energy within the network, and Wilhilm will send it back where it belongs—preferably with a one-way ticket. No more shadows lurking in the corners. No more Derek with his penchant for dramatic entrances. And, most importantly, no more deaths. Or at least, fewer of them.

Wilhilm takes a deep breath, the kind that suggests he's about to do something either incredibly brave or incredibly foolish, and begins the incantation. The words spill out, ancient and heavy with the weight of long-forgotten curses. The EyeStone responds with enthusiasm, which is more than could be said for most magical artifacts Wilhilm has worked with in his life. The EyeStone blazes to life, flooding the room with a light that makes even the shadows reconsider their life choices.

Seraphina begins to sing—a tune that is somewhere between a lullaby and a dirge, perfectly fitting for the occasion. It's a heady feeling, this blend of power and connection, and Wilhilm can feel it all—the euphoria of shared purpose, the tremor of fear that skitters along the edges.

But before he can bask in the glow of impending victory, a nagging sensation worms its way into his mind, a sliver of guilt that insists on being noticed. And then it hits —like an unwelcome guest at a party, Derek's memory barges in, darker and more twisted than ever. His laughter, sharp and mocking, echoes through Wilhilm's thoughts. *You always push too hard*, Derek's voice sneers, the sound of someone who's always got one more trick up his sleeve, even after death.

A vortex of shadows materialize beside Wilhilm. The shadows form eyes and something that resembles a hatchet face. Derek looks back at him. "*Yesssss. Thank you. I hope you won't regret that. Cheese is much safer than magic,*" he sneers.

Seraphina, lost in her magic, doesn't notice Derek's appearance. Wilhilm isn't so lucky. "Derek, this isn't the time!" A faint hint of desert sand with a slight hint of cheese is in the air.

"*Oh, but it is,*" Derek purrs. "*It's the perfect time. Look at her, so vulnerable, so open.*"

It's too late to stop. The air around Wilhilm shimmers with latent energy. The words of his spell, ancient and powerful, resonate in the space, creating ripples like stones thrown into a still pond. Slowly, ethereal runes begin to materialize out of thin air, each one glowing with an otherworldly light that pulses and flickers like the embers of a fire.

Wilhilm's heart races. This was what happened to Lysandra.

No, not Seraphina too!

His breath comes in short, sharp gasps, the weight of responsibility for her safety pressing down on him like a physical force.

It's like Lysandra, all over again.

The connection, a once invisible thread now feeling as heavy as a chain, resists his attempts, adding to the growing turmoil within him. The thought of failing her of being unable to shield her from harm fills him with a dread so profound it threatens to overwhelm his senses.

"Seraphina! Snap out of it!" She can't hear him. She stands there still, frozen in time.

Derek's laughter fills the room. "*You think you can control this? You can't even control yourself!*"

The chamber is thick with tension, the hum of arcane energies filling the air. The EyeStone's light has turned from pure white to a stormy gray. In the center of the room, Seraphina stands surrounded by a circle of runes, her determined face illuminated by their radiant blue glow. Wilhilm can feel the ripple of energies, like heartbeats in the darkness, waiting for the critical moment of union.

Suddenly, there is an abrupt surge of energy. A violent torrent of power spirals around Seraphina, drawing the turbulence of magic inwards, her as its epicenter. Her eyes widen in a glow of incandescent white as the rush of energy surrounds her.

"Seraphina!" Wilhilm's voice is almost drowned amidst the hurricane of brilliant light and sound. He can feel the chaotic thrum of a thousand voices. He fights to maintain the boundary, trying to prevent the energies from consuming her.

But it is too late.

With a deafening explosion, the streams of magic

converge, and Seraphina's silhouette stands against a blinding radiance. She is engulfed in flames.

A visceral scream tears from Wilhilm's throat. It feels as if the very fabric of his soul is being torn asunder. As grief threatens to pull him into the abyss, a deeper fury erupts from within.

With a thunderous crash, the stream of magic Wilhilm tries to control, explodes outwards. Every ounce of his power, every shard of his anger, every whisper of his sorrow, surges through the EyeStone network. The room quakes as the barriers between minds shatter, the individual thoughts and consciousness of everyone connected to the network fusing into one monumental hive mind.

CHAPTER 46

BEHIND BLUE EYES

Even as the tempest of his emotions spins out of control like a particularly indecisive tornado, the hive mind hums gently around Wilhilm, a vast ocean of thoughts and feelings that, quite frankly, has far too many currents for his liking. Somewhere within this mental maelstrom, Derek lurks, poised like a particularly smug shark, ready to take a bite out of Wilhilm's precarious state of mind.

Desperation pushing him forward, Wilhilm reaches out to the collective consciousness, that vast, interconnected network of minds. It's like trying to plug a leaking boat with a sponge, but it's all he's got. With a mental heave that feels like pulling off a particularly stubborn bandage, he lets loose his anguish into the hive mind, pouring out his pain like a river breaking through a dam. The collective bears the weight of his suffering, shouldering it like a particularly dreary communal burden.

Meanwhile, Seraphina is trapped within the embrace of the pyre—though embrace might be too affectionate a word for the cruel, magical flames that dance around her.

Her form flickers in and out, like a mirage on a hot day or perhaps a faulty lantern in a storm, her voice echoing through the ether with a haunting lament that would make banshees reconsider their career choices. The pain in Wilhilm's chest is searing, a burning sensation that has all the appeal of swallowing molten lava.

Lysandra.

Wilhilm's face prickles with heat. Beads of sweat form on his forehead and trail down his skin in tiny, meandering streams. The air is thick, it makes him cough. The figure within the fire, once petite and delicate, starts to twist and contort, expanding and darkening. Wilhilm's eyes widen, disbelief coursing through him, as Seraphina's form is devoured and in her place stands another. A towering, skeletal figure.

King Hasan ibn Azazel, the dreaded lich king.

Hasan dances his fingers through the air, the corners of his mouth turned upward. Dark, tattered robes billow around him. Withered flesh clings tenaciously to his spectral frame. A flicker of ancient recognition stirs within his hollow eyes.

The silver crown adorning his skull, once a symbol of mortal kingship, now represents his dominion over the realms of necromantic power. Engravings trace the metal, scenes of death and rebirth. Its gleaming surface reflects the light of countless spells, accentuated by the pale glow emanating from his undead essence.

"I hope you still love me," King Hasan says. Each word resonates with a faint echo, amplifying in the space around them, filling the chamber with an eerie, disembodied timbre.

What? How?

The realization is a blade to Wilhilm's heart. King

Hasan—has he freed King Hasan? Where's Seraphina? What did the lich do to her? Why has she vanished? Did he *kill* her?

"What's going on?" he whispers to himself, the words lost amidst the roaring flames and the sinister laughter of the lich king.

Wilhilm's fingers clench into fists, his nails digging into his palms. The one truth that stands stark amidst the chaotic whirlwind of his thoughts is this: The battle, the real battle, has only just begun.

"Thank you for helping me," King Hasan says. His voice is a haunting whisper that seems to come from everywhere and nowhere at once. It's a voice that has ordered the deaths of kings, turned allies into enemies, and reshaped the very fabric of realms.

Yes, thank you. Yesssss. The ugly voice continues to whisper in Wilhilm's mind.

"If it puts your mind at ease, I'm not really here. I can't leave my prison beneath the sands where you left me, for now."

"But you're dead... I saw you die..." Wilhilm says.

"I'm barely more than a skeleton now, but I still have life," King Hasan laughs. "And with your help, I'm growing stronger. You were so easy to manipulate. You played along so nicely. I nudged here, I nudged there, it all worked out beautifully."

"Where's Seraphina? Did you kill her?"

King Hasan laughs. "Come, look for her. You know where to find me. I didn't move."

"I will stop you..."

"You can't stop it now," King Hasan says. "You may not understand. And even if you could—if you interfere, you will hurt the world. My plan will make the world better.

More resilient. Something's terrible coming, and if you like it or not, I will be the salvation."

The ambient light in the chamber dims, replaced by a pulsating, omnipotent glow centered on Wilhilm. As the energies settles, the silence that follows is deafening. The fierce isolation that recently threatened to consume him melts away. It's replaced by a profound connection to something far greater than himself. Though Seraphina's voice is no longer with him and the EyeStone is no longer casting, Wilhilm is now the epicenter of a vast and interconnected consciousness.

Wilhilm is gone. Now, there is only everyone.

CHAPTER 47

STAYIN ALIVE

As Dakaria steps out onto the bustling street with her companions, a sense of foreboding permeates the air. She quickly sees why. The citizens of Tiringar no longer meander through the cobblestone alleyways. Instead, they exist in a state that borders between consciousness and a trance. Some stand frozen in their tracks, their bodies are rigid and unyielding, eyes staring blankly into the distance. Others wander aimlessly, their heads turning in slow, almost mechanical arcs from left to right, as if searching for something their minds can no longer comprehend. Their movements are hauntingly deliberate.

A group of screams pierce the air. Dakaria pushes through to see. At the center, a woman and two men stand frozen though flames engulf their bodies. The only sign they feel the flames is their contorted faces. Their agonizing cries mingle with the crackle of flames, painting a horrifying tableau of torment and suffering.

Dakaria can hardly take their eyes off the trio, only

dimly aware of the inky blackness trailing the other townspeople. Shadows clinging to their forms like malevolent specters.

"It's time we see the wizard," Mormak says.

"Will this... happen to us...too?" Gadisa stares at an unresponsive woman holding a basket in front of him.

"Might," Mormak sighs, pulling his sleeves over his hands.

"We might already be too late," Dakaria says. "I have a bad feeling about this."

"People become zombies or go up in flames, and you have a bad feeling about this? Wonder where that comes from," Mormak grumbles.

They hurry back to their inn and, even before they climb the stairs, they see shadows floating down the hall, curling and drifting through the room. They storm up the stairs and crash through the door to the Wizard's room.

Dakaria gives a shout. Wilhilm is locked in a desperate struggle with an insidious black cloud. Dark tendrils coil around his body, snaking through every crevice and orifice, as if seeking to infiltrate his very essence. It's clear he's in agony—his brow is tightly knitted and his mouth is open in a soundless scream..

"What do we do?" Gadisa asks.

"What do we hit?" Mormak asks.

Dakaria tunes her senses to the mystical energies pulsating within the room. With a firm resolve, she begins to weave her magic, channeling the essence of nature through her very being. Her eyes close in concentration, and her lips part as she releases a soft incantation.

The taste of swirling mana tingles upon her tongue, an intoxicating blend of sweetness and raw vitality.

Even as her spell is cast with unwavering intent, the room remains enshrouded in shadows. The curse lingers, defying her efforts to banish it. The flavors upon her tongue become a bitter tang of disappointment.

Undeterred, the druid delves deeper into her well of magic, seeking to understand the nature of the curse that resists her touch. She extends her senses again. The vast symphony of tastes accompany unseen forces at play. The darkness within the room takes on an acrid, smoky flavor.

She opens her eyes to see Mormak swing his two axes at the shadows. He hits with all his might, but his weapons just slide through them.

"I don't know what to do," Dakaria says.

"It all goes in there," Gadisa says, pointing at the EyeStone.

The EyeStone lays on the floor, as if dropped. The reflective surface shivers and ripples, as if disturbed by unseen forces. The never-ending shadows surrounding the mirror converge and vanish within its depths, swallowed by the abyss within. The rattling intensifies, sending tremors through the room, while the EyeStone groans under the weight of the magical disturbance.

Mormak turns his axes on the EyeStone, but his powerful blow is halted mid-air as if an invisible force protects the Echo Stone.

"We can't help him, those EyeStone shadows hold him down. We need that gnome," Mormak says. "If anyone knows how these things work, he does. We make him stop this."

"Ripple Dipple?" Dakaria replies. "We have to hurry, I don't know how long Wilhilm can to sustain this."

Gadisa bows down to speak to Wilhilm. "We'll be

back," he says. "We just have to make that gnome stop what's going on."

Wilhilm groans, giving no indication of him understanding.

The companions hurry downstairs, and the thronged streets of the city are just as chaotic and bewildering.

People wander aimlessly, their vacant gazes focused on an unseen horizon. Others, trapped in their own torment, release guttural cries that pierce the air, casting a pall of unease upon the surroundings. The companions weave through the crowded chaos, their path hindered by the tangled web of lost souls.

As chaos engulfs the city, the eerie phenomenon intensifies. It seems to Dakaria that more and more individuals are spontaneously combusting, their bodies becoming living pyres that consume them from within. Flames dance across the city streets, hungrily devouring everything in their path, transforming the once vibrant urban landscape into a fiery inferno.

The raging fires roar with an insatiable appetite, their fury spreading with unprecedented ferocity. Buildings crackle and crumble as tongues of flame leap from structure to structure, casting a hellish glow upon the darkened skies. Panic and despair permeate the air, mingling with the acrid scent of smoke and burning debris.

"Look... Something's odd about the way they move, it seems like they move into a pattern," Dakaria murmurs

"They form a circle," Mormak wonders, staring into the sky.

"I think it's forming a portal of sorts."

"The kind where monsters come through?" Gadisa says.

"No idea what's coming through, but I don't think it's something good."

The fires take on a purposeful semblance, forming a swirling vortex of searing energy, crackling with otherworldly power. Flames converge across the city like tendrils reaching skyward.

CHAPTER 48

IN THE AIR TONIGHT

As Dakaria, Mormak, and Gadisa approach the store for Cheese EyeStones, they encounter a bottleneck of confused citizens congregated in front of the entrance.

Dakaria stands at the fringe of the bustling crowd, her gaze fixes on a group of Neural Navigators leaving Cheese. They thread their way through the throng of people with an air of purpose and urgency.

Under their hoods, she sees their luminescent tattoos. The Navigators move with a grace that is both mesmerizing and slightly unsettling.

They are the custodians of the Nexus, guardians of knowledge. Their presence in the crowd is a stark contrast to the regular denizens of the city.

The crowd seems to part almost instinctively for the Navigators, their passage leaving a wake of whispered conversations and curious glances.

Dakaria feels a pull of curiosity. She remembers that the Neural Navigators had hurried to the inn back when she saw the twins self-combust.

"Hey you." She approaches the first Navigator, but he only pulls his hood down and turns away.

Well, if they won't talk to her, she'll make them talk. Dakaria closes her eyes and takes a deep breath, centering herself. She prepares to cast a spell that will compel honesty within its bounds. Her hands move through the air tracing the intricate patterns required for the spell,.

As the spell takes form, Dakaria senses the distinct aroma that accompanies her magic—a scent unique to each spell she weaves. The air fills with the smell of aged camomile. Intertwined with it is a subtle hint of sage, a cleansing herb.

With the final words of the spell spoken, Dakaria opens her eyes. The air within the invisible boundary shimmers faintly, touched by the spell's power. She turns her attention to the Neural Navigators.

"Tell me," Dakaria asks, her voice steady, "what do you know about the problems within the EyeStone network?"

The Neural Navigators, bound by the spell's influence, exchange glances. They seem aware of the magic's compulsion. Their expressions betray a hint of reluctance mingled with resignation. The scent of parchment and sage grows stronger.

In this moment, Dakaria stands resolute. She waits, patient and alert.

"We don't know yet what's going on," the first Navigator says, still hidden under his hood.

"There's demonic activity," the second one adds. "We detected it a while back, and when we heard about the self-combustions, we consulted the Nexus and found a connection going back to the Eldaris."

"The Eldaris? That was long before dragons ruled the world," Dakaria says. "How can there be a connection?"

"We may never know. Someone devastated the Nexus. They killed the guardian and a few Navigators," the first Navigator replies.

"As if someone doesn't want us to make the connection," the second one says.

"Don't waste time," Mormak urges. "We need to get in!"

Dakaria looks to him and when she turns back, the Navigators have gone.

She exchanges determined glances with her companions, silently agreeing upon a plan of action—storm in! With steadfast resolve, they forge a path through the crowd, calling out in measured tones to those blocking their way, gently nudging them aside to make room for their passage.

Inside the front doors, gnomes that run erratically through the shop while their EyeStones swirl into the air, adding to the portal that forms outside.

Mormak grabs a random gnome. "Where's your boss?"

The gnome points at the back of the shop.

In the back, a dozen gnomes converge against a door. They all pound against it.

"Are you all looking for your boss?" Gadisa asks.

"We don't know what's going on, or how we can fix it," one of the gnomes says.

"What's behind that door?" Dakaria asks.

"It's an intricate mechanism that requires the exact adjustment of more than a hundred cogs and wheels," the gnome says. "Dipple Nimble Retchbucket is in there."

There's a loud crash. "It's open," Mormak says, pulling his axe from the mechanism that regulates the door.

Despite the heavy door standing unlocked, it takes all three of them and half a dozen gnomes to pull it open. The room behind it is empty.

"What does that mean?" Gadisa says. "Where's Retchbucket?"

The gnome nervously jumps up and down. "How should I know? He was there, now he's gone!"

"How long has he been inside?" Dakaria says.

"Little more than a moon," the gnome replies.

"You're telling me he vanished a moon ago?" Dakaria says.

The gnome nods. "He said he needed some time to think about the next generation of EyeStones. Something about working with the input of our Zal'qaran sponsors."

Zal'qaran sponsors...? Right then, Gadisa walks into the room, then kneels down and picks up a broken staff.

Mormak glances at it. "Darkwood, purple heartswood. Traces of ash. Mithral," he analyzes.

Dakaria takes one the two parts into her hands, weighing it and looking at the runes. "A portal staff."

"He opened a portal? To where?"

Dakaria shrugs. "Hard to tell, but the runes are definitely Zal'qaran in origin."

"The Witchkings," Mormak murmurs.

"I thought they have long fallen," Dakaria says.

"Guys," Gadisa says.

"Witchkings never fall, they merely change," Mormak says.

"Guys," Gadisa repeats, a bit louder.

"Might be. It's evil so far we know," Dakaria says.

"Guys," Gadisa shouts. Both companions turn around to look where Gadisa points outside.

The EyeStones, floating in the air, almost finish forming the circle. As the portal begins to take shape, the fabric of reality bends, warping under the strain of interdimensional energies unleashed.

Sparks of otherworldly colors flicker within the inferno. The intermingling of fire and hidden forces heralds a cataclysmic event, an opening to realms beyond mortal comprehension.

Dakaria stands in awe and horror, her heart heavy with the weight of the impending calamity. With each passing moment, the portal expands, its edges pulsating with an eerie luminescence. She understands the dire consequences of allowing this gateway to fully manifest—it would inevitably unleash horrors.

As the portal reaches its peak, a violent rupture tears through the sky. The air crackles with energy as the portal expands, stretching wider and wider, until it can no longer contain the infernal forces pressing against it. With a thunderous roar, the barrier shatters, unleashing a torrent of dark energy.

A cacophony of demonic shrieks and cries pours from the abyss and fills the air. The piercing wails echo through the darkness, like the tormented souls of a thousand lost beings.

Dakaria experiences a sudden chill, not just a physical sensation, but a coldness that seeps into her spirit, as if the natural energies around her have been corrupted.

The wails are replaced by a whisper. It repeats only two words as it grows in intensity. "Wilhilm Grindtosser."

The whispers go quiet. Dakaria leans forward squinting to make out movement in the center of the portal.

Then, from the depths of the newly opened portal, a horde emerges, demons twisted and grotesque. Their eyes glow with a sickly malevolence, and their snarls reverberate with a haunting ferocity. Their clawed hands and gnashing fangs are primed for carnage, fueled by an insatiable hunger for destruction. They move with an unsettling grace, their movements fluid and unhindered, as they swoop down to the city streets.

"Wilhilm," Dakaria cries. "They're heading to Wilhilm!"

CHAPTER 49

BREAK ON THROUGH

Dakaria closes her eyes and touches Mormak and Gadisa. She calls on her magic and their skins prickle.

"You can move with immense speed now. Run, run as fast as you can back to Wilhilm."

Dakaria doesn't watch them sprint off. Instead, she closes her eyes once more and takes a deep breath, grounding herself in the essence of nature that always surrounds her. She commits a tiny particle of her soul to nature and receives magic in return, and one day, she will commit all the rest and become one with the world around her.

Her body shimmers with a subtle energy as she taps into the primal forces that flow through her being. With a whispered incantation, feathers sprout from her skin. Her arms and legs are replaced with wings and talons. Her senses sharpen, granting her the keen eyesight and acute hearing of the eagle she has become.

She stretches her wings, feeling newfound power and freedom. With a light leap, she takes to the air, soaring effortlessly amidst the currents, her feathers catching the sunlight with a shimmering brilliance. Dakaria glides effortlessly on the currents of the air, her wings spread wide, feeling thermals that rise from the fires below.

As Dakaria soars high above the city, her keen raptor eyes scan the maze of buildings below. She has to dart between thick clouds of black smoke to get a clear view. The city unfolds beneath her like a tapestry, each thread a street or alley, each knot a courtyard or square.

Her gaze is drawn to a particular inn nestled among the bustling streets. There it is. The inn's roof, a patchwork of shingles and thatch, stands out to her. She tucks her wings in, diving down with a precision and grace that only a bird of prey can muster. The wind whistles past her, a rushing sound that fills her ears as she narrows the gap between sky and earth at breathtaking speed.

She fans out her wings to break her descent, each feather catching the air to slow her flight. Then she glides down towards a landing spot, her talons extended ready to grasp onto a perch. With a final, elegant sweep of her wings, she alights gracefully.

She hops in through the window, where a fire rages. She turns back, and immediately coughs. Like elsewhere in the city, screams of terror mingle with the demonic roars. She steels herself and ducks in the window and allows her shape to return.

Wilhilm still lies on the floor, now unconscious. Dakaria shakes his shoulder and pats his cheeks but he's not responding. She hears Gadisa and Mormak climbing the stairs.

"I'm here," she calls out to them.

Then, she focuses on Wilhilm. Something happened. The shadows are retreating, Wilhilm struggles less. Carefully, almost reverently, she touches his skin. With a sudden jolt, Wilhilm's eyes spring open.

"What's... what's going on...?" he asks wearily.

"Nothing much," Mormak says. "Except your shadows somehow created a portal and demons are destroying Tiringar right now."

"Demons?" Wilhilm stares at them.

"We don't have much time, they're looking for you," Dakaria says. "Unfortunately, Dipple Nimble Retchbucket has disappeared. Seems like somewhere into the Zal'qaran desert."

"My prison beneath the sands," Wilhilm says. "Ishmaara, not again."

His confusion is replaced by fury. Dakaria could swear she sees the air around him throb with tension. His eyes now blaze with an anger as potent as any dragon's fire, the embers of his wrath igniting the darkness lurking within.

Every ounce of his outrage stokes this internal darkness, feeding it, allowing it to swell and surge. Like a tempest unleashed, the darkness surges forth, seeping through the pores of his skin, curling around his body in a shroud of roiling shadows. His hands tremble, not from fear, but from the immense power coursing through his veins, the sheer force threatening to consume him.

And then it explodes. The dark magic bursts forth, a wave of raw, uncontained power that resonates with the wizard's rage. The world bends and shudders under the weight of it, and for a moment, it feels as though everything will tear at the seams. A transportation gateway rips open and devours them.

CHAPTER 50

LOST ON THE DESERT

Stinging particles assault Wilhilm's skin and eyes. Every breath is a challenge, as if he's inhaling sand rather than air. His eyes clenched shut, he feels around blindly. His rage has quieted, and Wilhilm has no recollection of what kind of magic he exactly did.

He should have known better. For a moment, his anger got the better of him. He spent all of his life to carefully control his magic. He lost control once before and the results were disastrous. Now he lost it again—several times—, and the results are even more terrifying. Seraphina is gone (*what exactly happened to her?*), Tiringar probably has perished... and who knows what nest of demons he has created. He should have had better control. He needs to have better control.

Eventually, Wilhilm forces his eyes open. Visibility is a mere arm's length. A murky abyss of shifting sand obscures any semblance of the world beyond. Shadows dance and twist in the tumultuous gusts, haunting specters of a land consumed by the storm's relentless fury.

"Dakaria! Wilhilm! Gadisa," Mormak's voice cuts

through the air. Might be from the left, might be from the right.

"Where are you?" Gadisa shouts. "I can't see anything."

"It's night," Dakaria says. "It's night and we're in a desert."

A desert? Might it be... Could it be... was this the Zal'qara desert? Did his *rage* bringing him here to seek justice for Seraphina?

There you are, Wilhilm thinks. *So we see each other again.*

He kneels down and touches the sand. The mere touch sends chills down his spine, awakens the horrors in his mind. Then, Derek's voice cuts into his mind.

This is all your fault. You're the one that left too early, Grindtosser! I had plans, big plans!

Derek feels weaker now, for which Wilhilm is grateful, even though he feels Derek is still dangerously close to the driver's seat of his mind. He has much to do. Starting with locating the rest of the company.

Welcome back. This is where you will find your destiny. In the embrace of the sands.

The wind continues to howl, reducing Wilhilm's surroundings to a symphony of relentless force. The sand is a thousand tiny needles etching their mark on Wilhilm's skin. Everything tingles with pain. The sands shift beneath his feet, and Wilhilm feels panic rise in his chest.

In an instant, the sandstorm abruptly subsides as if nature herself had grown weary of her tantrum. The wind becomes a tender breeze. The churning sand settles, cascading to the ground like a golden curtain, revealing a transformed landscape. Moonlight pierces through the dissipating haze, casting a warm, ethereal glow upon the tranquil desert. It is a moment of breathtaking stillness, as if the world holds its breath, savoring the abrupt cessation of chaos.

The air, now clear, is tinged with the lingering scent of dust and the charge of a storm just passed.

Wilhilm's eyes, still stinging from the sand's assault, slowly adjust to the newfound tranquility. He scans the horizon, his heart heavy with concern for his companions. The storm had scattered them, each lost to the other in the blinding chaos.

Then, as if conjured by his fervent hope, figures emerge from the settling sands. First, the unmistakable form of Mormak, his stout frame and bushy beard coated in a fine layer of dust. He stands a short distance away, looking as surprised as Wilhilm feels, his eyes scanning the surroundings with a mix of bewilderment and relief.

Next to materialize from the sandy veil is Gadisa, his extensive form appearing almost as a mirage in the hazy aftermath of the storm.

Finally, Dakaria steps into view. Her cloak is draped around her like a protective mantle. She is the least ruffled of all of them.

Amidst the dusky twilight, Wilhilm's eyes catch a flickering dance of distant lights. At first, his mind wanders to thoughts of shimmering insects, enchanting fireflies illuminating the night. Yet, as the lights draw closer, their gentle glow solidifies and grows. A realization dawns upon Wilhilm. These lights are held firm by the steady hands of riders.

Torchlight paints their surroundings as the mounted figures emerge from the shadows. Wilhilm's eyes widen at the sight of the mounts these riders have chosen. Dune Serpents.

The Dune Serpents—a kind of gigantic serpents with

legs—are immense. The sinuous body of the first serpent undulates like a wave, each movement fluid and effortless. Its scales glisten under the moon's radiant embrace. The Dune Serpent in front leaves behind ripples in the sand, traces of its passage like a fleeting work of art. Wilhilm notices the creature's powerful limbs adorned with razor-sharp claws that dig into the dunes, granting it stability and control. Its eyes, bright and keen, seem to possess a wisdom borne of centuries of desert dwelling.

"We can only hope they have beer with them," Mormak says at the sight of the advancing company.

"*Man enta? Ma t'amal huna fil sahara?*" one of the riders asks.

"What's he saying?" Dakaria says.

Wilhilm takes a step forward. "*Kunna nuqida fi tufan arrimal*," he replies. *We were caught in the sandstorm.*

The speaker comes closer, the blue stripes on his head-scarf marking him as a member of the Asharii Nomads. The flickering light of the torch casts an ethereal glow upon his face and cast his strong jawline and the curve of his cheek-bones in high relief. His beard is well-maintained and the overall effect is one of quiet strength and resilience. The weathered lines make it hard for Wilhilm to guess the man's age.

"Sandstorm? There was no sandstorm," the man says, now switching to the Common Tongue. "My name is Kart'Ahed Uvhorz. Are you adventurers?"

Wilhilm nods and introduces each of them.

"Are you under contract?" Kart'Ahed Uvhorz asks.

"Under contract?"

"How do you say... on a quest?" Kart'Ahed Uvhorz clarifies.

"Not currently, no," Wilhilm says. "Not affiliated with anyone here, the least with your enemies whoever they might be, if this is what you're wary of."

"And you are a spellcaster? That's why you wear this fancy dress?"

Mormak snorts.

"They're just robes, but yes, I'm a spellcaster."

"Then, hereby I declare you to be in my employ, by the desert laws of the Asharii."

"What? You can't employ us just like that," Dakaria protests. "We have a say in that!"

"I followed the law," Kart'Ahed Uvhorz says. "I introduced myself, I asked about your current employ, you have none, I offered mine."

"Offered? There was nothing being offered," Wilhilm replies curtly.

"Well, do you want to be in my employ, or do you want to wander the desert alone, without water and without provisions and without directions?"

"He has a point there," Mormak chimes in. He directs his next statement to Kart'Ahed Uvhorz. "And just to be sure, is part of our payment made in beer?"

Kart'Ahed Uvhorz looks from Wilhilm to Mormak. "It can be arranged," he says.

"I'm in." Mormak smiles and bows. "At your service."

"What is your quest about?" Wilhilm asks. "I have my own business to attend to."

"It's nothing complicated," Kart'Ahed Uvhorz says, "I just need protection for my caravan for another three days."

"Didn't you have protection?"

"They are... how do you say...incumbent," Kart'Ahed Uvhorz declares. "Now, let's take you to our camp."

"Incumbent... what does that mean?" Gadisa asks.

"Probably massacred," Wilhilm says. "No doubt a massacre of the sort we will soon find ourselves in."

CHAPTER 51
TIME AFTER TIME

Cool winds swat at the tent Wilhilm and his companions take shelter in for the night, graciously provided by their new boss. Despite the gusty desert winds, the lanterns inside never flicker. Wilhilm takes note of the tent. It has a certain oriental charm, and once he comes around fixing his own tent, he would perhaps do some redecorating.

The elements are kept at bay. There's silence, just the community of friends. Are they still friends? Given what happened, Wilhilm feels too awkward to start a conversation, and neither does any of the others.

Mormak snores in the corner of the tent, his lengthy dwarven beard vibrating with each exhalation.

Wilhilm envies his relaxation. His own heart pounds when Dakaria murmurs words unfamiliar to him, her fingers dancing in secret patterns through the air. Before he can react, the ground beneath him pulses with energy. From the soil, a torrent of animated vines and weeds surge upwards. Wilhilm pulls back but they wrap around his ankles and crawl up his legs. They twist and wind around him with an insistent tug, pulling him downwards to root him to the spot.

The verdant fingers climb higher, encircling his waist and chest, making it harder to breathe. His muscles flex and tense, but the more he struggles, the tighter the green chains become.

Beneath the surface annoyance, a glimmer of respect emerges. *She has a lot of hidden talents*, he reflects with a mixture of admiration.

His eyes, one of the few parts of him that can still move, dart to Dakaria. "Ha ha, very funny, now I know you can do magic," Wilhilm says.

Dakaria ignores him. She puts up a circle of seven white stones around him, each glowing faintly with protective runes. Wilhilm's heart begins to thump uncomfortably in his chest, the beat resonating in his ears. This is looking like something serious. He feels his eyes burning, the shadows swirling all around him. The threat is building which means Wilhilm is losing control. What if she wakes up Derek?

If the demon takes complete control, they're all lost. Dakaria's playing with fire.

"Stop that, stop that now," Wilhilm says, now with a pleading tone and a hint of fear. He knows will happen if she doesn't.

Dakaria only continues to move with grace. She holds a small branch of yew in one hand and a vial of shimmering spring water in the other. "This will not harm you," she murmurs, her voice a mixture of determination and gentle reassurance. "We know the real Wilhilm is possessed. We seek only to speak to the true Wilhilm, to understand and help."

Possessed? He isn't possessed... Or is he? Derek is here,

that's for sure, and he's stronger than before. He's *kind of* present. But he's still in charge. Right? Wilhilm's throat is too tight for words. There's a glint of an owl's feather in her hand, and he finds it oddly comforting.

With practiced ease, Dakaria draws symbols of nature with the yew branch, connecting each glowing stone with an silver thread she weaves through the air. The symbols seem familiar to Wilhilm, though he can't quite place them. A sudden pang of sadness, a sense of loss, tightens his chest.

Dakaria approaches him and, with a surprising gentleness, pricks his finger, allowing three drops of his blood to fall into the vial. She holds it up to the lamplight and he watches as they swirl and dance with the spring water, his essence merging with nature's purity. The sight is strangely hypnotic.

The moment is shattered when Dakaria begins to chant. It's an invocation, a plea to the spirits of nature. Wilhilm feels a pull, an otherworldly force nudging against the barriers of his mind. The demon stirs within, restless and angry.

The druid sprinkles the water-blood mixture over him, her chant reaching a crescendo. Every droplet feels like a cool embrace, a soothing balm to his tormented soul. He's on the edge, teetering between his true self and the dark entity that's claimed him.

Suddenly, there's clarity. The demon's rage recedes like a nightmarish tide, replaced by a flood of memories, emotions, and thoughts. Wilhilm is fully himself again. Tears form, unbidden, as the weight of his actions and experiences crashes down on him. He gasps, overwhelmed by the flood of emotions but grateful for the brief respite from the demon's influence. This is how it feels to be free. He hasn't felt like this in *years*.

Dakaria's eyes lock onto his, filled with compassion and understanding. "Wilhilm?" she whispers, hopeful.

Wilhilm, his voice tremulous, manages to respond, "It's me... yes, but it has been me too before. I just think... I think, Derek isn't listening in right now. What did you do?"

"Who's Derek?" Dakaria asks.

"He's the demon you just suppressed."

"So, you're evil now?" Mormak says and suddenly sits straight up.

"Pretty much," Wilhilm says.

"What or who is Derek, what's possessing you? I can feel demonic energy," Dakaria says.

"Let it be," Wilhilm says. "We don't have time for that now, we need to save Seraphina. If she needs saving. She has to be *somewhere* around here. Abducted, lonely, waiting for rescue."

"You destroyed Tiringar with a demon horde, something possessed you..." Gadisa says.

Wilhilm watches the shadows dance over Mormak and Gadisa.

"You still have some shadows. These will... evaporate," Wilhilm says. His companions eye him sternly. When he tries to move, Dakaria's magic keeps him in check. "Fine," he sighs. "But it's not a nice story."

"Ours never are," Dakaria says.

"The thing is... I have a little demon problem."

"How little?" Mormak asks.

"What demons?" Dakaria asks.

"A few years back, you might have heard, the Three Warlocks of Zal'qara tried to tear up the planes..."

"Planes...?" Gadisa asks. "What is that?"

"There are different planes that make up reality," Dakaria explains. "We live in one."

"In one with little magic compared to the some of the others," Wilhilm adds. "Over hundreds of years, our ancestors figured out a way to tap into magic. We use tiny shreds of our soul to tear tiny rifts into reality, just enough to tap into another plane that has more magic, and pull it over to our side."

"So, everything around us is full of holes?" Gadisa looks around the ten, interested.

Wilhilm sighs. Explaining this might take a while.

CHAPTER 52
LE FREAK

Wilhilm shakes his head. "Those rifts heal fast, they're only open for a small amount of time. But the three warlocks, back then, they wanted to establish a permanent rift to a plane full of demons."

"But why?" Mormak asks. "Were they ale-making demons?"

"They did it for the usual reasons," Wilhilm says.

"So, for ale?" Mormak nods.

"For power and control. Anyway, the Patriarch enlisted the Academy, and the Academy recruited wizards to fight the warlocks, I was one of them. We traveled all the way to Ishmaara. Eventually, after lots of lives were sacrificed, and two of the warlocks had fallen, there was only me and... Lysandra, a... friend. The both of us were the last standing against Hasan ibn Azazel."

Wilhilm's chest tightens, the weight of memories pressing down, making it difficult to draw in a full breath. A familiar ache begins to swell within him, originating from the pit of his stomach and working its way up, threatening to strangle his words before they even form.

"What happened?" Dakaria asks.

"But it did work, right?" Mormak interrupts. "I mean, this plane seems still intact. The Three Warlocks are no more."

"It kind of worked. There was a little mishap, unfortunately."

"Spill it," Mormak says. "We don't have all day for your stories!"

"Lysandra... died. The last warlock was heavily wounded by then, but still very powerful. I had to pull more magic than I had ever pulled."

"Pulled from where?" Gadisa asks.

"From any planes. I don't think wizards really care where they get it from," Dakaria says.

"I used all the magic I could get, but my soul ripped in two, and when I thought I had defeated the warlock and closed the rift into the demon dimension, a demon slipped through and nested in me. I didn't know until recently. From the realm of the demon Azragoth no doubt, that was the domain the Witchking was fiddling with."

"Part of your soul is stripped from your body? And you are infested by a demon prince?" Dakaria asks.

"A demon prince? No, not at all. Just a minor demon very probably from Azragoth's entourage. He tries to use my soul as a bridge from the abyss."

"Minor doesn't sound so bad," Gadisa says. "We can get rid of something minor, right?"

"Just a minor..." Dakaria groans. "When dealing with demons, there is no minor evil, they're all evil!"

"The chap's name is Malphasar," Wilhilm says. "I call him Derek."

"You know his real name? What else are you talking about, you two?" Dakaria says.

"This and that," Wilhilm replies. "There's a lot of talk about world domination, and accepting the shadows... and..."

"And?"

"Cheese. He mentions cheese sometimes."

"How is this related to Cheese and their Echo Stones?" Dakaria says.

"I don't know either," Wilhilm says. "All I can do is guess. But it seems, King Hasan didn't die seven years ago as I thought he did. He turned into a lich. And since that gnome Retchbucket escaped to the desert, I guess, King Hasan still resides in the ruins of Ishmaara where he plots to exploit this EyeStone network to somehow call on demons."

"I hate those undead warlocks with their dark magic," Mormak grumbles.

"But how were you involved in what happened in Tiringar?" Dakaria wants to know.

"King Hasan needed me. Specifically, he needed the demon magic inside of me. I cast a spell called Soulshade which I thought would help me get rid of the demon. Instead, it allowed Hasan to gain back some of his powers. I'm not sure exactly how, but I guess that all of those years ago, I must have distributed his essence somehow across planes, and now he might have been able to puzzle himself together."

"What do we have to do to stop this? Demons broke through in Tiringar. If this continues, if every city goes through the same, this all will turn into a demon plane," Dakaria says.

"I'm not sure how the Witchking needs me," Wilhilm says. "This seems to be a chain event. He needed me to set it off once. But I'm still... connected."

“In theory, if I hit you with my axe, would this end things?” Mormak asks.

“I doubt it,” Wilhilm says.

“And if I hit the Witchking with my axe, how about that?”

“Perhaps you have washed yourself too often,” Gadisa chimes in. “It’s an underrated risk. Might have attracted all of those demons.”

“Cut it out, both of you,” Dakaria says. “What’s with your demon, Wilhilm? Is it sill there?”

Images of what has happened come up in Wilhilm’s mind. The once-majestic spires of Tiringar, now marred by the haunting presence of demons. It’s a hard thought to grasp. A heavy weight presses on Wilhilm’s chest, tightening with each breath. The Patriarch wanted him to promote Tiringar as a tourist destination and get rid of Cheese. A little late for that. Or is there a market for traveling to demon planes? Perhaps some adventuring tourists might be interested in that.

CHAPTER 53

LET'S GET IT ON

"Wilhilm, your demon, is it still there?" Dakaria repeats.

Wilhilm nods. "What do you think? That I can just shrug it off? However, now we're far away from Tiringar's magic undercurrent and from the rift. He's definitely weaker. Not a lot of magic he can siphon here."

"Is this... is this why you are so bad at magic?" Mormak asks. "Because there was a demon inside of you? When I think about the adventures and the dire situations we went through together, you did awfully little magic for a wizard."

"He's just not very good with magic," Gadisa says.

"It's complicated. When the demon slipped in, I think I knew what was happening, and I somehow managed to contain him with my magic," Wilhilm says. "I started out trying not to do magic all of those years, so the barrier around would not weaken. Only, the demon... its presence... it messed with my mind, and it made me forget that it was there, or even why I held back my magic. It seems, though, I still kept suppressing it. I've always feared the power of magic, its effect on my soul. All those thoughts... mingled somehow."

"Same result, right? If you don't do magic because you fear what happens or if you don't do magic because you want to keep the demon prisoner," Dakaria says.

"Let's circle back to making a plan. What can we hit?" Mormak says.

"I'm still connected to the network, thanks to that demon," Wilhilm muses. "I'm still the bridge between the demon's plane and ours. I can only guess that the plan seemed to be to use me as a bridge from the abyss to our world. When my soul ripped apart, the second half drifted off to the demon plane. But both halves are still connected. And this connection between me and the abyss, this constant connection, that is something I have and they needed. Or still need."

"So, we sever the... thread... the bond? A clean cut with my axe? Just point, and I hit," Mormak asks. The fabric walls of the tent billow slightly, then tighten abruptly as the wind outside picks up its pace. It's a low, haunting sound at first, like a distant chorus of forgotten spirits, rising and falling in an ancient rhythm.

"It's not that easy... my soul can't be cut in half just like that. We either get the missing part from there, or we put the part that's still here over there."

"And what exactly is your plan?" Dakaria asks.

For a moment, Wilhilm is silent. The wind is growing stronger now, transforming into a relentless, howling force that seems to sweep across the endless dunes outside. He can almost imagine the grains of sand being lifted, carried, and rearranged, an eternal dance of the desert reshaping itself.

"Well," he sets on. He coughs. "Well," he says again,

then pauses. "I figured it was impossible to stage a rescue mission for a missing part of the soul in the abyss. The sensible thing to do, for everyone involved, is to throw all of it just over the fence."

Mormak nods. "That's what I do when the ale gone bad. Just throw it away. Start a new keg. Makes sense to me."

"You can't... be... serious," Dakaria says. "There has to be another way."

"I don't understand. I still eat my snacks when they're spoiled. I don't like throwing things away," Gadisa says.

"You're eating rocks," Wilhilm says, pointing to the pile of pebbles Gadisa picked from the sands.

"I don't see your point, Mormak's eating rocks as well," Gadisa replies.

"Gems have important minerals, completely different," Mormak grumbles.

There is no use pushing any further, so Wilhilm turns back to Dakaria. "There is no other way. I have to sacrifice myself so the bridge will collapse and the demons can't feed any more power into the network. That still means you all have to defeat the Witchking, and I need to be banished with him."

"I can hit him with my axe, right?" Mormak asks.

"Yes, I told you before, I infused your axe with magic so you can fight ghosts and otherworldly creatures. You can hit liches with it too," Wilhilm says. "It won't do much good, though. King Hasan will regenerate right after you've hit him. He's basically unkillable. We need to find his phylactery first."

The canvas entrance of the tent flaps wildly, as if struggling to hold back the desert's breath. The sound of the wind is now a constant roar. It brings with it the faint, gritty taste of sand, seeping in through the smallest openings, while Dakaria hastens to tie the flaps back together.

"Fill-Actors? What do we fill actors with? What are they eating?" Gadisa says. "Sounds like it calls for a cocktail sauce."

"Phylactery. It's where the lich stores his soul," Wilhilm says.

"Again, what's it with these souls?" Mormak groans.

"We get to the ruins of Ishmaara. We find the phylactery. If we destroy the phylactery, you hit him until he's dead, that's how we defeat him," Wilhilm says. "I go to the abyss with him, the rift will close, there will be nothing left to allow him to return a third time. All that remains for you to do is to stop Retchbucket from meddling with the EyeStone network." *And I avenge Seraphina.*

"Hit him until he's dead, noted," Mormak says. "This is a good plan, a very good plan. Simple, yet effective. And I can remember it, which is always a plus in the heat of battle."

"I don't know if I... if we can give you up that easily," Dakaria murmurs.

Gadisa and Mormak look at each other. "You gotta do what you gotta do," Gadisa says.

"We have to somehow redirect the caravan to the ruins of Ishmaara, though," Mormak says.

"I don't think that's a problem," Dakaria says. "You'll be happy to know they've been lying to us."

CHAPTER 54

HOW WILL I KNOW

Dakaria lays out a map in front of her companions.

"That's the map I got from Kart'Ahed. That's where we are," Dakaria says and points at place in the map. Wilhilm tilts his head to better see what she's pointing at.

"So far out," he says. It's worse than he thought.

"You know what they say... Finding a gnome in a desert, that's like finding... a gnome in the desert," Gadisa says.

"Focus! I just started talking," Dakaria says.

"But we have a beautiful plan," Mormak says. "I hit it until it dies. Why talk more? Plans only get muddled by talking."

"Would everyone please listen?" Dakaria chimes in.

"We can't just hit it; we need to find the phylactery first!" Wilhilm says.

"And stop that Retch gnome," Gadisa adds.

"SILENCE!" Dakaria bellows.

An eerie hush descends upon their surroundings. The familiar sounds of the world around Wilhilm (and his companions as well) are muted, as if a veil of silence has been draped over their senses. Even the wind is quieter. Gadisa continues talking, but his voice is a mere whisper. Panic grips Wilhilm's heart as he tries to speak as well, only to be met with the eerie stillness of his muted voice. Then he sees Dakaria's face and realizes she didn't just express her annoyance with them, she did a spell.

"That's better," Dakaria says, her dampened voice reaching Wilhilm's ear like through a pool of water.

How? How did you do this spell and I'm still able to hear you? he wants to ask, but no words leave his mouth.

"I wonder why I don't do this spell more often. This silence, it's bliss. Like a gentle breeze on a summer's day. No, more like a cascading waterfall, washing away worries and immersing the spirit in pure serenity! No, I think, like a vibrant sunrise, painting the sky with hues of gold and filling the heart with a radiant warmth. Oh no, now I have it. Bliss like a field of wildflowers, blooming in vibrant colors and releasing an intoxicating fragrance, awakening the senses to a world of beauty and contentment."

Dakaria laughs. Mormak trims his nails with a knife but listens attentively. Gadisa is still trying to speak aloud.

"If you could speak, I would never have been able to finish these metaphors. So, anyway, before the spell runs out, as I said, we're here." Again, she points at the map. "That man, Kart'Ahed Uvhorz, said we're supposedly going here: Al'Alamayn. Which would mean we take this route."

Using her finger, she indicates a complicated mazed route toward the intended target.

"I overheard some of the guides prepping for travel in the morning. But they are preparing to go this direction. It just doesn't add up. If you asked me—we'll you wouldn't ask, I'm sure you'd quarrel about something, but I'd say the caravan is going in a completely different direction than what Uvhorz told us."

Dakaria looks up triumphantly. "But why? It does not make sense, does it? And, if you look at the water and the provisions, you will realize we stocked a lot more than we would have needed on the intended route."

Again, she points at the map.

"Because, there's a village here, and a village there. But look at the route I believe they're really on. Longer distances. More need for water and provisions."

Dakaria smiles at them, enjoying the fact that they have to listen to her for once.

"So, seeing my brilliant mind in action, you can surely deduct that I already have figured out what the intended target is."

Wilhilm can see there's a new, thrilling sensation coursing through Dakaria as all eyes in the tent focus on her presence. Her heart seems to beat a little faster from an exhilarating rush of excitement.

Dakaria returns to the map and puts her index finger on the map.

"There it is. That's where Ishmaara used to be."

"Goblin gifts," Wilhilm curses, as he feels his anger curse through him. "Goblin gifts!"

He tries to move, but Dakaria's vines still hold him in their grip. Everyone looks at him, and he realizes they could hear him.

"You just broke my spell," Dakaria says. "And I wasn't even finished!"

"That's a mighty curse," Mormak murmurs. "Didn't know you had so much filth in you."

"Focus," Dakaria says. "Don't you have anything to say

to all the revelations I just had for you? I mean anything except a filthy curse?" She eyes Wilhilm.

"I don't know...," Mormak says. "Do they have beer at that oasis?"

Dakaria groans and storms out of the tent.

"What's wrong with her?" Mormak says. "I don't want to go anywhere in the desert. I dislike every part the exact same amount. Makes no difference to me."

"She's worried that we're being played," Wilhilm says. The vines are cutting into his skin. He lets out a groan. "It just seems like it's more then coincidence. We want to go to Ishmaara. And we happen to run into a caravan that's trying to hide that they're going to Ishmaara just when we set out to Ishmaara ourselves."

Mormak nods slowly. "So, no beer?" He sighs.

"We don't need to do anything," Gadisa says, "except go along with the caravan, and we'll end up at Ishmaara."

"Probably," Wilhilm says. "Ishmaara has been devoured by the sands, we can't just go there, we need to find the entrance to a city that is beneath the sands. But if the caravan is heading that way, someone probably knows."

Dakaria is catapulted back into the tent, full of sand. She coughs. "It's a bit windy outside," she says. "But I still hate you."

"Can you release me?" Wilhilm asks.

She nods at him. "I will release my spell now. Steady. And warn us before the demon takes over again and opens rifts back to his plane. That really would be helpful."

The dense thicket of vines quivers as Dakaria raises her hand. Her fingers move with purpose, her motions fluid and deliberate. The air grows thick with the tangy scent of green, and the ground beneath Wilhilm vibrates gently, resonating with the life force Dakaria invokes. One by one, the tendrils respond to her silent call. They start to retract, wriggling and writhing as though sentient. The tightening embrace around Wilhilm loosens, the pressure from the vines ebbing away.

The final few tendrils caress Wilhilm's skin with a touch that's almost tender before they too, disappear. The ground of the tent is left undisturbed, with no trace of the botanical cage that had once been there.

Dakaria lowers her hand.

For a moment, Wilhilm listens into himself. Nothing. Derek still doesn't talk. But he can feel, the demon is still there. Waiting for more power. Waiting to resurface.

CHAPTER 55
BORN TO BE WILD

Wilhilm stirs from his slumber, the coolness of the desert morning seeping through the fabric of the tent. As his eyes adjust to the dim light, a sense of unease washes over him. The usual soft sounds of his friends' breathing are absent, their sleeping rolls empty. He sits up, rubbing the sleep from his eyes, his heart beginning to race. Where could they be so early?

Wilihlm's ears catch a muffled ruckus that pierces the quiet of the morning. The sounds are distorted, an odd mix of shrieks and shouts that seem to bounce off the canvas walls. In his half-awake state, Wilhilm's imagination takes flight, painting scenarios of distress or danger. Could it be a skirmish with desert bandits?

Wilhilm scrambles out of his sleeping bag, clumsily entangling himself in the fabric. He fumbles with the tent's cords, the noise outside growing louder and more frantic with each passing second. It sounds almost like... squeals of torture. He prepares himself for the worst.

Bursting out of the tent, Wilhilm is momentarily blinded by the bright morning sun. As his eyes adjust, the scene before him gradually comes into focus. There, in the middle of the desert, are his friends, but they're not in any danger. Instead, they're laughing, mounted on Dune Serpents, which are bucking and spinning in circles, clearly confused by their riders' attempts at desert racing.

"Hiyaaa, it's actually quite a graceful ride," Dakaria shouts over when she sees the wizard. "Come on, Wilhilm! Get on that one!"

Wilhilm approaches the majestic Dune Serpent with trepidation. It moves with a serpentine smoothness and the earth-toned scales blend seamlessly with the surrounding sand.

Wilhilm takes a deep breath, summoning his courage, before reaching out to touch the serpent's scaled hide.

The moment of contact is electric, and a surge of anticipation courses through Wilhilm's veins. He carefully positions himself near the creature's back, feeling the warmth radiating from its powerful limbs. With a deftness born of eagerness, he swings his leg over the Dune Serpent.

Wilhilm settles into place and grips the serpent's reins. He senses the creature's muscles tensing, ready to propel them forward across the desert landscape.

Wilhilm signals his readiness with a gentle nudge of his heels against the serpent's sides. The Dune Serpent responds, unfurling its body and gliding forward. Wilhilm's senses are instantly flooded with a rush of wind, the sand beneath him blurring.

Wilhilm spots Gadisa on a Dune Serpent as well. The beast strains to move forward, its breathing labored. Mormak bumps up and down on his own Dune Serpent, desperately trying to cling to the animal.

Then a different cry reverberates through the air, a primal and commanding sound that demands attention.

Wilhilm looks around until he can make out where the sound is coming from. He stares in astonishment at the sight of the loadbeasts. Sandstriders. He's heard of them. The creature's sinewy form stands tall on the desert horizon. Its elongated body is perfectly adapted to the arid landscape with its scales of earthy hues.

The Sandstrider's powerful hind legs, built for speed and agility, allowing it to navigate the treacherous sands effortlessly. With each step, the creature's clawed feet leave delicate imprints, a temporary mark upon the shifting dunes.

Instinctively, Wilhilm's hands search for his wand—the Sandstrider is more than a bit intimidating—until a towering figure casts a long shadow over the Sandstriders. There, covered in mottled, sweaty fur a huge female Feathermaul appears. Her brown and deep gray fur seems out of place in the desert.

Strapped to her side is a well-worn whip, its braided leather bears the marks of long years. She snaps the whip to the right of one off-course Sandstrider to correct it. Her eyes pan over the herd, looking for any other stragglers.

"You are our new spellcaster?" she shouts at Wilhilm.

He nods. "The Beastmaster, I gather?"

"The name's Fenric."

"Fenric? Doesn't that mean..." Wilhilm stops when her frown deepens. "Well, you know what, Fenric's a beautiful name. Great to meet you."

CHAPTER 56

GENIE IN A BOTTLE

Wilhilm's perched atop his Dune Serpent, squinting at the setting sun. The sun sits high and mighty in the sky, casting down its blistering judgement upon the desert and all who dare traverse it. He tries to ignore the heat of the sun in favor of watching two members of the caravan. One is Fenric, the other a scraggy man. They are clearly up to something; whispering to each other whenever they think nobody sees them, often accompanied by a third, a brawny loader who takes care of the Sandstriders when he's not whispering. Wilhilm can sense something is off.

"Do you think Dakaria's right? That this caravan might be fishy?" Wilhilm whispers to Mormak.

Mormak looks around and then leans in closer, "You mean other than the fact we're miles away from any ale, they're lying about where we're going, and we were forcefully employed? Nah, seems all normal to me."

"That's not what I—never mind," Wilhilm sighs. The old saying about trying to have a deep conversation with a dwarf is true: *Each keg of ale will add one point to their intelligence, points that dissipate in the absence of ale.*

Gadisa joins their conspiratorial huddle. "There *is* something going on. I found these," he says, producing a few smoke bombs and a vial filled with a suspicious-looking liquid.

Wilhilm squints at them. "Found?"

"You know how it is. Things have a way of moving toward rogues."

"What are they using it for? Planning a surprise party?"

Gadisa shakes his head. "Me thinks it's a sleeping potion."

"Ah, so it's a surprise sleepover party," Wilhilm mused.

"I'd use sleeping potions on guards if I wanted to acquire something," Gadisa says.

"Acquire?"

"Change ownership of items," Gadisa says.

"Oh, you mean *steal*."

Wilhilm looks around, and his gaze settles once more on the two familiar figures, still whispering like school-kids hiding a secret. What were they planning?

The caravan trundles on. The Dune Serpents plod ahead, trailed by the Sandstriders, each footfall creating a little puff of dust that dances into the golden horizon. They ride in silence for a moment. The orange hues of the sun paint patterns on Wilhilm's face, making his blue eyes seem even brighter. His lanky figure sways with the Dune Serpent's movements, his legs seeming far too long to be naturally dangling on either side of the beast.

"You'd think, given how long we've been riding, those two would've run out of things to whisper about," Mormak mutters.

"It hasn't been long," Wilhilm says.

“Time just seems to stretch without ale,” Mormak replies.

Wilhilm observes the other two riders. “They’re planning something,” Wilhilm says. “We better not eat anything tonight if they’re tampering with sleeping potions. I don’t want to be asleep when whatever they’re planning is transpiring.”

“No food?” Gadisa asks. “You mean, like no unreasonable amount of food?”

“No food at all. Because it’s poisoned. You’re the one that told us about it!”

“A little sleeping potion never hurt anyone if it comes with a tasty meal.”

“It literally sends you to sleep.”

Gadisa laughs. “It does send *you* to sleep. For me, it only sends my stomach to sleep.”

Wilhilm snorts.

“It does,” Gadisa says. “After a sleeping potion, I’m not hungry for two, three hours.”

“He eats rocks and horseshoes,” Mormak says. “I’m not surprised at anything he eats.”

“We don’t eat anything,” Wilhilm declares. “We need to be awake.”

In the stillness of the desert night, the Rogue’s snores make a peculiar symphony. They begin with a gentle whistling, much like the wind threading through a keyhole. Just when Wilhilm thinks that’s it, there is a sudden, guttural rumble, echoing the distant sounds of a sandstorm brewing. Occasionally, the pattern is punctuated with a snuffling, almost as if the Rogue is trying to sniff out hidden treasure in his dreams.

"He ate something," Wilhilm says in the semi-darkness of the desert night.

"Something big most likely. I wonder where he finds his meals," Mormak says.

"I don't understand how his mind works," Wilhilm muses. "One moment, he tells us the food might be poisoned, the next he eats that food."

Mormak shrugs. "I didn't even see what he ate. Just the aftermath, you know, gnawed-off bones and a hearty burp."

Wilhilm sighs, walks out of the tent, and lies down into the sand. He looks up into the sky. The moon attempts to comfort the vast desert with its gentle glow. He's just dozing off when chaos erupts. Shouts and the clang of metal echo through the night. Then there's the distinct sound of someone repeatedly saying, "Not the face!"

Wilhilm shoots up, nearly headbutting Mormak, who'd taken it upon himself to act as a human shield. "It's the three mutineers," Mormak hisses, while Wilhilm rubs his head. Mormak points at the trio. Through the darkness, Wilhilm can see they're grappling with the caravan leader, Kart'Ahed Uvhorz. Fenric's contours dwarf the caravan leader. The moonlight glints off an object that all four tug at in desperation.

"Not the lamp," Kart'Ahed Uvhorz says. He refuses to let go. "You're making a mistake!"

Wilhilm approaches them. "What's going on?"

"We will be rich," Fenric says, followed by a dark laugh. "Rich!"

"It's not that kind of genie," Kart'Ahed Uvhorz says. "It's evil!"

"He's trying to cheat us, take the lamp for himself, and leave us to rot in the desert, he lies to us, he's leading us straight to the cursed ruins of Ishmaara," the scraggy mutineer says with a tug.

And just like that, things fall into place. "You're hiding a genie lamp?" Wilhilm asks.

"A bit too late for hiding," Kart'Ahed Uvhorz says. "And I'm paying you for protection! Do some protecting!"

"Uh," Mormak chimes in. "Technically, the payment in ale is still outstanding, I'm not sure how legal it is to protect you. The guild has a thing against unpaid labor."

Wilhilm ignores the mutineer and says pointedly at Kart'Ahed Uvhorz "You're trying to take the genie lamp to Ishmaara. Why?"

"The gnome made me do it," Kart'Ahed Uvhorz says defensively.

"Gnome? Which gnome?"

"A couple of weeks ago, I was just where Ishmaara sank."

"It's bad luck, nobody should go there," Fenric murmurs.

"I thought to myself, well, if I'm here anyway, I could have a look around, you know, ancient treasures and such. Turns out, there's a gnome. Thinks he's super smart, building something. I see the lamp." Kart'Ahed gulps. "I should've known, never trust a gnome, they say. Anyway, when I was interested, he said I could have it for one gold. Cheap. Seemed a good deal. One gold for three wishes."

"But it didn't work?"

"The gnome said I had to get away from Ishmaara as far as possible before rubbing the lamp, something about not disturbing the ghosts of the old city or something. So, when I was far enough away, I rubbed it. But the genie... he corrupts wishes. I lost everything. My houses, most of my storage rooms, my wife. And I couldn't get rid of the lamp. When I would drop it, it just came back."

"That's all lies, you just want to frighten us," Fenric says.

"If you want to get rid of it, why you don't want us to have it?" the scraggy mutineer asks.

"That's not how it works. It would still bring bad luck to me, unless… I can bring it back to Ishmaara. At least, that's what a sorceress said when I asked her."

Or you could just gift it to someone, Wilhilm says, but doesn't dare speak it out aloud. Better not complicate things! "So, you want to bring back the lamp to Ishmaara and end its curse, but because nobody would go near the ruins of Ishmaara, you lied to them about where you'd be going," he says instead.

"It was a mistake taking it. It's a dark genie, everything one wishes for tuns into one's worst nightmare." The look on Kart'Ahed Uvhorz's face is desperate.

Fenric repeats, "You just want it for yourself! You led us into the desert, you lied to us. You never lie about your way when you're in the desert, that's the desert law. Everyone knows that."

Before anyone can react, Fenric, giddy with triumph, wrests the lamp from Kart'Ahed Uvhorz and rubs it vigorously against her fur.

A blinding light splits the desert night. The seemingly innocuous brass lamp leaks a thick, swirling mist of indigo. It's just a wisp, but the very air around it seems to grow heavy, charged with an electric tension that sends shivers up Wilhilm's spine. With a thunderous roar, the smoky tendrils explode outward, coalescing and solidifying at a rapid pace.

From this maelstrom, the genie forms. He towers above all present. His skin is a deep shade of blue, reminiscent of a stormy midnight sky. It ripples and shimmers as if made of liquid obsidian. His muscular form is adorned with ornate golden armlets and bracelets, which seem to float and dance around his wrists and biceps.

His attire, made of silk, billows around him like a dark storm cloud, his torso ending in a tail of smoke. It is the eyes though that are the most unnerving. A fierce, fiery orange radiates malevolence. They narrow with disdain and cruel amusement at the mortals before him.

The genie gives a booming laugh that sends ripples across the sand. As he stretches and rises, his fingers crackle with dark energy, arcs of eldritch lightning snapping between them. As he hovers above the ground, the sand beneath swirls and shifts, as if the very earth is cowering away from him.

CHAPTER 57
RUNNING WITH THE DEVIL

"Oh great," the genie says in a high-pitched voice. "What dumb wishes are you going to ask me to fulfill?"

Ignoring Kart'Ahed Uvhorz's frantic warnings, Fenric blurts, "We wish for an unlimited amount of wealth!"

"Nooooooo," Wilhilm and Kart'Ahed Uvhorz shout at the same time.

The genie smirks. "As you wish." And with a snap, a massive block of gold appears.

Wilhilm's hand shoots forward to pull back Mormak who has gone wide-eyed at the sight of so much gold.

The gold block rivals the mountains of Pirumanar. Even from a distance, the edges are razor-sharp and its sides perfectly smooth and flat, reflecting the sky and the surrounding dunes like a colossal mirror.

Wilhilm feels a gravitational pull towards it, an allure that is both mesmerizing and unsettling. He tightens his grip on Mormak.

"It's sinking," Dakaria says. "The sand can't hold it."

"It's what... something like 500 feet wide. Must be

more 60 million short tons of weight," Wilhilm murmurs. "It will probably sink forever."

The greedy mutineers, seeing their dreams slip away, lunge. They run toward the gold fighting each other to be the first to touch the gold. Fenric gets there first, reaches out triumphantly and caresses her prize. Almost instantly, her fur and her skin begin to rot, turning a ghastly shade of "not-alive-anymore". Her horrified scream underlines the old wisdom that with genies, one should always read the fine print.

The remaining two mutineers hesitate, their bravado crumbling faster than a biscuit in tea. It is clear they haven't thought this through. Actually, thinking doesn't seem to be their strong suit in general.

Wilhilm approaches with his hands raised. "Listen," he begins, trying to sound more confident than he feels, "how about we sort this out without more...rotting?"

The mutineers look like lost puppies in a desert storm.

"No mistakes this time. Do exactly what I tell you. Do you hear me?"

Both mutineers nod rapidly.

"Just wish for the genie to return to the lamp. Tell it as the rightful heir of Fenric to return to the lamp, just do that, do nothing else than that, and stay inside of the lamp until someone lets it out again. This is important. You can't fiddle with genie magic. Our best bet is to let it rot inside of the lamp forever."

The duo looks at each other and then back at the genie, who has conjured a sunbed and a drink. The scraggy mutineer takes a deep breath, "I... I as the rightful heir of Fenric, erm, I wish for you to go back into your lamp! Do that, nothing else than that, and stay inside of the lamp until someone lets you out again."

As the words leave his lips, a deep, spine-chilling silence blankets the desert. The only sound is the faint whistle of the wind against the sands and the almost imperceptible pounding of Wilhilm's heart. Every eye is fixed on the genie.

He lets out a guttural laugh, a sound so eerie it seems to rise from the depths of a long-forgotten abyss. Then, he starts to grow.

His form expands outwards, not just upwards but in every direction, casting long, ominous shadows across the dunes. The vast desert, which a moment ago has seemed endless, is now dominated by this titanic being. The swirling, ethereal mass of the genie becomes denser and darker, like storm clouds gathering on a horizon. The members of the caravan cower, their faces a palette of terror.

It seems that the entire world has been eclipsed by the genie's towering form. And then, with eyes that look down upon them like twin suns, the genie booms, "Do you truly believe I can be so easily commanded?"

The scraggy mutineer, his courage shattered, only stammers a feeble response.

Yet, as quickly as the terror has escalated, it shifts. A change comes over the genie's face, a subtle softening of those burning eyes. And then, almost begrudgingly, the enormous, terrifying entity retracts. The immense storm of malevolence folds inward, the darkness condensing, shrinking, pulling back into a more recognizable form.

With one last, lingering look, the genie's form spirals, twists, and condenses, rapidly shrinking in a whirlwind of color and sound. Then, with an audible pop, the genie is sucked back into the confines of the lamp.

A dark and booming “Party poopers!” hangs in the air for a moment.

Wilhilm turns to the mutineers, offering a small smile. “Next time, maybe stick to wishing stars.”

“We didn’t...” the scraggy one says.

“We weren’t...” the other mutineer says.

Kart’Ahed Uvhorz grabs the lamp. “I need to return the lamp to where we found it,” he says.

“You’re lucky,” Wilhilm says. “We need to find Ishmaara too. And that gnome.”

“Take the lamp, I gift it to you,” the scraggy mutineer says. He offers the lamp to him.

Wilhilm cries out. “No! What have you done?”

The mutineer looks at him quizzically. He really didn’t understand. “You can’t gift the lamp to me in the Zal’qaran desert. It means the lamp now belongs to me.”

“You seem the most competent,” the mutineer says.

“Where is it?” Kart’Ahed asks. He looks around frenetically. The lamp has vanished.

Wilhilm takes a look in his a small pouch, an artifact that can gold an almost unlimited number of things. The lamp sits on top of everything else.

“Crap,” Wilhilm curses.

CHAPTER 58
BLOWING IN THE WIND

Three mornings later, the vast expanse of the desert still lies before Wilhilm and his companions. This morning, as with every morning when the sun's first rays turn the skies a fiery orange, the caravan sets out, following the way to the fabled ruins of Ishmaara. And so far—much to Gadisa's displeasure—no Ishmaara.

"I don't understand," Gadisa complains. "If you lived here when it was still a city, and Kart'Ahed found the genie lamp in the ruins of Ishmaara, why can't we find it? One of you has to know where to look."

"Forget the ruins, look for ale instead," Mormak says. "First things first!"

Despite their bickering, Wilhilm often catches the Rogue scaling the dunes' peaks for fun. He claims it's to try and spy any unnatural formation or hint of the ancient city, but Gadisa has more fun than anyone in the caravan when he skis down the sand on his giant feet. More than once has he claimed to have spotted the city, only to be revealed as an illusion hours later.

Mormak often stops to kneel and taste the sand, hoping

to sense any vibrations or disturbances below, trying to find his way through the sands.

Dakaria attempts to communicate with the scarce desert fauna. On occasion, a lizard or a desert bird will approach, drawn to her aura. But the each conversation, as Wilhilm observes from afar, ends with a shake of her head.

The desert seems to have swallowed Ishmaara whole.

The caravan's men and women begin to murmur among themselves. The nights are the hardest. As they camp under a canopy of stars, the vastness of the cosmos mirrors the vastness of the desert around them, making them feel even more insignificant and lost.

On the third day, there is finally cause for celebration.

The group comes to a desert gorge. They're not only grateful for shelter from the winds, but Wilhilm is certain it's the same gorge that is so vivid in his memories—the last breath-taking sight he had before the sands swallowed the city of Ishmaara.

The walls of the gorge are sheer, dropping into shadowy depths below. The sun's rays barely penetrate its depths, casting eerie shadows upon on the walls. The gorge seems to have been carved by some ancient force, its walls smooth and winding.

Celebration turns to mourning as the days once more turn into nights and nights back into days and the elusive ruins remain just out of reach. Wilhilm can't help but wonder if Ishmaara might have been moved to another plane altogether.

The wizard is mid-thought contemplating the dwindling water supply when a peculiar sound echoes across the desert. It is a muffled sneeze, followed by another. Then another. The Rogue, with no eyes to shield from the blinding sun, is the first to spot the sneezing creatures. He tugs at Wilhilm's sleeve and points.

It's tiny creatures no taller than a dwarf's knee with oversized noses and sand-colored skin. They blend near seamlessly with the desert landscape, making them almost invisible to the untrained eye.

"They're... sneezing?" Dakaria whispers in disbelief, watching as one of the creatures takes a deep breath, its chest expanding, before releasing a powerful sneeze that blows a gust of sand into the air.

Mormak chuckles. "Ah! Sand Sneezers. Heard of 'em, never seen 'em."

"They're cute," Dakaria says. Carefully, she approaches the creature. "Hey you, over there, how are you?"

The Sand Sneezer remains standing, angling his head and watching Dakaria curiously.

"Bad," the Sand Sneezer grumbles.

"Oh, it has the mood of a dwarf," Wilhilm murmurs. "Splendid."

"What do you mean? It has no ale, what is it supposed to say?" Mormak chimes in.

"Why are you feeling bad?" Dakaria says and gestures the companions to stay behind.

"Allergic," the Sand Sneezer says.

"Allergic? What are you allergic to? Gold?" Mormak calls over. "Is there gold? Or ale?"

But the Sand Sneezer instead points at the ground.

"Are you allergic to Ishmaara? To the city beneath the sands?" Wilhilm asks hopefully.

The Sand Sneezer shakes his head and again points at the ground.

"I think it's allergic to sand," Dakaria says.

“Wait...” Wilhilm says. “You’re not serious. You’re allergic to sand? Why do you live in the desert?”

“We were born here, we belong here. The sands is where our ancestors are from.”

Wilhilm looks at the other Sand Sneezers, all of them sneezing.

“Did you ever try to move to somewhere else, somewhere less sandy?” he can’t help but ask.

CHAPTER 59

DOWN IN A HOLE

Instead of answering, the Sand Sneezers sneeze as one and the ground beneath them trembles. The Sand Sneezers, it seems, aren't just here to bemoan their medical status. With every coordinated sneeze, a whirlwind of sand spirals into the air. They converge into gaping sand geysers that threaten to swallow the caravan whole.

Dakaria, in a desperate attempt to communicate, tries mimicking their sneezes, which only results in her getting a face full of sand and a chorus of giggles from the Sand Sneezers. It is evident they find the whole ordeal rather amusing.

Gadisa attempts to engage, but every step closer is met with another sneeze and another shifting patch of treacherous sands. The caravan members are in chaos, their Dune Serpents bucking and goods flying through the air.

Wilhilm tries to direct the caravan away from the geysers. But the Sand Sneezers are relentless. It is like they are playing a twisted game, sneezing in unison to trap the companions further and further into the gorge's embrace.

Mormak, frustrated and out of patience, shouts, “Enough with the sneezing! We're not here to harm you!”

One of the Sand Sneezers, distinguishable by a peculiar tuft of hair on its head, approaches Mormak. It looks up, its beady eyes assessing him, before letting out the loudest sneeze yet. The ground quakes, and a massive sand geyser erupts right beneath the caravan, throwing everyone off balance.

As the dust settles, Wilhilm finds himself separated from the group, surrounded by the sneezing culprits. “Retreat!” Wilhilm shouts, but retreating isn't as simple. With every step they take, the sneezers continue their nasal assault.

Wilhilm’s eyes dart about, calculating the Sand Sneezers’ erratic patterns and the worsening scenario. Then it comes to him. Of course. If the Sand Sneezers would only gyrate the sand enough, it would uncover what lies beyond. Ishmaara.

“Let them take us downstairs to Ishmaara!” Wilhilm shouts over the tumult, his voice heavy with both determination and resignation.

His companions, each grappling with their own skirmish against the relentless sand eruptions, turn to him, expressions a mix of disbelief and alarm. The Rogue, caught in a sinkhole, frowns at Wilhilm, incredulity painting his features. “Have you lost your marbles?” he cries out, even as his boots sink further into the gritty trap.

Dakaria stares at the undulating sands as if trying to reason or communicate with it. “If there’s only sand beneath, we drown in sand. It could be our doom,” she warns, a vine whip coiling protectively around her.

Mormak grumbles, “I didn't sign up to be buried alive or taken by some sneezy sandy creatures!”

Wilhilm takes a moment, exhaling as the sands shift around them, making him feel as if the very desert is breathing beneath their feet. "Trust me, down there, that's Ishmaara, I can feel it," he urges, looking each of them in the eyes. "This might be our only chance to find the ruins. And it's evident we cannot fight off an entire desert of sand."

Shouts of panic from the caravan punctuate the air. Amidst the swirling grains and echoing sneezes, a mutual understanding begins to form among the companions. Despite their reservations, they slowly cease their resistance.

The Sand Sneezers, perhaps interpreting their submission as victory, surround them. A strange humming synchronizes among the peculiar beings. It vibrates through the sand. Wilhilm and his companions exchange final, resolute glances as the sands rise and enclose around them.

The world darkens, their senses overwhelmed by the grainy embrace. All sound muffled, all light dimmed. They feel weightless, suspended in an endless abyss of shifting granules. Time seems to stretch, the sensation eerily peaceful and terrifying at once.

There you are, finally, Wilhilm. Can you feel the embrace in the sands? Does it feel like home? O how the sands desired you.

Just as Derek's voice subsides, as suddenly as the onslaught began, they crash down on something. The sand deposits them unceremoniously onto a solid, cold floor. Coughing, spluttering, and shaking off the remnants of the desert, Wilhilm takes in their surroundings.

Kart'Ahed Uvhorz, the scraggy mutineer and another man of the caravan are down with them, the rest of the caravan must have landed somewhere else or perhaps escaped above.

The magic in nearby torches reacts to their presence and flickers to life weakly. The flames illuminate walls built from smooth cut sandstone. The middle blocks are carved with ancient symbols and pictographs. A small trench of brass is built into each side of the corridor and disappears into the darkness. Faded frescoes hint at forgotten tales, and a heavy silence pervade the air, broken only by their staggered breaths.

Wilhilm slowly gets to his feet, a triumphant glimmer in his eyes. "Welcome," he murmurs, "to the ruins of Ishmaara."

Mormak kneels and touches the inside of the trench, his fingers coming back tan and slick. "It's oil. We should not rely on those few torches around here for long. I bet this here will light the whole place up. But of course, I don't need the light. I've got the darkvision," he boasts.

"I've got darkvision," Dakaria shrugs.

"I don't have eyes," Gadisa adds.

They all just stand there staring down the corridor. A faint dripping sound comes through the dark, but beyond that, the tunnel is quieter than the desert above.

"Let's light it anyway," Mormak breaks the silence. "It'll be fun!"

The Rogue and the Druid stand over Mormak as he sparks a flint and sets the trenched oil ablaze. The flame zigzags across the floor, illuminating a tunnel that extends for thousands of feet. The trio lets out a simultaneous "Oooooh!" at the engineering marvel. For such a structure, the project must have been completed long before the sands above swallowed the land.

"What do you think it says?" Gadisa asks no one in particular, running his fingers along the ancient writing.

"There's only one person I know who could possibly read this," Dakaria says.

Mormak scoffs, "That wizard? Can he do anything? I, for one, I'm glad if he doesn't kill us."

"You know I can hear you," Wilhilm says. "Right?"

CHAPTER 60

LISTEN TO THE MUSIC

Kart'Ahed Uvhorz stands in the stone corridor, arms folded, a contemplative frown adorning his face. Two caravan guards stand at his side. Flanking the group are the Rogue and Druid, who join them in staring at the wall while Wilhilm attempts to read what is inscribed.

Mormak moves his face close the stone as Wilhilm traces the symbols upward before moving onto the next column of writing. A set of pictographs shows an oasis above them and then the tunnel to a large city.

"What does it say?" Mormak asks.

Wilhilm takes a swig of water from his skin, clears his throat, and begins to translate. "It says that in the reign of Kadoc'Al, a curse set upon the land scorched the trees and stripped the soil from the crops. The river dried up and the animals died. The king died. Kadoc'Ur, his son, performed sacrifices to their many gods. They, uhhh, they sacrificed their underwear?"

Gadisa squeals and covers his mouth with his hands.

Wilhilm reaches into his pouch, removes a small notebook, and consults the scribblings. "Nope! Not underwear! There's a small 'eye' symbol above the upside-down triangle. It's 'children'!"

Gadisa sighs. "Phew. Okay, we can relax. We do have underwear, but we don't have children."

"Anyway, so they sacrificed children of all ages using a cursed magic, which did not go over very well with Kadoc'Ru, the son of the son of Kadoc'Ur. And he... well, here they show a pictograph."

The wall shows a smaller figure wearing a crown kneeling and stabbing the king in his crotch, and the crown tumbling toward the young prince.

"Uhh, yeah, you can see here that Kadoc'Ur didn't survive his wound to... Oh, there's the word 'underwear!' Okay, well, moving on..."

"Stop, what is this about underwear? I don't want to lose my underwear." Gadisa lowers his voice, so only the Wizard can hear him. "You know I keep my stuff down there."

"Kadoc'Ru had a different plan... He had a tree in the court of the City of Ishmaara, and as long as the tree survived, the people there would have a reprieve from the judgment of the gods. But the water kept evaporating before they could get it back to the tree, so they built this tunnel."

Wilhilm scratches his head, "Seems like an awfully big project just to bring water to a tree but what do I know."

"How do you know this language?" Uvhorz asks. "Not even I know this language, and as a merchant I proud myself to know a lot of languages!"

The Wizard straightens himself out. "That's what we, errr, do. Learning languages and stuff. Part of becoming a wizard."

"Let's continue," Mormak says. "We can't stand here forever."

"Aye," Gadisa says.

Wilhilm looks down the dark pathway. For a moment, he thinks about the Ishmaara he knew, years before it sunk beneath the sands. "I'm back, finally," he murmurs to himself before venturing into the dark tunnel.

As Wilhilm descends deeper into the forgotten corridors of Ishmaara, his heart beats with anticipation. Each step through the twists and turns reminds him of his own past here. Each step brings him closer to ending the EyeStone. Closer to finding (or avenging... no, this sounds too cruel... it has to be *finding*) Seraphina. Finally, a chamber opens up before him.

The air inside is cool and still, as if untouched by time. The moment Wilhilm sets foot in the wide opening to the dungeon, a chill strikes the air. His torch flickers and the eerie shadows shiver on the ancient stone walls.

It's silent, except a rustle in the darkness. A whisper?

"Wilhilm..." The word slithers from some unseen crack. It curls around his ear. He pauses, taking a moment to ensure it's not just his imagination.

The hiss comes from above. "Hello Wilhilm..." Wilhilm jerks his head up, but there's nothing on the ceiling except for age-old carvings. Still, the voice seems to come from everywhere, even from the very walls that surround him. "Wilhilm, over there..." it beckons, causing him to turn swiftly to his left, then his right, searching for its source.

"Oh wow, this dungeon really knows you," Gadisa says.

"Back in my time, dungeons used to be silent," Mormak says. "We would have chopped any whispering dungeon to bits."

With every step, the murmurs grow louder and more

frequent. "So nice of you to visit, Wilhilm..." The walls pulse with a life of their own.

A distant, rhythmic drumbeat echoes through the chambers as Wilhilm and his companions venture deeper into immense chamber. The percussion grows louder, accompanied by the faint twang of string instruments. An air of anticipation fills the ancient stone vault, and the percussion merges with the whispers into some sort of song.

I remember all your spells
Magic rings and arcane wells,
Visions of a land,
A dream through a portal,
Winds shift the sand,
The desert's mortal.

Nightfall, then the break of day,
Mystic runes guide my way,
Staring at the skies,
I see an epiphany,
It's suddenly clear,
The power you gave to me.

Oh, Willy,
When you cast, you enchant without breaking,
But the dangers you'd sway,
Oh, Willy,
With your staff, you'd defend without quaking,
And we need you today,
Oh, Willy.

Lit only by dim torchlight, figures adorned in tattered wrappings and garish jewelry emerge, their eyes gleaming mischievously beneath their mummified countenances.

Wild, spiky hair protrudes from gaps in their bandages, and the sound of lutes and guitars melds into a frenetic desert rock rhythm.

The Rouge squints to get a better look. "They're... they're bards?" he whispers in disbelief.

"They're singing about me. This can't be bad, right?" Wilhilm says.

"It means they know you and they expected you; at least someone did," Dakaria says.

"It's bad," Mormak translates. "Very bad."

CHAPTER 61

I WANNA DANCE WITH SOMEBODY

"Who are you guys?" Gadisa adresses the tattered beings in the dungeon.

"We're the Pyramid Punks," the mummy replies. "We're here to greet you. Dead or alive."

"Greet us dead or alive, is that a thing now?" Mormak wonders. "I'm not sure that greeting us when we're dead makes much of a difference. Anyway, we're looking for something like... a soul container. No idea what those look like, but do you happen to know of one?"

"Shhh," Gadisa says. "That's a secret! If we advertise it, they'll know what we're looking for and hide it better!"

"And how are we supposed to find it when we're not allowed to ask?" Mormak says.

"First, let's defeat this enemy," Dakaria interrupts, "then we'll look for the phylactery."

"As long as they don't attack us with magic weapons, I don't see a problem," Mormak says.

"I do," Wilhilm says.

A strong chord struck sends a pulse of energy through the floor, more follow. The stones beneath Wilhilm's feet shift and change, reshaping the labyrinth around them. Even as the chamber sways, Wilhilm forces himself to blink hard to pay attention. The lyrics are mesmerizing, enchanting them where they stand.

Dakaria claps her hands over her ears, trying to resist the hypnotic allure of the song. "We need to get past them," she shouts over the cacophony, "or we'll be trapped here forever, lost in their twisted melodies!"

Mormak stomps his feet and claps. "Fight music with noise!" he bellows. "That's how my grandfather did it and how my great-grandfather did it!"

Wilhilm wonders if there really is a family history of fighting music in the Dwarf's blood, or if this just amounts to some kind of self-motivation. His own pulse races as the Punks strum their ancient, stringed instruments. Each note releases bursts of magical energy that manifest as gusts of wind and sudden spikes jutting out from the dungeon walls.

The air is thick with dust and the smell of decay, the atmosphere charged with the raw power of the Punks' music. The gusts of wind howl through the corridor, a tempest conjured from melody, threatening to knock Wilhilm off his feet. The spikes that emerge from the walls glint menacingly in the dim light, sharp and deadly.

"Is it a bad time to remind you of your protecting duties?" Kart'Ahed ventures.

"They protect us too, right?" the scraggy mutineer asks.

"Again, since there never has been any ale, we're not in your employment," Mormak grumbles.

Gadisa makes his move, his obese form surprisingly agile as he darts between the Punks. Wilhilm understands what he's after—he wants to snatch away their instruments and silence their chaotic symphony. Wilhilm watches, holding his breath.

But each time Gadisa nears one of the mummified bards, a crescendo builds, culminating in a burst of energy that sends the Rogue reeling backward.

Each thwarted attempt is a reminder of the Punks' power, the ancient magic that animates their desiccated forms and fuels their deadly music. The dungeon echoes with the sounds of battle.

Finally, Mormak gives up stomping and activates his EyeStone.

"Don't use your EyeStone," Dakaria warns. "Remember how it brought down Tiringar a few days ago? You saw the demons!"

"I'm not casting, I just want to show something," Mormak insists. He scrolls until he finds the cast he's looking for. "Do you know what that is?" he asks the mummies. "*These* are real musicians. Not the mummified sort that sings old songs."

The song wavers.

"Look at those moves! They're unbeatable."

The song comes grinds to a halt.

"I can do those moves," the first mummy says.

"I can do those moves too, they're not difficult," the second mummy says.

"I bet you can do them better than *him*," Mormak says to the second mummy.

"*Her*, can't you tell?" the first mummy corrects.

There's a certain roughness to Mormak's voice, like the rumble of rocks in a landslide, yet it's not devoid of warmth.

"Her do those moves better than me? That's not true, I'm the best dancer," the third mummy says. The mummy sports a leathered, decaying mohawk made from the remains of ancient fabric.

"I don't know," Mormak says. "I still think your girl here is better than you are."

"I am," the second mummy says.

"He's not," the first and the third mummy say simultaneously. They turn their kohl-rimmed eyes on their friend in disbelief.

"I guess we never know," Mormak says, "except, if you can... prove it?"

"Prove it how?" the first mummy says.

"A dance-off. Everyone takes turns and so you can see who of you is better."

"I'll start," the third mummy says.

"Ok, go on, Ziggy," the first mummy says.

Ziggy begins to dance, his movements an odd mix of graceful postures and frenzied moshing. The music picks up again as the other mummies accompany him. The discordant notes of the band's cursed desert rock fuels his fervor, and as Ziggy thrusts his skeletal hips and twirls.

A swathe of the millennia-old linen around his leg catches on a sharp edge of his studded armband. The linen rips with a dry, tearing sound, revealing the horrifying sight underneath: a patch of withered, mottled skin over jutting bones. Veins, long drained of blood, web across the exposed gray flesh. The sight is repulsive, yet mesmerizing.

"I think it's time to go, before they remember to focus on us," Mormak whispers.

Wilhilm couldn't agree more.

CHAPTER 62
MASTER OF PUPPETS

As Wilhilm, his three companions, Kart'Ahend and his men trudge through the dark, sand-laden corridors, the music fades. The fire channel doesn't continue through here. Instead, ancient torches lining the walls spring to life.

The deeper they go, the colder it becomes. The heat of the desert is now a distant memory. A damp chill crawls up their spines. The once whispering walls now remain silent, but the pull Wilhilm feels grows stronger. He feels there's something ahead. Something that calls out for him. And probably it was a very bad idea to follow that call. Still, he couldn't just stop.

Rounding a particularly tight bend, they enter a grand chamber, illuminated by a singular source: a massive obsidian obelisk standing tall in the center. It pulses with a dim blue light. Floating the obelisk in circles, connected to it by strands of shimmering energy, is a figure. He recognizes who it is.

Seraphina.

"Wilhilm," she breathes, her voice a siren's call, each

syllable dripping with a sweetness that tugs at his soul. The way she says his name, it's like a melody, wrapping around him, pulling him closer with an invisible thread. Her lips, though barely more than a wisp of light, curve into a familiar, tender smile.

But beneath the honeyed veneer of her voice, there's a tremor of fear, a subtle note of desperation that echoes in the hollow chamber. Her hands reach out to him, trembling slightly, as if she's afraid they might dissipate into nothingness.

"You're alive? You're alive!" Wilhilm says, not knowing what to think.

"Please, come closer," she pleads, her eyes wide and imploring. The urgency in her tone resonates deep within Wilhilm's heart. Then, something strikes him. Something's off. Seraphina's image flickers like a candle flame caught in a breeze. Yet her eyes remain fixed on him, pools of longing and sorrow.

"How are you alive?"

"I don't know what happened. One moment I was with you in Tiringar, the next I was here." The sound of her voice weakens his resolve.

She is alive, that's what matters.

Or is it a trick?

"Stop," Dakaria says. He feels her hand on his shoulder. "Don't rush anything. You know how it is with magic. Could be an illusion, something designed to trick us."

Seraphina shakes her head sadly. "But Wilhilm, you know me. You love me. How can I be an illusion?"

"Love?" Mormak grumbles. "All I'm looking for is ale. That's what I love."

"Did they... you know... errrr... kiss?" Gadisa whispers loudly to Dakaria.

She shrugs, then shakes her head. "I don't think so. He's an uptight wizard, after all. For his type, love is more intellectual than physical," she says.

"Why did Hasan target you? How did you get tangled up in all of this?" Wilhilm asks.

"Come closer and I can explain it to you," Seraphina says.

He ventures a step forward, but feels Dakaria's hand again. "Watch the vines of energy. Once you near the obelisk, they could reach you."

Wilhilm shrugs Dakaria off. "How did you end up here? I saw you burning away. It was... It felt terrible. So sad. I almost went crazy." Even as he says it, doubt creeps in. Is Seraphina real? Or does he just want her to be?

"Just one step closer. One and a half perhaps. Just a little closer," Seraphina says.

"I think I begin to get why Dakaria thinks it's a trap," Gadisa says.

"In the good old days of adventuring, they had at least the decency to put ale into every trap. Once I was trapped with a year worth of ale. Good days," Mormak says.

"If I was the evil guy, I'd make sure to have a buffet here," Gadisa says. "So, at least when Wilhilm gives into the blatantly obvious trap, we could have snacks and watch."

"I'm not falling for any trap," Wilhilm says.

"You just stepped forward, if only a little," Dakaria says.

"Did I? I didn't even realize."

"You don't mind if we stay back, right?" Kart'Ahed says, ushering his men back.

"Oh, Willy," Seraphina says. "You don't realize much, do you? Did you at least listen to my wonderful song? *With your staff, you'd defend without quaking, /And we need you today, / Oh, Willy.*"

Seraphina's voice darkens while she sings the song until it is a dark, unpleasant hiss. Her melodious voice, one that serenaded Wilhilm, now gives way to guttural groans.

The room, already dimly lit by the pulsating obelisk, darkens further as a tangible dread settles in the air. Seraphina twists and convulses violently.

Wilhilm stumbles back, eyes widening in horror. Her raven-black hair begins to float as if she is submerged in water, her hands clutch at her throat. The beautiful blue in her eyes bleeds away and is replaced by the vacant silver of someone else's eyes. Wilhilm can hear a series of soft cracks and pops—her bones reshaping, her stature changing.

Where Seraphina's smooth and soft features once were, the skin begins to stretch, her face becoming angular and more pronounced. It looks a lot like the last transformation, only faster, rougher. Her slender frame expands, her clothes tearing at the seams as her body grows taller and broader. She seems to pull energy from the room, dark tendrils wrapping around her.

"Did you truly believe—" her changed voice starts, now an amalgamation of both Seraphina's softness and an eerie calm that reminds Wilhilm of someone "—that it would be that easy?" A moment later he knows who.

Step forward. Let me out. Let me roam free. The demon growls in Wilhilm's chest. Suddenly, Derek's back!

Then, the transformation is complete. Before Wilhilm stands not the gentle, compassionate Seraphina, but King Hasan ibn Azazel. Dark robes drape his skeletal form, the withered flesh stretched tight across horribly visible bones. King Hasan ibn Azazel dances his fingers along the obelisk, eyes wide, the corners of his mouth turned upward.

"Welcome! So energizing that you followed my invitation! It's been so long since you paid me a visit. And the last time, you practically took the whole city with you." Hasan's voice booms, echoing throughout the chamber. It was deep, smooth, and unnervingly calm. "I must say, I was impressed by that display of power. And now, I need you again. To complete my biggest achievement yet."

Wilhilm steps forward, determination clear in his eyes. "What did you do to her?!"

"Her? But Willy, there was no her. There was only me. From the beginning. You saw it then, and there you are, still hoping. Adorable." Wilhilm clenches his teeth. "Remember, when I whispered in your ear to use the spell and open the rift? Me. Sometimes I just like to arrange my bones in a way a bit more feminine." He grins a skeletal grin.

CHAPTER 63
KARMA CHAMELEON

The air in the ancient, sand-choked ruin is heavy with a sense of inevitable, dreadful power. Hasan stands at the very heart of the buried city, his robes whispering of a time when they commanded respect and fear alike.

Wilhilm feels shock, and his shock quickly mutates into anger—a fiery, almost tangible thing that makes his skin tinkle and his left eye twitch in a most alarming manner. He clenches his fists, muttering words that could, under less furious circumstances, turn a pumpkin into a highly confused pigeon. "Duped!" he roars, his voice echoing off the stone walls, bouncing back at him with an almost mocking tone. "I, Wilhilm the Wise, Master of the Arcane Arts, have been... hoodwinked by a two-bit conjurer!"

Even Hasan seems to lean in, as if to listen to this rare admission of fallibility. The anger is hot, searing, but beneath it, creeping up like a guilty thief in the night, is shame. Deep, profound shame that sits in his chest like a leaden weight.

The sands around them, which until now had seemed

like solid ground, begin to tremble and shift as the Lich King raises one bony hand.

Wilhilm feels his cheeks flush a deep red, a stark contrast to his usual pale complexion, as the full weight of his folly crashes over him. He fell for the trick of some dead king.

And of Seraphina. If she ever existed. Tricked by his hopes. His love for Lysandra perverted by the Zal'qaran sands.

The motion of Hasan's bony finger is almost delicate, as if the Lich King is simply brushing away some persistent cobwebs, but the effect is anything but. The very earth shudders in response, and the sands above him through the holes in the roof begin to part, retreating in waves that ripple outwards from the Lich King's feet. Wilhilm watches in a mix of awe and sheer terror as the Lich King lifts his other hand, palms upward as though inviting the world to rise and meet him.

Gadisa, Mormak, Dakaria and Kart'Ahed shriek in panic, trying to cling to statues that start a dangerous swing.

The ground beneath them rumbles ominously, and Wilhilm stumbles, barely keeping his balance as the stones of the ancient city begin to move. With a slow, grinding sound, the slabs of ancient streets and the crumbling bases of long-buried towers start to rise, lifting Ishmaara upward.

The city ascends with the ease of a man stepping onto a stairway that he fully expects to appear before his feet. Hasan's skeletal fingers twitch and curl, guiding the ruins from their sandy tombs, coaxing them back into the light with the grim patience of one who has all the time in the world—and quite a bit beyond that.

"Mormak," Dakaria cries out, and Wilhilm watches a

statue coming down just right next to Mormak. Instinctively, he takes a step back, trying to calculate a potential trajectory of the big jackal statue just to his right.

As the city rises, the sands pour off the ruins in golden cascades, revealing columns, arches, and jagged remnants of structures that once ruled the horizon. The entire world seems to tilt, as though reality itself is being reshaped by the Lich King's will. Wilhilm clings to a crumbling pillar, watching in breathless disbelief as the ancient city reassembles itself beneath his feet, the bones of the past knitting together under the direction of the undead monarch.

The Lich King stands tall at the center of it all, his form silhouetted against the emerging skyline, as he lifts himself and the ruins upward with an almost casual flick of his wrist. The sands, so eager to bury the past, now make way for the sun.

Wilhilm hears Derek whisper. *Yessssss. Yesssss, this is it, the sands give back what they owe, they will be rewarded with millions of souls to come.*

Wilhilm's mind reels, caught between awe and the undeniable urge to flee, as he's standing beside the one who's making it happen. The city, once dead and buried, now starts to breathe again, and the Lich King, with the grace of a conductor finishing a symphony, finally lowers his hands, surveying his restored dominion with a satisfaction that seems to echo in the very stones beneath them.

"It's better to have our little discussion, while I'm not buried under tons of sand," Hasan smiles at Wilhilm.

Somewhere, there's a sneeze.

CHAPTER 64
SYMPATHY FOR THE DEVIL

"You destroyed Tiringar," Wilhilm says. "You destroyed the whole city."

"You did the heavy lifting. And it was just a little test of great things to come," Hasan says. "Didn't you feel the power? Didn't you feel the rush?"

"The rush of demons killing everything?"

"You focus on the wrong things, Wilhilm. Think of the hive mind! Can't you imagine what it means for us? Humanity connected, acting as one, casting our differences aside?"

"What for? To be slayed by demons?"

Now is the time.

"Forget the demons, they don't matter. Terrible, terrible things will be coming, Wilhilm. I know you can feel it too. Soul-rifting has a history of five thousand years. Five thousand years of magic that weakened the tapestry of the universe. So weak that dimensions will clash into each other. The hive mind can save us. And all we need is you... and your abilities."

"My abilities?" Wilhilm says. "You have the wrong guy. You know I'm weak. I always have been."

"Is this how the wizard intimidates people?" Gadisa whispers to Mormak. "By telling them he is weak?"

"There is a lot of talking where there should be more axe swinging and drinking," Mormak says. "Feels very wrong to me."

"You are not weak, merely unique. Just take a step forward and I will show you what you can do," Hasan says.

"Why do I have to come forward? Why don't you just come and get me?" Wilhilm says. "I have to do it voluntarily, is that it? Does it only work if I agree? If I choose to come? Well, then forget it. I will never!"

"You will leave us without protection?"

"Protection?" Wilhilm replies.

Oh yes. Yes. Let me protect. I am the protector, Derek whispers inside of Wilhilm's head.

"I told you, terrible, terrible things are coming, and we need to protect the fabric of the universe."

Wilhilm nods. "We need to protect it against you. You erected the EyeStone network. You channeled energy. People self-combusted and died. That was all your doing. By ripping apart these souls at once, powerful energy accumulated and ripped open a portal to the demon dimension. Magic 101."

Hasan continues to circle the obelisk. Beneath him, the shadows shift. "You make it sound so dirty, Wilhilm. Why do you think I did it?"

"Revenge."

"It must be a blessing to see the world in your easy terms. To see black and white, to see right and wrong. Not to see the shades, the gray, the sacrifices that have to be made."

"If we want to save the world, could we skip all of that banter, and go straight to the part where we learn what's going on?" Mormak says. "And then have some ale? And, if time permits, save the world?"

"Some snacks perhaps," Gadisa chimes in.

"That's what I'm doing: saving the world," Hasan says. "The people of Eldaris, they moved magic from here. For good reason. But when they disappeared, the dragons came back, they ruled the world. And they wouldn't just accept that magic was gone. They looked for another way. And they found one."

"Soul-rifting," Wilhilm says.

"Right, the way we all do our magic. Tearing off a tiny piece of our soul, thereby opening up a rift into a dimension where we can pull magic from."

"That's not how it works. It's more complicated than that," Wilhilm protests. "*Magalan's Treatise on How Magic Works* has three thousand pages!"

"I just summarized it for you," Hasan says. "But we never looked where we pulled the magic from, or where all of these tiny soul parts go to. Oh yes, we speculated, we wrote long essays, nevertheless we never cared to look. But I did, Wilhilm," He points to his chest. "I did. The night you did your thing, the night you thought you killed me, you pulled in more magic than I have ever seen. I saw the opening you created. And I chose to go through, to explore. To seek out the origin of magic."

"Quick question, did they have ale there? Asking for a friend," Mormak says.

CHAPTER 65
REFLECTIONS

Wilhilm feels his hatred against Hasan bubbling up, and at the same time, his words in a very strange way resonate with him. All his life, he has felt that magic was *all wrong*. That it was unnatural to sacrifice bits of one's own soul even for the tiniest of spells. And Hasan seems to confirm that something is fundamentally wrong with it.

No, absolutely not. This was not the way to think about it! This was madness. A plan to bring down the world, just to resurrect some fabled old-style magic that might have or might not have existed! They should kill him and be done with it. Save all of those lives he is sacrificing now just for magic. All the lives already lost in Tiringar.

Yet Wilhilm can't help but ask, "What is it, the origin of magic? Where did you go? What did you find?"

"I saw things, Wilhilm. Things I truly hope you will never see. Look what it did to me. There are things... a billion times worse than any demon you can think of. And they're coming. They're angry. So very angry, because we keep stealing from them. They've sent warnings, but we didn't understand their warnings. And now we will pay for what we did. We will pay for the thousands of years of magic we stole from them."

Despite himself, chills rush over Wilhilm. "Who's coming?" Wilhilm asks. He unconsciously steps forward.

Wilhilm suddenly feels the energy in the room prickle on his skin.

Now! Now!

Yessssss!

Wilhilm's vision blurs, the world around him dims into a haze of shadow and torment. Inside him, the demon surges like a black tide, clawing its way to dominance, trying to extinguish the flicker of Wilhilm's willpower. Each pulse of dark energy sends waves of searing pain through his being, the sensations raw and unnerving, as if his very soul is aflame. Wilhilm drops to the ground and grasps desperately onto a fragment of his consciousness, a glimmer of who he once was and who he strives to be.

The world around Wilhilm shivers, the edges of reality fraying as the demon pushes its way into his mind. Wilhilm's thoughts—normally a chaotic but manageable mess of half-formed spells, unfinished tea and craving for cheese—suddenly split open, revealing every dark corner he'd tried so hard to ignore. There, in the recesses of his consciousness, his sins and regrets line up like a parade of the worst-dressed nightmares.

The demon prowls through his thoughts, dragging out each unpleasant memory with a sickening delight. There's the time he accidentally turned half the village's chickens into explosive squawks. There's the little incident with the enchanted mirror that still haunts his dreams—literally. And there, in the deepest recess, is the shadow of his ambition, the unspoken desire for power that he has never quite managed to quell.

As Wilhilm reels from the onslaught, the demon begins its work in earnest, connecting him to something far larger and more terrible than his own demons. It's the hive mind again, but this time, it feels different. A lot different. Less *human*. The hive mind of demonkind opens up before him, an endless, writhing sea of malevolence and despair. It's not just a chorus of demons whispering their terrible truths; it's a symphony of souls, both damned and newly captured, all intermingling in a cacophony of suffering and madness.

Wilhilm's own voice joins the throng, but it's twisted, corrupted, as though his thoughts are being filtered through a thousand screams. He can feel the presence of other human minds, caught in the same trap, their individuality shredded and mixed with the seething mass of demonic consciousness. His thoughts are no longer his own; they are pulled apart, reassembled, and drowned in the collective hate and fear of countless others.

Every dark desire he has ever entertained is laid bare, magnified by the hive mind's relentless focus. His will, once strong enough to weave the fabric of magic, now seems like a feeble thread, fraying under the demon's relentless grip. The connection is complete, and Wilhilm feels his identity slipping away, dissolving into the sea of anguish that threatens to consume him entirely.

Lost in the vast, consuming shadow, his last thoughts barely discernible among the myriad voices that now scream in unison within the hive mind. The demon, roaring triumphantly, takes its place at the helm of his soul into the black abyss.

As the cacophony of voices within the hive mind roars

in his ears, something curious begins to happen to Wilhilm. The initial shock and terror is replaced by a strange, creeping warmth. It's as if he's been holding onto a heavy burden for so long that he's forgotten what it's like to be free of it. The burden of individuality, of responsibility, slips from his shoulders like a discarded cloak.

The countless voices in his head, once a frightening jumble, begin to harmonize. He can feel them melding together into something greater than the sum of their parts, a collective consciousness that pulses with raw power. It's overwhelming, yes, but also intoxicating.

For the first time in his life, Wilhilm isn't just wielding power—he is power. The hive mind draws him in, wrapping him in a blanket of dark comfort. There's no need to make decisions, no need to worry about the consequences of his actions. The hive makes those decisions, and Wilhilm simply flows with it, like a drop of water in a mighty river.

He is not responsible anymore. He feels the demons. He feels their slaughter in Tiringar. But he does not feel guilt. Not even the guilt about Lysandra's death can touch him anymore, and for once, he's free of the enormous weight it put on his shoulders. It's a profound sense of relief.

Wilhilm is part of something ancient, something vast. The demon plane stretches out before him, an infinite expanse of dark beauty and untold power. It calls to him, and he answers, his thoughts no longer his own but part of a grand symphony of malevolence and might.

But then, amid the countless murmurs and shrieks, something shifts. It's subtle at first—a whisper that isn't quite in tune with the rest, a thread of thought that feels oddly... familiar. Wilhilm's awareness hones in on it, and suddenly, like a bolt of lightning in the darkest storm, he feels it: the rest of his soul.

It's not just a memory of himself, not just some phantom limb that tickles with the idea of what he once was. No, this is real, tangible, a missing piece of him that's been somewhere else all this time, lost but not forgotten. The sensation is like stepping into a room you've dreamed of but never visited, a place where everything is just slightly off but still feels undeniably yours.

His soul, the part of him that was stolen, shunted, and left to drift in the demon plane, brushes against his consciousness. It's like finding an old book that you thought you'd lent out and never got back, only to discover it had been sitting on your shelf all along, just in a spot you never bothered to check. Except this book isn't just a book; it's a tangled mess of memories, fears, and the peculiar habit of humming when nervous.

The reunion is both exhilarating and terrifying. His missing soul doesn't come quietly. It drags with it the horrors of the demon plane, a thousand screaming voices clawing at his mind, demanding attention, demanding retribution. But it also brings with it a strange sense of completion, like finally slipping into a pair of shoes that fit just right after hobbling about in too-tight boots.

And yet, it's more than just a reunion. As the two halves of his soul reconnect, Wilhilm feels the hive mind react, its demonic tendrils curling around this newfound strength. The connection amplifies, and suddenly, he's not just a part of the hive—he's something more. Power surges through him, raw and unfiltered, the essence of countless demons now interwoven with the full, if somewhat battered, tapestry of his soul.

Wilhilm's thoughts swirl in a maelstrom of dark magic and identity. He is himself, and yet he is so much more. The hive mind roars, embracing this new depth of connection, but Wilhilm feels the tension building, like a balloon inflated beyond its limit. It's exhilarating, intoxicating, and utterly unsustainable.

And then, something happens. Somewhere, in a room next to where his body is, there is the dampened sound of glass shattering. Wilhilm thinks he can hear something like "Oops" clearly in Gadisa's voice.

A guttural sound of pure rage reverberates through the chamber. Hasan, once a figure of composed malevolence, now radiates surprise and fury. His silver eyes, previously brimming with confidence, dart to the obelisk, his brows furrowing deeply. "No!" he roars, the sound echoing, amplifying his anger and disbelief. "Who dares interrupt the source?"

CHAPTER 66

DEAD MAN WALKING

The demon, taken aback, snarls with anger, its grip momentarily faltering. Seizing this chance, Wilhilm channels every ounce of his willpower, weaving his memories, emotions, and desires into a radiant force that repels the encroaching darkness. The demon claws into his soul, is almost one with it. The more Wilhilm focuses, the more the demon's hold diminishes. With one last effort, he thrusts the demon back into the recesses of his mind, shackling it once more.

Panting heavily, sweat glistening on his brow, Wilhilm lifts himself to his knees, the world slowly coming back into focus. The weight of the internal battle still lingers, but for now, he remains his own master.

For a moment, Wilhilm simply stands there, panting, the echoes of the hive mind still ringing faintly in his ears like the lingering hum of an especially persistent mosquito.

"This big green brute just broke the connection and damaged some of our mirrors," a new voice booms across from the other room. "We're still on! I can fix it! I called the mummies in, so we have time for some repairs."

"Mummies?" Mormak echoes.

Wilhilm feels... lighter, somehow, as if a great weight had been lifted from his shoulders. There is a certain clarity to his thoughts, a newfound peace that he hasn't experienced in what feels like centuries.

And then it hist him.

That clarity, that lightness, isn't relief. It is absence. The comforting hum of his own thoughts, the familiar, ever-present background noise of his inner monologue, is gone. Utterly, completely gone.

Wilhilm reaches out with his mind, probing the recesses of his consciousness where his soul—his very essence—should have been nestled, secure and slightly grumpy from the recent ordeal. But there is nothing. No soul, no spark, no comforting warmth. Just a void, a gaping emptiness where everything that makes Wilhilm, well, Wilhilm, has resided.

He checks again. Perhaps his soul has merely taken a brief vacation, a well-deserved rest after the tumultuous events of the day. But no, the void persists, as vast and cold as the bottom of the deepest well. Wilhilm feels a strange sort of panic begin to creep in, the kind that starts as a nagging worry at the back of your mind and quickly spirals into a full-blown existential crisis.

King Hasan still stands next to the towering structure. The obelisk is now flickering erratically, like a candle resisting a gust of wind.

A hushed silence settles, and for a moment, time seems to stretch infinitely. Each flicker becomes more pronounced, casting unstable shadows that dance unpredictably around the chamber. Wilhilm, the companions, Kart'Ahed Uvhorz and his bodyguards, and even Hasan seem to hold their breath, anticipating the obelisk's next move.

With an abruptness that makes Wilhilm's heart leap to his throat, the pulsing ceases altogether. The chamber plunges into almost total darkness, save for a few torches placed intermittently along the walls.

Dust shakes from the ceiling, causing everyone to glance around in alarm. But Wilhilm's heart races for an entirely different reason. He's caught a familiar scent in the air—the unmistakable musk of ancient decay.

From the cavern's entrance, a tremendous figure emerges wrapped in centuries-old linens. Clad in the regal remnants of an ancient garb, the figure stands with an air of faded grandeur. Its haunting visage of eternally preserved nobility is framed by a headdress. Bejeweled with lapis lazuli and turquoise, it echoes the starlit skies. The central cobra rises proudly at the forehead, its hood expanded and encrusted with emeralds. Adorned in a tunic of deep blue, trimmed with gold, the mummy's form speaks of royalty, its arms wrapped in the style of the mummified dead. Bracelets encircled its wrists, a silent testament to forgotten opulence. Despite the tattered edges of its skirt billowing like shadows, the figure's stance is unwavering—a monarch or deity carved from the very sands of time itself.

Wilhilm's gaze turns to the headdress and the cobra.

A pharaoh.

The pharaoh.

"Kadoc'Ru," Wilhilm murmurs, remembering the depictions of him. An eerie blue luminescence fills the mummy's hollow eyes.

"This is the Mummy King we've seen on the wall," Wilhilm says.

Behind Kadoc'Ru dozens of mummy warriors march in

formation, their lifeless eyes gleaming with the same haunting glow.

The room, vast as it is, quickly fills with the mummy horde. Before Wilhilm or any of his companions can react, they find themselves circled, the cold eyes of the undead warriors watching their every move.

"I hate to mention it now, but I think we can ascertain that there's no actual protecting going on, and therefore, I don't owe you anything," says Kart'Ahed Uvhorz. "Just making sure we're on the same page here."

Kadoc'Ru gazes across the room at the captives. Once mighty in life, he is still mighty in death. He glances down at the bandages that wrap his body from head to toe, sees a tiny corner of the fabric curling up at the edge, and smooths it out with his finger. The corner pops back up. He tries to ignore it, but smooths it down again.

"Oh geez," he grumbles in a dry voice. "That's not good." He pulls at it, and instead of ripping off, the bandage peels back in a long swath with no end. He keeps pulling and peeling it until a section of graying dried skin is visible.

"My King!" his aide hurries to his side. "Please, my King! Stop!"

"It was sticking up–"

"Yes, but you mustn't pick at it!"

"We can match the bandages, can't we?"

"Well, we are out of crypt white. We can try using a shade of bone white, my King..."

The King tisks. "Oh great. The bone white will be slightly lighter than the crypt white. Everyone will stare."

The King and his servant glance at each other, an awkward silence between them. Finally, the aide gestures to the door and says, "I'm going to just go get the bandages now." He bows several times before scampering off.

Kadoc'Ru coughs, then looks around, obviously trying to get back in the mood. "Mortals," he hisses, his voice echoing eerily. "For the desecration of our holy halls, you are now my prisoners. The prisoners of King Kadoc'Ru, the King of Ishmaara."

King Hassan, who has stood politely through the whole exchange between Kadoc'Ru and his aid, now speaks. "I am King of Ishmaara." he says.

"From where I'm standing, it looks a lot like you are incapacitated. Your flesh is melded with this obelisk, right?"

"A minor inconvenience!"

"Our arrangement is crystal clear. If you are incapacitated, I fill in as the true king."

"That's why kings should die," Mormak says.

"We *are* dead," both kings say simultaneously.

"Not trying to be disrespectful but look at you. Two dead kings and you have to make arrangements," Mormak continues. "What if more dead kings turn up, or a living one for that? How do you take turns then?"

"Mortals do not need to occupy their petty minds with the benign questions of higher beings," Kadoc'Ru says.

From a dark corridor adjoining the hall, there is a sudden commotion. The distinct, rhythmic steps of mummies echo, interspersed with a lighter, more impatient tapping. A muffled voice can be heard, clear in its frustration deep, a guttural groan, sounding like a visceral testament to someone's prolonged deprivation. It's a hollow, aching noise that seems to echo from the very depths of a tortured soul, a raw and primal sound.

Two towering mummies emerge, clutching the arms of a familiar figure between them. It is Gadisa. The sounds come from him. Right from where his stomach is. Or should be. Wilhilm isn't really sure how the Rogue's unique body works.

"I'm hungry. Hungry!" Gadisa exclaims, extricating one arm from a mummy's grasp to wave dismissively. "No need for the rough treatment. I was just looking for some grub. One can't think properly on an empty stomach, you know."

"He was in the mirror room, disrupting the flow of energy, breaking some," a mummy reports.

"I told you. Those mirrors were irritating me. I saw myself multiple times," Gadisa groans. "And now give me something to eat!"

The mummies, unaccustomed to such demands, simply stare with their eerie, glowing eyes, their grip on the rogue unrelenting.

The Rogue sighs, rolling his eyes. "Look, I've been dragged through this dusty death-trap of a place, hounded by your mummy bards," he gestures toward the mummies in the room, "and have had one terrible day. The least you could do is fetch me a sandwich or something." He pauses, then added hopefully, "With cheese?"

"And perhaps some ale?" Mormak chimes in.

The hall, already tense from the confrontation with Kadoc'Ru, now contains a hint of bewilderment.

Hasan orders, "Kadoc'Ru, make sure you store them somewhere safe where they can't escape. I need the wizard later, after we fixed this thing here."

"I command my troops, not you!"

"Of course. Give any order you think is appropriate. But the right one!"

Kadoc'Ru coughs. "Store the prisoners somewhere safe, but don't hurt them!"

Wilhilm and his companions are outnumbered. Their weapons are useless against such numbers and the cold, unyielding gazes of the mummies give no room for negotiation.

"O almighty Kadoc'Ru," Kart'Ahed ventures. "Let's not be over enthusiastic here. It seems to me there is some quarrel with the bunch of these four. But I don't really know them. Just a chance encounter."

"So?" the mummy king hisses back.

"Confine these four all you want, but I have a business proposition for you."

"Wait... aren't you the merchant who was supposed to get rid of this evil genie for us? He was such a drag. Always complaining."

"Do you see him anywhere?" Kart'Ahed asks back.

Clever. He doesn't even lie.

"I see. Okay, you did the job. What kind of business proposition?"

"I couldn't help but notice the lack of crypt white linen. As it happens, I have a license for crypt white linen. My storage is full of it."

The mummy king ponders for a moment. "Right," he commands. "Take those four to the cells. I will deal with those other three personally."

The mummies march Wilhilm and his companions out of his room. Wilhilm stares back at Kart'Ahed, and somehow he senses it might be the last time he sees him. It feels strange to part with him in what feels like a betrayal and without good-byes.

The mummies usher them on. They are trapped, at the mercy of an ancient king and his undead army. And Wilhilm has lost his soul.

CHAPTER 67
CROSSROADS

The walls. The walls are definitely pressing in on him. Wilhilm puts his hands on the cold stone of the cell. As soon as he does, he realizes nothing is shrinking around him. It's only standard panic. The dankness of the cell, combined with the dread of what Hasan might do once he is back on track, gnaws at him. His mind races with thoughts of the EyeStone network, Seraphina's unnerving transformation and the utter and devastating loss of his soul.

He should not be allowed to do magic. The gods should have prevented him from ever getting close to magic.

The cold stone walls echo the chill in Wilhilm's heart. His thoughts are a turbulent storm. The revelation that King Hasan was Seraphina all along, a puppeteer in a macabre play of deception, gnaws at his already fractured sense of self. It feels like a betrayal of the cruelest kind, a manipulation of his deepest emotions.

The weight of his failures presses down on him. The memories of Lysandra resurface with a stabbing ache. The guilt floods forward with overwhelming intensity.

His magic took away the person he cared most about; it killed Lysandra. It gave a home to a demon, turning him into a vessel for destruction. Every attempt to harness it, to use it for good, has only spiraled into more despair. The realization is crushing.

In the dim light of the cell, Wilhilm still feels like the walls are closing in on him. He checks with a short push of his hand against the wall, just to make sure. The wall is fixed. But he's going crazy.

As despair threatens to engulf him, his eyes dart around the room, searching for any means of escape. It is then he spots them: his pouch, carelessly tossed into a corner by the mummies. From the outside, it just looks like a small and unimportant pouch, but really it magically stores all of Wilhilm's possessions. Well, most of them. He peeks inside. Among the items—the genie lamp. Its dull gleam is a beacon amidst his dark thoughts.

The genie within is a treacherous, cunning and malevolent through every wish.

There is a possibility there.

He could, perhaps, rid himself of his magic. Make sure the demon has nothing to feast on.

It may be the only way to break the cycle, to prevent further harm to those he cares about and to himself.

The thought is both terrifying and liberating. To be free of magic is to be free of the demon, of the guilt. It would also rob Hasan of any opportunity to use him for evil.

It could be the trump card he needs.

Rubbing the lamp could be like holding a serpent by its tail—dangerous and unpredictable.

You don't need the lamp, you have me, Derek whispers.

"I don't want you," Wilhilm replies. "I don't want magic. I don't even want myself anymore."

Don't give up just yet. Didn't you feel it? How powerful we are together? This King Hasan had a role, yes. But as for me, any wizard will do. It doesn't have to be this foul-smelling creature.

"Are you offering me a deal?" Wilhilm asks. He knows better, of course, than to take anything at face value. Demons lie and betray and manipulate. That's what they're made for. And probably made of.

Don't do anything stupid now, Derek warns, and Wilhilm that subconsciously, he already started to touch the lamp.

Wilhilm cautiously handles the lamp, the weight of his decision pressing on him. The surface is cold, metallic, and oddly reassuring. But the part that convinces him is that Derek wants him to put it down. So, he begins to rub the lamp in circular motions before he can change his mind.

A turbulent whirl of smoke erupts from the lamp's spout, filling the cell with a thick, acrid mist. As the smoke clears, there stands the genie, far larger than the confines of the lamp would suggest. Its eyes, glowing with an inner fire, lock onto Wilhilm's with a furious intensity. The genie's form is fluid, constantly shifting like a wisp of smoke, yet there is a palpable density and power to it. The very air in the cell crackles and thickens.

"So," the genie hisses, its voice dripping with disdain, "you again. Thought you could imprison me and be done with it?"

Wilhilm swallows hard. The genie's wrath is evident. Its form appears more tumultuous, and the color of its smoke takes on a darker, stormier hue.

"Ungrateful humans," it continues, its voice deepening, "Always demanding, always wanting. You release me, shove me back in, and then have the audacity to call upon me once more? You treat me like a wishing well."

"Technically..." Wilhilm begins.

The genie hisses. Wilhilm steps back, suddenly feeling very small and vulnerable. The genie might be his solution, but he's toeing a dangerous line.

In the heavy atmosphere of the cell, Wilhilm takes a deep breath, steeling himself.

"I wish for you to take my magic," Wilhilm says. "I don't want it anymore. I've lost everything."

"Then you should keep it and lose even more!"

"Hey, aren't you bound to fulfill my wish?"

The genie smiles mischievously. "There are laws for genie magic, and just wishing magic to disappear, that's not how it works."

Wilhilm nods. Of course. Genie magic has different laws. So, how can he use it? He think about it, and slowly, an inkling of an idea comes to him. An idea so audacious, it might just work.

"Genie," Wilhilm begins, his voice surprisingly steady, "I propose an arrangement, one that might entertain even a being as old and powerful as you."

The genie's eyes narrow, its form swirls with cautious intrigue. "Go on," it rasps.

Wilhilm smiles, showing no fear. "Have you ever wondered what it's like to be human? To feel hunger, joy, sorrow, the thrill of magic coursing through your veins? I offer you the chance to experience life as a human wizard, while I take on your role as a genie."

The genie's smoky form oscillates, clearly taken aback. "A human?" it scoffs. "I was one. Once. Long ago. Why would I want to return to that weak, ephemeral kind?"

"So, you love to be the wishing well of everyone? And you seem to like your little lamp. Is it comfortable? Do you like having to leave it when you are called upon, and then shoved back in, dependent on the whims of others? You've been trapped in that lamp for who knows how long. This is your chance to be free, to walk the Earth, feel the sands of the desert between your toes, taste the sweetness of fruit, and experience the myriad emotions of mortality."

The genie hovers in thought, its swirling form reflecting the whirlwind of its contemplation. It searches for a catch, a loophole in Wilhilm's offer. "And what would you want in exchange?"

"What can I have in exchange? You know as much as I do, once you leave the lamp, you need a replacement, and there is not much choice here, if I'm the one who wishes you free," Wilhilm says. "Just take my magic away."

"I can't take magic away," the genie says. "You should know that. The connection to your kind of magic will be severed, but genie magic will take its place."

"I don't want to do any more magic," Wilhilm says. "It only brought evil."

The genie laughs a dark laugh, puffing smoke through his nose and ears. "There's no good and there is no evil. But if this deal depends on you not doing any magic, I might ease your mind. Genie magic follows strict rules. Without a wish, you will not do any magic, and even with a wish, you have to carefully listen so you can use all the wriggle room the wish gives you."

Wilhilm thinks for a moment. It's not the whole package, but it sounds good enough for him. Trading places with the genie would bottle him up for good. He would be buried with the lamp for centuries. He would do no more harm.

After all, it was *his* magic that caused all of his. And *his* magic would be gone. "I am ready," he says eventually.

"You are aware that this is a binding contract? You can't just change your mind," the genie says.

Wilhilm nods.

CHAPTER 68

EYE OF THE TIGER

The genie scrutinizes Wilhilm, trying to find any deceit in his eyes. "I still don't see what's in it for you."

"Isn't that a question I would have to ask you? Isn't it the genie coaxing the wizard into trading places?"

"You are not normal," the genie says. "And I mean that in the best possible way. There's a lot of evil in you."

"Oh that," Wilhilm sighs. "That's technically not *my* evil. It's more of an acquired evil. A demon that slipped in, when I sacrificed my soul to banish his boss."

"Interesting. You're a returning high-stakes negotiator."

Wilhilm leans in, his voice firm yet persuasive. "You can trust me. Because as much as you distrust humans, I believe in their—in our—capacity to honor a deal. Especially one of this magnitude."

With a begrudging nod, the genie agrees, "Very well, Wizard. But remember, any treachery on your part, and there will be consequences."

In a forgotten part of the vast desert in the dimly lit, cold cell, the genie and Wilhilm stand face to face, their agreement sealed. With a wave of the genie's smoky hand, the air between them shimmers and distorts, becoming thick and viscous like molten glass.

Wilhilm's eyes widen as an alien sensation washes over him. It feels as if his very essence is being drawn out, unraveled thread by thread. He feels an intense lightness, a sensation of expansion. The walls of the cell, the cold floor beneath him, all of it blurs and loses substance. At the same time, a tremendous power bubbles up from deep within him, as if he is suddenly connected to the vast expanse of the universe. It's an entirely different feeling from the hive mind but equally exhilarating and terrifying all at once.

Simultaneously, the swirling form of the genie condenses, becoming denser. It is like watching storm clouds gather and solidify. From this dense smoke, limbs form, fingers stretch out, and slowly facial features appear. Sharp eyes, a prominent nose, and an unsure mouth. Soon, a man stands where the genie once was, draped in a loose-fitting robe of brilliant azure.

Wilhilm, now a being of pure ethereal energy, floats above the ground, casting a radiant glow. He tries to speak, but his voice is like a distant echo, reverberating through space and time. The sensation of omnipotence clashes with an inexplicable feeling of confinement. He is both boundless and trapped, powerful yet restrained by the confines of his new existence.

Meanwhile, the genie, now human, looks down at his hands, turning them over, flexing his fingers. He touches his face, feeling the contours of skin and bone. A deep rumbling emerges from his belly. He looks up at Wilhilm with confusion. "What is that? Is this body faulty?"

"It's hunger," Wilhilm's echoing voice responds.

"Hunger?" the former genie murmurs. He tries to

remember human experiences. ”I... I crave something. Something specific.”

Wilhilm, despite his new ethereal form, chuckles. “Ah, that would be the desire for food. Something savory, perhaps?”

“Cheese,” the genie-turned-man whispers almost reverently, his eyes alight with newfound excitement. “I want cheese.”

The former genie turns the door into a wall of gentle rain and leaves the prison cell. Wilhilm is impressed how easy magic comes to the genie, even in a completely new form. A Transmutation spell of that level, just with a whisk of a hand, *wow*.

Wilhilm looks down at his hands, now transformed. He has genie power. More than he ever wanted. But the best thing is he would not have to use it until someone found him. The world would be safe. Hasan’s plan spoiled. Wilhilm would be unavailable.

Doubt creeps into his thoughts. What if King Hasan found the lamp and would wish for his help? Would he need to oblige? Would he oblige, would he do what King Hasan needed? Damn. He should have given this much more thought.

Suddenly, he feels a gentle pull. It’s an unfamiliar feeling, starting at his feet and extending all the way to his head. He looks around and realizes, how his body flows back into the lamp.

What is this? Stop it!

Derek. His demon is still with him.

“This magic is not for you,” Wilhilm says.

But it calls out to me. It’s alluring. I like its... scent. It’s old, it’s powerful. And yet, it repels me, burns me if I go near it.

Wilhilm focuses to subdue the demon in his mind, and just like that, Derek disappears into some dark corner.

That was easy. Almost too easy.

The pull persists until Wilhilm is in the lamp. Now, he truly is removed from the outside world.

He just had to hope nobody would rub the lamp and let him out.

CHAPTER 69

WHERE THE STREETS HAVE NO NAME

Dakaria stands aghast in her own cell, watching as the door to Wilhilm's transforms into a cascading wall of gentle rain. The droplets glisten and create an entrancing display of refracted rainbows. She meets the Rouge's glance and he looks just as hopeful as she feels. Somehow Wilhilm's going to get them out of this.

A stranger—A wizard?— steps through the waterfall. He emerges without a hair out of place.

The Rogue's mouth widens with surprise. "How did he do that? And who is it?" He even forgets to continue his quarrel with Mormak about an old piece of cheese they've found on the floor.

"What's going on? Let me see!" says Mormak.

The stout Dwarf, his knuckles dusted with a fine layer of grime, approaches the cell door with measured determination. His weathered fingers reach out and clamped onto the cold, iron bars of the small window in the door. Through this narrow barred opening, faint torchlight from the corridor outside cast long, flickering shadows into the darkened cell.

Leaning in, he presses his bushy, ginger beard against the bars, his squinting eyes peering through the gap. His brow furrows deeply as he scrutinizes the dimly lit corridor beyond. Stroking his thick beard thoughtfully, Mormak says, “A door of pouring ale, that would certainly be the most useful spell ever composed.”

The strange wizard pauses, sensing their gaze, and addresses them. “Do you have cheese? I think I smell cheese.”

“Hungry, are ye?” Mormak asks through the door. He obviously looks around and disappears for a moment, before he returns with a small, moldy chunk of cheese. “I think I have what you want.”

“Give it to me!”

“I think I can arrange that. Can you do me a little favor in return?”

“What is it you want?”

“We have this little door problem here and you did wonderful work on the other door. But could you make it ale instead of water?”

“That’s all you want?”

“For this door, and for my two friends who have the same door problem. And in return, I’ll give you the cheese.”

The wizard’s face lights up, his craving evident. “Cheese? You do know how to persuade a man.”

“Do I know you?” Gadisa asks. “I feel like I know you.”

“You do look familiar somehow,” Dakaria says.

Mormak hands the treasured, moldy cheese over to the mysterious man. Then he holds his breath. How will he react? The wizard takes his time, smells the cheese. Eventually, he accepts the cheese with a gleeful grin.

“You've got yourself a deal, stout one,” he declares, taking a tentative bite and savoring the flavor with a contented sigh.

Mormak just winks, patting his now empty pocket. “A fair deal for a fair service!”

The man doesn’t reply but in moments the solid cell doors undergo the same mesmerizing transformation and become curtains of shimmering rain. The trio hesitate for just a moment to marvel at the spectacle, then Gadisa and Dakaria step through the watery barriers with ease.

Mormak steps through. Then tastes his lips. "Ale?!" he exclaims, eyes gleaming with delight. He steps back into the rain, head back and mouth open, savoring the rain.

The Dwarf gulps with gusto, the liquid gold spilling over his beard and down the front of his armor. His cheeks flush with joy as he revels in his bounty.

Dakaria, watching in bemusement, remarks, “Don’t take too much time. It will soon turn back into a normal door, and that’s definitely not the moment when you want to stand there.”

Gadisa rolls his eyes. “It's all fun and games until someone drowns in booze, or is halved by a door.”

When Mormak sings a tavern song off-key, Dakaria decides that’s her cue. She gestures toward Gadisa. “Take him, or we’ll lose him.”

With a swift motion, Gadisa grabs Mormak by the collar, pulling him away from the ale-rain. “Alright, that's enough for you!” he declares.

Mormak sputters, wiping ale from his beard and shooting Gadisa a look of indignation. “You can't interrupt a dwarf in the middle of his drink!” he protests. He pushes the Rogue off and turns back to his ale and bumps his nose on the wood and iron prison door that suddenly re-materialized.

"There you are," Dakaria says. "Would have gone right through you."

"Dead from drinking beer, it's a soothing thought."

"Where's Wilhilm? Why didn't he come out?" Gadisa asks.

Dakaria looks through the barred window. "He's not there. It's empty," she says.

"Can't be. They threw him into the cell just like us," Mormak says.

"Open it," Dakaria says to Gadisa.

"Me? Why me?"

"You're the Rogue. Isn't that what you do?"

"Oh. Right. But I couldn't get ours open. Hurt my shoulder."

"That's different. They expect you to break the door from the other side. Nobody expects you to break into a cell."

Gadisa crouches down, his hands moving with precision. One tool, a delicate silver pick, slips into the keyhole like a whisper. With practiced patience, the begins to manipulate the tumblers inside, his ears finely attuned to the subtle clicks and shifts of the lock.

As seconds turned into minutes, the tension in the air grow, but Gadisa remains focused. Beads of sweat glisten on his forehead. Finally, he sighs, sits up and throws himself with force against the door. With a crack, the lock loosens. Again, Gadisa throws himself against the door. The wood splinters and the door swings open.

"There you are. See, I got skills," Gadisa says.

Dakaria steps into Wilhilm's cell. The cell is mostly barren, save for his small pouch where he hides his belongings. A glint catches Gadisa's eye. It's the lamp, the one Uvhorz sought to return. Its surface shimmers even in the dim torchlight of the dungeon.

Gadisa kneels to pick it up.

"Do you think he... used it?" Dakaria says. She touches the lamp. Its weight and temperature feel odd, like it contains a living entity, much heavier than previously. But more curious than that is the feeling of residual magic clinging to it.

Gadisa turns to Dakaria, holding up the lamp. "This is the same lamp that that mutineer lot tried to snatch." He passes it around.

Dakaria squints, peering closely at the lamp. "Yes, as though a great power has recently been released... or contained."

Mormak, still slightly tipsy from his ale shower, belches loudly. "Ya know, I've been thinking. Didn't the wizard look kinda familiar, don't ya think?"

Gadisa's brow furrows. "You mean because that stranger's face looked exactly like that of the evil genie?"

"What if, just what if, they pulled a switcheroo? Genie becomes the wizard, wizard becomes the genie," Mormak says.

"You mean, the genie tricked the wizard, and now Wilhilm is trapped in the lamp?" Gadisa asks.

Dakaria's eyes widen in realization. "That would explain the strange behavior of that wizard... the hunger, the odd craving for cheese. Being trapped in a lamp for centuries might do something to you."

Gadisa, slowly piecing things together, clutches the lamp tighter. "So, you're saying Wilhilm is inside this?" He shakes the lamp slightly, expecting some response, but none comes. "Hello? Anyone in there? Anyone at home?"

Mormak nods solemnly. "It would make sense."

"Poor Wilhilm," Gadisa says, head down. "He never had a chance to give me all of his treasure."

"Why would he release that genie, knowing it would trap him?" Mormak asks nobody in particular. "He's the one that knew how dangerous the genie was from the beginning."

Dakaria shakes her head. "I don't know. Maybe he underestimated it."

"Do you think he's evil? I mean, he traded places with an evil genie. And he has a demon. He might be double evil now," Mormak says.

"We should be careful," Dakaria replies.

"All that treasure. Gone." Gadisa rubs his nose and sniffs.

CHAPTER 70

THREE WISHES

Curved walls of ethereal matter wrap the space like a womb around a babe. Wilhilm sniffs. It smells sweet inside. Rich silks and soft velvet pillows decorate the couch and the bed, and the lighting is warm like at a beach bath at sunset. Hookahs stand ready next to hand-blown stained-glass bottles filled with endless liqueurs and a mahogany chabudai adorned with diamonds that springs forth any food one may wish.

Wilhilm feels disoriented. He looks at his silken clothing, unsure how he got dressed in them. As if from nothing, an oval mirror appears, allowing him to see himself from head to toe. The garb is definitely Zal'qaran, but of a far older design. Something about the clothing is familiar, as if he'd seen it before. In a dream? A vision? A spell? Yes, a spell. But not one he wove. It was...

"The genie!" he says aloud. The memories come flooding back. Yes, this is the lamp, the prison that held a genie of immense power for centuries. There would be no escaping this extradimensional space.

He feels safe. For once in his life, there is no fear. The

place feels... reliable. Secure. Like strict rules keep everything in place.

Looking around at the food, wine, and hookahs, Wilhilm shrugs, "Meh, could be worse." He eats a grape from the table and watches another form in its place. A sip of wine from a glass becomes a gulp and then becomes a chug, but the glass never empties. "Yup, could be much, much worse."

Poking around the space, the wizard-turned-genie finds an eight-sided prism. He inspects its crystal form, the markings on each facet, the edges so perfect that it looks formed from a single piece. What the object does, he cannot be sure. A spell would answer that question, but Wilhilm cannot cast his own spells anymore. He cannot not use genie magic unless called out of the lamp. All that remains is some Divination.

How does he know this?

Shreds of knowledge that is not his seem to drift through his mind. The genie magic that courses through him grants insights beyond the mundane, revealing truths hidden to mortal eyes. Wilhilm focuses on King Hasan. What would his phylactery be? Where did he hide it?

Perhaps in that ancient tree that was mentioned in the inscriptions when they entered Ishmaara?

Just a moment later he can see what Hasan's phylactery is.

His senses wander outside and he watches a small mouse scurrying in the shadows. Seemingly inconspicuous, but with his enhanced vision, Wilhilm recognizes the subtle glow that emanates from the creature. The aura it carries is unmistakably that of Hasan's phylactery.

Memories flood back—glimpses of the mouse at Seraphina's side, darting beneath her robes, peering out from her collar. How had he never made the connection before? The tiny creature had been there, hiding in plain sight, every time she was around.

A pang of regret courses through him. Had he known, had he seen what was right before him, and if he had, could he have acted? Could he have ended Hasan's reign of terror sooner? Alongside the regret is a burning determination. The knowledge now in his possession could be the key to finally defeating the Lich King.

At that moment, the prism glows bright, so bright in fact that it makes everything else impossible to see. Wilhilm closes his eyes, and when he opens them, finds that he is floating in the air above a large fleshy wall with giant tubes running in and out of it. Giant drops of water trickle down its surface and patches of soot cling to it like a moss.

"How revolting," he says to himself.

A loud scream, followed by two more startles him.

The flesh wall is actually the stomach of a giant version of Gadisa holding a giant version of the lamp, sitting next to a giant version of Mormak and Dakaria. These massive forms of his friends stare back at him with mouths wide.

"What is that?!" Mormak cries out, pointing at Wilhilm.

"Guys? How did you get so big?" the wizard asks.

"How did you get so small? And where's the lower part of your body?" Mormak retorts.

Wilhilm looks down. His torso is still intact, though his skin has turned violet, while the rest of his body is swirling mist. He looks up. They're still in the dungeon. He smacks himself in the head. "I haven't figured out this genie thing quite yet."

Dakaria bobs her head. "Decent try. Just seems that the

genie is quite a powerful wizard now. I feel like that is going to be a problem."

"He didn't kill us instantaneously and enslave the whole city yet," Mormak adds. "Right now, he's more interested in cheese."

"Wilhilm," Dakaria asks, "What will you do?"

"The question is more likely what *you* are going to do. I can't do much anymore. It's better when I stay in the lamp. But I know where Hasan hides his phylactery."

"Not do much?" Gadisa says. "But you're a genie now!"

Wilhilm sees greed in his eyes, and the sight unsettles him so much, he instinctively retracts his hands from the prism and suddenly finds himself back in the lamp.

Interesting.

He seems to have been in two places at once. In the lamp and outside. Did he really go outside, or did he only appear outside? A kind of astral projection? There was so much to learn here.

~

"Let me have the lamp," Dakaria says to Gadisa.

"No!" he pulls it back. "It's my treasure! And it holds the ghost of my friend Wilhilm!"

"He's not a ghost, you big dummy! He's a genie now who can grant wishes."

"Then I will ask for the wishes!" Gadisa hugs the lamp. "I always liked him."

Mormak holds Dakaria back, "Just let him do it or we're going to become three pieces of well-done steak."

"How many wishes does one get? Seven?" Gadisa asks hopefully.

"Three. Everyone knows that. Three per person,"

Mormak says with authority. He holds four fingers up to underline his point, but Dakaria seems to be the only one noticing.

Gadisa rubs the lamp. He points at the tubes connecting his chest and his back and says, "I wish my hoses were stronger so that they won't get cut and I don't have to worry about deflating."

"No," Wilhilm protests, from the mouth of the lamp. "This is stupid! You need a plan to defeat King Hasan. And that Mummy King."

In a puff of magic, the hoses on Gadisa's body develop steel bands through them and the connectors become armored.

"Damn it," Wilhilm curses. "Don't waste my magic on stupid stuff!"

"Hey! This is not about you!" Dakaria admonishes Gadisa.

"Fine." Gadisa rubs the lamp again and says, "Since I miss my friend Wilhilm so much... I wish for all his treasure so that I can remember him better."

CHAPTER 71

DO YOU BELIEVE IN MAGIC

The sensation that comes with fulfillment of Gadia's wish is overwhelming. Wilhilm feels the power coursing through him, and with every beat of his heart, his form swells and he feels like he's pulled out of the lamp and into the dungeon. The walls of Ishmaara begin to feel like they're closing in, but it's not them, it's him. Wilhilm is growing, expanding, taking up more and more space.

"I think he's angry," Mormak says. "He looks angry to me."

Wilhilm's voice, once smooth and amicable, now rumbles with an otherworldly resonance. "You dare defy me?!" his genie form thunders, echoing through the cavernous dungeon. With each word, he expands. His head nearly touches the vaulted ceiling and his eyes glow an electric blue, casting eerie shadows around the chamber. Vast billowing arms extend, almost touching the walls on either side, and the whirl of his tail seemed like a tornado, swirling with intense energy.

Gadisa stumbles backwards, his bravado replaced with

fear. “Fine,” Gadisa says. “No need to get all upset. I retract my wish.”

“Just think about it,” Dakaria says. “You can help us. You have genie magic now. A unique kind of magic.”

“There’s no good magic,” Wilhilm says. “All kinds of magic end in desperation.”

“Mine doesn’t,” Dakaria says. “But genie magic has the most rules of any magic. And it’s temporary. Once the three wishes are up, they’re up.”

Wilhilm thinks about it. There’s some truth to Dakaria’s words. Indeed, genie magic does have a lot of rules. And a lot of mystery. He doesn’t quite understand where it comes from. Why it’s so powerful. And why those rules stay in place, what kind of power keeps them in place.

But no. There was no excuse to get back into magic.

“You don’t have to do much,” Dakaria says. “Just a little help for your friends.”

Wilhilm looks at his companions and realizes they need him. Even though he told them what the phylactery was, he knows they’ll find a way to screw it up. That was just how it is. They need him.

“I tell you what to wish for!” Wilhilm booms. Then stops for a moment. He resumes, his voice slightly lowered in thought. “No, wait, that doesn’t work in genie magic. I will tell Mormak what to wish for, and Gadisa, you just happen to overhear it, but if you wish for something, it’s your own free will. So, you better want exactly what I tell Mormak he wants. Do you understand?”

Gadisa nods. “I overhear wishes and I do something.”

“Good enough, I guess. Okay, now that that’s out of the way, listen carefully, Mormak. You just wish that you feel exactly where the mouse is that Hasan used to store away his phylactery. That way you will easily find it.”

"Me? Wasting a wish on a mouse?" Mormak shakes his head.

"Not you, Gadisa," Wilhilm says.

"Me? Why would I waste a wish on a mouse?" Gadisa asks.

Wilhilm sighs. He should not do magic. It would be better. But he can't let those three screw it up. He will have to give just a little more. Just enough so he could end this.

"Wouldn't it be a great idea, generally speaking, to have a wish like granting the genie the full extent of his magical powers, directed by his own free will, to achieve the following—first, stop the EyeStone network and those actively working to exploit it in a way that will bring imbalance to the current order of things; secondly, to close all rifts to the demon dimension that have been ripped open in the process in a safe and permanent manner. Oh, yes, and do all of that before the sun sets again, because without the time limit, the wish would not be valid, can't be too broad."

"This is a long wish," Gadisa says. "Chocolate would be shorter."

"Gadisa!" Dakaria intervenes, and Wilhilm is glad that he's not the only one to take the situation seriously.

"Fine. I wish... I mean, of course, coming from my own free will, I wish for Wilhilm to be able to command his magical powers to full extent, directed by his own free will, limited to the following—first, stop the EyeStone network and those actively working to exploit it in a way that will bring imbalance to the current order of things; secondly, to close all rifts to the demon dimension that have been ripped open in the process in a safe and permanent manner, and do all of this until the sun sets again."

"Your wish is granted," Wilhilm says.

DEEP within the lost city of Ishmaara, in a bustling workshop adorned with gleaming contraptions and whirling gears, Dipple Nimble Retchbucket dangles from a rope to toil diligently on his mesmerizing installation. Rows upon rows of mirrors, meticulously arranged, stretch out in a dazzling display. Each mirror is carefully positioned to catch and reflect the essence of a single Echo Stone at its center. He carefully lowers himself to the next Echo Stone and adjusts it.

The test at Tiringar has worked. They succeeded in ripping open a portal but it continues to send ripples through the whole network which impacted other locations. Dipple has to adjust the whole network to make sure their ultimate plan will work.

Unfortunately, a big green brute had waltzed in and wreaked some havoc, displacing mirrors, breaking a few of them. Fortunately, this creature can't disturb them now.

"A little more to the left," Albert the Mouse says. "Perfect." Albert the Mouse has done a lot of traveling between Tiringar and Ishmaara the last couple of weeks. More traveling than he did in his whole life up to that point.

"How do you know all this?" Dipple asks. "I have to write pages of calculations to get these measurements exactly right. You just seem to know."

"You have to smell the cheese," Albert says.

Dipple chuckles. "Right," he says. "Smell the cheese."

The gnome, diligently engrossed in their intricate installation, suddenly pauses, a perplexed expression crossing his face. Amidst the clinking of tools and the hum of machinery, an unmistakable scent wafts through the air —the distinct aroma of cheese.

"Demon energy, smells like cheese," Albert the Mouse says. "Once you know it, you can't unsmell it."

As the final mirror finds its place, a wave of anticipation fills the air. The installation, a feat of ingenious craftsmanship, allows the surface of one Echo Stone to be multiplied and mirrored across a vast array of others.

This will be the last installation they will ever do. Tiringar was only a small test compared to this installation. This will open up a rift so wide it will connect dimensions, extinguish life as it is known and create something new.

Something new and powerful. All the protection they could ever need.

With a flick of a switch, the mirrors come alive again, capturing the radiant energy of the central Echo Stone and distributing it among its mirrored counterparts. A wondrous cascade of light and magic ensues, as the reflections bounce and refract, creating an intricate web of interconnected energy.

As the room fills with the enchanting glow, the gnome gazes upon their creation with a mixture of pride and wonder. He has harnessed the power of mirrors and Echo Stones to create a mesmerizing network, allowing messages, thoughts, and magic to traverse through a myriad of reflective surfaces.

"Nice," Albert the Mouse says.

CHAPTER 72

MAN IN THE MIRROR

Wilhilm floats toward the heart of the EyeStone network, the mirror room. He feels like he's starting to get a grip on his genie body and this bizarre way of floating.

Delicate light from meticulously arranged mirrors illuminate thousands of Echo Stones, each whispering its own little tale. It's a symphony of silent voices, and the brilliance of the chamber is near overwhelming.

Albert the Mouse scuttles about in a corner, adjusting a mirror here and there, while the gnome, Dipple Nimble Retchbucket, scribbles some notes onto a piece of parchment, muttering to himself about angles and refractions.

Wilhilm takes a moment to survey the room, trying to understand the sheer complexity of its workings.

"Stop!" comes a voice from the corridor. Lich King Hasan enters. He managed to dislodge himself from the obelisk. His form, though skeletal, radiates an eerie aura, causing the very air to feel heavy and oppressive.

When he sees Wilhilm, for a fleeting moment, the unflappable confidence of the Lich King falters, replaced by a flicker of uncertainty. Wilhilm is surprised that anything unsettles the Lich, but especially that *his* appearance could unsettle the Lich.

King Hasan recoils slightly. His undead visage, usually an impassive mask, betrays a hint of perturbation. The certainty with which he had approached the ritual gives way to a guarded wariness. But the Lich quickly regains his composure, even when the initial shock lingers.

Hasan's bony fingers twitch, and with a flick, he sends forth tendrils of dark energy that slither through the air like a nest of particularly malevolent eels, each one snapping and hissing as it zeroes in on Wilhilm's ethereal form. These aren't your run-of-the-mill magical tendrils; these are the twisted, writhing threads of necromancy itself, each one hungry for life and power, with an appetite that would make a vampire look like a fussy eater.

Wilhilm tries to evade them, fearing they'd drag him down, kicking and screaming, into the cold, bureaucratic embrace of the undead.

As the tendrils close in, the ground beneath Wilhilm starts to tremble, and from its depths, a circle of ancient, ominous symbols begins to rise. They're shadowy silhouettes of long-forgotten hieroglyphs, each one flickering with an eerie, cold blue light.

This circle forms around Wilhilm, not merely trapping him but also sapping his strength, like a particularly persistent tax collector draining the last ounce of joy from his day. Each of these symbols is a tiny, insidious conduit for his power, working together to pull Wilhilm further away from the world of the living and closer to a place where he'd need a serious change of wardrobe and a newfound appreciation for the macabre.

Above, the dungeon's ceiling seems to collapse, but

instead of debris, a torrent of spectral souls descend. Spirits of those the Lich King has conquered over the eons, now enslaved to his will! They wail and scream, creating a roar that disrupts Wilhilm's focus. Each spirit attempts to merge with Wilhilm, to cloud his essence and dilute his power every time they sweep through him. One after the other, he has to focus to divert them, unable to focus on Hasan himself.

Amidst this onslaught, Hasan's hollow eye sockets gleam with wicked delight. He begins an incantation in the old language of the dragons. The words resonate with power, and the very fabric of reality seems to tremble. The goal is clear: to bind Wilhilm, to make the genie subservient, turning him into nothing more than a tool for Hasan's dark ambitions.

~

EMERGING FROM THE SHADOWS, the mummy king Kadoc'Ru appears in the mirror room, wrapped in ancient linens—part crypt white, part bone white—his every step leaving a trail of golden sand. Behind him, half a dozen mummies follow, their steps synchronized, heads lolling to one side in eerie unison. The very essence of death accompanies them and the air in the room grows cold.

Dakaria emerges from a small pathway, Mormak and Gadisa just behind her. She senses the dark aura and the imminent threat, stands her ground, eyes narrowing in determination. As Kadoc'Ru gestures forward, two of the mummies launch towards her with a burst of speed.

With a swift incantation, the Druid's hands shimmer with green energy. From her fingertips sprout vines, thick and thorny, to snake rapidly across the floor. As the mummies rush forward, the vines wrap around their feet and yank them off balance, causing them to trip face-first.

Dakaria gestures with a flourish, and the ground beneath the mummies starts to behave in a way that would make any respectable patch of earth ashamed. It softens and ripples, like a pudding that's been left out in the sun too long, before giving way entirely, transforming into a treacherous pool of quicksand. The mummies, already tangled up in the vines like badly wrapped parcels, find themselves in an even stickier situation.

They writhe and squirm, but it's no use. The more they struggle, the faster they sink, their bandaged arms flailing in a futile attempt to gain traction on what was, just moments ago, solid ground. Their ancient, dusty moans fill the chamber, echoing off the walls in a sort of resigned, undead chorus. It's as if they're lamenting not just their current predicament, but also the sheer indignity of being bested by a bit of dirt and some overenthusiastic foliage.

Kadoc'Ru, enraged by the defeat of his guards, takes a step forward, but Dakaria is ready. Drawing from the power of water, she conjures a torrential downpour within the room. To any other adversary, this might be a mere inconvenience, but to mummies, water is a potent weapon. As the water soaks Kadoc'Ru's wrappings, they become heavy, dragging him down. The bindings, aged and brittle, start to come apart, revealing desiccated flesh beneath.

With the mummy king weakened and struggling, Dakaria summons a gust of powerful wind. The force not only pushes Kadoc'Ru off his feet but also scatters the countless mirrors, disrupting the intricate arrangement of the Echo Stones.

Three more mummies emerge from the darkness. Their lifeless, decrepit forms cast long shadows in the dim light.

Mormak braces himself. The Dwarf lowers his center of gravity, digging his boots deep into the sand beneath him. "Mummies again? How many mummies do they have here?" the Dwarf shouts.

His eyes flash with an unyielding fire. Those who know him well understand that beneath his jolly exterior lies the heart of a warrior, forged in the fires of countless battles.

The air around Mormak heats up, the scent of burning embers pervasive. His dual war axes, passed down through generations of his clan, begin to glow. The engravings on the blades emanate a red-orange hue, pulsating rhythmically as if they hold the heartbeats of all his forefathers.

Without warning, Mormak releases a guttural battle cry. He lunges forward, a blur of motion. The first mummy, caught off guard, tries to raise its arms in defense. But it's too late. With a precise swing, Mormak's axe severs its arm, embers sizzling as they cauterize the wound.

Spinning on his heel, Mormak faces the second mummy. As it lunges at him, the Dwarf ducks and rolls, coming up behind it. He uses the momentum to drive his other axe into its back, the fiery energy of the blade consuming the dry, ancient wraps. Quickly, it is ash.

Emerging from his cyclonic assault, Mormak stands victorious, his chest heaving from the adrenaline. His axes slowly dim as he regains control, their energy spent but their mission accomplished.

"The mouse," Wilhilm's voice booms from somewhere. "You have to hit the mouse."

CHAPTER 73

PAINT IT BLACK

Dark shadows coil around Wilhilm like particularly malevolent serpents, each tendril writhing with the kind of enthusiasm that suggests it's been waiting all day for just this moment. They slither and twist, eager to wrap themselves around his heart and mind, with the clear intention of squeezing until something important breaks.

Derek, it seems, has managed to slip past the usually impenetrable defenses of gene magic with all the subtlety of a door-to-door salesman who refuses to take 'no' for an answer. And now he's back, and judging by the ominous way the shadows are converging, he's not here for a friendly chat over tea.

Wilhilm feels his heart drop like a stone in a very deep, very dark well. A creeping sense of doom spreads through him as the horrifying hunch dawns: in his desperate bid to gain power, his transformation into a genie has inadvertently done the magical equivalent of leaving the front door wide open and putting up a sign that reads, 'Demons Welcome!'

As the demon resurfaces, Wilhilm feels its dark essence intertwine with his own, siphoning off the potent genie magic coursing through him. The sensation is both violating and draining, like a parasite greedily feasting on his very essence. His luminescent form flickers erratically.

Desperation grips Wilhilm. His mind races, searching for a way to expel the demon, to regain control before it's too late. He can only guess the catastrophic potential of a demon wielding genie magic—it's a combination that could wreak havoc on a scale unimaginable, certainly tipping the balance in King Hasan's favor.

For a brief, heart-stopping moment, it seems as if the demon will engulf Wilhilm.

Now it is time to take sides. We will take the right one.

But then, suddenly, Wilhilm chokes. A violent cough racks his body, and his eyes bulge in surprise. It's as if he's swallowed a bitter pill or taken a deep gulp of rancid water. He sputters, gasping for air. The color drains from his face.

It stinks.

"The genie magic is still not to your taste!" Wilhilm realizes with dawning comprehension. There's a clear incompatibility between the ethereal, wistful essence of the genie's power and the raw, chaotic malevolence of the demon's energy. When forced to mingle, the two magics create a visceral, nauseating reaction. It's like oil and water.

Wilhilm doubles over, a retching sound escapes his throat as though his very insides rebel against the demon's encroachment. The demon itself seems to recoil in pain and disgust, its dark tendrils retracting rapidly, its power diminishing.

Wilhilm can hear the demon's frustrated growl, the realization that this host isn't as easily conquered as it had hoped. The genie’s magic acts as a shield, an unexpected barrier that prevents the demon from gaining a foothold.

Staggering back, Wilhilm manages a weak smile. “Seems like my last wish,” he rasps, referring to the genie's gift, “came with some unintended side benefits.”

In the dimly lit chamber, Gadisa's silhouette barely registers. He’s always had a knack for blending in, even in the most conspicuous of settings. But now, as the mummies converge, he draws upon a trick he picked up during his brief, albeit intense, training sessions.

With a flourish, he unveils the Dragonteeth Dagger, its blade dancing with a dark energy that appears almost... alive. It casts an eerie glow, but it’s not the gleam that the mummies should be wary of. It's the Rogue holding it.

Most would think him inexperienced, perhaps even call him reckless given his limited training, but what Gadisa lacks in formal education he compensates for in raw talent and instinct. With a slight grin, he performs a step so fluid, so swift, that he blurs into the very shadows around him.

As mummies close in, a feeling of overconfidence radiates from them. They have fought countless adversaries, but none like Gadisa. Their perception of the world around them does not register shadows as threats. But that’s precisely where they’re mistaken.

Suddenly, the chamber, filled with the eerie groans of the undead, has a change in atmosphere. There’s a brief shimmer as Gadisa, moving like liquid darkness, emerges momentarily behind one mummy. With a swift strike, he touches the Dragonteeth Dagger to the shadow of the mummy and the magic of his artifact unfurls. Almost instantly, the material world reacts, the armor tearing just where his blade touched its ethereal counterpart.

The mummy freezes, sensing a chill it hasn't felt in millennia. Darkness doesn't just wrap around it, darkness seems to seep right through the linen. Its limbs feel heavy, its motions sluggish.

In the dimly lit, echoey corridors of the dungeon, Mormak chases after the mouse, charging after the tiny creature with the same fervor with which he'd chase a dragon. The mouse zigzags between Mormak's legs. Every time the Dwarf thinks he has it cornered, it finds an impossibly small hole or crack to dart into. He finally reaches out to the small creature when it runs up a wall and across the ceiling, causing Mormak to scratch his head in disbelief.

"Come back here, you sneaky little...!" Mormak's shouts and grunts echo through the dungeon. He slips on a wet patch, crashing into a pile of crates. From atop a nearby ledge, the mouse squeaks as if cheering its own cleverness.

Drawing one of his axes, Mormak measures out the mouse's path. But the mouse has other plans. It dashes up his leg and perches on his shoulder, giving him a little nose twitch before diving away.

Mormak spins in circles, dizzy from the mouse's antics. A glint in his eyes, he makes one final desperate lunge, swinging his axe. The mouse, caught off guard, is clipped by the axe's edge. It goes flying against the wall.

The mouse squeaks in pain, and the squeaks turn into otherworldly shrieks. Its tiny, quivering form grows still, and an eerie silence descends upon the chamber as everyone pauses their own battles to turn towards the strange sight. The mouse's fur, once sleek and unassuming, ripples and darkens, giving way to an inky blackness that seems to pull the very light from the room. Shadows emerge, twisting and coiling around it like tendrils of smoke. These shadows seem alive, writhing with a mind of their own, and they dance about the mouse with menacing grace.

Mormak can only watch in horror as the mouse's body expands and stretches. Bones crack and reform. The tiny squeaks morph into guttural roars. Its eyes, once beady and innocent, now glow with a malevolent fire, piercing through the surrounding darkness.

The inky black gives way to scaled, armored skin, its once small limbs elongate and sharpen into deadly claws, and a maw filled with rows of jagged teeth emerges, dripping with an ominous, thick liquid.

It turns to snap at Mormak who brings down his axe on the head of the creature twice.

A brilliant crimson seam cracks the atmosphere. A ravenous maw of swirling red energy emerges. This rift pulsates, exuding a raw power that tugs at everything in its vicinity. Even as the transformed mouse-monster roars in defiance, the rift's pull becomes inescapable. Desperation is evident in the creature's glowing eyes as it futilely claws and lashes out, attempting to anchor itself. But its attempts are in vain.

With a force that shakes the very foundations of the dungeon, the rift gulps down the creature. The monster's harrowing cries echo, growing more distant and distorted, until they're muffled completely by the swallowing void. And then, as abruptly as it appeared, the rift snaps shut, leaving behind an empty space and a lingering scarlet afterglow.

CHAPTER 74
DEAD MAN'S PARTY

Hasan's power manifests like a dark storm cloud. A rising trumpet-like call pierces the darkness, sharp and jarring, much like the impassioned bellow of an elephant in heat. The cry blends sheer strength with a haunting, almost mournful tone.

Wilhilm was initially uncertain how to harness his genie nature but now feels it pulsating within him—an infinite reservoir of arcane energy that's been waiting to be tapped. He closes his eyes and takes a deep breath, allowing himself to be enveloped by the mystical power of his new form.

Deep in one corner of his mind, he feels his old anguish linger: a fear of leaning into the magic. But around him, the world begins to shift and ripple. He needs to go through with it, or he sacrifices the lives of his friends.

A radiant azure aura blooms around Wilhilm, shimmering with the sort of luminous intensity that suggests he might accidentally become the world's most magical light bulb. Intricate golden patterns begin to weave themselves across his skin, spiraling and curling like they're having a particularly artistic day.

He raises his hands and from his fingertips a cascade of glowing wish spells spills forth. Every single one tailored specifically to counteract Hasan's magic. A gleaming barrier forms, deflecting the dark bolts of energy Hasan hurls towards him. Where once his magic was a trickle, it's now a roaring river.

He uses a wish for the air to thicken, making it hard for Hasan to draw breath. With another thought, he turns the ground beneath Hasan into a quagmire, restricting his movement. He even summons illusory doubles of himself, leaving Hasan confused and overwhelmed.

But Wilhilm's masterstroke comes when he reaches into the very essence of Hasan's spells. With a sweep of his arm, he wishes for their reversal. Every curse, every hex that Hasan had placed on the battlefield is now turned against him.

Hasan, blindsided and drained, finds himself on the backfoot. The Lich King's once intimidating presence is now diminished, his spells backfiring or dissipating into thin air.

In that moment, Wilhilm feels the sudden loss of Hasan's phylactery. Mormak cries out somewhere in triumph. And then the realization hits him, like a slightly delayed thunderclap after a particularly bright bolt of lightning. The Lich King is vulnerable now. Vulnerable! The word rolls around in his mind like a rare, precious gem, gleaming with possibilities.

The thought brings a crooked smile to his lips. No more regenerating, no more rising from the grave like an undead jack-in-the-box. This time, it's for good.

Wilhilm, now fully empowered as a gigantic genie,

looks down at Hasan, a mix of pity and determination in his eyes, then snaps his fingers. "You're there, now you're gone," he says. Hassan dissipates into a black cloud, before he can even cry out. For a moment, Wilhilm feels saddened to see Hasan go just like that. Then again, it's replaced by an oddly satisfying feeling to unmake him just like that, after all of those years that Hasan has tricked and tormented him.

With a playful smirk, he conjures a miniature sandstorm within the palm of his hand. It's not the swirling, chaotic tempests one would expect of the desert but a delicate waltz of minute sand grains, each shimmering with a unique hue. The sands of time, some might say.

With a graceful motion, he releases the sands into the room. As each grain collides with a mirror, they stick to the surface, becoming a part of the glass. The room gradually darkens, the once gleaming mirrors now tainted with colorful specks of time.

Dipple watches in horror as the sands transform into an hourglass. Time itself seems to warp and twist in the room, and as each grain falls, a mirror cracks, its corresponding Echo Stone turning mute somewhere in the world.

Surveying his work and Dipple's appalled demeanor, Wilhilm recognizes him. It's the same gnome that sweet talked him into joining the EyeStone network in the woods. The one he caught with his golem. Or thought he caught. Probably it was a ruse from the very beginning. Perhaps the gnome even jumped into the golem to trick him. Hasan anticipated every move. Or almost every move.

But it's over. In a matter of moments, the room is filled with shattered glass and silenced stones. The EyeStone network is no more.

In this whirlwind of chaos, Gadisa's grip on the genie

lamp weakens. An unexpected blow from a mummy warrior forces the lamp to slip from his grasp, sending it spiraling through the air. Panic grips Gadisa as he watches the precious artifact begin its descent.

He darts desperately forward, his focus solely on the golden artifact. But fate has other plans. Just as he's about to reach it, an errant spell sends the lamp crashing into a cluster of exploding Echo Stones.

They're volatile, pulsating with the trapped essence of Ulthril. The moment the lamp makes contact, a blinding flash of light fills the room. The subsequent explosion sends shockwaves throughout the chamber, causing both allies and foes to stumble and shield their eyes.

When the dust settles and vision returns, a devastating sight meets Gadisa's eyes. Where the lamp once was, now lay shattered remnants, twisted metal warped from the explosion. The Ulthril from the Echo Stones, with its raw, untamed energy, has torn through the lamp's magic, rendering it beyond repair. The only thing tying Wilhilm to this realm is now broken.

There is a long fart.

"Sorry," Gadisa murmurs.

CHAPTER 75

SMOOTH CRIMINAL

The ebb and flow of magical currents, once as confounding to Wilhilm as a cryptic crossword in an ancient, forgotten language, now feels as natural as breathing—if breathing involved tapping into the very essence of the universe and occasionally turning mummies into harmless piles of dust. As he fires off wish spells with the casual precision of someone flicking crumbs off a table, the endless stream of bandaged menaces converging on him barely registers as more than a mild inconvenience.

He's not just casting spells anymore. No, that would be too simple. He's feeling them, like a musician who's finally realized that the piano keys aren't just black and white but a doorway to something far grander. Each spell pulses with the rhythm of the primordial, the ancient heartbeat of magic itself, and Wilhilm is the conductor, shaping it with his will as if he's been doing it all his life.

Then, a stillness envelops Wilhilm. It's not a stillness from the outside world, but rather an internal realization, like the sinking feeling one gets when a precious item is lost. He scans the battlefield and his gaze settles on the shattered remnants of the once-magnificent lamp. Even from a distance, the extent of its damage is clear. The pieces lays scattered and fragmented, like shattered dreams upon the cold, unforgiving ground.

A deep chill seeps into Wilhilm's heart, its icy grip squeezing tighter and tighter. The reality of the situation dawns upon him: with the lamp's destruction, the tether binding him to this realm is severed. The lamp was not just a prison or home, but his anchor, the very essence of his being. And without it, he will fade, becoming a wisp of memory lost to the sands of time. He will cease to exist.

With sorrow-laden eyes, he turns to his companions. "The lamp... it's gone," he murmurs, the weight of his words hanging heavy in the air. "Without it, I cannot sustain my form in this realm."

Dakaria's eyes widen in horror. Her usually composed face contorts in anguish. Gadisa stumbles a step back, the weight of the revelation almost knocking the wind out of him. Mormak stands as though rooted to the ground, his grip on his war axes slackening. Their faces mirror a shared sentiment: despair.

"But... there must be a way," Dakaria stammers, her voice trembling. "There has to be something we can do."

Mormak chokes back tears, his voice breaking, "We won't let you go, Wilhilm. Not without a good-bye ale, that is."

Wilhilm, despite his impending doom, manages a wistful smile. "I've cherished every moment with you all. But this... this is where my journey ends." The gravity of his predicament hangs in the air, thick with grief.

Amidst the quiet despair that's settled over the group like an unwanted fog—thick, damp, and entirely too persistent—a familiar yet decidedly different presence steps into the room. It's the original genie, though you'd hardly recognize him now, what with the whole being human thing.

Gone are the eyes that once held the infinite span of eternity; now they're filled with something far more mundane, though no less dangerous—a crafty, almost mischievous sparkle that suggests he's seen far too much and is perfectly happy to see a bit more.

He sweeps his gaze across the room, taking in the destruction with the practiced eye of someone who knows exactly how much trouble has been caused and is possibly a little bit impressed by it. Then, with the kind of low, appreciative whistle that one might reserve for a particularly well-executed bit of chaos, he lets everyone know that yes, things are bad.

"By the cosmic stars, Wilhilm!" he exclaims, clapping slowly, every strike resounding in the tense silence. "Now, that's what I call a proper display of raw, genie magic! I daresay, even in my millennia of existence, I've seldom seen such mastery. Well done!"

Wilhilm can't help but raise an eyebrow. This wasn't the reaction he expected.

The genie-turned-wizard grins, showcasing a wicked delight. "You've been a phenomenal genie, Wilhilm. Truly. And you know what the best part is?" He leans in, as if sharing a secret, "I'm absolutely thrilled it's you fading away and not me."

Wilhilm's eyes narrow.

Sensing the change in mood, the former genie waves his hand dismissively, "Oh, don't take it personally. It's just business. You see, I have... ambitions." A sly smile spreads across his face. "There are realms to conquer, empires to build. Now that I've got my human hands on magic I can actually use to benefit myself, the world is but clay in the hands of a master sculptor."

Wilhilm grits his teeth, fury and disbelief dancing in his gaze. The sheer audacity and callousness of the man's confession hangs in the air, stoking the embers of a battle that's yet to come.

"I guess there's no way to persuade you to trade places?" Wilhilm asks.

"That's the fun part," the genie says. "As the switch requires me to do it voluntarily, you can't trick or force me. There's no way you can come out of this alive. Good-bye."

Wilhilm's mind races. With genie magic, he knows there's always a backdoor. Always a way out. Always a trick. He just has to think of one. And fast. He feels his grip on the world around him weakening. The genie is right. No way of forcing him... except... except if Wilhilm would not be a genie and there would be a lamp present.

"Can't I just wish you to turn back into a human?" Gadisa asks. "Or wish the lamp repairs itself?"

"That's not how genie magic works," Wilhilm says. "You can't change my nature. And you can't use a genie's magic to switch places. It has to be done willingly."

"There must be something we can wish for," Dakaria says.

Wilhilm replays the conversation. There *is* something. A short moment where he almost had it it. A hint. Something. He has to find it again.

"If you weren't a genie and we would have a lamp, this would be much easier," Gadisa says.

Right. There it is.

"Mormak, quick, listen! Someone could wish for me to turn into a genie vessel."

“Someone? Who?” Mormak asks suspiciously. “O yes, him! Gadisa, you’ve heard the man.”

“What... why... why would I do that?” Gadisa asks. “You just said I can’t change your nature.”

“This is the exception because within genie magic, I would only adjust my nature. But wish whatever your heart tells you to wish,” Wilhilm says, then turns to Mormak. “Make him wish it, exactly like that,” he commands.

Gadisa sighs. “A genie vessel? Why? What would this achieve...”

Then suddenly realization dawns on the former-genie-now-wizard’s face. “Damn me. It means, you would not be a genie anymore. The spell would revert back, making me...” The man doesn’t finish the sentence.

Instead he rapidly sends a fireball at Gadisa.

CHAPTER 76
GO YOUR OWN WAY

"I wish for Wilhilm to become a genie vessel," Gadisa says. At the same time, the heat of fireball the genie hurled toward him, fills the room. Wilhilm wants to stop it, but no wish comes forward. Right. They didn't include anything about defending the group from the original genie in the initial wish

Then, suddenly, the fireball dissipates, just before it can hit Gadisa.

"Got it," Dakaria confirms, her hands up in the air and ready to defend.

Wilhilm waits for Gadisa's wish to have any effect. At first, nothing more happens. Then, the genie magic that surged like a roaring river through Wilhilm's veins wanes like a receding tide.

Each heartbeat is pronounced, the vibrant thrum of cosmic power growing fainter. The air around him seems to grow colder, the warmth of the genie's flame that once enveloped him, now slowly extinguishing. Colors lose their vibrancy, sounds their resonance, and sensations their intensity.

His limbs feel heavier, the buoyancy and levity of genie existence making way for a dense corporeal sensation. Every breath becomes more deliberate, every blink a conscious effort. There's a momentary dizziness, a vertigo as if the universe itself is spinning away from him.

Yet amidst this profound transformation, there's also a bitter clarity. The fleeting taste of ultimate power, the heady rush of bending reality to his whims, is replaced by a raw vulnerability, a fragility of mortal existence. It's humbling, grounding, and terrifying all at once.

Wilhilm is not just losing magic. He's losing a part of himself, a chapter of his life that, though brief, was transformative. The only time he could use magic without fear.

The original genie stands at the epicenter of the room, sensing the remnants of the magic that once made him formidable. He struggles, trying to move, probably trying to run away. But his human form begins to shudder, each tremor more potent than the last. Beads of perspiration form on his brow and his eyes glow with an azure luminescence.

A swirling mist envelops the genie-turned-wizard. It weaves and twines around him.

His body starts to elongate, losing the definition of a human form. Fingers merge, the torso expands, and legs dissolve into a swirling tail of mist and vapor. The features of his face blur and then sharpen, returning to their once proud and ancient visage. His mortal attire vaporizes into the ether to be replaced by ornate, shifting patterns of gold and azure that dance upon his formless body.

With a deafening roar, the transformation culminates. The entity before them is no longer a man but a magnificent genie, ancient and awe-inspiring.

But this newfound form doesn't linger for long in the

material realm. Wilhilm is now a vessel of untapped potential and power. He releases a vortex of energy that circles the newly re-transformed genie. The genie struggles against the magnetic pull but is inexorably drawn closer and closer to Wilhilm.

The room is filled with a bright, blinding light. Through the radiance, the silhouette of the genie is visible, shrinking and contorting as it's drawn into Wilhilm, through his mouth, his ears, his nose. The roaring energy reaches its crescendo, then, as suddenly as it began, it stops. The light fades, revealing a changed scene: the original genie, now once again in his rightful form, has vanished, sealed safely within the depths of Wilhilm, the new genie vessel.

No, noooooo!

For years, Wilhilm has felt the weight of the demon inside him, like a vice on his heart, a darkness that threatened to swallow him whole. Now, as he stands amidst the surreal tableau of genie magic and otherworldly entities, something changes.

Wilhilm cannot host a genie and a demon at the same time. Their magics are incompatible. By taking in the genie, the magic inside of him now expels the demon.

"Quick, his soul," Dakaria urges Gadisa. "Wish it back!"

"His soul?" Gadisa echoes, his forehead in wrinkles.

"Just do it!"

"I wish for Wilhilm's soul to return to his body."

A cold sensation spreads from the center of Wilhilm's chest, moving outwards. Wilhilm looks down in amazement as tendrils of shadow slide across his skin like spilled ink on parchment. They converge, the shadows gathering and writhing in a dense, swirling mass before him. To Wilhilm's disbelief, the shadows shape a small creature—a squirrel, black as the darkest night. Its fur ripples with the ethereal quality of shadow, its eyes gleaming red.

He stares at the shadow squirrel, eyes wide. A million thoughts race through his mind. Is he truly free of it? Can it return? But overriding those concerns is a profound sense of lightness. The burden he knowingly carried for so long and then struggled against is gone, replaced with a newfound freedom he's not felt in years.

Then, a sudden warmth runs though his body as if something inside completely itself. Breathing deeply, Wilhilm marvels at the sensation of his own unencumbered soul, the simple joy of existing without the overshadowing presence of the demon.

His soul... his soul knits itself back together.

There are few things in the universe more capable of producing a truly exalted sense of joy in a wizard than the return of his long-lost soul. This is not the polite sort of joy one feels when discovering a forgotten biscuit at the bottom of a tin, nor is it the mild satisfaction that comes from finally remembering the name of that obscure spell that turns potatoes into highly judgmental toads. No, this is a joy that explodes from within like a fireworks display that's been crossbred with a volcano—uncontrollable, ecstatic, and just a little bit messy.

Wilhilm, upon feeling his soul snap back into place like the final piece of a jigsaw puzzle that had been missing for far too long, experiences a rush of pure, unadulterated euphoria. It's as if someone had turned on all the lights in his mind at once, flooding every shadowy corner with the warm glow of life itself. Colors seem brighter, sounds richer, and even the dusty old spellbooks on his shelf appear to give off a faint, welcoming hum, as if pleased to see him fully intact once more.

The squirrel tilts its head curiously, almost playfully. It weak and not fully formed. The demon will not be able to sustain itself for long.

Then Mormak's axe crashes down on it and cuts the time even shorter.

"This was the demon, right?" Mormak asks.

Wilhilm nods, unable to speak and still overwhelmed with the sensation of freedom.

"Just to be sure, you can't eat demon, right? I feel a bit hungry," Gadisa says.

CHAPTER 77

BORN TO RUN

Dust clouds billow and swirl around the city of Ishmaara. The ancient stone walls and structures groan and tremble like the city cries out in distress. With every passing second, the ground quakes more violently, marking the city's impending collapse downwards, again into the unforgiving sands.

Gadisa takes the lead. His instincts serve the group well as he navigates the rapidly deteriorating alleyways, shouting out warnings at falling rock. His silhouette darts in and out of shadows as he guides his companions.

Mormak clutches his war axes with a grip born of desperation. Their sturdy, well-worn handles are slick with sweat from his palms, but Mormak's grip is unwavering, his knuckles whitening with the effort.

With each violent shudder of the ground, Mormak uses the axes to steady himself. He plants them firmly into the cracking earth, their blades biting into stone and sand.

Mormak's breathing is heavy, a rhythmic grunt with each exertion, as he navigates the treacherous terrain.

Wilhilm is still adjusting to the loss of his genie magic

and new life as a vessel. His heightened senses detect the arcane energy that seeps from the city's foundations, urging him to quicken his pace. His wand lights their path, its glow flickering with the instability around them.

Dakaria follows right behind him as they try to find the path of least resistance through the trembling city.

As they dash through one of the grand halls of Ishmaara, a massive column starts to tip ominously above them. With a shout of warning from Gadisa, the group barely sidesteps its crushing descent. They feel the rush of air and debris as it smashes into the ground behind them.

The hall leads to a once-majestic courtyard. The ceiling above splinters, releasing a cascade of jagged stone and sharp shards. Mormak shouts a dwarven battle cry and pushes Dakaria out of harm's way. Wilhilm tries to erect a brief magical shield, but recoils, unsure if he can do any magic without freeing the genie.

He's at the same impasse again. The demon is gone now. But just as he tried not to do any magic so he wouldn't release the evil demon, now he won't do any magic so he doesn't accidentally release the evil genie.

The group's breaths come fast and ragged. Every exit they approach seems to crumble just as they near it, forcing them to double back, to rethink, to find another way. The labyrinthine city now seems intent on becoming their tomb.

Finally, as they reach the main gates of Ishmaara as the grand archway above fractures. With a collective surge of adrenaline, they sprint. With a deafening roar, the arch collapses just as they clear it, a plume of dust and sand chasing them out into the open desert.

They don't stop running until the sounds of Ishmaara's

collapse are but distant echoes. The city of Ishmaara now rests even deeper under the sands of time.

The desert winds pick up, sending swirling vortexes of sand into the air. These tiny tornadoes dance across the landscape. The gusts carry with them the last whispers and echoes of a city being sealed away—the creaking of structures, the distant clang of falling walls, and the final sighs of chambers being buried.

Someone's sneezing somewhere.

CHAPTER 78

SHORT PEOPLE

Dakaria murmurs a druidic prayer to pay respect to the spirits of the city and the nature that reclaims it. Her eyes are misty but her voice is clear. Wilhilm commits the sight to memory, knowing that he's witnessing a significant moment in history. He watches Mormak. The Dwarf, tough as he may appear, shows a hint of sadness, having a deep appreciation for ancient structures and their legacy.

As the final remnants of Ishmaara disappear, the desert once again becomes a vast, uninterrupted expanse of golden sands. The city now lies hidden once again.

From the heat-distorted horizon, a dusty cloud emerges, growing rapidly in size. Within moments, the forms of riders become clear—Netherlings on the back of Dune Serpents, their horns pronounced against the backdrop of the setting sun, their eyes aglow with a mix of greed and malevolence.

"There's someone to save us," Dakaria exclaims.

"It's desert bandits," Mormak grumbles.

"They must have been lurking in the sands, waiting for

someone to turn up to rob," murmurs Gadisa, his grip on his Dragonteeth Dagger tightening.

Wilhilm turns to Dakaria. "I'm tired. Can you find the nearest oasis?" Two transformations, then fighting a Lich King as well as his own inner demon has drained him to the point of complete exhaustion.

Dakaria nods. She puts one hand into the sand and replies, "There should be one a few miles northwest of here."

The Netherlings close in. Their leader, a tall, scarred figure with a twisted horn, calls out, "What kind of sand storm was that? For a moment I thought I saw Ishmaara again. But now, it's end of the line, travelers! Hand over your treasures, and maybe we'll let you scurry away."

"Mormak, can you take care of our guests?" Wilhilm says. "I find myself in need of some rest."

Mormak sighs. "What would you do without me? You'd be lost, that's all I'm saying. You all owe me ale. Lots of it."

Mormak rolls his shoulders and cracks his neck. He steps forward, drawing his dual war axes. "Perhaps you didn't see the city sink? Or maybe you missed the part where we walked out alive? If I were you, I'd think twice about this."

The Netherling leader chuckles darkly, "It's four against...erm... let's say *many*, dwarf. Odds I like."

Mormak smirks, "Then let's even them out, so you can count more easily." With a roaring battle cry, he charges.

The desert sand churns as Mormak engages the Netherlings with ferocious intensity. His axes become whirlwinds, deflecting blows and delivering fierce counterstrikes. The Netherlings, confident at first, soon find themselves backpedaling, their numbers not offering the advantage they expected against the fiery might of the Dwarf.

With Mormak in his element no one else has to even brandish a weapon. Every swing, every step is calculated, a dance of war perfected over decades of battle. The Netherlings, for all their bluster, are caught off guard by the sheer power and skill of their singular opponent.

Finally, with six bandits knocked down from their mounts and the others hesitating, the Netherling leader signals a retreat, and the rest of them disperses into the desert.

Gadisa, meanwhile, takes the Dune Serpents of the Netherlings. “Looks fine,” he says. “We need something to ride. And there’s water and provisions in the bags.” He presents something that looks like a very dead beaver and shoves it into his mouth. “Peculiar,” he says.

Mormak, catching his breath, sheathes his axes and grins. “Told them they should've thought twice.”

“We should have bandits more often,” Gadisa says. “There’s quite a lot of loot on those mounts. And I thought we would end this adventure without any gold.”

Wilhilm, looking up from the map, nods appreciatively. “Well fought, Mormak. We have our path.” He points northwest. “The oasis awaits. Let's move out before more trouble finds us.”

“So, what’s with the genie?” Dakaria asks. “When someone strokes you, you set the genie free?”

“I don’t see that happening anytime soon. Enough time to do some research,” Wilhilm says. “Until then, I’ll refrain from doing any magic, so I won’t free the genie accidentally.”

“A wizard who can’t do spells. What else is new?” Mormak grumbles.

“Oh, I think a lot is new,” Dakaria says, smiling. She

links arms with Mormak and Wilhilm. “We’re stronger than ever.”

“But if we find food, I eat first,” Gadisa says.

“And if we find ale, I drink first,” Mormak says.

“And nobody stroke the wizard,” Dakaria reminds them.

YOU ARE AWESOME!

Thanks for reading *Craving of the Sands*! I can hear from the clinking noises your gold coins made when you purchased my book what an awesome person you are!

If you enjoyed my book, consider posting a review of it. These days, authors are inherently dependent on your good review on platforms like Amazon, BOookshop or Goodreads. Your review plays a vital role in enabling me to write more books in the future.

Also consider subscribing to my newsletter for news on my books, new rules supplements for table-top roleplaying games and single panel comic fun! If you subscribe now, you'll get a free e-book. Isn't that amazing? You'll find more on my website www.cearnachgrimm.com or at https://bit.ly/grimm-newsletter.

I'd also feel very honored if you'd follow me on social media (@cearnachgrimm).

ACKNOWLEDGMENTS

I would express my deepest gratitude to everyone who helped make the book happen (and laughed at it). I owe special thanks to W. Lawrence who co-wrote a short story with me in 2022, and part of that short story became part of the Ishmaara scenes in this book. I know, it sounds like a lot of parts. I'm very grateful for his wiling participation and the ideas and humor he brought into this project.

Over the years, I have written a dozen novels without ever publishing one, even though I published articles, short stories and comic books. This is the first novel that is being published. And even though I was under the impression that I know a lot about writing, I realized how little it actually was. How many skills I had to acquire to transition from draft to final manuscript!

It was a very humbling experience, to say the least, but by now I know better than to maintain I know anything about writing. I'm at the stage where I know that I know nothing, and that's something, right?

There is a great number of people who helped me in the process. My biggest believer, coach and cheerleader certainly was David Wolverton, also writing under David Farland, an established bestselling writer in his own right. Not only did he literally teach me a lot about writing, he also started editing my work, a process that was fun and educational and uplifting and everything you could ever hope it is. It came as a great shock to me when he died after suffering an accident at home. *Dave, wherever you are, I miss you.*

Gina Kammer helped me working through lots of the mess I came up with, struggling on my own after Dave's passing, and cleared the way to a cohesive story. I'm so thankful for her imagination, humor and story skills that helped to make the novel a fun experience.

When I approached publication, Rebecca Zornow took over as the main editor. She oversaw some major changes in the story with a meticulous eye for continuity and storytelling, helped me carve out considerably more of Wilhilm's character and his backstory, and when I thought I was done, my manuscript still came back with 2,102 comments, for which I will be forever grateful. It also, perhaps, explains my newly developed cheese addiction that may shine through in the finished manuscript. (Contrary to popular rumor, it did not replace my addiction to chocolate cakes, it added to it.)

Lionel Barter oversaw the final publication of the novel and some last minute changes as well as all the line edits and my later-than-last-minute changes on the proof pages. I imagine I'm hell to work with anyway, but in the context of many missed deadlines and zero experience on my part about the publication process, I'm quite happy that he didn't just strangle me and take my place. (*Or did he?*)

I also want to thank Michael for teaching me a lot about the publishing industry and for always being kind and patient. The Algonkian Writers Conferences he's running helped me along a great deal on this journey.

There's four very special people that need thanking as well. I need to thank Wilhilm, Gadisa, Mormak and Dakaria. They all stormed into my life quite suddenly—*poof*, and there, they were. They changed my life immediately. I posted the first Runebreaker single panel comics on Facebook, having next to zero followers. A week later, I had 5,000, and so many comments and encouragement.

Even now, years later, when I post a new comic, there's a lot of the names of this exciting first few weeks coming up in the comments. Thank you, fans of Runebreakers. You can't imagine how much it means to me that you bear with me, that you encourage and entertain me, that you engage with me. The world feels better with you in it.

I want to mention a few of you, those high up in my social media engagement list, as a stand-in for the many of you that gave me encouragement when I needed it.

Thank you Anne Brady, Ian Smolinski, Rob Pritch, Brent Wynn, Tez Boyes, Hellen Wood, Cliff Dixon, Roz Rosin, Marcus Wagner, Aaron Cazzola, Scribbilar Johnyai, Seán MacDonnchaidh, Gaming Mark, Sean Webb, Paul Suddeth, Ken Russell Barber II, Christopher Schuck, Jami Young, Tammi Bradstow, Mark Foster, Samuel Cowley, Michael Scull, Darrell Perrine, Peter Miller, Patrick Anthony, Mark Craig, Aaron McPherson, James D. Clifford, William Morey, Gene Flannery, Darrell Anderson, Kai Woodward, Sarita Taub, Susan Macdonald, Brian Holland, Frank Briant, and David Morr.

A NOTE FROM THE EDITOR

I tried hard. And I had help. But, unfortunately, a few typos might have slipped my tired eyes in one night or the other while compiling this book, so make sure you have the current version (or download a fresh copy if it's been sitting in your ebook reader for months.) It may have already been updated. If you spot a new typo, please let us know. We'll fix it for everyone. You can email the publisher at typos@nervousrocket.com and help us making a better experience for everyone.

Enjoy!

—Lionel Barter

Editor, Nervous Rocket

www.nervousrocket.com

LISTEN TO MORE BOOK RECOMMENDATIONS

Looking for your next podcast obsession? Then dive into the first episode of the new Dragons and Spaceships podcast! Host Brandi takes us on an incredible journey through fantasy and science fiction. Tune in now and join the conversation: https://www.youtube.com/@dragonsandspaceships - This podcast is sponsored by NervousRocket, the publisher of this book.

RUNEBREAKERS: REAL HEROES

Don't miss this comic book! The Runebreakers are a party of heroes, each with their own unique quirks and flaws, bound together by fate (and perhaps a little bit of bad luck). Together, they venture through enchanted lands, facing perilous foes and heavy puzzles (such as 'What does DO NOT TOUCH really mean?'). This printed comic book brings you the best of the webcomic that took social media by storm (a million views every week!) plus some additional never before seen panels.

CLASSIC SCIFI SERIES

Deep beneath the many-hued, volcanic sands of the Manalava Plains is an eerie world. And in this world, in a gem-encrusted cavern, is a pool of shimmering, iridescent matter, guarded by creatures from outer space. Into this unexplored region go two men following the shadowy trail of a vanished girl; searching down the corridors of time for a fragment of a departed age. Intent upon their quest they do not heed the silent voice that warns them of the great peril in the secret recesses of the cavern land. Lured irresistibly toward danger, the Earthmen discover that the interlopers from a far planet plan to use their superior powers to protect their lootings.

Also includes—

MARTIAN TERROR—Lolan, the Martian Sub-Commander, had no

choice. He sorrowed for Princess Mora's beaten, X-ray starved subjects. But when the desperate Venusians raised their empty fists, duty commanded him to cut loose his force-bolts.

And THE RED DIMENSION and THE PHANTOM OF TERROR.

Get your copy now at www.nervousrocket.com!